TO TELL ME
TERRIBLE LIES

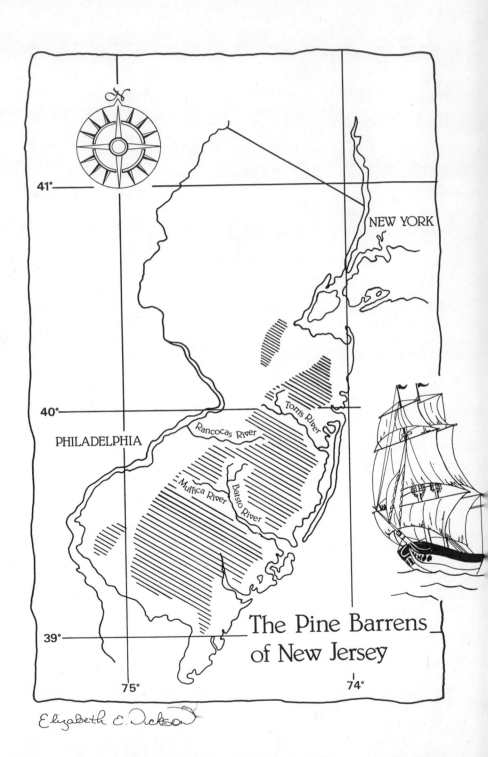

41°

40°

39°

75°

74°

NEW YORK

PHILADELPHIA

Toms River

Rancocas River

Mullica River

Batsto River

The Pine Barrens
of New Jersey

Elizabeth E. Dickson

A Romance of the Pine Barrens

TO TELL ME
TERRIBLE LIES

First of the Wainwright Chronicles
1778–1783

Katherine St. Clare

WAINWRIGHT PRESS
Emmaus, Pennsylvania

Library of Congress Catalog Card Number: 92-064334

Collector's Edition

Inquiries should be directed to
Wainwright Press
P. O. Box 288
Emmaus, PA 18049-0288

To tell me terrible lies : the
first of the Wainwright Chronicles /
Katherine St. Clare

Manufactured in the United States of America   ISBN: 0-9632830-1-4

1 2 3 4 5 6 7 8 9 10

To
Susan L. M. Huck
without whom there would be no book

to

the late Henry Charlton Beck
and George Agnew Chamberlain
whose books introduced me to the Barrens

and to

my mother, a red convertible,
and the hat we hung by a cranberry bog

with love

Contents

Will he never come back from Barnegat
With thunder in his eyes,
Treading as soft as a tiger cat
To tell me terrible lies?

Elinor Wylie
"The Puritan's Ballad"

Prelude

ONCE, SOME SAY, the Barrens were an island. Primordial oceans beat upon their shores when most of the eastern seaboard still slept beneath the sea. They seem an island still. Banks of white sand rise from tilled field and metalled roadstead as abruptly as though from the strand. The pellucid sky of the Barrens borrows light from the Atlantic. The soft air hints of salt.

Waves still lap the fringes of the Barrens—waves of traffic, shoreward bound. Eddies of commerce erode the island's edges. Here and there, great chunks have crumbled into the suburban swirl. No matter. Undismayed, the scrub oak and the pitch pine, the holly and the laurel, wait calmly to recapture their domain. They have done so before. With a swiftness that passes believing, the Barrens obliterate the insolent encroachments of men.

A few paces from traffic-choked highways, populous New Jersey dissolves into wilderness. Rank upon rank, the scrub pines range, green-black, to the horizon. The swish of traffic soon merges with the soughing of their branches. Cedar-water streams dark with tannin wend their brandy-brown way to salt marsh and thence to the sea. Swamps ringed by sentinel cedars breathe a stillness so intense that the splash of a fish-hunting heron seems an explosion of sound.

"Barrens," early settlers named this region—endless miles, endlessly scorched by fires long before the advent of men. The soil was too meagre for farming, the atmosphere too bleak to attract any but the loners and the lost.

Barrens? They appear so. But whence, then, the deeply grooved sand roads that crisscross these woodlands with ruts two centuries old?

ᴥ Deer scamper, surprised, from a hollow. Their hoofs
dislodge unexplained bricks.

ᴥ An iron sphere, old but unrusted, rolls from the shore
of a wilderness pond at the touch
of a fisherman's boot.

ᴥ By a crumbling stone wall, half submerged in leaf litter,
a vigil flame of daylilies keeps watch
over lives long extinguished.

Here, in this time-emptied wasteland, once throbbed an industrial heart. It pumped a stream of munitions to fuel a Revolution.

In time since lost to memory, lazy waterways mirrored the blaze of furnaces in blast. Giant water wheels creaked with their burden; showers of sparks lit the skies. The earth of clearings only deer now inhabit trembled to the hammer blows that forged a new nation's arms.

Now that bustle of industry is gone. Gone, all gone, as though they had never existed, are the forges and the primitive furnace stacks of blackened Jersey stone. Gone are the villages that served them, the "plantations" of ironmasters who ruled in feudal magnificence, the cottages of workmen who fed the greedy fires night and day. The Barrens have swallowed their ruins. In cities far away, descendants of colliers and sawyers forget the very meaning of their names.

Carters whose oxen hauled weapons to Washington's armies . . . the "rebel pirates" who "laughed in the Lobsterbacks' faces" as they flouted the British blockade . . . Tory spies who tallied the cargoes . . . "Refugee" bands that pillaged and plundered . . . all are gone.

A century ago and more, the forge fires died down in the Barrens. Thriving villages reluctantly surrendered to the forces of disuse and decay. The villagers scattered. Here and there, rust-flecked iron headstones in overgrown graveyards bow in mourning over those who stayed behind. And in unmarked anonymity near modest Quaker meetinghouses lie the victims of shipwreck and storm.

Somnolent in sun, glittering in snow, the Barrens savor their solitude. All is loneliness.

But wait! Pause, if you will, and linger. Succumb to the lure of the trails carved by coaches that lurched from Long-A-Coming to the sea. Trace the grooves of place-names on weathered cedar signs: Speedwell Furnace. Martha. Atsion and Batsto. Aetna. Calico. Dabble your feet in amber waterways by the ruins of disintegrating dams. Finger the mottled bark of pines warm with the memory of fire.

Breathe the resin-scented stillness and catch whispers of long ago.

Do you hear them? The rustle of silken petticoats . . . the scuffle of dancing feet . . . the rat-a-tat-tat of hammers . . . the clangour of a forge . . . hoofbeats . . . shots . . . a muffled cry of warning . . . the echo of a sigh.

Here, in these forsaken wastelands, lived men and women who loved and lost as we. Their passions burned as brightly as the forge fires extinguished by time. Limpid waters still shimmer with their reflections. The crowns of the pines toss restlessly, tormented by their dreams. The Barrens brood, haunted by their presence, their raptures and their agonies, their passion . . . and their pain.

BOOK I

Stuart Brandon

C H A P T E R ❧ 1

F ROM THE MOMENT she saw the seagulls, Serena knew this was no
ordinary day. Or did it begin last night, she wondered, last night,
in Father's study, with the family long abed? With two men—Father
and the stranger—in whispered consultation?

The light from their single candle had throbbed with the forge hammer's blows. It had pooled in the stranger's brandy, transmuting it to
moulten gold. And in his eyes she had seen . . . No! I'll not think of him—
whoever he is, and whatever he wants here. She forced her thoughts
back to the gulls.

Laughers they were, a few herring gulls among them. They circled
Weyford Lake, unwontedly silent. Most were adults with sleek grey backs,
their white breast feathers phosphorescent in the dawn. A youngster or
two remained disguised in the mottled browns of adolescence, adult only
in the arching grace of his great wings.

A few miles eastward, whence the gulls had come, the sun leapt angry
from the surface of the sea, bloodying the water and feathering the clouds
with flame. In Weyford's orchard, bare trees stretched chilblained fingers
toward the warmth of the fire in the sky, though the apricot light had
yet to tint the leaden waters of the lake.

Black Susan had not come to stir the fire, and Serena's breath hung
frosty in the air. A lacework of ice rimmed the pitcher on her washstand,
and the flannel-wrapped brick that last night had warmed the linens lay
morning-cold and useless beneath the featherbed. Serena scarcely noticed
the chill. She watched the gulls and, absently, traced her fingertips along
the flowing "W" debossed on the iron windowsill. I'm never cold, she
thought proudly—not like Prue with her everlasting sniffles. And that's
why, last night . . .

The image of the stranger stole back into her thoughts. Dark, he had been, with an air of brooding about him. The shadows had etched harsh lines into his face. Was that but a trick of the firelight? The lithe lines of his body had nothing of age about them. The tilt of his chin and the set of his cloaked shoulders bespoke the habit of command.

And I in my nightdress, she thought now. That light in his eyes—was it only the candle's reflection? Would I have withdrawn so quickly, without the book I had come to seek, had Father not been there, his brows sweeping together in that frown I know so well? And why is each second of that encounter—and the other times I've seen the stranger, coming always by night and by stealth—acid-etched into my memory?

Forget him! she adjured herself again. Think of this day. It's as good as certain that Father will order a blowout. Surely Father will let me watch them pour the final heat! Delightedly she hugged herself, curling her pink toes in the coarse black hairs of the bearskin that spread from bed to window—a wild, woodland note in the otherwise feminine room. "Can I have it, Father?" she had begged. "You know it's for me, for all that Enoch offered it to you." Old Samuel seldom withstood her for long. Triumphantly, she had borne her prize past her mother's mild protests and Prue's icy stare.

The mantel clock chimed seven. Serena pulled the quilt off the bed and swathed herself in it until only her toes and the frill of her nightdress peeped from beneath its folds. She tugged the tawny mass of her hair free to spill in tangled waves to her waist and padded back to the window to curl on her "lookout" seat. The leaded panes of handmade glass lent their own special shimmer to the dawn. As she watched, the last of the stars twinkled out. Deep blue night receded before opalescent day. The lake had become a mirror. The gulls, settling down upon it, glided serenely above their reflected selves.

❧   ❧   ❧

Wainwright house stood upon a rise, its grounds sloping down to the lake shore. From this eminence, Serena could see her world—the iron plantation of Weyford. The lake and the dam with its sawmill. The workers' village across the bridge. And beyond, beside, behind, the humped shadow of the Jersey Barrens—acre upon acre, mile upon mile of pitch pine, scrub oak, and laurel threaded by streams dark with the tannin whose action produced Weyford's ore.

Pines rimmed the lake, their mottled trunks warmed to red by the rising sun's fire. Beyond them, billows of smoke smudged the sky as giant hammers drummed their martial greeting to the day. Here was Weyford's core, its clattering, clanging, charcoal-fired heart—the iron furnace and the forge. Day and night its fierce beat pumped a stream of arms to Washington's Continentals. The ironworks never slept. So long as the waters could move the creaking wheels, the Revolution's lifeblood would flow.

On the lakeside walk of iron flagstones white with frost stood Serena's father. Samuel Wainwright, too, watched the gulls. Long attuned to the vagaries of Jersey weather, he knew what their presence here portended. A storm was coming from the sea. Even now a northeast breeze freshened at the storm's insistence. From the chimneys in the workers' settlement, smoke was beating down to the ground.

It is time, Old Samuel was thinking as the salt wind stirred his white hair. Time—and past time—for the winter to turn freezing. The furnace had stayed in blast long past the usual date, devouring Christmas and the New Year festivities in its panting greed for more bog ore, more charcoal, more oyster-shell flux. Every cannonball poured, every load of shot shipped, meant hope for the coming spring campaign. Soon the roads to the west of the Barrens would freeze. Wagons bound for Washington's encampment would jounce and sway in the rock-hard ruts, but the carters need not fear that the iron-bound wheels would be mired. Coastal shipping was all but paralyzed by the guns of the British blockade; still, the Army would be supplied.

The Lord giveth, thought Old Samuel. But He also taketh away. He paced restlessly, the iron flags ringing with his footfalls. Frozen roads meant frozen streams. The water wheels would creak to a halt—and the furnaces with them, lashed captive in shrouds of ice. We have done well this season, he thought proudly. Since the British struck Chestnut Neck, the men have poured a ton and more a day. But now there's snow in the air—I can smell it. Snow, and bitter cold. Today we must blow the furnace out. The men will welcome the respite, patriots though they be. It is punishing work to raise ore from the stream beds and cast it into artifacts of war. Now it is time to take to the woods, to hunt fresh meat for our larders—a deer or two or perhaps a bear, still fat from a summer's feeding. Time, too, to cut ice from the lake and to mend hard-driven machinery. This morning's charge must be the last. We can tap the last heat at sundown, and cool the furnace lining before the snow. Pray God the men restrain themselves and stay sober enough for the tapping.

His decision taken, Samuel turned on his heel and stamped toward the Big House.

🦚 🦚 🦚

ON HER CUSHIONED perch high above him, Serena hugged herself. I was right! In the light of her knowledge of Old Samuel and the works she had traced the line of his thinking. He was planning to blow the furnace out. And that meant a frolicking—a special celebration to mark the work year's end. There would be dancing at the White Stag, too, and a feast of roast venison and plump oysters from Barnegat Bay. This year, Father will surely let me watch the blowout. Didn't he have me draw the gate to start the water wheels? On April fifteenth—my eighteenth birthday, and the start of the smelting season. Of course I must be present when it ends.

Old Samuel disappeared from view, striding around the corner to his countinghouse. The air shook with the peals of the Big House bell that summoned all hands to their labours. Serena hastened to dress.

CHAPTER ❧ 2

S ERENA RUSTLED down the stairway, well aware that she was late. The dining room doors stood ajar. A fire had been kindled on the hearth, and the family were ranged about the table. Samuel, his heavy ironmaster's hands already folded for the blessing, frowned as Serena slid hastily into her chair. A dimple flashed at the corner of her mouth as she smiled a conciliatory greeting. Despite himself, Samuel smiled back. Then he bowed his head and cleared his throat with the hacking cough that seemed part of his speech.

"Oh, Lord," he began, "we Thy servants humbly thank Thee . . ."

As she bowed her head with the others, Serena glanced toward the foot of the table. She suppressed a smile. Her mother's look of pious abstraction meant that, surreptitiously, she was easing her cramped feet out of her red heeled kid slippers and burrowing them into the shawl beneath her chair. Mother, thought Serena, I need no words to know what you are thinking.

The fire was crackling cheerfully, but cold seeped through the many-paned windows to eddy about one's ankles. Draughts ruffled the fire into fretful puffs of smoke and twitched at the table's linen cloth. Anna Wainwright was missing the snug double casements and cosy tiled coal stove of her rooms in her native Vienna. *Ach!* she thought, in the language that never quite left her, how American houses are cold.

Anna's small head with its coronet of greying chestnut braids tipped sideward as Samuel droned toward his amen. Beneath dutifully lowered lashes, her bright brown-eyed glance slid from one to the other of her daughters.

Prudence, the elder, sat sedately, hands folded, eyes cast down. Her wispy curls, an indeterminate brown, were sternly subdued by her cap. The well-modelled lips were closed tightly. Not a fold disturbed her lawn fichu, but her forehead bore permanent creases that belied her twenty-three years.

Serena sat as quietly as Prue. Yet everything about her bespoke motion. Her snug-fitting gown of russet wool seemed to embody the fire's warmth; the first rays of the sun made moulten copper of her hair. All her repressed excitement glowed in the topaz eyes that tilted provocatively at the corners. Her throat and her slender wrists were pale, as befitted a lady, yet they seemed faintly dusted with gold, as though summer had lingered to caress them. Modesty would find nothing to criticize in Serena's choice of attire. But, thought Anna, one sees not the clothing. It is the body beneath them that one senses.

Beside Serena stood an empty chair.

". . . and most devoutly we thank Thee. Amen." His duty done, Samuel tucked his napkin into the ample folds of his waistcoat and reached for the platter of smoking ham that Black Susan offered to him.

"Serena," said Prudence, "you have forgotten your cap." The unspoken "again" plummeted through the air, burdened with the weight of a thousand such reminders—of garments flung aside and samplers left unfinished. Unheeding, Serena had skipped and scampered through her childhood. Prudence, always a step behind though five years the elder, had trailed disapprovingly in her wake.

"Oh!" Serena put a hand to her head and started to rise.

"Sit! Sit!" said Anna. "Eat before all is cold."

Prudence tightened her lips but said no more. Silence reigned at the table while each addressed the food. Serena fell to with appetite, piling ham upon her plate and reaching for a bowl of crisp potatoes. Prudence nibbled at a biscuit, her eyes fixed far away. Samuel stoked himself as methodically as he might feed one of his furnaces.

The profusion of dishes set before them bore witness that Anna, too, had sensed the onset of hard winter and a day of heavy work to come. Weyford was nearly self-sufficient, but nearby farms bordering the Bay augmented its bounty. Wainwright House was famed throughout the Barrens for its food.

This morning there was bacon as well as ham, home-cured under Anna's direction, pungent with woodsmoke, and lean. No need to waste precious grain on the hogs when the scrub oaks were laden with acorns. Eggs lay snugly waiting beneath their quilted cosy. At each place steamed a bowl of hot oatmeal, a dollop of butter and honey melting in the centre, a jug of thick cream ready to pour upon it. Preserved crane-berries from nearby bogs glowed ruby in a crystal dish. In pewter mugs placed ready to hand, juicy apples sputtered in their bath of heated cider. Staunch patriots that they were, the Wainwrights no longer drank tea.

Samuel finished before the others, impatient to get on with the day. Beneath shaggy white brows his keen blue eyes fixed the gaze of each in turn. He coughed. "You have all heard the bell?" It was hardly a question. "Today we blow the furnace out."

Serena dropped her fork with a clatter. Prudence gave an ostentatious start. "Father!" cried Serena, "I knew it! There's a storm coming, isn't there? Oh, please, Father, may I watch the last heat poured?"

Samuel hesitated. This unwomanly interest of Serena's! Best, he thought, to stamp it out as he would a vagrant coal from the forge fire. Then his features softened as he regarded his younger daughter. Her eyes were bright with expectancy, illuminating her whole face. "Perhaps, . . ." he began.

But Prudence broke in. "Oh, Serena, have you no dignity? To wallow in that filthy, smelly hole? You will ruin your garments in the smoke and soot. And the men! Have you no care for your position? It was bad enough when you were a child—running to the forge whenever Mother or I let you out of our sight, pestering the men to tell you their yarns. But now you're a woman grown. How *can* you hang about with those ruffians? Don't you see how they all look at you?"

"I see how they *don't* look at you. That's the burr in your backside, I shouldn't wonder."

Seeing the red flush spread over Samuel's face, she added quickly, "Oh, come, Prue! Don't be such a sobersides. I'm only jesting." She turned pleadingly to Samuel. "*Please*, Father, let me go. I've never watched a blowout."

For some moments Samuel did not answer. His gaze, turned sombre, was fixed upon the empty chair. Sam should be here, he thought—here, not shivering at Morristown with the Continentals. Why did he forgo his ironmaster's exemption when he knows I've need of him at Weyford? His mind swerved from the answer—that Sam hated the making of iron, that the red billows of smoke, the soot and the clangour repelled him as surely as they magnetized Serena. He sighed. Serena should have been a boy. Was I wrong to send her to the Hightstown academy? Did Mistress Mansey encourage these unseemly preoccupations? Best that she marries—and soon. At this thought, another occurred to him. Perhaps . . .

"Very well," he conceded, "you may go. I expect to tap the furnace near sundown. But by then whoever is not working will be well into his applejack. You may watch, but you must keep your distance. I shall send Caleb Sawyer to escort you. Remain in the house until he comes to fetch you—or I'll not have you watching at all."

Some of the light ebbed from Serena's eyes. "Caleb Sawyer? Why must I have him for nursemaid? With that scrawny neck and that scraggly ginger beard he looks like a half-finished chicken. No wonder the Princeton patriots tarred and feathered him. They were only putting on what God forgot." She giggled.

"I'll not have sacrilege at this table! And see you don't mention Princeton to him. It is not an episode he cares to remember."

"That I'll warrant," agreed Serena, heedless of her mother's warning look. "Maybe that's why he skulks against walls." She laughed softly again. And maybe, she pondered, that's why his hind end tucks under when he walks for all the world like a whipped hound's tail.

"Enough, Serena. Caleb Sawyer will escort you, and that is the end of it. I'll not have you maligning the best clerk I've ever had. More's the pity your brother never took such liking to the forge."

"*Liking?* Then why does he duck his head like a turtle every time the forge hammer strikes? Come now, Father—liking? I've known him cringe at a tapping as though the fire were live and like to eat him. And how can you be so trusting of a man who never looks you in the eye? All you ever see is the top of his balding head, even when he's walking by himself. You would think there were diamonds in the ground." Serena paused. "Father," she said solemnly, "Caleb is so furtive I shouldn't wonder he's a spy. After all, isn't he a Tory?"

"No, he is not a Tory. He is merely British-born, and his accent tells against him. Where do you get such notions, Serena? A spy? Would a Tory toil night after night in the forge office?"

"He might, if it suited his purpose." At her father's black look, Serena subsided. "He might, too," she muttered rebelliously. "If *someone* isn't spying, why are we losing so many loads of shot? You might think the Refugees read every bill of lading." And what might the stranger have to do with that? she thought suddenly. But no—he comes by night, true, but there is nothing furtive about him, that I'd swear.

"Enough!" bellowed Samuel, stung at last to rage. "Caleb Sawyer is like a son to me—far more of a son than Sam has proved himself. Caleb is devoted to the ironworks. You don't find *him* out hunting deer when the account books need attending. Nor hanging about the White Stag, either. Caleb's as good as my right hand. It's a share in Weyford he'll be getting, the day he is wedded to you." He stopped abruptly.

"Wedded to *me?*" This Serena had not heard of before. She drew breath to protest, but Prudence forestalled her.

For once the mute Prudence had found words enough to say. She glared, white-lipped, at Serena, her pale eyes wide. Two spots of angry colour blazed in her thin cheeks, and the tip of her nose quivered with indignation.

"Caleb Sawyer is an admirable man!" Her bodiless voice trembled. "A fine, cultured gentleman, Serena. How dare you slander him? How dare you suggest that he's disloyal? For shame!"

Oho! thought Serena. So that's the lay of the land. Well, Prue can have him, and welcome. I'd sooner bed old Jake Buzby than that spinster in whipcord breeches. Prue looks like a rabid weasel when she's angry. Serena opened her mouth to say so, then held her peace. Her father's purple face warned her he was an inch from an explosion that would shatter all her plans for the day. Let Caleb Sawyer walk out with her, since that seemed to tickle his fancy. She'd rid herself of his chaperonage soon enough.

A sharp look from Samuel silenced Prudence, also. He turned back to Serena, who took care to look suitably docile. "Very well, then, daughter. I will send Caleb for you when the heat is ready to pour."

Chair legs scraped on the shining pine boards as Samuel rose from the table. Time to work. The others rose and followed. By the stairway the three women paused. "Serena," said her mother, "your cap and apron you will be needing. Work there is much today."

Behind Anna's plump back, Serena thrust her tongue out at Prudence but then wrinkled her nose to signal truce. Moving quickly and lightly, she started up the staircase. Her skirts were held with a twist of the wrist to reveal just a glimpse of slim ankle. Her fingertips caressed the burnished wood of the bannister; her hips swayed with sinuous grace. Prudence stood motionless, watching her sister. Her skirts of serviceable grey hung limply about her flat hips; her sharp features twisted as scorn fought with envy.

Anna, catching sight of her expression, was shocked at its venom. *Ach, die Prudence sieht es auch.* The Prudence sees it also. Anna quelled a shiver of premonition. The slender figure crossing the landing radiated an aura unmistakable to any woman, irresistible to any man: a sensuality the more compelling for being beyond volition.

CHAPTER ✺ 3

W HEN CALEB CALLED at the Big House, darkness was flooding the sky. In its wake swept the gathering storm, its ramparts gilded by the last rays of the sun. Empurpled outriders astride the freshening wind had gained the outposts of Weyford. Behind them streamed banners of palest jade, as though the restless Atlantic, impatient for battle, had risen to join the skies.

Descending the stairs of Wainwright House, Serena paused on the landing. Caleb stood by the fire in the drawing room, talking with Prue. In a rocker sat Anna, her hands busy with knitting, her eyes above her spectacles fixed on her older daughter. Comprehension showed in her gaze.

Why, Prue looks almost lively, thought Serena. It came as a surprise. Day by day one forgot that Prudence resembled Serena — as an artist's study in watercolour wash might resemble a vivid oil. Everything about Prudence was almost and not quite. Her face was pale. Her hazel eyes were so clear as to seem without colour, fringed by the palest of lashes. When she was happy they gleamed with light — but Prue, thought her sister, is seldom happy. More often her eyes gazed inward, cast down in sullen reflection, or blazed, white-rimmed, with angers she dared not speak aloud. Prue's eyes were a shade too close together, her nose a shade too sharp. A weasel, I likened her to, thought Serena now. It's true.

As Serena entered, Prudence fell silent. Her animation dropped from her like a purloined garment guiltily shed. Caleb did not notice. His eyes on Serena, he stepped forward with a jerky little bow. Prudence scurried away.

Look at him, thought Serena. The very hunch of his shoulders bespeaks his disapproval. He thinks this no excursion for a woman. What a sorry specimen he is: gaiters sagging about those skinny shanks, that thinning

hair, that scraggly beard. I suppose it's his gesture to the festivities to
eschew that woolen cap he's wont to wear over his ears.

"Good evening, Master Sawyer."

"Good evening, Mistress Wainwright." Again that jerky bow. The surprisingly full, red lips beneath the ginger beard were curved in an almost boyish smile.

I cannot abide him, thought Serena. The way he smears his eyes over my body all the while they're so humbly cast down. What can Father be thinking of, to wish me wedded to this creature? He's as furtive as a ferret.

Anna's thoughts were much the same. How can it be that my Samuel is so blind? Just so does he refuse to see that it is the Prudence who should marry soon—soon! before her soul it is burnt by angers she thinks to hide from us all. Never will she forgive her sister if the Serena marries first, and marries the man she herself—

Anna sighed. She had confronted her husband this morning, after the scene in the dining room. Impatient to be gone to the furnace, Samuel had scarcely attended her words. And once he perceived her intention, her effort was doomed.

❦ ❦ ❦

"SAMUEL, TO ME you must listen this one time. For the Serena, the Caleb is not the right man. Her spirit he will crush. *Ach!* so righteous he is, so—*Wie kann ich's sagen; kleinlich*—small of mind. The man you think him he is not. You, husband, you see always what you want to see. But in the Caleb there is something I trust not, something—*Ach, Gott!*—it frightens me. If it is your wish that he be of our family, if that must be, think then of the Prudence. She—"

"Nonsense, woman. Is it to talk twaddle that you keep me from my work? Serena has spirit indeed—too much spirit. Caleb will calm her down. He will tame those wild notions she has gotten from Mistress Mansey. He will teach her to be as a woman should be: handmaiden to her husband."

"*Nein* . . . No. Husband, it is wrong you are. The Serena is not one to submit. Fight him she will, and you will lose her."

"Lose her? Nonsense, Anna. To what? To whom? She is my daughter; she obeys me, as the Lord intends. And I say she will marry Caleb Sawyer. She needs taming, and I need him about the works. Now that's an end to it!"

"But the Prudence—"

"An end of it, I say. I will hear no more of this, Anna!" And Samuel was gone.

🍂 🍂 🍂

STRANGE IT IS, thought Anna now, remembering how suitors had flocked to Serena when her childhood was scarce behind her. And none could satisfy Samuel. Men from fine Philadelphia families had ridden away from Weyford disappointed, like as not with a flea in the ear. No man was good enough for Serena but one. And that the one her sister wanted, the Lord knew why.

Now Prudence moped extinguished in a corner. Serena's festive attire had Caleb's full attention. And well it might. She had chosen a gown of heavy indigo wool to shield her from the cold. But the bodice fitted trimly, and the full skirt swayed like a bell. A snowy linen collar, daintily embroidered—Prue's handiwork—set off Serena's fine skin, though Prue had been quite right in predicting that the soot would make short work of it. Row upon row of small velvet bows rose and fell with her excited breath, and a blue grosgrain sash circled her narrow waist. Her cuffs were of softest deep-blue velvet, the last of a privateer's stores.

The rich hue of the velvet made splendid contrast with the gold lights in her hair. It was gathered demurely in a thick coil at her neck, but stray curls hung loose about her ears. Leaving her velvet bonnet in the wardrobe had cost Serena a pang, but she knew that the winds at the furnace site would rip the plume to shreds. A fringed scarf would better protect her from the shower of ash that would be falling. Pearl studs gleamed in her ears as she handed Caleb an old woolen cloak to put about her shoulders.

The task took uncommonly long, but at last his clinging hands fell away. Bidding Anna and Prudence good evening, the pair stepped out into the night. From the veranda they looked down toward the lake, where the glow of furnace and forge stained the far waters crimson. "Let's hurry!" Serena said.

But when they reached the plank bridge that would take them to the workers' settlement she paused. "Wait." She turned and stared behind her, up the rise. There stood Wainwright House, dominating Weyford, solid, substantial, its bricks laid in orderly courses, the Virginia creeper Anna had tended softening its angles and disguising its newness. The white underbark of the giant sycamore that guarded it—legacy of a far older structure on whose foundations the Big House was built—shone faintly with the last of the ebbing light. The windows glowed softly, shutters hospitably wide. Through the fanlight over the carved front door flickered the candles of the hall chandelier, lit for this occasion. The house wore festivity well. Only the widow's walk—a room, really, built on the roof—spoiled its felicitous proportions.

Dusk hid the structures beyond it, deserted now, and swathed in shadows: the countinghouse and store, relics of an earlier time, small and shabby; the weathered cedar shed where Caleb inspected the char-coalers' loads before sending them on to the works; the angular bell tower beside the office, blackly piercing the sky. Behind the house, unseen from this vantage, lay Anna's garden; beyond it stretched pasture and orchard.

Behind Weyford enclave loomed the Barrens: endless miles, endlessly scorched by fires long before the advent of men. Pine and scrub oak, holly and laurel, in soil unfit for the plow. White sand trails snaked through the perimeter, leading here to a cellar hole, there to a clearing, but the interior was known only to the deer. From swamps guarded by the lances of cedars, streams coiled their way to the salt flats, leaving behind them the deposits of limonite that had brought men to the Barrens to make iron.

The Barrens are so vast, thought Serena. And Weyford, for all it's grown so, seems so small. She shuddered for no reason. Then she turned and went on. The planks of the bridge trembled with the force of Weyford River as it tumbled over its dam to seek the sea. To the right lay the smooth darkling waters where the gulls of this morning now floated asleep, ghostly shapes barely visible in the gloom. To the left, by the sawmill, the fallen waters churned and frothed, spume hovering wraith-like above them. The sound seemed louder than usual, and in a moment Serena grasped why. The forge hammers had gone silent. Their metro-nome blows had ceased.

"We must hurry," she said again. Caleb said nothing, his store of amen-ities exhausted. They paced the wide sand road between the workers' cottages. Here and there someone called a greeting. Simon Crabtree, Serena saw, had left his gate open again. Old Samuel would have some-thing to say about that: Last time he had fined Simon twopence. It was hard to rein her steps to the pace set by Caleb's decorum. Every fibre within her strained toward the distance where a shower of sparks lit the sky. Her unwonted apprehension, like her resentment of her escort, melted in the warmth of her anticipation.

They picked their way through the trees that screened the lake shore and emerged in a vast burnt-out clearing. Acres of cutover stumps and discarded branches littered what had once been forest floor. Each year the voracious furnaces consumed near a thousand acres. The itinerant colliers had been pitching their huts farther and farther away, and men less foresighted than Samuel Wainwright — who at least made a gesture at replanting — were already scrambling for accessible timberland. Weyford's hundred thousand acres seemed less ample than a decade ago.

✎ ✎ ✎

THE FURNACE DOMINATED the clearing. Three stories high, thirty feet to a side, it towered over the casting shed huddled at its base like a suckling beast. As night deepened around it, flame shooting from its stack smeared the sky with lurid light. Shadowy figures darted about, ministering to its demands. The hellish scene pulsed with its monster breath as leather bellows as big as a man fed icy blasts into its fiery heart.

Barrow after barrow was trundled up the ramp to dump flux, fuel, and ore into the gaping stack. By the quay wooden shallops rocked gently, done with their work of bringing ore from the swamps. Sweating men shovelled frantically to supply the returning barrows while, nearer the furnace, others — faces black — shovelled charcoal and oyster shells brought from the bay. It was a filthy business, primitive and crude, harking back to a time when men in breechclouts squatted before crucibles of clay. It was a wasteful business, too, leaving much ore unsmelted. Beyond the furnace giant stamping hammers, water-driven, crushed slag to recover ore.

So near the furnace it seemed they must soon be consumed by its heat, gutterers smoothed the channels in the sand into which the molten iron would run. No time now for such frills as the flowing script "W" debossed on the firebacks for which Weyford was justly renowned. Only "pigs" were being poured tonight, to be recast later as cannonballs. Even so, each two-foot pig would bear the mark of Weyford — a "W" hastily scratched into its belly before it hardened. Old Samuel was proud of his iron; let no lesser ironmaster pass off Weyford pigs as his own.

The pace was slowing. Soon the elements — carbon and oxygen — must do their work unaided. Men from the forge, whose work was done, gathered near the casting shed: forgers, slitters, and stampers with lines of fatigue etched black on their fire-tinted foreheads. One by one, the barrow men were joining them, thick-muscled giants one and all.

So streaked with soot were their faces one could not tell white men from black. Two Lenni Lenape from the Indian mission at Brotherton blended with the handful of Africans escaped from the South. Cold as the night had become, not a man wore a coat, and sleeves were rolled

high on sinewy forearms. The fierce breath of the furnace scorched
their faces while the wind froze the sweat on their backs. Lung fever
was a constant hazard, and every year one or two coughed their lives
away despite the efforts of their wives and the Black Doctor, summoned
from Lumberton.

A bulky figure detached itself from the group and hailed Serena and
Caleb. It shambled toward them, tilting ever so slightly. Jake Buzby was
celebrating early. A black mongrel, mostly hound, loped beside him.

"Evenin', Miz Serena. Come to watch the blowout?" The deep voice
was muffled by layers of clothing and mellowed by the applejack in which
it was constantly steeped. "This be Cinders," Jake continued. At the
sound of his name, Cinders gazed soulfully at his master. "He be doin'
right good at his learnin'. Gettin' so he can sniff a breakout surer'n any
man."

Serena bent to fondle the floppy ears. Jake's fire dogs were a legend in
the Barrens. Other colliers kept watch themselves when their earth-
daubed ricks were afire. Smoke coming too fast through the chinks sent
them running to add sod lest the wood burn too fast and consume itself.
Wood must cook, not burn, to make charcoal. Smoke coming too slowly
meant a scramble for more fuel. Moreover, there was danger of a breakout that could set the whole forest afire: Thousands of acres had been
lost in this way.

Jake's dogs were trained to sniff breakouts. With one of them standing
watch, Jake was free to attend to his jug of Jersey Lightnin' or one of the
blowzy women who kept him supplied with knit jerkins and other comforts. Jake's harem was as famous as his fire dogs. "I be t'other side of sixty,
but a man for all that." If the dog started yelping, Jake would shamble
forth and attend to the necessities, cursing as he did so.

"He seems a likely pup, Jake," said Serena. "Yes, this time Father
relented and let me come. Did you bring your coal in already?"

"This mornin' I brang it, good 'n early. Then I be waitin'. Knew a storm
be comin'. A frolickin's not a thing I want to miss." Jake squinted toward
the stack. "It'll blow soon," he said, with the certainty of accustom.

Jake and Serena were friends of long standing. Many a roasted apple
had she wolfed by his fire while his tales of the Jersey Devil sent shivers
down her spine. "Half so tall as a man, he be, with wings like a bat and
claws like a dragon. Born down Leeds Point way, they say. Some nights
ye can hear him a'howlin'."

But now, as Jake rambled on, embellishing the exploits of Cinders,
Serena wondered at Caleb's restraint. This smudged giant, clothes dusted

with the soot of his trade, words slurred by his premature libations, was hardly fit company for Serena as Caleb understood "fit." Long since, she had expected an outburst. None had come.

A clutch at her arm explained the silence. While Serena gave his master her attention, Cinders had sought distraction. He had begun investigating Caleb. Now he was nibbling at the drooping gaiters and pawing in friendly fashion at Caleb's shins.

The effect was electric. Caleb's eyes bulged. His expression was frozen. The fingers clutching her elbow were trembling. Teeth clenched, body rigid, Caleb fended off the harmless Cinders as though he were a mastiff out for blood.

Serena's eyes danced with amusement. Convulsively, embarrassed into action, Caleb flung out his foot. "Get that mangy cur away from me!" Caleb's voice cracked; the timid kick fell short. Cinders retreated, baffled. In a falsetto quaver that drew all eyes toward him, Caleb cried, "Do you hear me, Buzby? Get him out of here. Now. Before I throw him into the furnace."

"Yessir, Master Sawyer, sir." Jake touched his forehead in a burlesque of subservience. As he lurched away, his eyes met Serena's. Laughter seemed certain to explode. Dog and master retreated to the fringes of the crowd. From somewhere among the watchers came a snicker. Caleb ducked his head and turned away from Serena, affecting to watch the work.

❧   ❧   ❧

THE TENSION had heightened. Night and storm lent their touch of fantasy. Slag spilled from one of the tapholes to seethe upon the ground. Brittle chunks glowed darkly orange, netted with black where they crusted. Blue flame danced over the slag heap, as scurrying figures made ready for the blow.

Samuel Wainwright had come down from the bridgehouse, done with his exacting task of gauging the proportions of the charge: so much charcoal, so much ore, so much shell. His dark-glass spectacles swung on a chain about his neck. Beside him stood Enoch Price. "Best weigher I've had," boasted Samuel. The reticent giant with the brawny, scorched arms bade fair to be a wizard at his art.

And art it was. Like a master chef, Enoch doled out the ingredients of the "soup." Too much of this, too little of that, and the pigs might harden too brittle, a cannon might explode in the field. Weighing the quality of the charcoal, the purity of the ore, timing each addition, took more than

scales. "Enoch," said Samuel, "has the eye for it." The eye, too, for the
subtle shades of colour, the intensity of light, that told the ironmaster
when the soup was ready to pour. Young though Enoch was, the ironworkers knew him for their own.

Now both men watched the progress of the heat, shielding their eyes
again with their spectacles of coloured glass. First smoke, then flame
belched from the furnace stack in faster and faster succession. The wind
had risen to a gale, and great sheets of fire twisted free of the central column and tore themselves to tatters in the night. As the exultant flames
surged and ebbed, lighting one and then another of the faces turned
toward them, the treetops that ringed the clearing capered in a dance of
their own. The earth shuddered with the might of the forces unleashed
within the crude stone crucible. The furnace panted faster and faster,
throwing flame ever higher as its labour neared fruition. The roar of
elements colliding submerged all speech and all will.

Samuel gave the signal. The furnace foreman seized his lance and
pierced the fire's heart.

The brightness of noon lit the clearing. Its farthest reaches shone
white, bringing high summer to warm the winter night.

A satiny liquid thick as cream streamed from the taphole into the
waiting troughs. Pinwheels of sparks danced above it while whirlwinds
of flame pursued it through the night. Ghosts of forgotten eons whose
decay had formed the limonite joined in frenzied dance upon the pyre.
A glowing white river whose touch meant death flowed docilely into the
waiting moulds. As it moved, it cooled to crimson. Already its outermost
branches were crusted with deceptive grey. On and on flowed the river,
a ton of nature's savagery tamed to serve the purposes of men. Shadowy
figures guided its course with dipper and ladle. Then it slowed to a trickle
and stopped. The glow died down.

A sigh of relief shook the watchers. They had grappled with Nature —
and won. The blast was over. Now let the storm come! Slag rakes and
tampers flew into the air, their owners heedless of the safety of their
heads. Roars of jubilation burst from furnace-parched throats. Word
had reached the Big House, and the bell sounded peal after peal.

Blown out! Seven months of twelve-hour days and twelve-hour nights
were over. The tenders of the flames could have their rest. Now they
could take their women sleighing, or lounge in the White Stag telling
tales. White teeth shone in sooty faces as grins stretched the tension
from pursed lips. Jake Buzby seized Mike McGuire and whirled him in
an impromptu reel. His partner, a wizened gnome shrivelled by years in
the mould house, was hard put to stay on his feet. Others joined in.

Soon one of them would splash into the lake, now silvered with ripples raised by the wind.

Someone had brought cowbells. Sticks and crowbars hammered iron kettles. The irregular din sounded counterpoint to the unceasing clang from the belfry. "I'll never forget this!" cried Serena. Within the depths of her body, memories of flame roused wild sensations. Exhilaration seized her, and she tugged Caleb's arm as though to draw him into the dance. He jerked away. The rebuff brought her back to the moment.

"I'll dance with you, Miss Serena," said a husky figure by her side. It was Enoch.

"Know your place," snapped Caleb. "Have you no respect?"

"Respect is for people who earn it," said Serena. She smiled at the bashful giant who had watched her so yearningly for so long. The spirit of the scene had transformed him, melting his shyness away.

Caleb was bristling. With relief Serena spied her father emerging from the bustle near the taphole. He pointed first to her, then to Caleb.

"Caleb—Father wants you," she said urgently.

Caleb hesitated, his glance shifting from her, to Enoch, to Old Samuel.

His employer beckoned imperiously.

Caleb swallowed hard. "Come with me, Price."

Serena shook her head. "No—Enoch can stay and protect me. Father would expect that."

Still Caleb hung back.

"Hurry!" she said. "You know how impatient he can be."

Samuel Wainwright had started toward them, beckoning yet again to his clerk.

Caleb made his decision. "Wait here, then. Don't stir until I come for you." Dodging among the celebrants, he was gone.

ⅇ ⅇ ⅇ

"THAT WILL FETCH HIM awhile, if I know Father." Serena smiled at Enoch, a dimple flashing.

Enoch seemed tongue-tied. The daintily voluptuous figure had not been so close to him before. Beneath the brimstone stench from the furnace, he caught a breath of verbena from her hair.

"There's dancin' tonight, Miss Serena. Master Sooy, at the White Stag, he's made ready. Two fine bucks be hangin' a week now, and there be bushels of oysters brought up from the bay. Old Hank, from Tuckerton, he's brought his fiddle, and he's promised to play his air tune—the one that danced the Devil down."

Serena smiled. Like as not Fiddler Hank found his "Devil" at the bottom of his jug of rum. Then her eyes turned wistful. Folk tale or not, she'd never heard his "air tune." And her feet itched for the dancing she knew would continue long past dawn. "Enoch, you know Father will never let me go." Then the evening's enchantment overcame her. It seemed almost a sin to let this night end like any other night of the year. Supper and prayer and bed—while two miles away windows blazed with light and rafters rang with merriment?

Caleb was threading his way back to her. In a moment her chance would be gone.

"Listen, Enoch," she whispered hastily, "I *will* go with you tonight. But Father must never know of it. I cannot meet you till nine—by then they'll all be abed."

Enoch hesitated. Defying his redoubtable employer might cost him dearly in the end. But to dance with Serena? To have her to himself on the way there? And he would find words to tell her he wanted her as his wife. And to tell her father, too. For Old Samuel respected competence more than birth. And perhaps he would never learn of this escapade.

"The dancin' be barely begun then!" He could hardly believe his luck.

"I'll meet you by the shallops at the farther dam. I may be late—wait for me!"

"I'll wait, Miss Serena. I'll wait till midnight if need be."

Enoch hurried off into the darkness. Serena turned to Caleb. She accompanied him sedately back across the bridge and left him at the door of Wainwright House.

C H A P T E R ❧ 4

S ERENA, holding tight to Enoch's arm, stepped into the clearing by the White Stag. The storm was well under way, and a flurry of snowflakes pursued them as they sought the shelter of the porch. The wooden sign with its white stag creaked to and fro above their heads. A few Jersey wagons stood about the clearing, horses hunched against the cold. "Look!" said Serena, "I'll warrant they'll not sleep in Tuckerton tonight, or even Long-A-Coming." The Tuckerton stage stood empty near the dual-tracked sand road. The team had already been unhitched, and now a hostler struggled to unload some heavy baggage from the roof.

"They'll be glad to doss down two to a bed," said Enoch. "Always allowing Master Sooy has room. Likely they'll not mind biding—listen!" As the tavern's oak door swung wide to admit latecomers, sounds of merrymaking burst into the night: the scraping of a fiddle, shufflings and scufflings and laughter, the clank of pewter tankards on the trestles. Candlelight spilling through the windows gilded the weathered boards of the porch. "Let's go in!"

"Wait! My slippers." Hanging onto Enoch for balance, Serena tugged at her fur-lined boots. The change of footgear gave her a moment to catch her breath. On the loose sand of the curving trail from Weyford, every step had taken the effort of three. She stowed the boots beneath a window. Her feet in their supple kid slippers tapped in time to the muffled music. But still she hung back, smoothing her hair, settling her shawl. Now that she was here, trepidation seized her.

At last she nodded to Enoch. They swept into the room on a torrent of noise that subsided abruptly at their entry.

"It's old Wainwright's daughter." Swift as a bay wind over reeds the whisper spread through the tavern. Enoch peered over the heads of the crowd, seeking an empty table. Serena studied the scene, her lowered

lashes screening her eyes. The long, low-ceilinged room was full of men —
a few known to her from the furnace crew, some whose soot-stained
faces proclaimed them colliers, a handful who might be farmers, and, at
a table by the fire, a party whose elegant garments proclaimed them
travellers from the stage. Here and there a flash of colour betrayed a
woman's presence. But these were not the goodwives of Weyford, long
gone to their virtuous rest. Nor yet were they farmers' wives. These were
"Pineys" for the most part, colliers' women and daughters of backwoods
hunters. And their rigid faces told Serena they considered her out of
place.

Her face burned. Her gown of fine claret wool, whose snug fit and
deep neckline had goaded the goodwives to hissing in the holly-decked
drawing room of Wainwright House at Christmas, now seemed ostentatious. Serena clutched her shawl about her, but its Oriental fantasies
of jade and crimson, azure and gold were scarcely less conspicuous than
her gown. For a moment she wanted to run. Then she swallowed hard,
lifted her chin, and gave Nicholas Sooy a dazzling smile as the host of
the White Stag scurried through the crowd to greet her.

"Mistress Wainwright! You honour our house. What word from your
brother?" Bowing, smiling, talking easily, Nicholas Sooy led her to a
choice seat in a corner. A tiny man, slender and courtly, the very reverse
of the traditional stout host, he tried to put Serena at her ease as his
mind raced to encompass this aberration. What can she be thinking of?
he mused, appalled. Surely her father cannot know she has come here.
To observe a muster with her brother in broad daylight — yes, of course.
But at night? And on such a night? Sooy's thin lips beneath his trim
Vandyke narrowed in resolution: I must see that she comes to no harm
here. He settled Serena at the table, then motioned to Enoch. "What do
you wish? Oysters? Venison? I trust my guests may have left you a few
morsels. Something to drink?"

"Cider, please," said Serena, fearful of drinking strong spirits.

"Bring Mistress Wainwright a Stewed Quaker first," said Enoch. "And
one for me. Some oysters, too. And then the venison."

"The very thing on a night cold as this one." Sooy bustled away.

Serena's cheeks cooled a bit as the hubbub rose and onlookers resumed
their conversations. If some of them gossiped about her, at least she
could not hear them. Letting her shawl drop from her shoulders, she
looked about the room.

The White Stag was ablaze with light. In sconces along the walls, the
flames of bayberry candles dipped and swayed with the draught of the
merrymakers' passage. Above the teakwood bar — hewn, it was said,

from ships' timbers salvaged by the wreckers at Barnegat—tin whale-oil lamps dangled, threatening the heads of the drinkers. Near the door was a space cleared for dancing. There sat old Hank on an upturned keg, twisting the pegs of his fiddle, ear close to the strings to test their tune. Trestle tables heaped with oyster shells had been shoved together helter-skelter in the remaining space, and the smell of roast venison hung tantalizing upon the air.

Here came Master Sooy bearing two tankards of hard cider. At his heels trailed a lackey with a tray on which reposed a platter of oysters and two apples highly polished. A third man trotted to the fireplace and returned brandishing a pair of red-hot pokers.

"Two Stewed Quakers," pronounced the host. Setting the tankards on the table, he plunged a hot poker into each. The tart liquid sizzled and frothed, foaming over the edges of the mugs. Sooy dropped the apples into the boiling cider and they in turn sputtered and popped. "Stewed, indeed," said Sooy. "Do not the Quakers deserve it for calling Weyford cannonballs Devil's pills?" Serena laughed. Indeed, a Quaker captain had used just those words in refusing to carry the shot.

Enoch cracked the oyster shells and handed them to Serena. Savouring the briny juice, sipping the frothy cider, she began to enjoy her adventure. Enoch, somewhat daunted by his temerity in having brought her here, seemed to have little to say. Snatches of neighbouring conversations bobbed briefly to the surface, then swirled away.

"It be blowin' a nor'easter, sure."

"The Barnegat Shoals be claimin' their own tonight."

"An' the Barnegat wreckers'll pick 'em clean by mornin'."

Knowing laughter greeted this sally. The storm held first claim on conversation. Even so, the Battle of Chestnut Neck clearly remained a source of hot contention, for all it had happened months ago. The British had taken the Neck unaware, destroying a goodly portion of its "nest of Rebel pirates" before setting out for Weyford. But an alert farm lad had seen the Redcoats crossing the Mullica River. A ragtag force of iron-workers, hastily summoned from their beds, had ambushed the British and saved the furnace and forge. For all that, loss of the privateer fleet had dealt the Patriots a heavy blow.

"Drownt. Has to be," said a gruff voice behind Serena, apparently referring to one privateer's captain. "Not been seen since. Went down with his ship, more'n likely."

"Be missed, he will. None of t'others had his spirit. Remember the time . . ."

"Rowed a whaleboat right under their noses . . ."

"Sailed the *Mary Ann* right up the Mullica . . ."

"Auctioned off her cargo while the Lobsterbacks tried to get the range . . ."

"Sent the captain back to 'em in a rum barrel marked 'here's a toast for King Georgie'."

"Aye, that be a man. Who's to laugh in the Lobsterbacks' faces now?"

Serena turned to Enoch. "Who is that they speak of?" If he answered, she did not hear him. The colour drained from her face. She gripped the edge of the table so hard pain shot from her knuckles to her elbows.

The fiddler had started playing, and some of the crowd near her table had thinned as dancers took the floor. For the first time her view was unimpeded. A door she had not noticed opened beyond the stairs. And the man sidling through it? That hunch of the shoulders, the wool cap about the ears—Caleb Sawyer. He leaned down to talk with a stranger seated half-hidden in a secluded nook.

For some moments they remained deep in discourse. Then the stranger rose, his elegant back still turned. There was nothing of the Barrens about his dress. Stepping back, Caleb scanned the room. And now he saw her. His face flushed nearly purple. His eyes narrowed in a malevolent glare. Then he half-ducked and turned away.

Why, he's as afraid of me as I am of him, thought Serena. But why? "Enoch, there's Caleb Sawyer. Please—clear the way for me. Perhaps I can prevail upon him not to tell Father."

Enoch shouldered a path through the crowd—but too late. Caleb had scuttled down a passageway. Serena did not try to follow. My cap is surely over the windmill now. Well, then, by God, I'll enjoy this night. The least Father will do is lock me in my room for weeks. A scrawled piece of foolscap fluttered on the planks. She picked it up. The few words she read in a glance made her pale. She looked quickly round and thrust the paper into her bodice. Old Hank was well into a rollicking reel. "Dance with me, Enoch. Did you not ask me here to dance?" Enoch took her hand and guided her to the floor.

&a &a &a

"DANCE, MIZ SERENA?" It was little Mike McGuire of the furnace crew. With a partner near his own size, Mike stepped smartly enough. But before they could finish the figure, another man cut in. Serena tossed her head back. Her cheeks were flaming. The cider had affected her more than she knew: Her feet had a will of their own, sliding and tapping to the rhythm of the reel. Now the dancers skipped in a circle, many joining hands. Then a gigantic barrow boy swung Serena round and round. Her feet left the floor, her skirts swung wildly.

"Play your air tune, Hank," called a collier. Sweat flew from Hank's face. His bow was a blur of motion as he sawed away faster and faster. Likely it seemed indeed that the Devil had been danced to exhaustion. The dance accelerated madly. Serena could scarcely breathe. Faces whirled past her. Enoch. Master Sooy. And—Caleb, slit-eyed with jealous animosity. Now, what . . . ? The thought was swept away.

Suddenly the fiddle quavered to a halt. The dancers stopped. Jolted out of her enchantment, Serena tried to find her balance as her partner set her roughly on her feet. Enoch sprang forward and steadied her. The tavern door was open. The candles sputtered in the draught, setting monstrous shadows to capering about the room. By the doorway, by the stairs, in the passage to the kitchen stood men armed with pistols and clubs.

"Joe Mulliner," someone whispered. "Might've known he'd not miss this frolic."

Mulliner's was a name Serena knew. The goodwives in the drawing room spoke of him often. Leaning forward, bonnet to bonnet, speaking in the aspirate whisper that relishes another's misfortunes even as it deplores them, they recounted his many crimes. Mulliner's was the largest, and apparently the best organized, of the outlaw bands that ravaged the Barrens. Calling themselves Refugees, professing British sympathies, they were in fact wont to prey with a fine impartiality on Patriot and Tory alike, plunder their aim. Lonely farmsteads near the coast had learned to fear them. Occasionally a fat bullock or two found its way to the British commissary, and there were those who gave accounts of Refugee spying, but for the most part pillage and arson were matters of pure sport.

Rather less dishevelled and more debonair than his rivals, Mulliner conducted his sorties with a flair the others lacked. His eye for a pretty woman was fabled throughout the Barrens, and the patrons of more than one tavern had been held at pistol point while he danced with the fairest among them. Even churches were not safe from his incursions, and it was said one wedding had been halted because he demanded to kiss the bride. This woman—so the goodwives whispered—blithely abandoned her lacklustre groom and was last seen riding pillion with Mulliner. After such forays, which had earned him the sobriquet "dancing desperado," he was said to retreat to an island on the Mullica, evading

interception of his orders by tying them to the collar of his dog, whom
he trained to swim the river by night.

The man now shouldering his way into the White Stag was massive: six feet tall and broad in proportion, dressed all in black. Unlike his minions, he scorned to wear a mask, and his clean-shaven face glowed ruddy in the light. Tousled red curls fell to his ears; these, and the red silk scarf at his throat, were the only touches of colour about him. Pistol in hand, he surveyed the company. His brown eyes gleamed with amusement.

"Sure," he said, "but it's hurt I am to see such a fine frolickin' held without me. Well, it's never too late, eh lads?" More of his men poured into the room, taking up positions by door and window. Someone shut the door, and the flickering light steadied. Mulliner swaggered to the serving bar. "Host—it's a hard ride we've had tonight, and we've a mighty thirst. Draw me a drink."

He took the pewter mug from Sooy's trembling hand, tasted, and spat. "Pah!" The mug rolled on the floor. "Applejack! And not well aged at that. Is this the White Stag? Or is this a jug tavern, Sooy? Do ye be savin' the Barbados for the swells? To the cellars, man. Bring us something worth drinkin'. Follow him, Gimp—see he tries no tricks."

Sooy flushed. To call the White Stag a jug tavern amounted to the grossest insult. Of these disreputable establishments, isolated on lonely trails, travellers said, "No matter what drink you order, it all comes from the same jug. And no matter how many in your party, you sleep in the same bed." The ruffled proprietor of the White Stag soon emerged from the cellars, slim bottles under each arm, a cobweb in his beard.

Mulliner took a swig. "Ah, that's better." He wiped his mouth on his sleeve. "The finest Barbados. I'll wager you got that from one of our brave privateers. Here's to the British captains! May they send what's left of that scurvy lot to the bottom of Barnegat Bay!" He tilted the bottle to his lips and swallowed noisily. "A bottle for each of the boys, Sooy. Mind you keep your wits about you, lads. And now, ladies, who has a mind to dance with me?"

Serena tried to edge into the crowd, but the movement caught Mulliner's eye. He walked toward her, his heavy footfalls setting the boards to trembling. "What have we here? A little red rose? A finer flower than I've seen in these parts before." While Mulliner was drinking, the watchers had relaxed a little. Now the tension in the room swiftly rose again.

Mulliner reached to tip up Serena's chin. Enoch sprang for him. The next instant he lay bleeding on the floor. Two ruffians leapt forward to hold him down. Another grabbed Mike McGuire. He struggled gamely, but his captor was twice his size, and flashed a knife. The crowd stirred restlessly, but no one else came forward. "Play!" called Mulliner to the paralyzed fiddler. He took Serena's wrist and yanked her onto the dance floor.

Serena looked around, beseeching someone to help her. A few men, embarrassed, shuffled their feet. The women's faces were stony. One woman, a short, plump redhead, stared brazenly at her. As plainly as words, her expression said, "You came where you don't belong. Now take what's coming to you."

Serena's heart was pounding so hard her throat pulsed with its beats. Her head swam, her hands turned to ice, her feet would not obey her. She stumbled. "Whoa, there!" said Mulliner. "What a shy filly we've got here. I know how to warm up those hands." He seized her and held her to him. The buttons on his waistcoat pressed into her breasts. Mulliner's finery did not bear close inspection. He smelt of tobacco, rum, horses, and stale sweat. Serena struggled to breathe. Mulliner tipped her head back, hand in her hair, and kissed her.

She wrenched herself free. "No!" She began to fight. Her fists pounded his chest. Her feet flailed at his shins. He held her off one-handed, laughing. Then she brought up her knee. The blow hit home. But she was too short, too off balance, to disable her giant tormentor. He bent over briefly, face purple, but as she turned to run away he seized her fiercely by the waist, nearly bending her double. "By God, bitch, you need taming! And I'm the man to do it."

Mulliner grabbed a cloak from a bench and flung it over her head. Blinded, she fought at the smothering folds. As she managed to free her face, Mulliner slung her over his shoulder and burst through the door. As he crossed the inn yard, the snow almost blinded him. Several inches had piled up on the ground. He slipped once and nearly dropped her. "Cover me, men! Cut their horses loose and take their britches. Empty their pockets. Then scatter and ride like hell."

He flung Serena across the horse's shoulders. She kicked and squirmed. The horse shied nervously. "Lie still, wench—ye'll have us both trampled." He was in the saddle now, jerking her upright. At once the horse was in motion. Serena looked back toward the tavern, hoping against hope for rescue. One man had managed to slip past the guards in the commotion. He stood on the porch, watching. It was Caleb.

Then Mulliner's body blocked the White Stag from view. He spurred the horse to a wild gallop. It plunged down a narrow trail that twisted and turned through the darkness.

Now here they turned, now there, for an endless time of which Serena lost all counting. Once the hoofs spattered through water; more than once the horse slipped and nearly lost its footing. Branches lashed at Serena; snow pelted her face. Her body was sore from the constant jolting, bruised where Mulliner's fingers dug into her ribs. On and on they went, through the wild night, over this trail and that, deep into the Barrens.

At last they slowed to a near halt. Now she could hear the soughing of branches and, closer by, an irregular clicking sound pitched higher than the moan of the wind and thus audible despite it. Before her muddled wits could place the sound, a pitch-black structure loomed before them. The horse halted. Mulliner pulled her roughly down and bore her triumphantly inside.

CHAPTER ❧ 5

"JOSEPH MULLINER, you are a fool." The words swept into the chamber on a blast of air as icy as the tone in which they were uttered. Then the heavy door shut with a crash.

Serena gasped. The voice was one she knew.

In the depths of the fieldstone fireplace, dying embers flared. Smoke billowed toward the timbered ceiling; fugitive snowflakes sizzled on the hearth. On the stand by the tumbled bedstead, a candle guttered and died.

The bedstead lurched, its rope springs creaking, as Mulliner scrambled to his feet. Steel flashed in his hand, then vanished as he straightened, tucking the knife into his boot. "Brandon? Be that you?"

Straining against the bonds that lashed her to the bedposts, Serena peered around her captor's bulk. A tall, slim man stood by the door, his cloak swirling about his knees, a pistol in his hand. Shadows crisscrossed his features; firelight made sparks of the melting snow in his dark hair. For a long, still moment, he held Mulliner's gaze. Then, with deliberate slowness, he thrust the pistol inside his cloak and stepped into the light.

Serena struggled to raise her head. Her throat tightened; a cry of grateful welcome rose to her lips. *It is he! The stranger. Father's midnight caller—come to rescue me.* But her greeting died unuttered as the newcomer sent her a glance full of meaning. *Be still!* he ordered, as plainly as if he spoke. *Be still—you do not know me.* Serena sank back, wondering at her instant comprehension of his thought.

"Brandon," said Mulliner again. For all his bulk he seemed to sense himself subordinate, chastened as a stablehand caught tippling. "What the hell—?"

"*Captain* Brandon. I do not recall giving you leave to address me as a familiar. We were to meet here, Mulliner, *alone*. I gave you no leave to

make free of my belongings, nor to place *my* quarters, *my* bed, at the
service of your . . . impetuous romps."

"What be it to you how I pass me time?"

Tearing off his cloak, Brandon flung it at a bench. He circled the room with his glance, acknowledging the signs of struggle. He gave Serena another warning look. Still puzzled, she held silence. "And rough the sport with which you choose to pass it." In contemptuous dismissal, he turned away to warm his hands at the fire.

Mulliner stirred. "But—"

Brandon whirled to face him, his eyes blazing with the fury he had so far kept in check. "You blundering jackanapes! Were it not for this storm, the whole howling pack from the White Stag would even now be upon us—and that Tory catspaw with them. Months of hiding gone for naught. And why? You hear a fiddle, you spy a pretty face, and you lose what little head you have. Well then, by all that's holy, why not tumble some collier's doxy who might welcome your infamous attentions? Must needs you seize upon the daughter of old Wainwright himself? And abduct her into the bargain?"

"If it's Wainwright's daughter she be, what were she doin' dancing with the barrow boys? I thought she—"

"You thought! No, Mulliner, we're in this pickle precisely because you did *not* think. Not thinking is your way of life. And one day soon it will be your death. The dancing desperado indeed! You'll do your dancing on Gallows Hill with the hangman calling your lay. But I'm damned if I'll dangle from some British mast because of your escapade. I'll not have the British learn I did not drown at Chestnut Neck. I'll not have this place found. Not by the Patriots. Not by those who choose to seem such. Still less by the British. Nor will I be hounded from hummock to hill while the *Audacious* is fitted for sea. The worst night's work I ever did was to hire your Refugee ruffians."

Serena listened in a daze. Freed of Mulliner's weight, she breathed deeply at last. The mists of terror, pain, and unaccustomed drink lifted, and she struggled to think. That lean countenance, taut now with anger; the confident bearing of that lithe body clad in linen shirt, breeches, and boots: Indeed, this was the man who came to Wainwright House by night and haunted her thoughts by day. His words suggested that he had stumbled upon her plight upon arriving for some clandestine meeting. What commerce had he with Joe Mulliner?

More quietly now, authority supplanting annoyance, Brandon continued. Mulliner stood subdued, head cocked in an attitude of listening. "Your fool's luck has brought you the snow to cover your tracks and confound your pursuers. By the time they recovered their wits and their horses, you were well away. The swamp path will have frozen solid – take it. Ride like the devil, and perhaps you can reach the Quaker bridge crossroads before them. Let them think you have taken her westward. Lure them as far as the strength of your horse will let you. Then you can . . ."

❧ ❧ ❧

RELIEF FLOODED through Serena, sweeping Brandon's curt orders beyond her mind's grasp. Soon her captor would be gone, and she set free. Eagerly she gulped the cold, fresh air that had swept Brandon into the chamber. Instinctively she sought to wipe from her lips the traces of Mulliner's kisses. The thong binding her wrist cut off the gesture. She knew that Brandon's arrival had spared her an ultimate shame, the nature of which she understood but dimly. But – who *is* this Captain Brandon? Why did he come here? Why is Mulliner afraid of him? He is, I know he is. And *why*, damn him, is he lounging at his ease by the fire, chatting with that ruffian as though they were allies of long acquaintance, accomplices if not friends?

Her thoughts raced frantically down a dozen blind trails, then swerved to her own predicament. What must Brandon be thinking? She felt the hot, shamed blood coursing through her cheeks as she realized how she must look to him now: not Samuel Wainwright's daughter, sheltered and aloof, but some strumpet tossed down for a tumble. The skirts of her gown were crumpled about her knees. The lace at the neckline was in tatters. Her hair, torn from its bodkins, lay in tangled skeins about her shoulders. Her slippers were lost, her stockings flung aside, her petti-coats lying torn upon the floor. Only her tightly laced bodice, its whale-bone impervious to her captor's tuggings, had spared her lying naked in Brandon's sight.

She twisted her body, trying to burrow into the quilts. Sensing her movements, Mulliner half turned, and over his shoulder she saw Brandon shake his head. Swift as an eyeblink the message passed: Do not attract his attention. We want him away.

"Mulliner!" snapped Brandon, "make haste or you've no chance to evade them."

A flurry of movement, a clink of coin, a last, muttered colloquy by the door. Then the screech of heavy hinges and, felt as much as heard, the groans of branches tortured by the wind. For some moments the storm was a living presence in the room. Then a muffled sound of hoofbeats

rose above it. They ceased abruptly as Brandon shut the door and slammed
home the bolt that Mulliner, in his mad haste, had left unfastened.

For a few moments more Brandon ignored her. He did not approach
the bedstead. Instead, he went back to the fireplace and tossed in some
pine cones to rekindle the embers. Then he threw on some logs and
swung the crane nearer the blaze.

Some formless doubt kept Serena silent. Nothing in her sheltered life
had prepared her for this moment. When first she had seen the stranger,
his glance had touched the secret places of her body and stirred quiescent
fibres of her being, setting them to vibrating with unfamiliar yearnings.
Now, beneath her leaden cloak of weariness, those fibres resonated, setting her to shuddering, not with fear but with tension of another sort,
unexplained, unresolved, unreleased. This encounter had found her taut
and trembling, poised at the threshold of long-forbidden knowledge —
knowledge of what it meant to be fully a woman. However it ended,
could she ever be a carefree girl again?

Then he turned. He snatched his cloak from the bench and flung it
over her. Only then did he bring a taper from the fire and relight the
candle by her side. He drew a knife from his boot — so he, too, carries a
knife, thought Serena — and matter-of-factly, with four swift strokes,
severed the thongs that bound her.

Serena sat shakily upright, clutching the cloak to her breast with her
arm as she rubbed her tingling wrists. "Water," she whispered. "Please."
He brought a flagon and held it to her lips as she gulped thirstily. "Thank
you," she said faintly, wiping her lips with the back of her hand.

He nodded. Then his face changed. His features hardened. His eyes —
blue, she saw, the colour of distance — became remote. He straightened
and backed away from the bed. His left hand resting lightly on the frill
of his linen shirt, his right staying a phantom scabbard, he bowed as
impeccably as though a ballroom lay at his back. "Good evening, Mistress
Wainwright. You seem distressed. Pray, excuse the impetuosities of my
late companion. His manners equal his discretion, if not his taste."

He straightened then, the stern set of his lips belied but little by the
faint trace of a quiver at their corners. "Please pardon the liberty of my
addressing you in the absence of a proper introduction. The occasion
appears to require it. My name, Mistress Wainwright, is Stuart Brandon,
late of His Majesty's service and now captain of my own fleet, however
small. Your name, as you see, I already know. And now . . ." He looked
down at her accusingly. "Pray tell me, Mistress Wainwright, how you
propose to resolve the predicament in which your willfulness has placed
me?"

C H A P T E R ⟡ 6

T HE WORDS STRUCK Serena like a splash of cold water. Never thinking that this had, at least in part, been his intent, she struggled to
her feet, wincing at the pain that shot through her cramped limbs. "My
willfulness? *Your* predicament?" A sudden lightening of his expression
reminded her of the cloak. She quickly wrapped it round herself and
confronted him squarely with what dignity she could. And suddenly, as
though the upright posture had cleared her brain, she realized fully
whom she faced.

Fragments of memory, snatches of conversation, had swooped like
summer moths, elusive and tantalizing, beyond her mind's grasp. Now
they coalesced. And she knew that her rescuer—or was he her adver-
sary?—possessed a subtle wit that made Mulliner's bluster seem the
posturing of a child.

The White Stag, she thought. What were they saying about some
privateer? Of course: Captain Brandon. Captain Stuart Brandon. This
is the man who's set Barrens tongues to wagging with tales of his raids
and the womenfolk to twittering with rumours of his looks. It was he
who rowed an eight-man whaleboat up to the *Mary Ann* one pitch-dark
night and captured captain, ship, and crew. His privateer fleet cruised
Barnegat's channels to leave His Majesty's wiliest captains stranded
upon the shoals—until the raid on the "nest of Rebel pirates" left Stuart
Brandon sword in hand upon a blazing deck, a British boarding party
before him and a powder magazine at his back. The explosion had hurled
him overboard and he had drowned—or so it was said. "Who's to laugh
in the Lobsterbacks' faces now?" they had asked one another at the
White Stag.

The answer stood before her. Captain Stuart Brandon: alive and in
hiding.

His glance acknowledged her recognition. "Precisely, Mistress Wainwright. *Your* willfulness. Had you retired like a lady to your virtuous
bed, you and I would not have met so precipitately. Nor would Mulliner
be riding through the storm as for the midwife. We'd all be asleep, and
not"—he smiled slightly—"together. And soon you'd be waking at Black
Susan's call."

How well does he know me—and the ways of Wainwright House?
What connection is there between him and my father?

"Well, Mistress Wainwright? Now what are we to do?"

Serena rallied. His mocking demeanor enraged her; the anger it kindled
annealed her pride. "So this is the brave Captain Brandon, scourge of
the British fleet. I'd not have thought you placed so easily at a loss. The
answer is simple. Take me home and be gone about your business—
whatever that business may be."

Home, she thought longingly, her anger spent. I want to be home: to
wake up in my own familiar room with the light of the lake rippling
upon the ceiling and the dawn of a new day breaking outside. To be
with Mother, with Father, even with Prue. How strange that just this
morning Wainwright House seemed a prison. *This* is the prison, this
gloomy chamber with its sooty walls, and he—in him I sense a gaoler
more formidable than the abductor he so tersely dismissed.

Thinking of the bright promise with which this day had dawned, she
fought to hold back her tears.

Brandon had been watching her closely. "Home?" he said, one eyebrow
raised. "In this?" As he spoke, a fusillade of sleet assaulted the door. The
gale howled in the chimney; a branch crashed upon the roof.

"Yes, damn you! Home!" Serena's temper snapped. She lunged for
the door. Brandon was there before her. He watched with a quizzical
smile as she struggled with the bolt, a massive affair of wrought iron.

"Permit me." With a flick of the wrist he shot the bolt back. The door
blasted open as he sprang aside, pulling her with him. "Pray, look." The
heavy door slammed against the wall as the wind rushed into the room.
Snowflakes whirled up, down, here, there, stinging her face and bared
throat. Her hair whipped about her ears. Her torn skirts fluttered as the
storm snatched insistently at them, urging her into its frigid embrace.
Snow was piled knee-deep in a drift upon the threshold.

Serena nearly lost her footing as Brandon forced the door shut and
threw the bolt. He stood with his back against it, gripping her shoulders,
shaking her gently with each word. "You surprise me, Mistress Wainwright.
I had not judged you a fool. Where, pray, did you intend to go—barefoot
into the bargain? And how would you find your way there? The trails by

which Mulliner brought you here defy seasoned woodsmen in broad daylight. How did you hope to retrace them in darkness and in storm?"

Serena drooped, stunned to silence, her teeth chattering. Melting snow trickled between her breasts, setting her to shaking at its icy touch.

"Besides," Brandon went on, "I have taken considerable pains to let the British think me dead. Foolhardy as it was for the impetuous Joseph to have brought you here, I fear I must insist that you remain. A pack of avengers in hot pursuit of me would be most damnably inconvenient."

Serena raised her head. "Take me home, then—as far as the finger-board—in the morning. I'll walk from there. They don't know you were part of this. They need never know—the others. Father . . . Father already knows you're alive. He'd not tell. But I won't tell even him—I swear it. I know what you've done for the Patriot cause and now"—she flushed—"for me."

"Pah! You—a woman—keep such a juicy tidbit to yourself? Women are born with their tongues clacking and die with them clacking still. The day a woman keeps a secret is the day cats can fly."

"But I promise—"

"Women's promises! Not worth the breath they waste making them." His face hardened. He seemed to look through and beyond her, his gaze bleak and cold. "No," he said, "I'll not stake my life on the word of any woman."

"Damn you!" Head up, eyes blazing, Serena sprang at him, kicking at his shins, pounding her fists upon his chest. "Let me go! Let me go!" He grabbed at her wrists, fending her off as she sought to claw his face. "Let me go!" Her voice rose. "I want to go home—home, damn you! I *will* go home." With the fury of an animal in its last throes she twisted and kicked and fought.

He did not strike her as she half expected. He merely caught her flail-ing arms and forced them slowly to her sides. Her burst of strength was soon exhausted. Her struggles subsided. "Home," she whispered. Then the tears came. Her body shook as her sobbing mingled with tremors of exhaustion and chill.

Brandon hesitated. Then, with an awkwardness of unaccustom he drew her to him, cradling her against his chest, stroking her heaving shoulders, saying nothing. At first her body stiffened, resisting. Then she succumbed to the warmth, the strength, the comforting male scent of him. Awkwardly still, he smoothed her tangled hair. When at long last she quieted, he half guided, half carried her to the bench by the fire. Retrieving his cloak, he draped it over her shoulders, holding it round her as she strove for calm.

When he saw her clutch its edges to draw it round her he moved away

and busied himself about the fire. She sat huddled in the folds of fine
worsted that smelt comfortingly of leather and tobacco smoke, thinking
vague thoughts of her father, feeling spent.

As at a great distance, she heard him moving about: the whoosh of
the bellows, the crackle of rekindled flames, a scrape of ironmongery—
soothing sounds, all. Her eyelids drooped.

"Here." He tipped a mug of steaming tea laced with brandy against
her lips. The strong draught burned its way to her vitals. Then he set a
bowl and a sliver of soap on the bench and poured out some heated
water. Wringing out a linen cloth, he rubbed it with soap and handed it
to her. In a daze she took it, thinking only to wipe her face and hands.
But Mulliner's image lurched into her consciousness, and she rubbed
with the cloth until her skin burned, scrubbing and scrubbing at her
face, her throat, her mouth—again and again, her mouth.

"That's enough." He took the cloth from her and dropped it into the
bowl. Her face smarted from the harsh cleansing. Still, she felt the better
for it. She looked up at him then. How had he known? "I'd feel the same,"
he said simply. His compassion, unexpected now, totally at variance
with the man he seemed to be, overwhelmed her as his sarcasm had not.
Tears, released by the brandy, coursed unchecked down her face.

He reached down and pulled her to her feet. His lips twisted in the
ironical smile she had already marked as uniquely his. "You have borne
yourself bravely, Mistress Wainwright. I'd not thought to see such courage in a woman—nor such sentience. I thank you for that." He flicked
the tears from her face. "Come," he said softly, "it's near daylight. You
are cold and weary. Drink up: It's time you were abed." She drained
the last of the brandied drink. Already his features seemed distant and
indistinct.

He picked her up and carried her to the bedstead. She made no protest:
The capacity to protest seemed drained from her. Her limbs felt heavy,
bonelessly limp. She sensed practiced hands at her back, loosening her
stays. Feebly, she moved to protest. "Don't be a fool. You'll never sleep
in that Iron Maiden. How women bear such nonsense, I'll never fathom.
Here—take this. It seems I've a dearth of nightdresses on hand, but this
will serve."

He stripped off his shirt and dropped it on the bed, baring the muscled
torso and shoulders of a swordsman. "I'll absent myself while you make
ready." He moved off into the gloom, then glanced back. "Fear not for
your virtue, Mistress Wainwright. I've no need to steal from you, here,
what is offered me freely elsewhere." She heard the scrape of hinges and
the closing of an unseen door.

Anger at his arrogance briefly renewed her strength. She stripped away the cruel stays that cut off her breath and dug into her flesh the deeper with each moment that passed. She tossed her shredded garments aside and, finding a utensil beneath the bed, attended to her body's urgencies. Weariness again engulfed her. The sounds of the storm, ignored these many minutes, seemed louder in the hush that had descended upon the chamber. She slipped on the shirt he had given her. The warmth of his body still clung to its linen folds.

Drowsily she slid beneath the quilts. Dimly she sensed him reentering the room. Forcing her leaden eyelids apart, she saw him bending over her. His face was in shadow; she could not read his eyes. "Sleep," he said softly. "In the morning I'll see what's to be done."

He turned away. Serena felt herself poised in that glassy seeming stillness with which Weyford River plunged over its dam. Then she closed her eyes and was swept down and down into swirling, amber-tinted darkness.

C H A P T E R ❧ 7

W HEN AT LAST she awakened, Serena knew at once she was alone. Not even the wind broke the silence. The fire had dwindled to a few tired coals, and the air felt musty and chilled. As she grew accustomed to the dimness, she saw streaks of pale light at intervals along the walls.

Blinking, she fought for alertness. An unaccustomed languor urged her back to sleep. Her body felt spent and sore, as though covered by one vast bruise. Her head was aching; her tongue felt furry. Her brain was fogged like the air about her. Scattered thoughts trundled through her mind like recalcitrant carts of ore.

"Cold . . . so cold." Her words hung frozen in the stillness, suspended on the vapour of her breath. Instinctively, she tugged at the quilts, trying to draw them about her. It was then that she realized she was naked but for a man's shirt. Fast upon that knowledge came the memory of the night.

She sat up abruptly, head reeling. Pain pounded her temples. Her limbs felt stiff and sore. Where the leather thongs had bound her, red wheals circled her wrists. What have I come to? What is this place? And Stuart Brandon? What will I do when he returns? For he will return; I know it. Even to herself, she feared to voice the thought that came to her—that night's passing had somehow left her less able to withstand him than before.

She took stock of her surroundings. The massive bedstead on which she sat was roughly hewn of oak. Four crude bedposts, bark still clinging to them, rose to a lofty canopy. From the posts dangled strips of deerhide. As she glanced from these to her reddened wrists she blushed in mingled panic and shame.

"I'll think of that later," she whispered. "There's no time now." Her shoulders straightened; her chin assumed its customary tilt. She drew a deep breath and held it, alert for any sound of hoofs. She heard only the whispers of the diminishing wind.

She threw the quilts aside, surprised to find they were silk. Clutching at a bedpost, she came dizzily to her feet. Instead of the planking she expected, her bare toes encountered a rug. Even in this dim light it glowed: topaz and tourmaline, garnet and gold. Just for a moment, she paused, wondering, but the cold on her near-naked body cut short her reverie. Her teeth chattered. Goosebumps sprang out on her skin. Her clothes were nowhere to be seen. Very clever you are, Captain Brandon.

Suddenly the touch of his shirt on her skin became alien. She pulled it over her head and flung it from her.

I've some tricks of my own, Captain Brandon. Tensed against the shivers that rattled her teeth and roughened her movements, she tugged at the bedclothes. A sheet would serve. The sheets, she saw, were fine linen. She wrapped one around herself and tied it, toga-fashion, at her shoulders. It floated loosely, dragging on the floor. Though touching the thongs that dangled from the bedposts cost her a quiver of revulsion, she ignored it. She picked at the knots with panic-hastened fingers. Brandon might return at any moment. There! the thongs were loose in her hands. Tied end to end, they formed a crude sash that held her makeshift garment together. Decently if gracelessly covered, she set out to explore.

Not very hopefully, she tried the stout door. It was a crude affair of planking joined by iron studs of a dimension that suggested massive thickness. With both hands she tugged at the crosspieces, breaking a fingernail as she struggled. The door gave all at once and she staggered, her weight pulling it wide.

Grey daylight flooded the chamber. Her eyes watering, bare feet stinging from the snow that fell onto the floorboards, she grasped the doorframe and looked out. The snow was still falling, though lightly. It was everywhere, weighing down the trees, piled in shapeless mounds upon the forest floor. A trail of footprints, already drifting in, led along the brick wall and around a corner to where, she assumed, the horse had been quartered. Of her arrival with Mulliner, no trace remained.

Clearly this structure had once been a home—shuttered windows flanked the entrance. But beyond the stoop, where a clearing had been, ranged a thick stand of third-growth saplings, their slender limbs a lacework of white. Two full-sized trees stood among the scrawny newcomers, twin catalpas flanking a path that was no more. Long, curved seedpods dangled from the branches, clicking drily in the wind. A memory stirred

in Serena. I heard that sound last night, she thought. I do know where I
am. This is the old sawyer's place where Father and I once picnicked.

Old Samuel, ever eager for new holdings, had brought her here once years ago. The place had been a ruin even then, forsaken and desolate, its millrace dried up, its water wheel broken, rusted machinery scattered about. The outbuildings had already crumbled away and part of the roof had fallen in. The Barrens had set about reclaiming the site, and creeper vines were everywhere. Only the catalpas, exotics planted when the place was new, had survived.

On that bright June morning when first she had come here, orange daylilies had flamed in the rubble, the last spark of some woman's hopeful gardening, as alien as the catalpas. Serena, in her solitary wanderings, had seen such ruins elsewhere in the Barrens, which, in a few short years, could obliterate a generation's planning.

I'm but a half day's walk from home, though the trail was a faint one even then. But I can get home—I must, when the snow melts. If Stuart Brandon will not budge and Father has not found me.

She shut the door—a late addition, surely, not the formal portal she remembered—and looked around again. Yes, now one could see the outlines of the windows in this room she had thought to be sealed. But they were shuttered inside as well as out, and chained to boot. Captain Brandon, she thought, is very chary of intruders, unlikely though they would be to investigate this ruin. Any chimney smoke seen from a distance would be thought the work of a collier.

Fire, she thought. I need warmth. Then she saw what had escaped her attention. On a bench near the fireplace were bread, cheese, and teapot. Food first, she amended her thought. I'll think the better for some sustenance. She fell upon the food. Cold though it was, the tea refreshed her, and the bread was surprisingly good. How thoughtful my absent host is, she thought sardonically. I must remember to thank him. But I see he's taken the fire tools. Only the bellows remained. With these and some sticks of kindling, she coaxed the fire to life. When warmth began to seep through her, she resumed her exploration of the room.

Like the bed, the room was a blend of opulence and rusticity. The gold and cobalt glaze on the teapot—Meissen, like her mother's—glowed in the flickering light. The smooth wooden handles on the bellows were inlaid with mother-of-pearl. Pewterware gleamed on the mantel, and hangings warmed the shabby walls. Even her untutored eye recognized the rugs as Persian. A brass lamp swung from a beam.

Then the wall behind the bedstead caught her eye. Next to a rough cupboard was a door. That must be where Brandon had gone last night while she undressed. She lit a candle and pushed the door open, half fearing what she might find. Shadows fled up the walls as she entered. The chamber, though, was much like the one she had left, only further sunk into desuetude. The far wall had been shored with heavy timbers. Sea chests stood about. Most were padlocked and piled high in a corner, but one was open. A plume stirred in the draught; a glimmer of silk caught the candle's light.

Navigational charts were pinned to the crumbling walls, and more were piled in rolls upon a mahogany desk that straddled the room's near corner. A fireplace on the far wall showed signs of recent use. *It's true, then. He is planning some campaign against the British—a campaign more likely won if they believe him a menace no longer.* Her breath came faster. *Oh! she thought, to be able to fight as the men can—as Sam can, on the battlefield; as Father can, at his furnaces; as Stuart Brandon can, on the sea in open battle, or at night by cunning and stealth; to counter British tyranny in a manner immediate and real, not sitting primly by the fire knitting footgear for the troops. Oh, Father! Why cannot you see what I am? What I could be?*

A sound from outside broke her reverie. Hoofbeats! Stuart Brandon was returning. It seemed suddenly imperative that he not catch her in his quarters. Her heart pounding, she made for the doorway, her feet tangling maddeningly in the folds of her improvised gown.

❧ ❧ ❧

TOO LATE. He came upon her from behind, through some entrance she had failed to see. Catching her as she stumbled, he turned her round. "Good morning, Mistress Wainwright. I trust you slept well?" His glance took in her makeshift dress. "Well enough, at any rate, to go exploring. Women and cats—neither can rest until they know every detail of their quarters. Tell me, Mistress Wainwright, is your curiosity satisfied?" With a casual manner she sensed as false he quartered the room with his eyes.

"You need not fear, Captain Brandon. I've not touched your things— nor would I. It seems you know me less well than I'd thought."

He nodded. "Apparently so. You surprise me." He concluded his scrutiny of the room; finding nothing disturbed, he appeared to relax. He took off his cloak, shaking the snow from it. "Come, we've much to discuss. But first—" He proffered a bundle. "Your garments, Mistress Wainwright. I fear the worthy Joseph has left them the worse for his attentions."

She recoiled. The very sight of the claret wool made her gorge rise.

"So," he said, "I take it you don't wish to redon them?"

Her only answer was a shiver of revulsion.

He nodded slightly. "Very well then. It seems you find yourself in need of apparel." He walked to the open sea chest and began pulling out feminine garments. A sea-green moiré with lawn fichu. Silks and laces and delicate embroideries. Azure and crimson, sapphire and jade. He draped them over the trunks and boxes, the rich colours of the fabrics pooling on the splintered floor. "Have you no preference? The fashion-starved ladies of Philadelphia would barter all their husbands' riches—and who knows what else besides—to be offered such a selection."

Serena said nothing.

"You surprise me, Mistress Wainwright. I would have said you have an eye for a fine gown."

Whom were these gowns made for? wondered Serena. Sumptuous as the fabrics are, elegant the styles, they are not new. They're at least ten years older than the styles in Mother's pattern books—and those have been in the sewing room since before the Declaration.

As Brandon rummaged at the bottom of the chest, she caught a glimpse of ivory satin and a spiderwork of veiling. He snatched back his hand as though the gleaming fabric burnt it. "Margaret." His lips shaped a name that Serena could not hear, as his eyes shaped a vision she could not see. The woman who appeared in his mind's eye had none of the warmth he sensed in Serena. Hers was a beauty carved in ice, sheathed in scorn he had not noticed until too late. Mistaking coldness for purity and hauteur for strength, he had given his heart and received her pledge to marry. Then her trousseau had come back to him in this trunk, borne by the same messenger as her letter. She had married a man far wealthier than he—a man, moreover, who could bestow on her the title that the bend sinister in his coat of arms denied him. Abruptly, he snatched up the scattered garments and hurled them pell-mell into the trunk. He slammed down the lid, stepped aside, and brushed his hands together as though ridding them of some stain.

"No doubt you are right, Mistress Wainwright. Silks might be a trifle ostentatious in such humble quarters as these." He opened another chest, pulling out some cord breeches, a striped jersey, and a shirt of undyed Osnaburg. "Here—" Digging deeper into the trunk, he retrieved a fringed sash, some striped hose, and a pair of buckled shoes. "You can wear these. Then come in by the fire. We've a problem to discuss, you and I."

SERENA DONNED the jersey and breeches. She pulled on the coarse hose and clumsy shoes, then pulled the roughly woven shirt over her head. It hung loose, nearly to her knees, and she tied it with the sash. Then she tightened the shirt's lacings closely around her throat and returned to the main chamber.

He was seated by the fire, gazing into the flames, hands round his crossed knees. The room had assumed a more cheerful mien: The brass lamp had been lit and candles burned on the mantel. But his expression was remote, the lines of his face were grimly set. Her tiredness returned, and with it a sense of foreboding. Her every muscle ached with the longing to find some warm place and sleep and sleep and sleep. Damn him, she thought, why this constant duel of wits? She drew a deep breath. "Captain Brandon," she said, "it is time you took me home."

He looked up then. "Indeed? And what makes you believe you still have a home to go to?"

Something in his expression made her pale. She sat down on the bench opposite his and gripped its edge hard.

"I have been to the White Stag," he said. "Mulliner has led them a chase. They were far from here when the snow drove them home. Now there are no tracks to follow. But it would not matter if there were. In your place, Mistress Wainwright, I'd hope for little from the village."

"Father—"

"Your father has told them not to search for you. Indeed, he has said that if you set foot in Weyford village he will turn you out himself."

"I don't believe you! He would never—"

"You forget, my dear, that your honoured father is a man of irreproachable rectitude. Sin and ye shall be forgiven—by the Lord, mayhap, but not by Samuel Wainwright. Someone—no, it was not I—has persuaded your father you departed the White Stag with Mulliner by your own volition. Indeed, that you arranged to meet him there. The Lord our God is a jealous God, they say—and Samuel his servant a more jealous master still. 'Strumpet,' I'm told, is the word he used. Though 'harlot' may be nearer the mark."

"But that's monstrous! How could he believe . . . Who told him such a lie?"

"I do not know—though I can guess. But it matters little who told him: The point is, he believes it. No doubt your sister Prudence has already set about stitching an 'F' for fornication to adorn you, should you be so ill-advised as to return."

"How much you seem to know about Prudence. And my father. And, for that matter, about me."

"I learn what's necessary to go about my business and to protect myself from unpleasant surprises. And you, Mistress Wainwright, would have done well to do likewise. Had you done so, you might have spent last night in your own bed rather than in mine."

She blushed at the implication. So the warmth she had sensed in brief moments of wakefulness had been the warmth of his body. "What do you . . . Oh, what is the use." She made a move to rise, but her knees were too weak to support her. Confusion set her head to spinning. Is Stuart Brandon lying? But to what purpose? And how could Father banish me unheard? Who would tell him such a tale—and from whom would he believe it? She remembered, then, the look in Caleb Sawyer's eyes when he had encountered her at the White Stag—the malignant force that had leapt the distance between them. Caleb! Father would believe *him*. But what has Caleb to gain by disgracing me?

Her eyes swept the room as though imploring its walls to give answer. She saw a crumpled paper on the floor near the bed. Half bemused, she plucked it up and smoothed it. The motion seemed vaguely familiar. This was the paper she had picked up at the White Stag, thrust into her bodice, and forgotten. She held it up to the firelight.

Cannonballs—3 waggon loads.
Grapeshot—12 hogsheads.
Cannon—2.
Camp kettles—2 dozen.
To Morristown 20th next. By Quaker bridge and Red Lion.

Her hands trembled; her breath came faster. "Caleb Sawyer!" she cried aloud. "He *is* a spy!" The spidery hand was Caleb's: She had seen it a dozen times. So her careless remark at breakfast had been truer than she knew. Father must see this. He must know at once. We must not lose even one more load of shot.

Then, all at once, her mind linked the import of this paper with the tale that Brandon had recounted. If Caleb thinks I suspect his spying, he indeed has much to gain by my disgrace. He has Father's confidence; were I to return with my tale after a whole night's absence, is Father likely to believe me? But—this paper. Can Caleb explain that away?

"Captain Brandon, I *must* return home. For there's news I must give my father before the twentieth next. Look!" She handed him the paper. "Caleb Sawyer—or the stranger he was meeting—dropped this at the White Stag. It's proof he's a spy. You're a Patriot—you can help me. We must expose him at once!"

She stood tensely while Brandon scanned the paper. His expression did not change. "You think the ingenious Caleb could not explain this?" Before she could stop him, he crumpled the paper and threw it into the fire. It flared, blackened, fell in flakes onto the hearth. "A belled cat kills few starlings. As a liar, Caleb is the peer of most and the superior of many; as a spy he is sadly inept. Better to have him at Weyford than caught and replaced by someone with a brain for the business."

"You knew?"

"Of course."

"Then why did you not warn Father?"

"Your father, Mistress Wainwright, is a superb ironmaster whose talents at dissembling are nil. Surely you know that subtlety is beyond him. Moreover, he is willfully blind where Caleb Sawyer is concerned. Did he know, all hope of foxing Sawyer would vanish. And you underestimate the glibness of Sawyer's tongue and the extent of your father's wrath if you believe that paper would win you forgiveness. Your father, Mistress Wainwright, is not a forgiving man. And that is our predicament."

"He'll forgive *me*," said Serena proudly, "when he learns I've done nothing shameful." Nothing shameful? She thought again. She remembered her father's stern features, his relentless condemnation of "sin," the near jealous fury with which he had despatched any suitors of hers from Weyford. Her glance fell from Brandon's. She remembered that a night and most of a day had passed. She took a deep breath. "Father loves me. How could he believe ill of me on so slight an evidence as Caleb Sawyer's word—for it was Caleb who told him that, wasn't it?"

Brandon looked at her then, and his eyes held compassion. "Othello strangled Desdemona on so slight an evidence as a handkerchief—and on the word of a man that any but a jealous fool would see as a knave and a liar. It seems that those who love trust the loved one least of all."

Serena swallowed hard.

Brandon marked her comprehension. So, he thought, she has read Shakespeare's work. In this, too, she is different from the others. "Well, Mistress Wainwright, what are we to do? Shall I take you back to Weyford— to your father's tender mercies and the goodwives' wagging tongues?"

What manner of man is this? she thought. Why does he shift between kindness and scorn? Then, unbidden, the message of her body leapt to her mind's awareness. The look in his eyes had changed. Its meaning reverberated through her, setting her nerves to quivering as they had on that moonless night at Weyford when first she had encountered this man. Her weariness receded; a restless warmth lingered, suffusing her body and sapping her will.

"Well, Mistress Wainwright?" His voice had hoarsened. His eyes had darkened, their pupils wide. It was a look she knew only too well—the look he had given her at Wainwright House. It woke in her a response beyond volition. In the deepest recesses of her womanhood she felt an aching sweetness, an unidentified yearning. She struggled not to show it on her face. But he saw.

Oh, dear Lord, he knows—knows I neither want to leave this place nor lose him. He is so much that I have longed for unaware. He is of that wider world I sense but cannot reach. Her breath came faster. Her pupils, too, widened, dark with a desire she did not quite comprehend.

He watched her, silent, for a moment, then rose from the bench and drew her slowly to him. He tipped up her face and looked down into her eyes—eyes the colour of brandy, a deep, clear amber like the shallows of Weyford River when the sun of high summer warmed the sands. Flecks of jade floated in their depths, as though the essence of pines, sea, and sky had been distilled there. Now they were clouded with confusion and pain. You've the face and body of a woman grown—a beautiful woman. And you've both brains and bowels to complement that beauty. But you're still a child. Your world has changed forever through one rash act—and you've yet to realize it fully. He sighed. Almost reluctantly, he stroked her hair, roughened silk still faintly scented with verbena, electric with the vigor of youth. Then his fingertips gently traced her features: her brow creased with the first hint of an adult sadness, her cheekbones, her chin, and at last her lips. "Perhaps time will cool your father's wrath. Stay here then, until the *Audacious* sails: here, in the forest, with me."

Dazed, she could not answer except with her eyes.

"Stay here." His voice was muffled now, his lips against her skin.

Still she said nothing. But she moved closer and clung to him.

Gently he began untying the laces at her throat.

☙　☙　☙

NIGHT AND DAY and night again passed before the sun appeared. It rose on a shrouded silence. Mile upon mile, the Barrens glistened. Deer huddled, drowsy, in what shelter they could find; smaller creatures dozed in their burrows. An occasional bird chirped greeting to the dawn from within a needled refuge, then was still.

To the east the Atlantic spent the last of its rage in a froth of green-blue breakers netted with white foam. Cresting waves spun veils of spume tinted pink by the light of breaking day. At the tide line of the beaches, where the white sands met the grey, threads of ice stitched tangled seaweed to a lacework of broken shell. Dune grasses bowed beneath their silver burden, and in shallow bays behind fragile barrier islands the wind spent its last breath in teasing the reeds. Ice, splintered by their restless swaying, tinkled counterpoint to the surf's subsiding roar. On diked lands bordering the bays, cattle clustered for companion-ship and warmth, their breath hovering white in the air.

The vast Barrens wakened slowly as the sun rose from the sea, coaxing the pines to release their spicy fragrance into the gentled air. In the swamps and bogs, decaying ages warmed the waters, sending coils of mist to swath the sentinel cedars and to bead each needle with shim-mering pearls of light.

Dark, winding streams gurgled past icy shallows from their spring-fed, swampy sources to the bays. Only the streams broke the sombre ranks of pine, warmed here and there by the brown of oaks still clinging to the leaves and life of summer and—near the swamps—by hollies berried red. At intervals along the rushing waters, woodsmoke proclaimed the presence of men—the clustered chimneys of forge villages and the iso-lated huts of colliers.

The storm had sobbed itself to extinction with petulant tears of sleet. As the sun rose higher and the sky turned radiant blue, each pine needle became a prism, distilling a rainbow into the pellucid air.

At Tuckerton, at Waretown, at Barnegat, at a dozen lesser coves and bays, ice-sheathed masts and spars spread a tracery of fire in the sky. At Chestnut Neck, blackened corpses of burnt vessels glistened in their slick winding-sheets.

To the west of the Barrens, at the confluence of trails whose ruts cast blue shadows on the unsullied snow, was Cooper's Ferry. Across the Delaware River, moated by its ice, lay Philadelphia. In cobbled streets where bonfires had once welcomed independence, sentries trudged, grumbling at the cold. Stragglers huddled at braziers to warm their red-dened hands. Behind the brick walls of the city's snug homes, Patriot and Tory alike fed their fires, counted their shrinking stores, and pondered the outcome of the lengthening war whose rallying cry had been written at their doorsteps.

On the Jersey side, at Morristown, the ragtag-and-bobtail Continentals gathered at fires where camp cauldrons cast at Weyford hung steaming. They complained, as soldiers will, of the discipline of Baron von Steuben, newly come to train them, and the continued vexing absence of their pay.

At Weyford village, at Batsto and Gloucester and Aetna, at all the furnaces that fed on the living fuel of the Pines, the water wheels had halted. The furnaces rested, their fire subdued to embers and to ash. The hammers lay silenced, the casting sheds deserted. By Weyford landing, cannonballs awaiting shipment mounded innocent as eggs beneath the snow. The White Stag slept, shuttered and secretive, its revelers long gone to their rest.

Deep in the shrouded forest, exhausted by passion as fierce as the storm's, cradled by the strong arms that held her, Serena slept too.

CHAPTER ✍ 8

THE HORSE'S HOOFS stirred up a cloud of white dust as Serena and Stuart Brandon rode toward the sea. The white sand trail stretched before them, sparkling in the sun. Spring had flung its pastel gauzes over the sombre Barrens. Even as a few scrub oaks clung stubbornly to the last year's leaves, whortleberry bushes on the forest floor stretched blood-red fingers turgid with sap toward the warming light. In the low-lying wet spots the winged seeds of the swamp maples glowed like ruby glass, and the air was pungent with skunk cabbage unfurling its shoots of acrid green. Such standing pools as had not been dried by the un-wonted daily sunshine of the past few weeks mirrored blue skies and fleecy clouds.

The day was uncommon warm for April, and the exertion of the ride had flushed Serena's cheeks. Beads of moisture clung to the fine hairs of her upper lip and trickled between her breasts. Intoxicated by the sun-light, the motion, and the faint hint of flowers on the breeze, she turned her winter-pale face to the sky: sun-dazzled, sweat-silvered, heat-dazed. She wore breeches and rode astride, Brandon's body firm behind her, her awareness of her freed breasts intensified by his encircling arm. Her feet were bare, her clumsy shoes stowed in Brandon's bedroll. Her hair was bundled carelessly into a nautical cap.

✍ ✍ ✍

"WERE IT NOT for that hair," he had said to her this morning, "you'd make a passable lad—at a distance. Though close inspection would give you away. Here—hide that mane." He had tossed the cap to her, laughing. Then his laughter had faded abruptly. "Better you had been a lad," he'd said. "Better for Weyford—and for my peace of mind."

His interest in Weyford seems insatiable, she thought—like mine. He listens when I speak of what I would do there, were I a man and free to be Weyford's master. He does not scoff, as Father did, nor tease me, as did Enoch. Indeed, such patience is unlike him.

"Why do you ask me so often about Weyford?"

"Mere curiosity, Mistress Wainwright." Never, even in the transports of passion, had he abandoned that ironical address. She had not been deceived in this instance. The intent look about him when she spoke of Weyford belied his insouciant reply.

Now, as they traversed a sun-splashed stretch of trail, the horse passed under a sassafras tree. Serena snatched a handful of yellow-green florets and crushed them between her fingers to release their lemony scent. She brushed the fuzzed surface of a budding leaf against her lips, then his.

What bewitchment keeps me with Stuart Brandon, waking each dawn to a resolve to return to Weyford, whatever the cost, then sinking each night once more into his bed? What keeps me in thrall to this enigmatical adventurer whose sapphire eyes turn to flint if ever I seek some glimpse of his soul? Is it his looks? His exploits? The sense that with time and patience I might stir his heart as I know I stir his body?

It is all those things, she thought. But still more it is drowsy mornings when we lie sated in bed and talk together as equals, when he forgets his contempt for women and listens to my dreams. It is his books which I read in his absences, and what he says of them when he returns. For Brandon had often been absent on errands he forbore to explain, while she, once the snows receded, explored the surrounding Barrens and brought back woodland treasures to adorn their quarters: holly branches thickly berried for the pewter mugs on the mantel, the first arbutus, yellow-tasseled witch hazel, and osier twigs crimson with spring's quickened blood.

Now, lulled by his nearness and the sun's beneficent warmth, she let the leaves she had been fingering drift like feathers to the ground. Dreamily stroking the horse's sleek flanks, she let her mind float freely, pondering the days past and their meaning for her future. Her lad's attire: How did I endure women's clothing? No wonder men can do what women cannot: They can *move*. Ensnare a man in corset lacings, tangle his feet in petticoats, make him ride sidesaddle, and see how nimble he is then! She thought of the trees she had tried to climb, the brooks she had tried to leap, with those ever-hampering skirts forever about her legs — and of her mother's despair at the damage that ensued when Serena's clothing clashed with her proclivities.

Mother, she thought — does she miss me? Does she, too, think I rode off with Mulliner like a wanton, and wonder why? Were I to go to her, even now, and explain to her: Could she intercede with Father and win me back my home? But explain what? That for months I have lingered in the arms of a man whose very glance turns my bones to water? The snows were deep and fell one upon the other as I have not seen them fall in all my life—but the last one melted weeks ago. Will anyone truly believe I could not have come home, had I willed it?

In her time with Brandon she had seen him to be planning, not for one ship but for a fleet. Clearly he contemplated a series of sorties against British shipping come spring. His brusque, grudging replies and the evidence of her own observations informed her how thoroughly he planned. He spent much time poring over charts, and it was obvious that his frequent absences were connected with spying of some kind. Her own knowledge of the woods surrounding Weyford and the twisting, secretive rivers and coves might have helped him. But not until the last week or so had he paid her comments much attention.

❧   ❧   ❧

"LOOK," SHE HAD SAID two days ago, pointing to one of his charts, "there's Forkèd River. Its course does not run that way. There are smaller streams the chart does not show. Nor is that the true shape of the cove. The estuaries shift, you know, with every storm, and move with the years and the seasons. I was near there last year on Big Sea Day, and I *know* there is navigable water that does not appear on this chart."

Serena had looked wistful as she spoke. Big Sea Day had been the high point of each summer, when the populace of Weyford and the other forge villages followed Indian paths of an earlier time on a pilgrimage to the sea. The trails to the shore were thronged with wagons full of merry-makers keen for the taste of clams dug fresh from the sands at the ebb of the tide. Once they had ferried in relays across the shallow bays, the admonitions of stern preachers were forgotten. The villagers steamed their catch in seaweed, even as the Indians had before them, drank the briny clam broth, quaffed cider and ale, and cavorted barefoot upon the broad sands. Not even the nearness of the British fleet had quite quenched this yearly festival. Sober goodwives were known to shriek like children as the cold surf splashed their ankles. For once they forbore to scold about the young, who stole in couples through the dunes to sheltering hollows beneath the wind-stunted junipers. Serena sighed. She could almost hear the gulls, feel the shuddering of the sands pounded by the surf, smell the bracing air.

BRANDON HAD BROUGHT HER back to the present. "Very well then, where are they?"

"I cannot show you on the map—they are too hard to find. I am sure the contour of the land lies differently from this chart."

"And what would it serve me to know it?"

"I know—do you think me deaf and blind?—the *Audacious* must be nearly fitted. Where is she? At Barnegat?"

His eyes narrowed. "And what, pray tell, makes you think that?"

Serena sighed impatiently. "Where else? The wharves at Chestnut Neck are near destroyed. Besides, you're too likely to be seen there. Tuckerton is certain to be alive with Tories. And Waretown? Well, perhaps. But at Barnegat you have the protection of the Shoals. The British are unlikely to venture near them. You might escape attention. I wonder, though—" She had been about to ask why he had established his own hiding place so far from that of his ship. But she had not told him how precisely she knew where they were.

"But the secrets of the coastline are known to you, of course. So they teach navigation now at Hightstown? And coastline geography, too?" He stood for some moments, studying the chart. "Well, you've a fair sense of strategy—for a woman." His ironical smile did not quite remove the sting. "Where did you learn it? Haven't you spent your days as a fine damsel should—stitching at tapestries and cutting up reputations?"

"You know how I've spent my days—" She closed her lips tightly. Damn him! It's clear he seeks to profit from my knowledge—even as he twits me for having it. Why must we so often be at sword's point—and always because of some jibe about women? Why does he hate us so? And why should I tell him what I know—*or* how I know it? He'll only find some new way to scorn me. And yet, if he loses his ship . . .

She tossed her head. "With spring come, the British will grow more bold. They struck Chestnut Neck. Well-protected by the Shoals as Barnegat is, they may yet seek it out. What if they sortie against the shipworks? Suppose you could hide the *Audacious* until she is ready to sail—hide her deep in the Barrens where the Lobsterbacks can never find her?"

He looked at her speculatively. "You know of such a hiding place? How can you be certain it will serve?"

"I know what draught an ocean-going ship needs. And how she could be towed to such a spot. If you think me a fool, that's your concern—and

if it so turns out *you* are the fool, that's your concern, too, I'll warrant."
She started to turn away.

His face tightened; his nostrils flared. "Fool!" Margaret's voice shrilled
down the decade since their parting. "Fool, to let that stinking old goat
marry your mother for her money. Fool, not to get your hands on the
Stuart title. Do you think you're the only heir spawned on the wrong
side of the blanket? Your father acknowledged you a Stuart — why not
press your claim as first-born? Priests can be bought, parish records
altered. Papers could be lost — and others found to your advantage — if
you'd the brains and bowels for the business."

He had looked at her as though he had not seen her before — as, indeed,
he had not. "What need have I for a title, let alone one purchased at the
cost of dishonour? I've wits enough to make my own way. In the Colonies,
if not in England."

"Fool!" Curious how he'd not noticed the sneer in her voice, the emptiness behind her eyes. "I'll not slave by your side in some hovel in the
Colonies. Have you no pride?"

His eyes turned inscrutable. "Too much pride to stake my worth on
some meaningless piece of parchment."

He had not seen her again. Why then, he wondered, his gaze coming
back to the present, had he carried that cursed trunk about with him
like some albatross slung about his neck? His eyes lit with grim amusement. Not Margaret, but a very different woman stood before him now.
He would be a fool, indeed, were he to spurn her counsel at this strident
ghost's behest.

"Very well, Mistress Wainwright. Show me your hidey-hole. We can
set out for the shore tomorrow. I've a mind to show you the *Audacious*.
It's unlikely anyone at Barnegat will recognize you in that attire — you
can ride with me. It will be an overnight journey, though, with Captain
carrying two."

✥   ✥   ✥

AND SO THEY HAD set out. The warm weather made travelling easy, for a
blanket on the ground served for bedding. Last evening they had camped
by a small lake. At sunset the peepers had begun their serenade: sleigh-
bell notes from every tree, underscored by the bass of the bullfrogs who
hid in the greening grasses by the shore. The sun vanished beyond the
charcoal-sketched trees, trailing its crimson cloak. The sky darkened to
amethyst and then to deepest blue. The first star hovered low on the

horizon, and an occasional fish feeding at the surface set its light to rippling across the placid lake.

Here, in the still evening beneath the darkening sky, Brandon seemed younger, less sardonic, more human. They had sat companionably enough, crunching on the last of the bread he had toasted over the fire, sharing a flagon of ale and swinging pine branches to ward off the swarms of gnats.

"Phew!" He spat out a gnat that had drowned in his ale. He seemed almost comical in his disgust.

Serena dimpled. "Be glad it's only April. At least they're not mosquitoes. Have you heard Jake Buzby's stories about our Jersey giants? But no — you've not met him."

Brandon seemed of a mind to indulge her. "What stories?"

Serena settled herself with her legs tailor-fashion and her hands on her knees. Suddenly she appeared to have three chins where one had been and a substantial belly in place of her slender waist. "Well," she said, in a fair imitation of Jake's bass rumble, "I be settin' near the forge one day when the fire be burned out and the skeeters be comin' in swarms. Clouds of 'em, there be, buzzin' an' whinin' and bitin' till I be fair distracted. Ol' Mike McGuire, he be with me, and a-swattin' and a-scratchin' like to die. Now Mike, he spied a camp kettle lyin' near the water — it be the biggest kettle Weyford made. So big it was, oxen wouldn't haul it, and that be why it be layin' by itself. He took out for that kettle with the skeeters buzzin' after 'im, and they made 'im fightin' mad enough to lift it by hisself and crawl right under. I thought he had a good idee, but ye know, Miz Serena, I be too big to crawl under no kettle. Well, them skeeters set up a buzzin', madder 'n' hell at bein' done out of their supper. And first thing I knowed, they was hovrin' over that kettle. And they drilled in their snouts 'n' drilled some more, till they was well sunk in, like. Then they flapped their wings all together and flew that kettle away."

Brandon laughed. "And then they came back, I'll warrant, and made a feast of poor McGuire."

"They did. Jake swore Mike was 'all swole up fer days'."

Still smiling, Brandon sat looking out across the lake, his knees drawn up, arms folded round them. Emboldened, Serena leaned toward him. "Stuart — why was Joe Mulliner coming to your hideaway? You said — that night — 'the worst night's work I ever did was to hire your Refugee ruffians.' *Did* you hire him? *Why?*"

He scowled. For a moment she thought he would not answer. Then he uttered a short, mirthless laugh. "How affecting that my every word should be etched upon your memory, Mistress Wainwright." He picked up a pine cone and tossed it into the water, then leaned back to watch the ripples grow and spread across the lake.

She waited, saying no more. Abruptly he went on, "The worthy Joseph had his uses. As a decoy of a sort. His raids upon Patriot farmhouses had far more of greed about them than they had of Tory fervour. He was easily dissuaded from real pillage by judicious allotments of gold. His Refugee reputation lulled British suspicions. And when their own trains of raiders were raided in their turn—well, you take my point, I'm sure. They were unlikely to suspect him. But of late he has grown too greedy—and too careless. His escapade with you was sheer folly, bound to bring the wrath of the worthy burghers down upon him."

He looked at her then, his eyes gleaming in the last of the light. "But it has had its compensations, has it not, Mistress Wainwright?" He stretched out a hand to her. "Shall we retire? Tomorrow will be a full day."

ﾞﾑ ﾞﾑ ﾞﾑ

RIDING NOW on the last leg of their journey, Serena smiled to recall how they had laughed together. Brandon seemed a different man when he laughed, the deep furrows between his brows easing, his blue eyes alight. Then her smile trailed off into a look of reverie. The somnolent air, heavy with spring, Captain's sleek muscles flowing smoothly between her thighs, Brandon's arm beneath her breasts awoke the new-found flame that seemed never to sleep, only to smoulder, ready to flare anew. She leaned back against the length of his body. Her nipples grew harder; her loins began to tingle. Her heart beat faster; all her body was afire. Now, she thought. Right here, right now, by this roadside, in the soft sand, in the sun. I want you now, inside me, all over me. Now.

As though he felt her fever, he drew rein. Together they slid to the ground. The horse moved away to crop some grasses at the trailside. Brandon flung down his cloak. This time Serena was the supplicant, running her hands through his dark hair, across his back, under his shirt, over his shoulders and chest, then sliding them down, down, into the waist of his breeches, twining her fingers in the wiry hairs where his maleness stirred to meet them.

Down, down, her fingers slid. She felt the silk-smooth column, exploring it with fingers that seemed all sensation, feeling it surge at her touch. Then they were lying on the cloak, twined fiercely together. One of her hands was tearing at his shirt, the other at her own, pulling and tugging to remove the last barrier between her breasts and his naked flesh. Then, one arm around him, pressing herself against him, she grasped his hardness with an insistent hand and urged it toward the void within her that throbbed and ached to be filled.

Suddenly he tore free of her. He pinned her to the ground, tearing at her breeches. His supple hands grasped her hips and held her helpless as he plunged into her readiness again and again and again, thrusting, probing, deeper, ever deeper, as though he would know every secret of her body by means of the sensations of his own. His mouth devoured her breasts, then moved to her lips, sealing off her cries, bruising and insistent. Harder, deeper, he moved inside her, filling her to bursting, always increasing the pace.

His mouth took her breasts again, sucking greedily, his teeth on her nipples sending darts of flame through her belly, between her thighs, inside her womb. She pivoted to meet him, grasping his buttocks, urging him yet deeper. He forced her legs back, thrusting himself still farther within her. His eyes were closed, his mouth was drawn. Then he exploded inside her, his maleness convulsing in the ultimate spasms that sent his seed in heated spurts again and again into her deepest core.

The cords of his neck were strained, his muscles rigid. For endless moments he hung poised above her, as her body began its own spasms, wave upon wave, surpassing the fierceness of his. At last he collapsed upon her, spent, as the throbbing of her body subsided in rhythm with the tremors of his own. Then they lay quietly together, their mingled sweats drying in the sun, their heartbeats slowing, their consciousness returning, their persons separate once again. He drew away from her, sat up, and turned his back.

"Mistress Wainwright, we've dallied here too long. It's a long ride yet to Barnegat." There was a coldness to his tone that puzzled her. Avoiding her eye, he rose. He collected her scattered garments and tossed them toward her. "Dress—and quickly." He stood with his back to her, tidying his person, then leaned against Captain, arms folded, all but tapping his foot in impatience. His face was closed: She might be a stranger. It was hard to believe that moments before they had been straining together on the ground. The easy rapport by the lakeside, the instant they had been as one just now, might never have been.

When she was dressed and had bundled her hair once again beneath her cap, he assisted her onto the horse, mounted behind her, and started off without a word.

For some hours they rode in silence. Preoccupied, confused, Serena paid little heed to the surroundings, her body still afloat upon the ebbing tide of rapture, her spirit chilled by Brandon's sudden turnabout. What did I do? I could swear that he reached a pitch of feeling he had not known with me before. Was it my forwardness? Did that offend him? It did not seem so—he seemed to welcome it. Then why has he retreated into his fastnesses?

She twisted round as best she could, straining to see his face. It looked remote, ungiving. He stared straight ahead, gaze fixed on the trail. The arm wrapped round her waist was meant only to steady her, its sinews taut, its hold impersonal, almost painful.

They rode past another small lake, then into a thicket of holly. The shade was deeper, the air almost dank under the closely massed trees. As they emerged, Serena glanced up. The sky above the trees was brighter, bleached almost white. A new scent mingled with the familiar odour of pine: salty, bracing, laden with moisture and a rich hint of tar. Serena straightened, gripping the horse's mane, and sniffed rapturously. "Oh!" she cried. "The sea!" She yearned forward, trying to look ahead.

Brandon did not answer. The last of the woods fell away. The sky opened out, the palest of blues with just a vestige of haze. The trail led through a salt marsh. Reeds higher than their heads swayed and rustled in the easterly breeze. The track on which they rode had been filled in; crushed shells, packed hard, lay atop the ruts, slightly higher than the black muck on either side, from which rose the sulphur odour of decaying vegetation.

The trail took a sharp turn. The reeds parted to reveal broad waters, bluer than the sky, stretching to the horizon. They had come to Barnegat Bay.

CHAPTER ❧ 9

A T THE BASE of the trim village street dwelled the soul of Barnegat: a huddle of silver-bleached shacks dwarfed by a forest of masts and dominated by the Bay. Serena hurried after Brandon, trying not to stumble over coils of rope and piled-up stores. The air was vibrant with the clang of hammers upon chisels and the screech of sawblades slicing through white cedar. The smell of tar was everywhere, its thick pungency cut by the sharpness of turpentine and the spiciness of wood shavings, all underlaid by the brackish odour of the marshes.

They had left the horse well back of the village, tied to a tree near the Quaker meeting house. On foot they would attract less attention. Now Brandon set a brisk pace over the warped boards of a wharf, peering ahead for a sign of Captain Dennis, his shipwright. Spying a rotund figure up ahead, he gestured brusquely to Serena. "Wait over there."

Serena perched on a coil of rope and watched the bustle around her. Men were everywhere: swarming up masts, dangling on scaffolds against curved hulls, wielding brushes heavy with tar, sawing and banging and scraping. Farther down the wharf a few struggled with folds of heavy canvas, while across from her a merry group rested comfortably, their backs against some pilings, unwrapping pasties and passing a jug amongst them. Gulls wheeled and screamed overhead, swooping over the men's heads and up among the masts again, anticipating scraps. A young lad dressed much like Serena detached himself from the group and walked to the edge of the wharf, tearing a crust of bread into pieces and tossing them to the gulls, who fought noisily over them.

Brandon was talking with a short, stout man who waved a massive curved pipe to underscore each word that issued from a mouth completely hidden by moustache and beard. His coat and waistcoat had almost the look of a uniform, and a thick gold chain spanned his ample paunch.

When he removed his hat to scratch his head, apparently stymied by some query of Brandon's, Serena saw that all his hair was on his face: His pate shone in the sun. Soon he turned and marched toward the end of the wharf, Brandon following.

After the isolation of the past months, the noise and movement around her confused Serena and excited her too. She took deep breaths of salt air, savouring the mingled aromas, letting the bustle about her become one with the slap of the water against the pilings. The sea air was an intoxicant, the sun a soporific. Serena drowsed.

A shadow crossed her face, startling her to wakefulness. Brandon stood over her. "Don't be misled by his popinjay looks," he said. "Captain Dennis is the cleverest shipwright in Jersey. He comes of a long line of shipbuilders down about Cape May. Now, come with me. I'll show you the *Audacious*."

❧　❧　❧

BRANDON HIMSELF rowed the dory. The wind had freshened with the nooning, and the boat bobbed over waves crowned with white. Captain Dennis had called a temporary halt; no workmen were to be seen. The *Audacious* rode calmly at anchor, the rake of her lines beautiful and deadly, stripped of all excess. The masts of white cedar reached proudly for the sky, the bowsprit leapt forward, eagerly cleaving the air.

No one was aboard. When Serena had negotiated the rope ladder and landed lightly on the deck, she paused and looked around, her eyes sparkling. Everything was clean and new. Except for some canvas-covered stores and the ubiquitous coils of rope, the deck was immaculate. They climbed to the afterdeck. Here, too, all ornament was absent. No carvings interrupted the smooth curve of the taffrail, and only the turnings on the spokes of the ship's wheel showed the touch of the woodcarver's hand.

Brandon moved toward a cannon already mounted on its moorings and flipped back the canvas cover to show Serena the "W" of Weyford on its barrel. "When was it poured?" she asked.

"Right after the British struck Chestnut Neck. I watched the casting and tested its trueness. We worked by night, using only the most trusted men."

"Why that? The men are Patriots."

"You forget Caleb Sawyer. He has his informers, never fear."

"You've known about his spying that long? And left him to do mischief?"

"I have my reasons. Some I've told you, some I haven't. Come—see my quarters."

His cabin was not yet fully furnished, but the fine carvings along the hull contrasted sharply with the clean-lined spareness of the decks. The hand-rubbed ornament on the mahogany captain's table pleased the eye and beckoned the touch. Serena traced the curves of an oak-leaf border. "You do yourself well," she said.

"There's no need to clean blood from the decking in this cabin," he said bluntly. "If the fighting reaches here, the ship is done."

Serena swallowed. "I'd forgotten. This is a fighting ship."

"Indeed. Let the fat British merchantmen waste deck space with folderol. In the heat of battle, space for one's sword arm is all that matters."

"Can we go out on deck?" Serena tried not to think how the ship would look with blood running out the scuppers and wounded men writhing in the thick coils of cannon smoke.

He laughed at her queasy expression. "I fight to win—but I also make careful plans. You'd be surprised what can be won bloodlessly with a little foresight." She remembered his escapade with the whaleboat. It seemed a lifetime ago she had heard it recounted at the White Stag. She followed him back to the open deck, recovering her spirits as she squinted up the tall masts to the dazzling sky. The rocking motion of the deck under her feet brought a delicious unsteadiness.

Then she espied the crow's-nest, high atop the main mast. Her topaz eyes gleamed, their depths emerald with the water's reflection. Before Brandon could guess what she was about, she had sprung up on the wooden cleats and begun to climb. Brandon leaped to stop her, but the ship lurched slightly, giving her just time enough to scramble out of reach. Glorying in the freedom her lad's attire gave her, she moved rapidly up the mast.

"Come down, you fool," called Brandon. "You'll break your neck!"

"No, I won't! I've climbed my share of trees. I want to see the coastline."

"Well, fall to your death, if that's your pleasure. I'll not climb to your rescue if you panic halfway down."

Serena kept climbing, her face flushed with the effort. The mast was higher than she had thought. The wind, stronger at this height, tore at her clothes, flattening them against her body. On she went. Strands of loosened hair escaped her cap and whipped about her face, stinging her eyes and making them water. The higher she climbed, the more sickening became the mast's gyrations. Giddily, the *Audacious* danced to the water's motion.

She did not look down. The circular crow's-nest loomed above her at last. As she grasped a sheet and hauled herself safely up, the wind snatched off her cap and sent it spinning away. Her hair tumbled down, streaming free, gleaming in the sun like coppers freshly minted.

When she had caught her breath, she stood and looked about. There, she thought, is the world I grew up in. How different it looks from here — how different the horizons! Below was the Bay, the whitecaps on its surface visible even from this height. Beyond it to the east stretched the barrier islands, flaunting their breastwork of dunes. The darkly massed junipers on their leeward side looked like mosses at this height and distance; the delicate tracery of the beach plums was spiders' work. The white strand stretched for miles in each direction, lace-edged with still whiter surf. The slender thread of the shoreline was broken at intervals by inlets, Barnegat Inlet to her right, Crane-berry to her left.

Beyond the curling points of the islands lay the Shoals, where fiercely churning currents scoured the sands of the ocean floor. The seething cauldrons where the waters contended sent vapour high into the air. And this is near calm, thought Serena. What must it be like in a storm!

Many a proud vessel had foundered in the Barnegat Shoals, driven aground by storms, caught in treacherous currents when her captain misjudged the shifting channel. Some said such ships were lured by the lights of wreckers who waited on the dunes to pilfer the cargoes. The sands were littered with the bleached bones of ships, now buried, now exposed at the whim of the winter northeasters. And more than one cottage along the Bay was furnished with a luxury scarce reflective of the means of a fisherman or salter.

Dazzled by the sun on the waters, green-blue still with the chill of winter, and dizzied by the pitching of the ship, Serena turned her gaze landward. Below her lay Barnegat village. The Quaker meeting house was scarcely visible behind its shelter of trees, but the modest markers in its burial ground gleamed white — far more of them than the population would account for, for here, as in the unmarked trenches behind the building, were buried many victims of the Shoals.

From the marshes on either side of the village rose columns of smoke and steam where the salters tended giant cauldrons, boiling down salt water from their diggings beneath the turf. The giant pans in which salt slurry was drying were shrunk by distance into dishes fit for dolls. Narrow tidal streams, unseen at ground level, wound their serpentine course through the mud flats, slick and black at this time of year, soon to be blanketed in acid green by the marsh grasses.

To the west was the dark bulk of the Barrens. There seemed to be no end to them, no trace of the roads that wound through them. To her right rose the Forkèd River Mountains, blue with distance, their modest height of a hundred feet or so exaggerated by the Barrens' flatness. Here and there on their faces she could see the scars left by sawyers cutting cordwood to fuel hearths as distant as New York. On the seaward slopes of the mountains, the wreckers were rumoured to place their phantom lights, luring ships from far out at sea. For years there had been talk of a lighthouse here, like the one far north at Sandy Hook, but this plan, like many others, must now wait the resolution of the War.

Serena's face was smarting with sunburn and stinging from the wind. Her eyes burned. The discomfort of her body and the uneasiness of continual motion had eroded the excitement of discovery. She prepared to descend, for the first time looking down. Her stomach lurched. The ship's deck appeared smaller than the perch she was crouched on. Looking shoreward to steady herself, she saw the cluster of wharves, the bustling figures on them foreshortened to the shape of waterbugs scurrying on Weyford Lake. A few men stood clustered at one end of the longest pier, staring upward. Her long hair, streaming like a pennant in the wind, had attracted notice. In the shadow of a pile of cordwood crouched a figure whose lines seemed familiar.

I must get down, thought Serena. He will be furious — and rightly. Avoiding attention had been a crucial part of his plan. She took a deep breath, gripped the sheets tightly, and groped for the topmost cleat. Descending was much harder than going up. The wind was stronger, threatening to tear her from her foothold. She dared not look down to estimate the distance, for each glance increased her vertigo.

Halfway she froze, both arms wrapped round the mast so tightly she thought her muscles would crack. Sweat ran down her face and trickled from her armpits. It drenched her shirt, increasing her chill as the wind sucked the moisture from the cloth. Her stomach heaved as she fought not to vomit. Brandon's words came back to her: "I'll not come to get you if you panic."

Not that she believed him. He would come to her rescue if only to mock her for her failure. Damn! she thought. I'll not give him that sport. She drew a deep breath, then another. Calm yourself, she adjured. You've climbed trees. Pretend this mast is one of them, and the ship below you solid ground. So long as you're not fool enough to fall, it doesn't matter how high up you are. She forced herself to let go the mast, one arm at a time, and to grasp the sheets again. Her knuckles white, she let herself down. One step. Two. It was easier now that she had started. Another cleat . . . another, taking deep, cautious breaths all the while.

When she dared to look down she was a few feet from the deck. Suddenly exultant, she leapt the last distance, landing lightly, knees bent, in front of Brandon. Her teeth began to chatter, her knees to shake. But she smiled in triumph as she looked up at him. She had done it. And the sight of far horizons had been worth the fright. "How beautiful the *Audacious* is! Oh! to go to sea in such a ship—to see the wide world beyond the Barrens."

For just an instant she thought she saw admiration in his eyes. Then it was gone. He scowled blackly, thrusting a scarf toward her. "Tie up your hair," he said. "Don't you know how you've endangered us?" Roughly seizing her arm, he marched her toward the ladder.

CHAPTER ❧ 10

THEY STOOD AT THE END of a logging trail, near the summit of the Forkèd River Mountains. From this eminence they could see the whole harbour where they had been only yesterday. Dawn had brought another day of sunshine, a touch colder than the days preceding. They had camped the previous night in virtual silence, after a gruelling twilight climb spurred by Brandon's wish to confuse anyone who might be tempted to follow them.

Serena had felt uneasy, the memory of that hunched figure on the wharf tugging at her consciousness. Whoever it was had vanished by the time they returned from the *Audacious.* Only a few idlers had grinned slyly as Brandon and his "cabin boy" passed. The knowing leers had faded under his icy stare.

But he was still surly this morning, his display of annoyance surely greater than her innocent prank had deserved. Suppose people saw she was a woman—who, at that distance, would recognize her? Who, in Barnegat, would even know her? By the time they had reached the wharf, her disguise had been back in place, augmented by a rough jacket and hood that Brandon had found in the dory.

Come now, Captain Brandon, she thought now, your angry snit is absurd. The more so when I sensed your response to me when we sheltered together for warmth in the night. He had not touched her, though. And the fatigue of the day's adventures had made her glad enough to rest.

This morning's another story, thought Serena. It's too beautiful a day for your sulks, Stuart Brandon. As they descended the slopes, she pondered how to breach his defenses. They reached the flat ground and began to follow the course of a small stream. I know, she thought, nearly giggling. She directed him in monosyllables as she plotted her revenge.

⚘ ⚘ ⚘

THEY EMERGED from a thicket onto the bank of a larger stream, twenty, perhaps thirty feet wide and, by the look of it, shallow. Wiry grasses stirred at the bottom, piercing the litter of last year's leaves. Their movement, and the faintest dimpling of the water's surface, showed the direction of the current. The white sand on the bottom was plainly visible, each rounded pebble was clearly defined.

"We have to cross here," said Serena. "Have a care for your boots — best take them off."

"They'll dry," snapped Brandon. "Let us be about our business."

Serena hung back. Brandon stepped into the water — and went down and down. He was nimble enough to avoid plunging face forward, but when he recovered his footing he was standing in water chest high. Serena, on the bank, doubled over with laughter. He doesn't know everything, she thought. No Barrens native would be fooled by that water. "Swim forward a bit," she called. "You'll find it deep enough to float your ship!"

Then her courage failed her. He was furious. His eyes all but shot blue sparks at her as he swam toward the bank. Then he lunged. She turned to flee. Too late. He grasped her ankle and pulled her into the water. She landed with a splash, bobbing up just long enough to see that he was laughing as he ducked her under the water again.

Coming up for air, she shrieked. The water was so cold it burned. Gasping, she made a dive for him, reaching to trip him. The current swept her against him, and he went down, too. Now both were drenched, both laughing. "I told you," she sputtered. "I told you. Now do you believe me?"

"So you did, Mistress Wainwright." The dousing seemed to have cooled his temper. "Shall we discuss it on dry land?" Their teeth were chattering. The current had swept them a few yards down the stream. He clambered up and stretched out a hand to help her. Together, dripping, they struggled to where Captain stood waiting. Brandon pulled some blankets and dry garments from the saddle roll. Dragging her with him, he moved to a sheltered spot where sunlight dappled the forest floor. The thick carpet of pine needles felt warm and comforting on her bare soles.

Wrapping a blanket around her shivering form, she began to unfasten her soaked shirt. The cloth was plastered to her body, limning her nipples, puckered with cold. Wet hair streamed to her waist. Seeing him struggling with his boots, she dropped the blanket and went to his aid.

Back toward him, she bent and grasped his boots, feeling one foot, then the other, braced against her buttocks as she tugged. Now both stood barefoot. They began to peel off their wet garments, neither looking at the other. Serena's body tingled with the cold and her awareness of his nakedness beside her. As she reached for the blanket to dry herself, she felt his hand on her wrist. "We have better ways of getting warm," he said.

❧ ❧ ❧

IT WAS EVENING. The plaintive call of a dove mourned the fading of the light, while, high in an oak that caught the sun's last rays, a wood thrush warbled evensong. Smoke rose lazily from their campfire, its pine scent mingling with the charred aroma of roast fowl, as Serena and Brandon ate together by the stream. The gently rippling water held the last light of the sky, the woods were dark and still.

Chewing the last of a chicken wing, Serena bent to the water and rinsed her fingers and her lips, seeing herself mirrored in the silver surface. Then she lay back on the blanket, staring at the darkening sky. They had tramped through the woods that afternoon, keeping to the stream bank, clambering over fallen logs, as Serena showed Brandon how the stream, with many twists and turns, sought the river mouth. Its depth was astonishing. "Yes," conceded Brandon, "if we clear a fallen tree or two and wait for the tide, we can lower sail and let longboats tow her in. At full moon we can do it by night."

Now he sat beside her, meditating on his plans. For many moments neither spoke, as the night deepened around them. From the woods came the small rustlings of night creatures aprowl; a large bird flapped across the sky, its call the essence of loneliness. The stars came out. Serena lay half-dozing, exhausted by the day, her hair, which she had left loose to dry, fanning out on the blanket about her.

When she opened her eyes, Brandon was leaning over her. The glow from the fire lit his face; his forehead was furrowed, his eyes were deep in shadow. The stern line of his lips had softened. "Quite the strategist, aren't you?" he said. "You were right, you know." He pulled a blanket over them to fend off the growing chill, then resumed his scrutiny. Gently his fingers traced the tilt of her nose, the curve of her cheeks. She closed her eyes and felt him touching her lashes, softly stroking her lips.

Gently, gently, barely touching her, his hands traced the curves of her body. Then she felt him unfastening her shirt. Now his fingers were warm on her naked breasts, caressing, exploring, never pausing, as her clothes seemed to melt from her body at the touch of his caressing hand. He moved away for a moment, then his naked flesh met hers. Still he moved gently, entreating, not commanding, his fingertips still exploring her body, the smooth and the rough, curves and crevices, skin and hair and delicate membrane.

He held her against him, and she felt his swelling maleness, but with no urgency, no insistence, only warmth and the ceaseless explorations of his hands. He seldom kissed her at such moments, but now he did so, softly, and his lips moved down her throat to her breasts. He touched her hardened nipples softly with his tongue, flicking it round and round, back and forth over their tips. As her breasts rose on the crest of her quickening breath he suckled them gently in turn, his tongue still teasing the nipples as they lengthened and tightened in his mouth.

She lay back, her mouth open, feeling the pulse of desire in her throat, her belly, her inmost being. Her hips moved, her thighs opened. She sensed, rather than saw, that he was gazing down upon her face again. Then she felt his mouth move downward along her body, kissing, sucking, lightly biting. She moaned, seeking for his hand to place it back on her clamouring breasts.

Then his hands were between her thighs, his fingers moving, seeking then finding the place where her womanhood hid. She felt his tongue probing at the centre of exquisite sensation, searching, stroking, sending beneficent fire along her nerves to her very fingertips. She could not lie still. Her hips moved restlessly as she sought to keep contact with his mouth, lest she lose these sensations she had never felt before. She lay back, neck arched, muscles straining, eyes wide open, staring, tense with expectation.

Then his tongue, thrusting and probing, moved inside that nether mouth whose secret lips trembled at its touch. In and out his tongue moved, faster and faster, fanning the fire within her, stretching the exquisite tension tauter and tauter until she could endure it no longer. The spasms began. The secret lips quivered, then convulsed, opening wider to beg him come within. He entered her then, deeply, deeply, feeling the quickening waves within her sweeping his maleness into the maelstrom of her desire. In the moment before he felt himself leap and spurt within her, he looked down into her face. Her love was writ plain there; her eyes, meeting his, glowed with its reflection.

His body arched. "Serena!" he cried. "Serena!" And lost himself within her. Wave upon wave swept her body, surging higher and higher, deeper and deeper, until the tide crested, bearing her at last to a halcyon shore

where she floated, spent, upon the diminishing ripples of passion's lan-
guorous ebb.

Long after he slept beside her she lay awake, staring at the sky, watching Orion wheel his course across the heavens while the dog star Sirius pursued the receding night. As the sky was lightening to grey, two deer came down to the water and lowered their heads to drink.

🪶 🪶 🪶

THE NEXT MORNING he barely spoke. With brusque motions he loaded their gear upon the horse and obliterated the traces of their campfire. For the first time he placed her behind him, where she could not see his face. He set off without a word along a trail that she knew headed westward.

Through her arms about his waist she could feel his muscles quivering with tension. She longed to lean against him and feel his body against her breasts, but unsure why, she dared not. When the motion of the horse brought their bodies into contact, he jerked away.

It seemed that they rode on forever, hour upon hour through unchanging terrain. Pine, oak, pine again, whortleberry and laurel, here and again a sweetbay magnolia when the ground beneath them turned damp. The sky was a dull grey, neither sun nor cloud, the shadowless light bringing winter's bleakness back to the monotonous trail.

What has happened? thought Serena. She remembered the previous night, the look in his eyes as he gazed down at her, the tenderness of his lovemaking, the tone in which he called out her name. It seemed a dream. Yet the lingering warmth of her body, the reminiscent tremors coursing through her, told her the night had been real. It was the day that smacked of nightmare, as the lengthening miles spun out beneath the horse's hoofs and never a word passed between them.

When noon came he groped in the saddlebag and passed her a hunk of bread, neither stopping nor slackening the pace. Later he paused briefly that they might relieve themselves, then hustled her back onto Captain and rode on. Questions she ached to ask him stuck in her throat. Once she raised a tentative hand to stroke the back of his neck. He shook her off.

A blaze of anger coursed through her. How dare he use me this way, whipsawing my feelings with his shifts to and fro? His ironical remoteness was easier to bear: It warned me to keep up my defenses. Now he has invaded not my body but my soul. She felt vulnerable and raw, every nerve exposed, every sensibility tied to his whims. Well, no more! Next time I'll withstand him. A lingering tremor deep within her gave the lie to her resolution.

At last he drew rein. They were at a place the Pineys called a fingerboard—the intersection of many woodland trails. She looked about. This was familiar ground.

"Get off," he said. Without thinking, she obeyed, her muscles stiff from the hours of riding. The horse moved restlessly. With unwonted viciousness he curbed it. Then he pointed down one of the trails. "You're but a few miles from Weyford. That track leads to Jake Buzby's charcoal pits. Weyford lies beyond them—which, being an expert woodjin, you undoubtedly know."

"But—" She started to say she could not return to Weyford, so long absent, and disgraced. Something held her back.

A strange light shone in his eyes. His hands gripping the reins were white-knuckled. "The *Audacious* will be ready to sail soon," he said. "There's a war to be fought—fought and won. I've no more time for dalliance—no need for a woman to while away spare hours. I'll have no hours to spare." Turning from the look in her eyes, he groped in the saddlebag. "Take this." He held out a deerskin sack.

She did not move. He looked into her face then, wincing at its white stillness. Deep inside himself he felt a twisting pain. Don't let her go! cried something within him. This is a woman like none you've ever known. You must not lose her, the inner voice implored him. Seize her . . . hold her . . . take her away with you, lest something irreplaceable be swept forever from your grasp. For an instant he wavered. His grip on the reins loosened; he tensed, ready to spring from the saddle and take her into his arms. Then—No! he cried in the silence of his mind. I'll not hazard my heart. I'll not let her ensnare me. Not this woman. Not any woman. I'll not love her—I cannot permit myself to love her. But you do love her, said the voice. No! he cried silently. No! To silence the voice, he thrust the sack at her again. "Take it," he said harshly.

This time she took it, impelled by his urgency. It was heavy for its size, and her wrists sagged. Her numbed fingers felt the shape of coins—gold, by the weight of them. Instinctively, she threw the pouch down. The drawstring loosened and some guineas spilled onto the sand. "I don't want your money."

"Better take it." He drew a deep breath. Margaret, he adjured himself. Mother. Remember. They're all alike—this one, too, I'll not be betrayed again. And she would betray me; it's only a matter of time.

Summoning his anger to sear away his pain, he said, "Take it, Mistress Wainwright, as earnings. I never said you didn't give full value."

Serena's face flamed. Her throat constricted. How can he say these things? What has come over him? I'll not cry, she told herself. Damn him! I'll not cry.

He watched her for a moment, his face remote and grim. "Farewell, Mistress Wainwright. Have no fears for your future. You can wheedle yourself back into your father's good graces — and if not, well, a woman of your talents cannot fail to find a protector."

She opened her mouth in angry protest, but she could force no words from her closed throat. She stood as if paralyzed while he wheeled Captain about and started back down the trail they had just travelled — back to Barnegat, she thought, back to the world, to his ship, to the sea.

The horse began to canter, then to gallop. A cloud of white dust fogged the trail.

She remained motionless, watching, as the dust slowly sifted to earth. The trail was empty. Already twilight was falling. All around her, the Barrens grew dark. She stood there for a long time, eyes fixed upon the spot where last she had seen him. Then at last she bent down and retrieved the sack of gold.

CHAPTER ❧ 11

WEYFORD APPEARED deserted. Long before she entered the village, Serena sensed something to be wrong. The furnace should be in blast by now, but no thumping of slag hammers greeted her approach, no shower of sparks lit the sky. Furnace and forge lay dark and still. On the gently rippling waters of the lake, the moon laid a path that led nowhere. The line of Durham boats bobbed empty by the shore, the mill wheels and wharfs were silhouettes pasted on silver.

What could have happened? Serena wondered. The lake must have thawed weeks ago; the spring campaign must be under way, and orders for arms were piled high on Father's desk at season's end. Has the War taken an unexpected turn? Heaven knows that in these last weeks I've given little thought to the fortunes of the Patriots. Stuart surely had news, but not I.

She limped on. Her bare feet were blistered. She felt tired to the bone, less from her walk than from the strain of the events that had culminated in Brandon's desertion. From habit she followed the path that led her through the village. Here were some signs of life. A dog barked. A curtain stirred at a window. One or two cottages showed lights in their dormers. But the ironworkers retired early when no frolic was afoot. Not a human soul greeted her as she crossed the bridge and climbed the long slope to the manor.

Wainwright House! Had I thought to see it again? What welcome awaits me?

Here, too, darkness and silence reigned. One window on the second story showed a candle; downstairs no light could be seen. Wait! A faint glow on the bark of the sycamore tree reflected light that must be coming from the back sitting room. Now she saw that the windows were shuttered.

Serena crept onto the porch. The iron steps were cold on her bare feet. Through a crack in the shutter she peered into the sitting room. Her mother was there all alone. Mother! The sight of Anna in her rocker, familiar from thousands of evenings stretching back to her first memories of childhood, made Serena's eyes sting. Rubbing the tears away with the back of her hand, she stole around to the rear entrance.

Samuel's countinghouse was dark. No men clustered by the company store, waiting to buy provisions when Caleb had tallied their credits—or, at this time of year, debits. It took most of the summer for all but a few men to earn back their winter's supplies. Nor was Caleb about. But the door by the path from store to house was unlocked. Serena slipped in. Familiar scents enveloped her. Beeswax and turpentine, bayberry and pine smoke. The faintest hint of indigo from the dyed curtains in the passage. Traces of spice from the kitchen belowstairs—clove and cinnamon, cardamom and nutmeg. Home.

Anna sat by the cold fireplace, her head bowed over her embroidery hoop. But her hands were still. She was dressed in black worsted, a black shawl over her shoulders. The heavy skirts of her gown fell in sculptured folds to her feet . . . her feet! The red-heeled slippers were gone. Felt house boots had taken their place.

What can have happened? thought Serena again. Since earliest childhood, first in the modest home now occupied by Caleb Sawyer, then in the grandeur of Wainwright House, the tap! tap! tap! of those dainty red heels had signalled Anna's passage. To Anna, those slippers were a talisman, a link to the Anna Meissner of Vienna, long ago: a poor country cousin, all but a servant, consigned to the meanest bedchamber in the mansion of the haughty von Reithofers. She had been chaperoning Minna, the youngest daughter, wearing one of Minna's cast-off gowns, when the visiting American had asked her to dance. And she had left Vienna without a backward glance to follow the lanky barbarian to his raw new land across the sea.

It had been a long journey. First to the snug pastures and blue hills of Pennsylvania where Samuel mastered his trade, then to this infertile wasteland where not only a broad ocean but miles of scrub pine and swampland stretched between her and the life she had known. Did Mother ever regret it? Serena asked herself now. I think not. But Anna had insisted upon these slippers, grimace though she might when they pinched her chilblained feet. And Samuel, practical no-nonsense Samuel, had replaced each pair as they wore out.

Serena entered. Anna looked up. Light from the single candle sputtering in the tall carved stand sparkled in the tears on her cheeks. *"Ja?*

Was vollen Sie, Knabe?" What is it you want, boy? The needlework fell to the floor. *"Die Serena!"*

Serena ran to her mother and fell to her knees. "Mother! Oh, Mother!" All the pent-up tears of the long, long day, the long, long weeks, shook her body. She cried as she had not cried since childhood—perhaps not even then, her arms about her mother's waist, her face in the soft lap where she had nestled so long ago. For long moments Anna said nothing, stroking Serena's hair.

Then Serena felt her mother's body first tense and then recoil. Anna drew her hand away. "Serena—to do this wicked thing—how can it be? How?" Anna gripped Serena's shoulders and held her off. "A robber who murders and plunders. And with him you ran away. *Ach,* yourself you have ruined. What becomes of you now?"

"But I didn't run away with him, Mother. Let me explain to you. I—"

Footsteps sounded in the hall. "Who is here? Has Caleb returned?" Prudence hurried into the room. "Is it Father?" She stopped. *"You!"* A dozen emotions waged war in the compass of that single syllable: apprehension, spite, contempt, envy—and love, however attenuated. All the conflicting passions Serena had always sensed in Prudence fought for supremacy as she stared at Serena.

There is anger there, thought Serena. But there's fear there, too. Fear of me. But why?

Prudence took a quavering breath. "How dare you? How dare you show your face here, with Father coming to bring Sam's body home? Hasn't he enough to bear? Hasn't Mother?"

"Sam—?" And then everything fell into place. The emptiness of Weyford. The silence at the ironworks. The shuttered windows. Anna's tears.

"Yes, Sam. Our brother—or had you forgotten? Our brother, who went to fight the British while you sported in taverns and flung yourself at men's heads. Sam is dead. He led a party of raiders against a British supply train. They blew off his head. They—" She put her hands to her face, sobbing.

"Mother," said Serena. "Oh, Mother, I didn't—"

Prudence raised her head. The cords in her neck stood out; her eyes were wild. Tears streamed unheeded down her face. "Don't speak to Mother!" Her hand shot forward and gripped Serena's wrist. The long, bony fingers were icy. She jerked Serena up, whirled her about, gave her a push. "Get out!" She pointed to the door. "Get out! Go back to your Refugee lover! Go anywhere! But get out of Weyford before anyone sees you here. You've no right here, no right to talk to Mother. Get out!"

"Sam," repeated Serena, stunned. She barely heard what Prudence

was saying. "Sam." Her tall brother with the careless laughter who took
her part and abetted her pranks. Sam, who had taught her to slip through
the woods like an Indian, to bait a hook, to light a campfire, always wary
lest his father or Prudence catch them out. Sam, who had hated the
ironworks, who had seen the war as a chance for adventure, a chance to
get away from their father and the burden of the works that he knew
would someday fall upon him. Sam—and with him Samuel's plans for
the ironworks. Old Samuel would be inconsolable.

"Father—?"

"Don't speak of Father," said Prudence. "You broke his heart—and now
this. I told you—get out. Before he comes back, before he sees you."

Anna stirred in her chair. *"Nein."* No.

Prudence stared at her mother. Serena still stood in a daze.

"Ach, nein," Anna repeated. "To us the Serena has come back. Here is
her home—here her father is master. It is not for you or me to put her
out. She will want to say farewell to her brother. She must stay for—for
the services."

"She has no right—"

"A right she has—yes. To Sam she is . . . was sister. My daughter she
is—and the daughter also of my husband."

"Father has disowned her."

"So he has done—in her absence. Now what she says he must hear—I
must hear. It is for that you have come, *nein, Kindchen?*" Is that not so,
child?

Serena nodded numbly. I suppose that is what I came for, she thought.
What else can I do but tell Father . . . what should I tell him? The question echoed through a void from which all thought had somehow vanished. She swayed on her feet.

"So tired she is," said Anna. "Call you the Susan. We will help her to
her room. Her father she cannot face tonight—and that she is here you
are not to tell him. With the . . . with the Sam he will want to sit up this
night." Anna's face crumpled. She bit her lip and drew a ragged breath.
Prudence made no move. Anna struggled to her feet. "Susan!" she called
into the hall. "Susan!"

"You were always Mother's pet, weren't you?" Prudence hissed. "Wait
till tomorrow. If you think you'll get round Father, you're mistaken. If
there's any justice, he'll throw you back in the muck where you belong."
Again her eyes held that strange hint of fear. "He will. I know he will."

"Komm, Kindchen." Anna stood in the doorway. Behind her bulked
Susan with a candlestick. "Come to bed."

Her room looked smaller than she remembered it. Smaller, but still familiar. There were her lookout window, her bed, with the bearskin still beside it, her special ivory comb upon the dresser. The testered bed looked cool and clean. She sat on a hassock while Susan bathed her feet, cooling the blisters, stroking on a healing salve. The stained shirt and trousers fell from her; she felt soft folds of linen touching her face. Then she was under the covers, between verbena-scented sheets, beneath her head a pillow with the whipped-cream softness of goosedown, soft, so soft, as soft as the darkness that lay like folds of velvet upon her eyes. She slept.

ح‍ ح‍ ح‍

FATHER HAS AGED, thought Serena. Or is it just that it's months since I've seen him, and now I see him more clearly? Samuel's hair had been white for as long as she could remember. But always it had sprung vigorously from his high forehead, thick and crisp. Now limp strands hung about his ears and draggled on his high collar, yellowed and dingy. The broad shoulders slumped, his skin seemed to be too big for him, his corpulent middle had lost its solidity, an old man's belly sagged below his waistcoat. His eyes, shadowed with fatigue and grief, glared at her from beneath thick, untrimmed brows like those of an angry owl.

They had met, perforce, in Serena's room. The drawing room and library were thronged with mourners assembling for the funeral. Serena had not been allowed downstairs. Shortly after dawn Anna herself had brought up a tray. "Your father I have told of your coming," she whispered. "No one is to be seeing you, by his orders. Here he will talk to you, after the breakfast."

Now Anna stood in the background, twisting the fringes of her shawl through restless fingers. Anna, too, had aged. The last traces of chestnut in her coiled braids had faded to brown; a network of lines etched her face. Her eyes were swollen with weeping: for her son, for Serena. Even for the sake of the funeral she had not been able to force her red-heeled slippers on her dropsical feet. Her shuffling gait made her seem a different woman.

Serena's breakfast sat queasily in her stomach. She had wakened early: confused, wretched, sick with apprehension. Weariness hung about her like a pall, made all the heavier by her grief for her brother. Watching her father move heavily toward her where once he would have stamped commandingly through the room, she felt the bruise that seemed lodged in the region of her heart swell and throb painfully. "Father—" She could not bring herself to say "good morning," though the sun streamed

through the windows and the birds sang full-throated in the branches of
the sycamore tree.

"Well, Serena," said Samuel, forbearing to greet her. "You show a want of taste, not to speak of feeling, to come here at such a time."

"I didn't know—"

"That seems likely. Rogues, I suppose, pay scant mind to the deaths of heroes."

"I didn't know. But if I had, I would have come the more swiftly. Do you think I would not want to bid Sam goodbye—to comfort Mother, and you, if you would let me?"

"Small mind you've paid to your mother's comfort all these months. Or mine. And what solace can we find in the tears of a harlot who's trampled our reputations in the dust? Sam is gone. Gone. My *son*." Samuel bowed his head, tensing his whole body to hold back the grief that threatened to overwhelm him. Behind him, Anna burst into tears.

"Oh, Father, I'm so sorry, so sorry about Sam." Her own tears stinging her eyes, Serena stretched a hand toward her father's heaving shoulder. At her touch, he flung up his head and struck her hand away. "Don't touch me! And as for saying goodbye to Sam—you'll not go near him or his grave. I'll not have you profaning his memory."

"Father, I've not done what you accuse me of. Please, let me explain."

"I need no explanations. Caleb Sawyer has told me enough of your scurrilous ways. Slipping off to taverns, night after night. Roistering with those Refugee scum, laughing behind your hand at us all the while. Thinking yourself very clever, no doubt. Then running off with that ruffian bold as brass, with the whole village watching and snickering at me." He pulled a bandanna from inside his vest and blew his nose noisily. "May the Lord forgive your shameless behaviour—I cannot. Why did you come back to parade our shame before the village? Did your bandit paramour desert you?"

Serena swallowed hard. Though not the truth, it came near enough. "Father, it's not as you say. I've done wrong; I've hurt you and Mother— and I'm sorry. More sorry than I can say. But it's not as you think. I did not run off 'night after night'. I was there at the White Stag for the first time, for the frolicking. Enoch can tell you—"

"Price? I sent him packing. And lost the best ironworker among them. And that, too, must be laid to your account."

"You believed Caleb, but not Enoch?"

"Caleb has no reason to blacken your name. Caleb was deeply attached to you—he was nearly betrothed to you. It was agony for him to tell me these things, but who else would?"

"Who else indeed? And they're lies. Lies befitting a Tory spymaster who—"

"Silence!" thundered Samuel. "Blackening his reputation will not give you back your own."

"But I've proof . . ." Serena faltered. The paper Stuart Brandon had burnt was long gone—and Brandon was right. Her father's need to believe Caleb would outweigh any proof she could offer, the more so now that so much time had passed. "Let me see him, then. Let him repeat these tales of his to my face."

"Caleb is away. He had business in Barnegat."

Barnegat! The cold weight in Serena's stomach plummeted as her mind made the connection it had failed to make at the wharf. "Barnegat? How long has he been there?"

"Since three days past. He returns for the funeral."

That crouched figure on the wharf. Caleb Sawyer! He had seen her with Stuart Brandon, then. Oh, dear Lord, thought Serena—how much does Caleb know? The *Audacious*—he's seen the *Audacious*. I must warn—

"Husband," said Anna hesitantly, "should we not be hearing the Serena out?"

"Hear her out? Hear more lies? With Sam lying dead in his coffin? The facts are plain. She went to the White Stag. She rode off with Mulliner—a hundred people saw her. She's been gone three months and more. Don't be a fool, Anna."

"But we have only the Caleb's word that she went of her own will, only the Caleb's word that many times she had gone there. The Master Sooy has told you she had not—"

"Nicholas Sooy is a good friend. He tries to spare our feelings."

"But—"

"Enough!" Samuel turned back to Serena. "You're fortunate indeed. Caleb has told me that if you return, he'll overlook the stain upon you and will marry you. As his wife and prospective mistress of Weyford you may in time live it down with the life of prayer and repentance Caleb offers you."

"Mistress of Weyford? Then Caleb is to be your heir—that shifty-eyed turncoat?"

Samuel lunged forward and grasped her shoulders, shaking her until her teeth rattled. Her stomach lurched. She prayed not to vomit in his face. "Stop!" cried Anna. "Husband, stop!" He let go abruptly. Serena reeled backward. She clutched a bedpost for support, struggling not to cry, to control the heaving of her stomach.

"Strumpet!" said Samuel. "Defy me again, and I'll turn you out in the swamps where you belong! You've no right in this house, no right in this room. Your presence here defiles us." He coughed, breathing heavily. His hands shook. "Were it not that the Lord adjures us to forgiveness, you'd not remain here another instant. Were it not for your mother's softheartedness you'd not have spent a night in this room." He turned to his wife.

"Anna! Serena is to stay in the tower room. Have a pallet set up for her there. The wind is rising; the woodland is a tinderbox. Let her pass the time in firewatching until Caleb returns. Have her food brought up there. And lock the door."

"That will not be necessary, Father. I'll not run away."

"Lock the door, Anna. See to it quickly. We must greet our good neighbours who have come here for Sam's sake." He left the room.

Serena stood rigid, still clutching the bedpost. Her face was very white, but a spot of red burned on each cheek. Her eyes smarted.

Anna patted her shoulder timidly. "*Kindchen*, beside himself he is. His heart it is broken. And now the Sam is— Wait. Wait a few days. Then it may be—" She shook her head sadly and turned to go.

Serena waited until her mother had shuffled out. Then she ran to the slop jar in the corner. When the spasms of nausea at last subsided, she got shakily to her feet. Taking a linen towel from the washstand, she soaked it, wrung it out, and wiped her face and her trembling hands. Black circles danced before her eyes like swarms of monstrous gnats. She sat down on her bed and laid her head on her knees, praying for the faintness to pass.

The signals of her body could no longer be ignored. I'm with child, she thought.

She looked up. Prudence was watching from the doorway. On her face apprehension fought with triumph. Clearly, she had heard and seen everything. Serena stared at her bleakly across the chasm that had opened between them.

CHAPTER ❧ 1 2

S ERENA TWISTED and turned on the narrow cot. Moonlight flooded the tower room through the windows that lined its walls, spilling silver on the plank floor and charcoal in the corners. The wind that had been rising steadily over the past days shrieked and moaned incessantly, worrying at shutters and whistling through cracks. It was a dry west wind that bore no promise of rain but whipped the last moisture from the crackling-dry Barrens where the snows of winter had long since been drunk by the thirsty sands.

In the weeks Serena had been home, the few spatters of rain that had fallen had dried before they could penetrate the litter of pine needles and last year's leaves. The tips of the oaks showed tender new growth — silver, crimson, mauve, and moist, fresh green — but Samuel had been right; the Barrens were a tinderbox. So was Wainwright House. The air was crackling with tension.

Restlessly, Serena sought a new position, some place of repose on the crumpled linen damp with perspiration and tears. The square tower room, an enclosed widow's walk, was a hotbox in the daytime, when sunlight poured in unobstructed. At night, with wind rattling every pane, it was draughty and bleak. Until the unnatural heat of the past few days, Serena had often been cold.

Now she got up and took a turn round the windows, scanning the horizon for any sign of flame. There was none. Nor, looking toward the furnace, could she see any sign of activity, though the paralysis that had followed Sam's death had now lifted. Colliers' carts rumbled across the bridge by day, stopping near the store so that Caleb might assess their loads and credit the accounts of the drivers. Clumsy skiffs floated down from the diggings, heavily weighted with ore. But furnace and forge were silent, their fires extinguished soon after they had been lit. The

risk of forest fire was too great.

Fire was a constant Barrens hazard. At times like this, when the forest floor was strewn with fodder for flames that winds could whip to gigantic heights, the danger multiplied a hundredfold. The vegetation of the Barrens was inured to the fires that repeatedly swept vast acreages, often leafing out with renewed vigor when the understory had been cleared. The structures of men were less adaptable.

Lightning, attracted by the iron in the soil . . . an instant's carelessness with flint and steel . . . a stray bit of moulten iron escaping from the furnace stack . . . each could bring disaster. And, since burnt-over timber was good for little but charcoal, a dishonest collier intent upon cheap purchase might indulge in a spot of arson that the wind could fan into a holocaust of smoke and flame.

No wonder, then, that cautious Samuel had built the tower room astride the roof of Wainwright House in defiance of the architect who protested, with some justice, that it ruined the mansion's fine proportions. "Smoking rubble has no fine proportions," said Samuel. And in seasons of greatest danger, the tower room was occupied night and day. Only through constant vigilance was there any hope of extinguishing a fire, for once it took hold it would burn unabated until nature's rains put it out.

With Serena confined in the tower, the firewatchers were assigned to rooftop scoutings. The constant vigil was hers alone. She took it seriously, making frequent rounds of the windows, from which a wisp of smoke or, at night, the smallest flame, might be visible miles away. It passed the time. And time went slowly, so slowly that she nearly lost count of the days that trundled monotonously by, with little to do but read Shakespeare's plays, which Anna had smuggled up to her. Committing favorite passages to memory helped to pass the time.

The days were endless, the nights hideous. What shall I do? she asked herself. Where can I go? What paths are open to me? Echoes of her last talk with her father pursued one another through the corridors of her mind.

"I have spoken with Caleb," Samuel had told her on the day after Sam was buried. "He holds to his offer to marry you."

"But I won't marry him. I *can't*. He repels me."

"So. A good man repels you while the Pine Robber wins your embraces. May the Lord forgive you. Well, Serena, you can marry him. And you will. Let it be your salvation."

"No."

"Serena, I will not turn you out, though you deserve it. You will stay in this room until you agree. But I warn you—my patience is not endless." Samuel turned to go. He seemed drained, his anger exhausted, obduracy taking its place. "When you are ready, tell your mother. I'll not speak to you again."

Now Serena paced the room, her thoughts circling the track they had long since worn in her brain. Stuart Brandon. The child to come. Her mother. Caleb. Prue.

Prue — she thought now. If Prue guessed, she has not told Mother. But how long will it be before my condition is plain for everyone to see? She tried to remember. How long since my last flux? Once while I was away it happened. But twice? No, not twice. And the sickness? That has only plagued me since I came home . . . came back to Weyford. Then I've a month, maybe two if I'm careful, before anyone will know. If, that is, Sister Prudence continues to keep silence. Why hasn't she spoken? I should think she could scarcely contain herself at this new chance to proclaim me her inferior.

And what of Stuart Brandon? What would he say if he knew I'm to bear his child? Thoughts of Brandon merely added to her torment. At times in the long, lonely nights her dreams of him were so clear that she woke hearing his calm, clipped voice, feeling his hands upon her body. The desire he had roused and the lingering vibrations of passion stirred longings in her that would not be stilled. She would lie face down upon her bed, pressing her swollen breasts against it, moaning softly, remembering, remembering, until her body found its own surcease that let her sleep but left her still empty, restless and unfulfilled.

At other times her anger triumphed, driving desire from her body and supplanting it with rage at how he had used her. And yet . . . and yet. She recalled words he had spoken, looks that had flashed between them, conversations about the ironworks, about the *Audacious*. He spoke with me, she thought, as no one ever had, saw things in me that no one ever saw. She relived long, lazy mornings in that great rustic bedstead when she had lain in his arms and poured out to him all her thoughts and hopes and dreams. And always she remembered the silent rapport and passionate rapture of that twilight hour beside the woodland stream, the look in his eyes on that final wild night when at last he had cried out her name. How can I forget him? she thought, tossing restlessly through night after night.

Now, sitting on the edge of her cot, twisting her hands in bewilderment at her predicament and the paralysis in which she seemed entrapped, she remembered that night by the stream, remembered his eyes and the unwonted tenderness in them. Will he come to me, she thought, on one of his visits to Father? She knew he would not. But perhaps . . . perhaps if he knew about the child, he would help me. How could he have

meant the things he said when he left me, after that night? And now . . . I
must find him and tell him. For the child is his as well as mine; he must
be told.

Tomorrow, she thought. Tomorrow I will think of how to find him.
She lay down on the cot, staring at the sky. When the moon had long set
and the sky was grey with dawn, she sank at last into a sleep that brought
no rest.

☙ ☙ ☙

"KINDCHEN —" ANNA EMERGED, puffing, from the narrow passage where
the precipitous stairway, its treads shallow as a ladder's, entered the tower
room. She leaned against the doorjamb, blinking in the brightness, hand
pressed to her bosom as she tried to catch her breath.

At the sound of her mother's voice, Serena slammed the casement
shut, cutting off the shrill cheeping of the finches who were fighting
over her breakfast. At pains to conceal the nausea that made it impossible
to swallow, Serena had been feeding her meals to the birds. Watching
their fierce contentions over bits of bread and scraps of bacon lightened
the dreary hours.

Serena had grown thinner. Her cheeks were pale, her eyes deepset in
smudges of weariness; a few fine lines marred the smoothness of her
brow. There was no mirror in the tower room, but she had no need to
consult the glass to know that her features were taut with strain. The
loose fit of her simple gown of indigo homespun told her plainly how
much weight she had lost. How long before it filled out again with the
bulge of the child within her?

"Good morning, Mother," said Serena. Can I tell her? she wondered.
Can I trust her? Or will I merely give her more pain to bear? How could
she help me if she knew? And how long before she does know?

"Serena. *Ach, Kindchen!*" Anna twisted the lace fan she had pulled
from her ample bosom.

"Sit down, Mother. I'm sorry I cannot offer you a chair."

Anna sank wearily onto the cot and sat for a moment, fanning herself.
Then she patted the spot beside her. "*Komm, Kindchen. Setze dich bei
mir.*" Come, child. Sit by me. Serena hesitated. German was the language
of her childhood, the secret language that she and Anna shared, the
language of songs sung just for her.

"*Röslein, Röslein, Röslein rot, Röslein auf der Heide.*" Rose, small rose,
sweet rose so red, rose upon the meadow. Down the years came the echo
of Anna—a younger, vibrant Anna so different from the extinguished

woman who sat before her now. That Anna had worn her gleaming chestnut braids in a coronet about her head. Her eyes shone with life as she strummed her clavicord in treasured afternoons of leisure, chanting Goethe's wistful lyric of love and loss to a tune of her own devising.

"*Heidenröslein*" had been Serena's favorite, for by then she had been old enough to understand the poignant allegory: A youth destroys a lovely rose for love of it, plucking it greedily from its stem, taking it far from its native heath to where it must languish and die. Now, as Anna's German stirred this memory, Serena's eyes brimmed with tears that she quickly turned to hide, gazing unseeing out the window.

Oh, Mother, she thought. If only I could sit by you as I once did, and snuggle against your shoulder, and ask you to mend my hurt. But something in Anna's manner held her back. That, and a fear of giving in. If once she succumbed to Anna's touch, if once she let the tears flow unrestrained, she would be lost, swept away, at their mercy, her will dissolved by grief, her resolution destroyed by her sense of duty. She swallowed hard, downing the knot of tears that hurt her throat. "I'd rather stand."

"*Kindchen,* for weeks now your father waits. Little patience has he always. Now it is gone. Can you not do as he wishes and let us forget what you have done?"

"Do as he wishes? Marry that . . . that creature who has filled Father's head full of lies that he might have me in the guise of Christian charity? Mother, *you* must know, though Father can't or won't see, that Caleb has itched to paw me from the day he first set foot in Weyford. And now he sees his chance to bind me to him before God, with chains of obligation and guilt. And to bind Father, too, and the ironworks. He wants them as much as he despises the work, and he wants me and despises me, too. Can't you see that?"

Anna hesitated.

"Mother," pleaded Serena, "don't lie to me. You've seen how he looked at me, how his eyes crept all over me as his hands twitched to grab at me. You've seen him all but slaver behind that beard of his when he knew Father would not see. Must you and I mince words with one another?"

At last Anna sighed. "A long time now have I seen it. I have seen, too, how you dislike him. First I thought, it is only that he is older. Fine looks he has not. Fine speech he has not. But that he wants you—such a bad thing is that?"

"A peculiar kind of wanting that is—a wanting that never looks one in the face. And besides . . ." She stopped. Remembering Brandon's comment —"A belled cat kills few starlings"—she let the issue of Caleb's spying rest.

"*Ja*, his eyes, something strange there is about them. But your sister—"

"Prudence wants him—let her have him." But, thought Serena, he does not want Prudence, though Prudence is the elder and stands to inherit the works. He only wants me.

"The Prudence has not brought disgrace to us. She has not broken your father's spirit—and my heart. Her good name, it needs no redeeming. *You* need it."

"Mother—*you* say that to me? Not really knowing what has happened? Father will not listen. Won't you?"

"Your father you do not understand," said Anna, ignoring Serena's plea. "His favourite you were, his darling—yes, more than the Prudence, more even than his son. Proud he was of you, your spirit, your beauty. He indulged you. He spoiled you. He let you play by the works—*Ja*, he knew more than you think. To Mistress Mansey he paid to send you—it is I who begged but he who sent you. Such freedom he gave you—a trouble to him it became. He believes not that women should have learning. He thinks it is not God's design. And how have you now repaid him? He has lost the Sam, too. He has now no son to leave his life work to. All but *verrückt* . . . crazy . . . he is with sorrow. And the Caleb—he means to make him a son, to save the ironworks for his grandchildren."

"Then Father is a fool."

"Serena!"

"Yes—a fool. He knows everything about making iron—and he knows nothing about people. His blind trust in Caleb will be the ruin of Father." Serena whirled to face the window again, breathing fast. "And as for love—" She choked. Gripping the windowsill, she fought to control her voice. "As for love," she said bitterly, "if Father loved me, he at least would hear me out."

"Because he loves you, he fears to hear. As I do. If what you could tell would not hurt us more, you would have told it."

The child, thought Serena. Can I really tell Mother I'm bearing a bastard? That soon all of Weyford will see my disgrace? That spiteful tongues will wag all over the Barrens—even more than they do now? With a child beside me to remind them, the goodwives will never forget.

"Serena, the way we have found for you, you must take. The Caleb you must marry now. It is your father's order—if with chains he has to bind you while the lines are read."

"No!"

"The Caleb has asked to see you. This afternoon he comes here. What he wants you must do for all our sakes."

Serena turned to face her mother. "Very well," she said, "I've a word or two for Master Caleb." I'll stave them off, she thought. And somehow I'll get away. I'll find Stuart Brandon; he must be near Barnegat still. She clenched her fists. "Mother, there's but one thing you can do for me — since you will not take my part. Let me see Caleb alone."

"*Ja.* Your father I will talk to. Now I go." Anna heaved herself to her feet. At the stairs she turned back. "*Ach, Liebchen.*" She drew a ragged breath. "We love you — I, and your father, too. Angry he is now, and stubborn. But he loves you. Can you not see that we want what is best for you?" Anna held out her arms. Tears trickled down her face.

Serena's face was set. She made no move toward her mother but stared stonily at her, her eyes dry, until Anna dropped her arms and hobbled down the stairs.

When Serena heard the door to the stairway close, she dropped her face into her hands and sobbed bitterly.

❧ ❧ ❧

THROUGHOUT THE DAY the hot wind rose. The sky took on a sullen cast, grey tinged with ochre and sulphurous green. Dry leaves and loose pieces of lumber skittered across the ground. On the lake shore and below, near the countinghouse and store, the wind rushed up behind the men and set their leather aprons to snapping like flags. Dust rose in spirals that whirled across the open spaces.

High in the tower, Serena watched as Caleb approached, threading his way through the colliers' carts. The wind snatched his hat and sent it cartwheeling toward the lake. A lad chased it and brought it back to him. Then Serena lost sight of him as he neared the house. Yet her senses, honed by the wind and her own apprehension, told her the instant he entered the passage door.

He no longer comes a-calling like a suitor. Now he enters the back passage as a familiar. Master Caleb is riding high. But I'll unseat him. I will. I must. She moved from the window to the centre of the room, drawing herself to her full height as she heard the stairway door open.

She had pleaded with Samuel, through Anna, that she at least be allowed to confer with Caleb in the drawing room, not as a prisoner in this barren eyrie. Samuel had refused. "She'll not set foot in this drawing room until she comes to stand before the pastor, with Caleb Sawyer by her side." But at least Anna had sent Susan up with some respectable clothes. In pale apricot silk with a lace frill about the throat, Serena felt more like herself. The warm tint of the gown lent colour to her pale

face. She stroked the smooth fabric to give herself confidence—it was so
long since she had worn a fine gown.

Caleb was clumping up the steps. He had gained no grace during her absence and nearly fell into the room. He's dressed for courting, thought Serena. The elegant coat and brass-buttoned vest were new, and so were his knee breeches.

He stood with his hands behind his back, under his coattails, nervously flapping them. "Good day, Serena. Do you find your new quarters to your liking?" From under his brows, his gaze swept the barren room, lingering on the simple cot, the few belongings stacked on the bare floor.

Serena said nothing. The slimy cur, she thought. No "Mistress Serena" on his lying tongue now. He thinks he's brought me low. He knew in what quarters he'd find me, and why I would be there. But if he thinks to twit me about my downfall, he'll get no satisfaction from me.

"I should think you would be eager to improve your position," he continued, "but your father informs me you've spurned my generosity."

"Generosity?"

"I'm generous, I think, to accept you as my wife, to offer you a respectable place here, to give you an opportunity to live down your escapade, to overlook . . . many things." He looked her full in the face for a moment. Then he let his glance travel to her waist.

He knows, thought Serena. He knows I'm with child. How? Prudence, of course. Prudence must have told him. How else could he be certain? But Prudence? Mealy-mouthed Prudence speaking with a man of bastardy? I'd not have thought her capable of it. Telling Mother, yes—but a man? Does she think in this way to discourage him at last, to bind him to her side in my stead? Ugh! How can Prue bear the thought of his touching her?

Caleb was watching her closely, his eyes furtive yet intent. His face had reddened slightly.

His forehead looks like worms writhing, thought Serena in disgust. For a moment she saw another face overlaid on the one before her—the grey-blue eyes, direct and clear, the implacable lines of forehead and brow, the head held proudly high. Stuart Brandon. A quiver passed through her taut, stretched nerves. Her face softened, her eyes glistened.

It was only for an instant, but Caleb saw it. His own eyes glowed with that malignant light she had seen in them once before—at the White Stag. Desire was in that look: a twisted, thwarted desire, intense yet suppressed, festering and evil. For the first time, Caleb frightened her.

Still he watched her. He narrowed his eyes, calculating, speculating. His body seemed to coil, snake-like, into itself. Then his thin neck stretched forward, his beard quivered, his lips curled, as he prepared to strike.

"If you think to go to your lover with your bastard, you'd best change your plans. Stuart Brandon is dead."

Serena felt the blood drain from her face. She swayed as the room circled round her, swooping and pitching. The ceiling. The windows. The baleful glare of the sky. Caleb's face, shrinking and expanding, advancing and receding, bobbing in and out of her vision like some grotesque air-filled bladder on a string pulled by a child. Caleb's eyes with their look of triumph danced before her, seeming to come closer and closer, though he stood as though rooted in his place. Beads of perspiration dewed her forehead. A black veil hovered near her eyes.

She managed a deep breath. Her vision cleared a little. Caleb made no move to help her as she stumbled to the cot and sat down, bringing her head to her knees. The faintness passed. She sat bolt upright, bracing herself with her hands.

"Dead? I don't believe you. How could he be dead? And how could you know if he were?" The satisfaction in his eyes told her what she had confessed.

"No one has told you the news while you've been . . . resting here. The British fleet attacked Barnegat. His ship was not fully fitted out" — Caleb looked at her meaningfully — "as you well know. The storm — the storm on the night you ran off from the White Stag — closed off his bolt-hole at Crane-berry Inlet. They ran him aground. They took the *Audacious* with all hands. They tried him at sea — for piracy. They hung him and buried him at sea."

It took all Serena's will to remain upright. Her icy hands gripped the thin mattress of the cot, her nails shredding the frayed edges of the coverlet. Her gorge rose; she felt the taste of vomit sour in her mouth. I won't. I won't be sick before him. I won't let him know what this means to me. I won't think of it myself. Later. Later, when he has gone, but not now. Not before him.

Shakily, she stood up. She braced her knees and fought for balance.

"Now don't you think," said Caleb, "you should reconsider my offer?"

Serena raised her head. Her face was dead white. Her eyes were enormous, the pupils black. "You scurvy liar! I don't believe you! You've lied to Father, lied to Mother, lied and lied and lied! You lie whenever it's to your advantage. And if it *is* true" — her breath caught in a sob — "if it is true, still, I'll never marry you, never let you lay your hands on me. Never — if I die for it." She darted forward and spat in his face. "Get out of here!" Her voice rose to a shriek. "Get *out!*"

Caleb stood rigid, shuddering, her spittle running down his cheek. After a moment he raised his arm and wiped his face on his sleeve. "You bitch! You'll pay for this—and your bastard, too. I offered you help, and a good name for your brat, and this is how you serve me. You'll pay for this, Serena. By God, I'll make you pay!"

He turned and stumbled down the stairs.

C H A P T E R 🔊 1 3

C ALEB SAWYER STALKED blindly through the main hall of Wainwright
House. Above him the draught from the rising winds set the
chandelier's prisms to chiming.

Anna Wainwright came out from the drawing room. "*Herr Sawyer!*
You have spoken, then, with the Serena? What is it that she—?" He
brushed past her and jerked open the door to the back passage. In the
stillroom was a basin and ewer. He splashed some water into the basin
and scrubbed at his face, rubbing and rubbing until his cheek was chafed.
The spot where Serena had spat on him burned like a brand.

Still rubbing his cheek, he stormed to the store, ignoring the idlers
who clustered by the stove as though it were winter and they in need of
heat. He plunged into his cubbyhole through the door behind the counter,
which was cluttered as always with goods: A wheel of cheese with a
wedge cut from it. Jugs of molasses. Sacks of meal from the gristmill. A
loaf of sugar. A tin of needles. Blockade-run papers of the new machine-
made pins.

He slammed the door shut and went to his counting-desk. For once,
his buckram-bound ledgers, his dusty papers, the brass inkwell and sharpened quills failed to calm him. His face still burned. His breath rasped in
his throat. He clung to the edges of the table, panting. Spittle frothed
on his lips as his tongue sought epithets equal to his anger.

"Bitch!" he said aloud. "Whore! How dare she refuse me! She *cannot*
refuse me. She is to be my wife—my *wife*. Mine. To be in my power. To
do as I say. And when she is . . . when she is . . ."

She has always laughed at me. Even when she spoke most courteously
I could sense the laughter behind her eyes, those amber eyes that capture the sunlight and make it her slave—as I would make her mine. I
know what she thinks of me. She thinks I'm not a man. But I'll show

her—I'll show her. Desire lay like red-hot bars across his flesh. His manhood stirred feebly, but stirred, as it never did except at sight or thought of Serena. He cupped his hand under his crotch and felt the softness there grow firmer, harder.

When she is mine—mine in the eyes of God and of Weyford, *my* property, *my* chattel, alone with me in my own house, shuttered and safe behind the cedars beyond the dam, then . . . then. . . . He thought of the glorious tawny hair he had seen flying free in the wind at Barnegat. I'll make her take it down. She must take off all her garments and stand naked before me, with only her hair for raiment. And I'll make her lean over me and brush it over my body, every part of my body.

And if she refuses? She will not refuse for long. A shudder shook his body, a vicious tremor that erupted from deep within him. He clutched his manhood more tightly and felt the yearning ache in his loins. He pictured Serena's white skin, and that teasing shadow where her breasts began. He thought of the hand-coloured pictures in the books hidden at home in a secret cupboard—of how her breasts would thrust forward if he bound her hands tightly behind her back.

She will not refuse me, he thought again. How pale her skin must be where the sun has never touched it. And if she defies me . . . if she dares defy me, I'll lay red welts on that skin with the lash. The welts will form a crisscross pattern of heat on that cool skin, and I'll trace it with my fingers, with . . . I'll make her take me in her hands, in her mouth, and then—surely then—I'll be able to . . .

And if I cannot? The brass-inlaid case in his bedroom came to mind, with its velvet lining and its implements of ivory—the case sold to him by a seaman who had brought it from the Orient where, the man had said, such implements were commonplace. If I cannot have her with my body, still I will have her. And she will submit to me. His eyes glazed, his hand moved frantically as he thought of what he would do, how he would use her.

He came out of his trance. His anger flared anew. She has spurned my offer of marriage. And her father, for all his promises, is still her pawn. Will he really force the marriage? How can he? Well, perhaps Pastor Haines will perform a forced service if he's told of Serena's condition.

Serena's condition—a bastard in her belly and that pirate the father. And my name, Caleb Sawyer, not good enough to baptize the brat. He shook with fury as he remembered the wharf at Barnegat—the two of them there, laughing in the sunlight, the ductile thread that bound them all but visible despite the black looks of her paramour, his angry impatience with her prank.

What intimacies they must have shared, the two of them, lying with their heated flesh pressed together, Brandon's hands and mouth all over her, exploring those secret places of which Caleb could only dream. What had she done with him, said to him, her breath sighing in his ear as he plumbed the hidden depths of her? What tacit remembrance of acts done in darkness charged the space between them as they moved through the sundrenched day?

He slammed his fist against the table. The inkwell jumped in its holder. Some quills fell to the floor. "Damn her! I'll make her pay!" Then he saw someone standing in the doorway. Tim—the lad who had retrieved his hat and who did about the store for him.

"M-M-Master Sawyer," Tim stammered, frightened at the rage on Caleb's face. "Jake Buzby be here with coal fer ye."

Buzby! Another beneficiary of Serena's smiles and dimples. She was laughing with Buzby at the blowout. That drunken woodjin, smelling to high heaven of smoke and applejack. "I'll take care of him," he said aloud. He stalked toward the door. Tim ducked out of the way.

Jake Buzby was beside his creaky wagon, leaning against it and chewing a straw. His face and hands were powdered with charcoal dust; the coal was stacked perilously on the wagon bed. The dog Cinders was perched on the seat. The wind blew a cloud of charcoal dust into Caleb's eyes. Dust settled on his fine new coat and blackened his fresh linen stock. As he drew nearer the cart, Cinders, perhaps recognizing his scent, gave a short, sharp bark and started up.

"Set, dawg," said Buzby. " 'Day, Master Sawyer. Got a right good load fer ye. Two cords there be—mebbe more."

Caleb brushed busily at his cuffs, glancing warily at Cinders. He wrinkled his nose at the applejack smell that habitually accompanied Buzby. This stinking sot, he thought. And she laughs with him.

He affected to examine the charcoal, though his gaze was blurred by anger. "A good load?" he said scornfully. "Two cords? If there's one and a half there, I'll be surprised. Don't you think I know a short stack when I see one? And it's like as not hollow in the middle."

Jake bristled. "I don't be peddlin' short stacks. I got me reputation."

"Pah! A reputation as a sot." The anger that seared his bowels melted Caleb's caution. "Look there! And there!" His skinny finger jabbed toward the wagon. "Burnt through, not seasoned. And here! Not even charred. Fine lot of pigs we'd cast with this."

"And a fine lot ye know about ironmakin' of a sudden. *And* about coalin'. Ye bin takin' lessons off Miz Serena?"

Caleb flushed crimson. Cinders, sensing contention, jumped down from his perch. Tongue lolling, still friendly, but alert, he pattered toward Caleb.

Caleb backed off, toward the front of the wagon where the swaybacked horse shifted idly from foot to foot. "Buzby," he said, "I've enough of your swindling. Next thing we know, you'll be burning off our own timber and trying to peddle it to me. Take this worthless stuff and dump it in the river. That's all it's good for."

Jake glanced round at the ring of watchers who had gathered at the sound of raised voices. Then he narrowed his eyes and looked deliberately at Caleb. "That be good coal, and ye know it. Took me a week to cure that load, watchin' every minute that the woods don't take afire. Them that's honest themselves don't see no need to call an honest man a swindler. Whut ye plannin' Master Sawyer? Whut plots 'n' schemes ye up to now?"

The crowd stirred.

"That be tellin' 'im—'im an' his cheese-parin' ways."

"Warn't no given' short counts when the Old Man be doin' the countin'."

Caleb's thin hair whipped in the wind. His high forehead flamed. "Silence, lout! Take your nag and your cur and be gone. You there!" he turned on the watchers. "Be about your work if you've a mind to keep your jobs. Buzby, do you hear me? Go!"

Deliberately, Jake spat on the ground by Caleb's foot. Caleb sprang forward and grabbed Buzby's shirt. The hulking old man stood his ground. "Cinders," he said quietly, "tell Master Sawyer good day."

Cinders dashed toward Caleb, ears jouncing, tail wagging. "Get away!" shouted Caleb. "Get away!" He backed off, kicking wildly with one foot. He heard snickering. He whipped his head around to see who was laughing and lost his balance. His arms flailed wildly. He went down between the horse and the cart.

"Whoa!" called Jake. Had the horse bolted, Caleb would have been dragged and killed. But the horse set all four feet firmly on the ground and lifted its tail. A cascade of horse droppings plopped on Caleb's waistcoat.

At sight of his purple face the watchers scattered. Buzby bowed in a manner almost courtly and stretched a hand to help him up. Caleb struck it away. He scrambled to his feet, a shower of manure flying from his garments. "Buzby, I'll kill you for this."

"I takes a lot of killin'."

"I'm warning you. Don't show your face at Weyford again."

"I be stayin' away when the Old Man tells me to. Not afore."

Caleb looked down at his clothes. The stench that met his nose was overpowering. As he turned to go, he looked up at Wainwright House. A casement was open in the tower room, and Serena was leaning from it, laughing. "You, too," he cried angrily, his words torn away by the wind. "You, too. You'll regret this. I'll make you pay. Just wait."

Her laughter pursued him, peal after peal, as he ran for the shelter of his lodging.

⫷ ⫷ ⫷

AT SUNSET the wind died down. The lull brought no respite from the tension. Heat, sullen and oppressive, settled over the Barrens. Midges swarmed in the shallows, and early mosquitoes whined about Caleb's ears as he skulked past the row of workers' cottages. From windows open upon the warm night he heard voices and laughter.

They're laughing at me. At the figure I cut. At the way that drunken sot made a fool of me. The spot of fire in his brain grew and grew. He felt its heat on his forehead, on his flesh. And then he felt himself back in Princeton, being carried along Nassau Street, the jeers of street idlers mingling with the taunts of the students who bore him roughly toward the edge of town. "Tory! Tory!"

He felt the stickiness of the tar on his skin, the sting of burns, the prickle of feathers, the ignominy of being naked before these hooligans. His skin had burned for days from the tar and the repeated, frantic scrubbings with brush and turpentine. He had had to shave his scalp, his beard, all the places on his body where the tar stuck and stung. Not until all traces of his ordeal had been eradicated had he dared venture out from the home of the Loyalists who had sheltered him, to seek another position now that the College would no longer employ him as clerk.

Now the remembered burning of his skin mingled with the fire in his brain until he felt his whole being aflame with humiliation, thirsting for revenge. He came to the dam and stopped, leaning on the bridge rail in the twilight. Atop the hill he saw a light in Serena's tower.

Swift with springtime, fed by springs deep beneath the cedar swamps, Weyford River surged over the dam. He did not see it. The water roared as it tumbled from the spillway. He heard only Serena's mocking laughter, the laughter of the watching idlers, the laughter of the whore he had once hired in a futile attempt to prove his manhood. Laughter, always laughter, dogging his footsteps, echoing down his days. The boards beneath his feet shook with the force of the water; his hands upon the railing shook with the force of his rage.

"I'll make them pay," he whispered. The roaring waters swept his words away. "I'll make them pay." The thought had obsessed him all day. But how? Slowly the knot of anger that had squeezed thought from his brain uncoiled into a burning fuse that lit an explosion in his mind.

Fire! he thought. Fire was the answer. Fire as searing as his rage. With fire he'd avenge himself on them all. Serena—let her laugh when her father was ruined, her home destroyed, and she a beggar. That old sot Jake. And his drooling mongrel, too. And Old Samuel into the bargain— Samuel, who had failed him.

Fire! Now his mind, frozen so long, was working at fever heat. I must plan it well. Let them think it old Jake's doing—by design, or by carelessness. His drunkenness is known to all.

The ironworks will be destroyed. No more munitions will slip seaward by the creek or set out on their long journey over land. The British will be spared the risk of battle: They'll conquer Weyford without hazarding a man. And I—I will be rewarded. Generously rewarded, when I get word to Lipcote. I'll be rich! And no muddling about with filthy furnaces, sweating out iron drop by drop.

I'll be rich—and Samuel Wainwright will be penniless. He's sunk everything he has into Weyford. And when Old Samuel is driven to the wall, I'll claim the burnt acreage and a fortune in charcoal. And Serena? Without her father's fortune behind her, we'll see how long she laughs at me. Again that dark shudder coursed through him, as scenes from his afternoon's musings danced again through his brain.

Fire! He all but felt the heat of the flames fanning his face. Tonight, he thought. It must be tonight. The Barrens loomed, parched and sweltering, tinder waiting for a spark. Moving for once with decision, Caleb pelted up the hill toward the store.

CHAPTER ✍ 1 4

ARRIVING AT JAKE BUZBY's clearing, Caleb paused, panting, to wipe the sweat from his face and to listen. He heard no sound of human activity, only the maddening whine of the mosquitoes and the faint snapping of coals in the charcoal pits ahead. He rubbed his aching forearms, flexed his cramped fingers, and picked up the jugs of turpentine that had dragged at his shoulders the last hour. Two miles on these sand trails seemed like ten, and days spent hunched over his counting-desk ill accustomed him to walking. He settled the packet of venison, well laced with cyanide pilfered from the engraver's shop, more firmly under his arm.

Quietly he stole along the last few yards of trail. The clearing opened before him. Two ricks of charcoal were burning—two separate pits. Fool! he thought, to burn charcoal in these dry woods. The mounded structures, taller than he, were outlined by an orange glow. They looked like giant beehives, their combs dripping fire.

Caleb had no attention to spare for the beauty of the spectacle before him. Beyond the ricks he saw Buzby's crude hovel. I'd best make sure he's sleeping. Caleb moved stealthily around the firelit circle. He saw a small shadow moving against the glow: Cinders, on his rounds. Will he bark and betray me? Then he realized that Buzby had trained the dog to respond only to variations in the flames.

From Jake's hut came the sound of loud snores. Clutter surrounded the hovel: empty jugs, fragments of crockery, axes, a saw, other tools of Jake's trade. Wood chips littered the floor of the clearing, mixed with dead leaves and pine needles. Only around the charcoal pits had Buzby made some attempt to keep the ground clear.

A breeze had sprung up, drying the sweat from Caleb's forehead. Good, he thought. He tested the wind's direction. It had shifted since the morning; for weeks the wind had blown from the west. Now it blew easterly, directly toward Weyford village. That will spread the flames faster, thought Caleb. Again he felt the burning, in his chest, in his gut. The significance of an east wind escaped him as he thought of the flames leaping toward Wainwright House, crackling hungrily, devouring all before them.

But first . . . He swallowed. Time to eliminate the dog. He moved back to a spot near the charcoal ricks. He unwrapped the meat, holding it before him. Would Cinders remember him as friend or foe? "Cinders?" he called softly. "Here, doggy. Here, boy."

He heard a questioning whine. Then Cinders loped toward him. As the dog neared, Caleb began to sweat. His throat tightened. His hands shook so badly he could scarcely hold on to the meat. He was no grown man, but a boy of five again, clinging to the trunk of a cherry tree in the Squire's garden. And the dog coming toward him was no docile hound but a pair of fierce mastiffs who barked and howled beneath the tree, snarling, slavering, snapping their massive jaws inches from his toes. He felt the rough bark of the tree against his cheek, heard the rustling of the leaves as it shook with his trembling, the low branch on which he cowered sinking nearer and nearer those gaping mouths, those fearsome teeth. And he heard the laughter of the Squire and his cronies, watching at a distance, making no attempt to curb the dogs. "Caught us a poacher laddie, eh, boys?" cried the Squire . . .

Cinders stood a yard away, head tilted questioningly. "Here, doggie," urged Caleb, his teeth chattering. "Come here, doggie, I've something for you." Summoning all his will, he stretched a hand toward Cinders and patted him gingerly on the head. Reassured, the little dog came forward, sniffing at the meat. Caleb set it gently down and backed away. The dog snatched eagerly at the venison, carrying it a few paces away before biting and tearing at this unexpected treat.

It took but an instant. A stifled howl burst from Cinders. Then he fell. His body jerked, twisted, almost rose into the air with the intensity of its final spasms. Then it quivered and lay still.

"That's one of them done." Caleb picked up the turpentine and moved toward Jake's hut.

ە ە ە

SERENA KNELT BESIDE the cot, her head on her arm. Her glee at Caleb's mishap had long since ebbed. So had the anger that had buoyed her up through the confrontation with her enemy. Her hair tumbled about her bowed shoulders, her body sagged with weariness and despair. She had cajoled Susan into bringing up her "comfort gown," a faded, washed-out nightdress of flowered muslin, worn to softness. Her fingers rucked its thin fabric into pleats, then smoothed it, then rucked it up again.

She rolled her head restlessly against her arm, pressing her closed eyelids against her skin as though to rub out the vision that obsessed her: Stuart Brandon, hanging, the long, lean body jerking at the end of the rope, then swaying, swaying, as she had once seen a hanged convict at Woodlington gaol, his face purpling, his tongue thrust out, his eyes starting from their sockets. And then, when that dreadful swinging to and fro ceased at last, being cut down and dumped ignominiously into the sea. Down, down, the body would go, weighted perhaps — yes, it would have to be — till it rested on the sandy bottom, rolling gently in the deep sea swells. And the crabs . . . Stop!

She felt the feeble retching of her stomach, long since emptied in violent spasms. And beneath that, beneath the images that haunted her, beneath the feeling of stunned surprise, the throbbing in her head and the ache of her knees pressed against the hard board floor, was pain — a pain in her heart that shocked her with its intensity.

Why am I not glad to hear he's dead, after the way he used me? Why do I feel this void inside, growing and spreading, where his image had been? He used me — and he left me. He would never have sought me out again. And if I had sought him, found him? What then? What hope had I of his protection?

Why did he shun me again and again — just when he had been close to me? Yes. It was when we had been closest that he turned brusque, even cruel. Why? Why did he run away from me — and why am I so sure he was running away? And sure, too, that somehow we would have met again?

"Would have met —" Is he really dead? Have the British really hanged him? Perhaps Caleb lied: He has lied so often, each lie entangling me more tightly in his web. Perhaps this, too, was a lie. No . . . no. He believed what he was telling me. That vindictive glee I saw in his eyes — triumph over Stuart, over me — was real enough. Stuart Brandon is dead. Oh God! he's dead. "Take him and cut him out in little stars, and he will make the face of heaven so fine . . ."

She rocked to and fro in her pain, wrapping her arms tightly round herself, her head bowed, eyes blinded by tears. She clamped her hand over her mouth to stifle her sobs, lest anyone hear and investigate.

Mother . . . ? Oh, to bury her head in Anna's plump shoulder and sob

out her grief and despair. There was no one to share it, no one to tell, no
way to ease her pain and confusion with a flow of words poured out to
an understanding ear. No one close to her even knew that she had met
Stuart Brandon. And if I tell, she thought, if I explain what he's done,
how can I account for this grief, this pain that begins in my chest and
surges through my body until my very fingertips throb? Why grieve for a
man who seduced me, used me, then abandoned me, pregnant with his
child?

His child. He did not know about the child. Now he will never know.

She flung herself down and wept without restraint.

When at last she arose and went wearily to the window, it was twilight.
Pale flashes of heat lightning flickered in the east.

The child. It must not be born here at Weyford a bastard. Nor will I
place it at Caleb's mercy as surrogate father.

What can I do? Where can I turn?

Enoch? He was in love with me — I know he was. Where did he go
when Father turned him out? To Batsto? To Aetna? Neither's so large a
plantation as this. But he's a good iron man. Any plantation would welcome him, perhaps with a more responsible position. I could . . . But
could I? She remembered Enoch's shyness, his deference, his transparent
joy at having her on his arm, the way he handled her as though she were
glass. Could she go to Enoch and ask him to be father to her bastard? Or
worse, go to him, saying nothing, cajoling him into marriage, and then
watching his eyes when the child was born and the calendar told its own
story? No, Enoch, she thought. You deserve better than that.

And there's this, she told herself sternly: You know that the thought
of being touched by any man but Stuart Brandon makes you shudder.

What of my mother's people, back in Bethlehem? She thought of the
tight-knit Moravian community, tucked snugly among the Pennsylvania
hills, where once, years ago, she had visited. The Wednesday night
prayers, the sternly kept Sabbath, the interminable blessings before
meals. No. There was no place for her among those staunch and sometimes dour people. Better Weyford than that.

Where, then? Who? How? She remembered the sack of gold. Lighting
a candle, she pulled the leather pouch from the crevice in the wall where
she had hidden it. Sitting on the cot, tailor-fashion, she shook the contents out into her lap. The coins glittered in the candlelight: Spanish
dollars, guineas, some foreign coins she had not seen before. "Five . . .
ten . . . there must be fifty coins here!"

In the currency-starved new nation, it was a fortune. Fully enough, she thought, to keep her until the child was born, to pay for its birth and a short breathing space thereafter. Stuart Brandon had abandoned her, true, but he had not left her without recourse.

But where shall I go? And what shall I do when the money is gone? It will not last forever—prices rise daily. I will have to earn my bread somehow. But how? What work is there for a woman, except as a barmaid or a whore? Or perhaps as a servant. Somewhere far from Weyford, where I'm not known. But who will take a servant with an infant? And what future will the child have as a serving girl's brat?

She put the coins back into the sack and hid it away again. She blew out the candle and went back to the window, gazing to the west, where Philadelphia lay, and all the wide world she had first glimpsed at Hightstown.

Hightstown! And now the darkened window seemed to reflect the face of Mistress Mansey: the dark hair, grey at the temples, pulled back neatly from the high forehead, the dark eyes, round, alert, drooping slightly at their corners, the narrow nose, the well-modelled lips held firmly shut.

& & &

On her last day at the academy, Mistress Mansey had sought her out. "Here," she had said, proffering a silk-wrapped packet. "Take these with you, Serena."

Watching her teacher, Serena gently unwrapped the silk. Books: some cheap editions of the plays of Shakespeare and one volume bound in softest calfskin. Gently she opened this last and read the title page: "The Poetical Works of John Donne." On the flyleaf was a quotation, inscribed in her teacher's hand:

For Serena Wainwright—

"Death be not proud, though some have called thee
Mighty and dreadful, for thou art not so,
For those whom thou thinkst thou dost overthrow
Die not, poor death, yet canst thou kill me."

—Virginia Mansey
Hightstown Female Academy
January, 1777

Serena had looked up inquiringly. "You have an unusual mind, Serena," said the older woman. "That is both a gift and a curse to a woman. There are many kinds of death: A mind can die because it is starved or because it is smothered, because it is sapped of its wealth by those who take from it and give nothing back. If you have these books and can ponder the thoughts in them, your mind will not die of starvation back among those who may not see its worth."

"But these are your books," said Serena. "And they are precious to you—I know they are."

"They will be the more precious in your possession, for I'll know they will keep the flame of your mind alive when otherwise it might dwindle and go out."

"Then thank you. I shall take good care of them. I promise."

"Promise me rather that you will wear them out." Mistress Mansey smiled. "And then find a use for that mind."

"How, back in the Barrens, where even a woman like Mother is good for naught but a wife?"

"I came to America from a village more remote than Weyford. And I found a use for mine. Finding sparks and fanning them, feeding the fires in minds like yours that might otherwise have died out for lack of fuel."

❧ ❧ ❧

MISTRESS MANSEY! thought Serena now. She would help me—hide me, perhaps, until the child is born. Then—perhaps I could learn to teach the younger girls, find a place in her school. Is she still there? The school, Serena knew, had been first closed, then used to quarter Hessian soldiers from the troops holding Trenton. And the town had been terribly battered as first one army, then another, fought through it. Was Virginia Mansey still there?

I'll find her, resolved Serena. I'll get to the White Stag—no, I'm too well known there. Well, Atsion, then. The stage stops there. I'll buy my way to Long-A-Coming and from there—to Lumberton, perhaps, or Mount Holly. And northward. Even if she has left Hightstown, someone there may know where she is. Someone must.

Renewed energy coursed along her nerves. She paced the room, making plans. Somehow, whatever she did, she must retrieve those books and take them with her. And she would need . . . she went to the windows, pacing the circuit of them. At the eastern bank of windows she paused. Over there. Near Jake Buzby's clearing. Was that a charcoal rick? Or—

A tongue of flame leapt skyward.

Serena flung the window open. "Fire!" she cried. "Fire! Fire!" No one was about. She stumbled down the narrow stairs and pounded upon the locked door. "Fire!" she called. "Fire to the east! Let me out! Oh, please, let me out!"

She heard running footsteps. Someone turned the key. *"Kindchen! Komm helfe uns!"* Come help us. Anna ran on. As Serena crashed through the door of the stairway she heard the Big House bell clanging wildly.

❧ ❧ ❧

CALEB DROPPED the flaming brand into the wood chips he had soaked with turpentine. Buzby's hut went up at once, its flimsy sides engulfed in flame. The fire raced along the turpentine trails he had laid, crackling gaily, heading for the brush. It devoured the litter of pine needles and leaves, relishing it, thriving on it, growing and growing.

Caleb capered after it, waving his arms like some mad priest invoking Lodi, the god of fire. His shadow danced with him, grotesquely elongated, first before, then behind, as the light shifted at the whim of the leaping flames.

Now the fire had reached the trees. Flames raced up the trunk of a pine, feeding greedily on its oozing sap. Up, up they raced, along the branches, into the crown. For an instant, each needle glowed, a separate filament of orange light. Then, with a roar, the whole crown burst into flame. Then the next.

The fire leapt from tree to tree, easily bridging the small rushing stream that marked the end of old Jake's holdings. The wind, steadily freshening, whipped it along. Glowing pine cones dropped from the branches to set new fires on the ground. A burning branch broke loose and crashed to earth. At once new flames surged skyward.

Behind Caleb, a human torch staggered from Jake's hut and rolled in agony on the ground, its screams all but drowned out by the roar of the fire. Caleb did not turn. Still he continued his mad dance at the base of the flames. His rage had found full expression. He and the fire were one—the burning within him and the burning without. "Now they'll pay," he cackled. His words were swept away in wind and flame. "Now they'll pay."

Now the treetops were a mass of flame, the tree trunks glowing columns. And on the ground . . . on the ground. Caleb looked around. There was fire in front of him, fire behind, low, angry, crackling flames that raced toward him from every side.

Whence had he come? Where was the burnt ground on which he

would find safety? Where was the brook? That way? No, that way. Smoke blinded him, burning his eyes, scorching his lungs. He stumbled now this way, now that, crashing into tree trunks that burst into flame as he reeled away, tripping over vines that became red-hot coils of wire. Sparks showered down on him, burning holes in his clothes, stinging his forehead.

He turned back the way he had come — thought he had come. Where was the clearing? Where was the trail? Then he saw the stream, its dark waters dark no longer, but scarlet with reflected flame. He could hardly breathe for the pain in his nostrils, his throat, his lungs. Then he felt a searing heat at his ankles, at his knees. His breeches were afire.

He screamed as the pain reached his thighs — screamed and ran, beating madly with his hands at the flames between his legs, running and screaming, screaming and staggering, until he plunged into the water and was still.

CHAPTER ❧ 15

THE FIRE WINGED through the springtime forest, an arrow aimed at Weyford's heart. Leaping easily across the upper portion of Weyford River, the head fire raced along the shores of Weyford Lake. Lateral fires followed its course, fanning wider and wider, consuming leaf litter and brush. Whortleberry and sheep laurel raised their arms in supplication to the flames, only to be engulfed. The fronds of bracken fern, new-green, tender, moist with spring, blistered and blackened, contorted and fell. Glowing red whiskers of moss crumbled to ash on the scorched forest floor.

Whipped to frenzy by the winds of their own passage, the flames of the head fire bounded treetop high. Black smoke belched from the crowns of pitch pines exploding with boiling sap, while the long, fringed flowerlets of the black oaks floated like orange glowworms back to earth.

Squirrels, racing to the topmost branches of the oaks, trembled and chittered at the tongues of flame that scampered up the tree trunks more nimbly than they. Panicked creatures fled the fire, fox and bear, deer and wildcat, raccoon and weasel and vole—predator and prey companions in fear. The agonized shrieks of the losers in the race were lost in the cacophony—the roar of the wind, the snap of falling branches, the crackle of the flames, the sizzle of boiling sap. Frightened birds flapped over the burning acres, flock upon flock, parent birds frantic as their nests burned below.

Smoke filled the night sky as the fire splashed crimson on the bellies of the clouds that scudded along with the east wind, hiding the face of the moon.

Already the upper reaches of the lake had become a pool of flame, silhouetting human figures that scurried along its banks to try to stem the fire—or, failing that, to snatch what they could from the path of its hungry advance. Weyford village was a cauldron boiling with men. Old Samuel stood at the bridge, his white hair flying in the wind, shouting to be heard above the rumble of wheels, the cries of frightened children, and the incessant pealing of the bell calling its tocsin across the empty miles.

"McGuire! Take a crew to the furnace—the fire's not there yet; you've time. Draw the gates; start the mill wheels; keep them wet. Throw everything loose into the lake—we'll salvage it later. But the sheds will go up like kindling. Wet them down. Use the pump." Against the contingency of fire, Samuel had devised a pump worked by the furnace bellows.

The diminutive Irishman nodded, blinking in rhythm with his employer's gruff commands. He turned to go. "And, McGuire," said Samuel, "don't worry. We'll save your house if we can."

Mike cast a brief glance toward the village street where his house, and those of his fellows, stood tinder-dry and vulnerable in the most likely path of the flames. "Best pray for rain," he said. He hurried off across the bridge, beckoning his cronies to follow.

Samuel took stock of the activity. Bucket brigades toiled on both sides of the lake, women and men together, to wet down the roofs of the houses. Crude arrangements of ropes and pulleys were hauling heavy buckets to the roofs of the countinghouse and store. The barns? he thought. The piggery? Too far, perhaps, from the lake to be saved. Someone had best herd the cattle to the lake shore.

"Seth," he called to a sturdy figure in farmers' homespun that emerged from the thickening smoke. "Hitch up. Start plowing a firebreak around the orchard. Get someone else to work between the houses and the lake. Blindfold the horses if need be. But hurry!"

Samuel coughed. The smoke, carried by the wind, was making it hard to breathe, hard to see. Already sparks were flying through the haze—sparks, and chunks of flaming debris. He looked toward the sky, but the smoke obscured it. Was the easterly wind bringing rain? It was their only hope to save the works.

The planks of the bridge thundered with the tramp of many boots. Help—some none too steady on its feet—had come from the White Stag, summoned by the pealing bell. "Thank the Lord," said Samuel. "Come this way. You, lads! Collect every bit of sacking you can find. And you! Load those hogsheads on the wagons there. And the sacking, too. Take them along the lateral fires—take axes to cut your way through. Beat out what you can."

Samuel stamped off to see that wet sacking was sent up to the roof of Wainwright House and that watchers were posted to pounce on any spark. The cedar shingles were paper-dry after the months-long drought. He looked back once more to the workers' habitations. McGuire was right — pray God it rained before the fire came near them. As he watched, he saw laden women and children — and some men, too — making for the trail to the White Stag: fleeing. Whatever few possessions they most treasured — a bit of silver, some porcelain, bundles of clothing or household goods — they intended to save them. Fools! thought Samuel. They'd do better to make for the lake.

He looked to the east. A rim of fire outlined the dark mass of the nearer trees. "Anna!" he called, running up the slope to the house. Where is Caleb? he wondered, pausing to cough. He should be here. I need him to save the store accounts. "Anna! Come help me in the countinghouse!" He felt the pain of effort in his chest as he hurried up the stairs.

By the front door he paused, his breath whistling in his throat, looking down the slope to the frantic bustle by the bridge, then up at the tranquil glow that shone through the many windows. Wainwright House! His passion, his pride. Built with his first large profits, the first fruits of his expansion — the fruits made possible by that infusion of capital ten years ago. What will become of that venture now? More pressing concerns swept the thought away. "Anna! We must prepare rations for the fire fighters. And," he whispered on a half-sob, "we must prepare to abandon Wainwright House."

❧ ❧ ❧

POISED WITH ONE FOOT on the stairs, Serena heard her father enter. No, she told herself, I'll not go down. Not until they call me. And they won't call me. She swallowed a knot of tears that rose to choke her — I'm not one of them any longer. I've been too long away, too much has happened. I've caused too much grief.

From downstairs came sounds of preparations to depart. Running footsteps. Slamming drawers. Anna's voice, sharpened, agitated. "Prudence! The silver — the plate. Down the well we must put it; it is too heavy to carry. *Ach, Gott!*" The crash of breaking crockery echoed up the stairwell. "It is butter I have on my fingers. Susan! Another kettle we must put on the fire. Bring you the cider from the stillroom. And the fresh bread. So long as this house stands we must be feeding the men who try to save it." Her steps receded toward the kitchen passage.

Serena hurried down the hall toward her room. This is my chance to get away. I must not lose the opportunity. There are hundreds to fight the fire, she told her conscience, hundreds much stronger than I, with no unborn child to think of.

What shall I take with me? The portmanteau in the attic? No. I've ten miles, fifteen, to walk. I must take only what I can carry—some undergarments, a gown or two, some food, if I can slip unobserved into the stillroom. And the books—Mistress Mansey's books. And the gold. I'll tie that around my neck again.

The full skirt of her nightdress tangled about her legs. Oh! for the freedom of movement of her days with Stuart Brandon, the boy's breeches that freed her limbs from the clinging impediment of skirts. What had happened to them? She pulled open the carved walnut wardrobe. There they were, crumpled in a corner and forgotten.

She ran back to the door of the room and closed it, turning the ornate brass key. Swiftly she shed her nightdress and donned the rough garments—comforting now, familiar as her own skin. Working by touch in the semidarkness, lit only by the skyglow from the windows, she braided her hair, pulled the cap down over it.

Now for the packing—a pillowslip would do; she dare not be too long about it. A simple dress, another. She brushed the silks and fine wools in the wardrobe lingeringly, her sensitive fingertips identifying each gown by its feel. I'll use some of the gold to have new ones made, she thought—gowns more befitting a teacher. A change of footgear. She would need her stoutest shoes for the walk ahead. The ivory comb. The miniature of Anna, young, bright-eyed, wearing a satin ball gown. The books, wrapped in a second pillowslip.

What else? She glanced about the room. The bearskin—how can I leave it? And the ivory-backed brushes, the hand mirror that matches the comb. And . . . and . . . She swallowed hard. Will I ever see this room again? Or Mother or Father?

She went to the window where she had watched the dawn on the morning of the blowout. Could it be that but a few months separated her from the girl who knelt at that window? The sky beyond the orchard, tinted apricot then by the rising sun, was now lit by a baleful false dawn. The apple trees, their outlines fuzzy with blossoms and new leaves, would likely become gnarled skeletons once again, blackened and charred, with no knobby promise of buds at their tips.

The forest, she thought sadly, the beautiful springtime forest starred with dogwood blossoms in the clearings. It will be scorched and shadeless, those pitiful spars of burnt trunks standing watch among the ashes of burnt creatures. Then she remembered walking with Sam at the fringes of just such a scene: a small fire that one, mercifully contained, but hot and fierce while it burned.

"Look, Serena," he had said. He touched the trunk of a scrub pine, blackening his fingers. "See that knob—and this, and this. Wait and see.

In a few weeks you'll see green here. The Barrens are used to fire. And look here." At the base of a scorched chestnut oak, he scratched away the black debris. White shoots were thrusting up from the earth.

"You'll see. Wait a few years and you'll have a fine drunkards' gaol again." They both laughed. Many a drunken woodjin had been tossed into the palisade of a many-trunked chestnut oak to sleep off the effects of his "clandestine retreat." And some months later, when they had passed the site again, verdure greeted them, only the sooty char of the tree trunks revealing where the fire had passed. That, and the feathery plumes of the cedars, grey and brittle, in the swamp where the fire had halted. The ghost trees would stand there for years.

Perhaps, thought Serena now, perhaps the forest will heal. And Mother and Father, too, when the fire has died down, and the rains come, and new growth hides the scars. And my memory will be pale and distant, like the ghosts of those cedar trees.

She picked up her bundle and headed resolutely for the stairs.

❧　❧　❧

"JOE! JOE! Wake up!" Grace's plump breasts quivered as she crouched over Joe Mulliner, vigorously shaking his shoulder. On the other side of the broad bed, Honour stirred sleepily. "Wha—?"

Grace and Honour, twin sisters, had often served as butt for Mulliner's jests. "I've had Grace," he would crow, "and I've had Honour. I've had so much Grace and Honour they be plumb wore out!" He would roar with laughter, slap whichever of their well-padded rumps was closest to hand, and call for another ale.

"Joe!" Mulliner reared up. Lights danced before his eyes. His head seemed fair ready to split open. He fell back, swinging a massive arm in Grace's general direction. The blow flew wide. The girl had instinctively ducked.

"Be still, woman! Don't ye know what a head I've got on me?"

"Grace," mumbled Honour sleepily, "come back to bed. It must be the middle of the night."

"No! Joe, get up! Come look—to the west. The sky's all over red. T'would be near Weyford, I'd reckon. A tremendous fire there must be."

"And what's that to me?" But Mulliner hauled his huge form from the bed. He swayed as he came to his feet, clutching his forehead. Then he straightened and shuffled to the window.

His island hideaway had a slight incline at its centre—not much, but enough to allow Mulliner to scout the surrounding terrain. Trees lining

the shore blocked most of the view, but—"Ye be right," he said. Low-
hanging clouds to the west glowed redly. "T'would be a monstrous blaze
would light the sky like that. Hand me my britches."

Grace collected scattered garments from bedpost and floor. "Honour,
throw me Joe's boots."

Yawning widely, Honour fished under the bedstead. She flung herself
up, a boot in each hand, her coarse black curls bobbing. "Here! And
here!" Her bare breasts shook with each throw. Then she flounced back
down and pulled the quilts over her head. "Why are you so put about?"
Her voice was muffled by the bedclothes. "You've seen fires before."

"They'll be fleein'," said Mulliner. "All up and down the Weyford if
the fire's big enough. And leavin' choice pickings fer me and the boys."
He struggled into his boots, stuffed his shirt into his breeches, and shoved
his pistols into his belt. "Be good, girls." He slapped Honour's rump and
bent down to plant a kiss on Grace's pert nose. The top of her head
barely reached his collarbone.

"Hey, boys! Up with ye! Saddle the horses! We've a fair ride to make!"
He clumped along the hall, hammering at doors. "Let's be going!"

Grace crawled into the bed and curled up beside Honour. In a few
moments, the women heard hoofbeats and then splashing as the horses
forded the stream.

ᔰ ᔰ ᔰ

OLD SAMUEL WORKED at the head of a line of men, lifting the heavy wet
sacking, swinging it at the flames. The advance scouts of the head fire
licked at the litter of the clearing near the works. Suddenly a fierce gust
of wind sent up billows of smoke and whipped a sheet of flame toward
the men. Samuel turned and ran with them, his chest heaving as he
coughed, choking on the smoke, his nostrils full of the sickening smell of
his own hair burning where sparks fell upon his head.

"Here!" he shouted. "Form a line here!" He bent over, shaken by a
spasm of coughing. Now the flames raced in every direction, leaping
across the hastily shovelled breaks, crossing their own path, chasing one
another, chasing the men who flapped the sacking wildly to protect
their ankles from the fire.

Now the furnace and forge were at their backs as line after line was
abandoned. The water wheel had stopped, its mechanism jammed.
Sweating men tried feverishly to work the bellows pump by hand, sending uneven spurts of water toward the base of the flames. Others milled
about the casting shed, running to and fro from the millrace with sacking

that they soaked and then passed to the men on the shed roofs.

The fire seemed to pause for a moment, the flames fighting amongst themselves as the swirling gusts of wind sent them in conflicting directions.

Samuel's face was black with soot. His shirt was torn and scorched, his white hair frizzled and charred at the ends. "Don't give up, men," he cried. "There's rain coming. Do you feel that wind? The Lord is sending us rain. If we can but hold the fire here—"

He ran toward the flames, swinging the heavy sack. Then he tottered. Mike McGuire saw him falter and ran toward him. Samuel's face, made lurid by the flames, seemed to crumple. He stared sightlessly, eyes glazed. His right eye drooped. His right jowl sagged as though phantom fingers tugged it downward. His lips twisted sidewards. The sacking dropped from fingers suddenly become claws.

He pitched forward as the first drops fell.

CHAPTER ✍ 16

THE FIRST RAINDROPS pelted the back of Mulliner's neck as he pounded toward Weyford at the head of his Refugee band. "Pull up, boys!" He reined in the horse and looked skyward. Wind whipped his hair and set his cape to flapping. The horse shied, and he yanked viciously at the bridle. The horse stood still, its neck arched tensely.

In the months since his encounter with Serena, Mulliner had changed. His features had blurred and thickened. His ruddy good looks had coarsened, his brown eyes were bleary, ringed by puffy flesh. His massive body was running to fat, a bulge at his waistline now clearly perceptible. The swaggering good humour of the "dancing desperado," the jovial deviltry that had marked his escapades, were vanishing. He danced no more at taverns. Through the Barrens fled rumours that his pistols now were used not to frighten but to kill and had more than one corpse to their credit. His curbing of the horse showed a savage temper that had not marked his actions before.

The skies opened. Rain came down in sheets. The men pulled their capes over their heads, sheltering as best they could in a clump of pines. Muttered curses rose from among them, barely audible beneath the drumming of the rain. "Shut up," snapped Mulliner. "Gimp, ride with me. You boys be stayin' here. Keep yer powder dry." He laughed harshly and set off, rain streaming down his neck, guiding the horse up a sparsely wooded slope. Gimp gamely accompanied him, digging one knee into the horse's flanks, his bad leg flapping uselessly. The taciturn, lame old-timer had been Mulliner's man since long before his outlaw days.

For some ten minutes Mulliner and his companion scrambled up Apple Pie Hill. When they reached the clearing at the top, Mulliner scouted its perimeter, shielding his face against the rain, which now fell steadily. "Look!" To the northwest the glow in the sky dimmed, even as they watched, as though some giant hand had snuffed it out. "Damn! It'll smoulder for days, but the worst of it's over. Our hares'll be guardin' their burrows by the time we get near Weyford."

The two scrambled back down the slope. "Boys, I've a change of plan for ye. With the fire doused they'll be goin' back to their homes. Slim pickin's fer us then, I'll warrant."

"Devil take it, we bin rousted from our beds and made to ride hell fer leather—fer nothin'."

"Wild goose chase."

"One more of the Chief's cracked schemes."

"A warm bed and a hot woman behind me and a cold wet ride afore."

"Damn. I've a mind to—"

"Shut up, boys. There's yet a way of makin' the ride worth yer while."

"Dare tell."

"What be it?"

"The Mount Holly stage be leavin' Atsion 'bout now. They be runnin' at night now fer fear of British raids. It'll be crammed with fat geese ready fer pluckin'."

"Wild geese?" Someone laughed disagreeably.

"Tame enough for you, I'll warrant. Ride hard, lads, and we'll be catchin' it when it's left Red Lion."

"We never be robbin' no stage."

"Afraid, are ye? Old crones at a farmstead are easy game—a brace of fat merchants puts the wind up me brave laddies."

"We been't skeert."

"Come on, then—the men among ye. The chicken-hearted—go back to yer beds. But we'll not be sharin' the swag with ye."

Mulliner swung the large chestnut around and rode off without looking back. One by one the men fell in behind him. Urging the horse to a canter, he stood in his stirrups, peering ahead through the mist. Then he swerved onto the trail that would bring him to the main road a mile beyond Red Lion.

❧ ❧ ❧

SERENA TRUDGED over the Quaker bridge, so weary she zigzagged from rail to rail. The quickened waters gurgled beneath the bridge; the rain stung her face and plastered her clothes to her body. The coil of braids upon her head was sodden beneath the soaked cap; had she had a pair of shears about her she would gladly have cut them and flung them into the river. Each seemed made of lead, bowing her neck and straining her aching shoulders.

How much farther? The trail to Atsion had never seemed so long.
The rain pattered on the leaves, beating a tattoo: Hurry! Hurry! Hurry!
If the rain had put the fire out—and that seemed more than likely, given
the intensity of the deluge—she might even now be missed.

Her reason told her none would search for her—in the confusion
reigning at Weyford it might be hours before someone realized she was
gone. But reason was drowned out by that insistent patter: Hurry!
Hurry! Hurry!

Her tired legs tried to obey. She was chilled through, and the cold,
which at first had refreshed her, now brought a desire to sleep that was
well-nigh irresistible. Is there somewhere I can stop, take shelter, close
my eyes for a few minutes—just a few minutes?

The White Stag was far behind her now; she had passed it before the
rain began. The tavern had been alive with lights and voices: Pineys
fleeing the fire, their possessions bundled on their backs. The inn staff—
those who had not been sent to help Weyford fight the fire—moved
among them with food and ale that Nicholas Sooy had ordered given
out. Children wailing, women chattering, their voices roughened, pitched
high with fright and exhaustion, grunts and squeals from a few Piney
hogs who ran free amongst the crowd, the bass rumble of men's voices,
and faintly, faintly, in the distance, the alarm bells—Weyford's now joined
by the nearer bell from the small church at Pleasant Mills.

Someone here might recognize me. Cautiously, she had moved to the
shadows, skirting the clearing, then setting out on the trail to Atsion.
There, with luck, she might board the Mount Holly stage. The stages
were running at night now—good! The darker it is, the less chance that
someone will see through my disguise.

She judged she was halfway when the rains came, turning the low
places to muck that seeped coldly into her shoes as she slipped and
slithered along. The five miles or so she had hoped to cover in a bit more
than an hour stretched endlessly ahead in the mists that rose as icy rain
met sun-scorched earth.

The rain settled down to a steady beat. Water dripped from the branches
that arched across the trail. The mist swirled, wraith-like, shifting and
coiling into vague, threatening shapes, transmogrified by her tired mind
into visions of infinite dread. No habitation, no light, no sign of life
appeared on either side of the trail. She stumbled mechanically along
the ruts, too tired to avoid the puddles by walking on the road's sandy
crown.

How far have I come? How long have I been walking? With no stars to
help her judge the time, her trek seemed a journey through a void where
no sign marked her passage, no progression could be seen but an endless

series of steps with no past, no destination. Step. Step again. Set one's mind to a rhythm of another step, then another, then another. Count the steps? No, that will make the road seem longer, since I've no idea how many must be taken.

Despite her resolution, her steps slowed. She had begun to look for a place—any place—where she might shelter, when spots of light, rainbow-ringed, danced before her in the mist. Fuzzy shapes emerged. A house. Two. Candlelight in their windows. A cluster of dwellings. Then many lights, many windows, voices, the snuffle of horses. Atsion Inn. No sound from the forge here, no signs of fire about the furnace, whose Quaker owner had shut it down lest he be compelled to make munitions.

"Atsion Inn. Est. 1765. Thos. Gaither, Host." Serena passed beneath the sign, moving faster now, her fatigue forgotten. She heard cries and the jingling of harness from the courtyard behind the inn. The stage was in. It must be loading for the trip to Lumberton and thence to Mount Holly. She hurried round the corner of the building, keeping to the shadows.

Yes. There it was—a closed coach, thank the Lord. Not long ago the stage line had used open Jersey wagons that left the passengers at the mercy of the elements. The closed coaches, cramped and springless, were an advance, though it was said that a traveller might have a stone's weight pounded from his frame between Philadelphia and Tuckerton.

"Hostler! What's the fare to Lumberton?"

"Inside or out?"

Serena hesitated. Outside would cost less. But inside she could perhaps curl into a corner for the sleep she craved, cramped, perhaps, but out of the rain. And the driver might be more curious than tired passengers would be. "Inside."

"One and six, lad. There's room for but one." The hostler, a scrawny youth with wisps of hair draggling, straw-like, beneath his woolen cap, turned partly away, looking toward the coach. "The driver's mounted. Hey, there! Wait! One more for Lumberton."

"Hurry it up, then."

Serena groped in the folds of her soggy bundle. Thank the Lord I thought to put some small coin aside. She wanted no eyes on the leather pouch nestled damply between her breasts. "Here." She tried to keep her voice pitched low. The coins disappeared into the grubby hand.

Serena swung herself into the coach. The hostler banged the door shut. Room for one, thought Serena, was wrong by half. She wedged herself into the corner by the door, beside an ample matron whose chins rested on a massive bosom that quivered with her snores. No curiosity

here, thought Serena with relief. She stowed her bundle securely under
her feet.

The other two passengers were plainly merchants, perhaps bound home from Tuckerton, where some privateers' prizes had been auctioned. One was as fat as the other was thin. Serena amused herself by wondering which, if either, was the spouse of the goodwife by her side. The fat one, she guessed. Were it the thin one they'd be sitting side by side.

The coach jerked as it started forward. As it passed near the inn, light splashed momentarily over Serena's mud-spattered clothes and smudged face. The thin man, nattily clad, with a dapper frill about his bosom, looked her over with some distaste. "Fleeing the fire, lad?"

Serena affected not to hear. Indeed, the creaking of the coach, the rumble of wheels, and the pounding of hoofs as the driver whipped his nags to speed would have made it difficult to reply. The coach jounced, flinging her first against the soft cushion afforded by her seatmate and then against the hard door. Serena braced her feet against her bundle, wedged herself as best she could into the corner, and let the comforting darkness engulf her.

ᴥ ᴥ ᴥ

MULLINER CALLED a halt. They had made good time on the serpentine trail, for the rain had compacted the sand. It was hardly likely the lumbering stage could have beaten them. They were just to the west of Red Lion. The stage, thought Mulliner, might take on extra passengers or freight at the inn there. Better to waylay it between the inn and Lumberton, before the woods thinned out and farmlands afforded poor cover.

"Let's be scoutin' the trail fer a bit."

The men were grumbling amongst themselves again, tired and surly after their hard, pounding ride. Mulliner ignored them. At least the rain had stopped.

They rounded a thickly wooded curve. Here the trees were taller, the understory was more luxuriant. The thick, grooved trunks of oaks predominated, interspersed with the glimmer of laurel pale in the misty night. Spurring his horse ahead, Mulliner saw the land open out; stands of third-growth saplings, sassafras by their citron scent, scattered on higher spots of the water-logged open ground. Beyond lay what appeared to be cropland.

He rode back to the waiting men. "Here be the spot—after they round the curve. The driver will be slackin' off a bit, I'll warrant, expectin' open land ahead. We'll block the road. Gimp! The lanterns!"

Relieved to be provided with a definite objective, the men dismounted. Mulliner set them to piling fallen logs and brushwood across the roadstead. When the barrier was completed, he checked the lanterns and settled down to wait.

⋙　⋙　⋙

THE STOP AT RED LION had been a short one; the stage paused only long enough for the driver to water the horses and pick up a parcel or two. Serena longed to stretch her cramped limbs, but the driver called down to them not to dismount. Her companions barely stirred, then lapsed back into noisy slumber.

Serena rubbed her bruises. Her elbows, her shoulders, her forehead where it had knocked against the wall as the stage jounced violently through a puddle—every part of her felt black and blue. So tired was she that her sleep had bordered on unconsciousness. Limp and uncaring, she had let herself be flung about. Now she tried to will herself back to sleep. The miles will seem shorter if I do not tally their passage.

She could see nothing by peering through the window except mounded shadows of laurel and bear oak and once in a while, where the forest thinned, the silhouettes of individual trees against a sky tinged faintly grey. They were at full speed now, lurching and swaying.

"Whoa!" The horses stopped short. The stage swayed wildly, nearly overturning, the passengers, loose-limbed with sleep, flopping about like rag dolls. Serena pitched forward, nearly into the fat merchant's lap. Then the stage stopped, canted sideways, one wheel in the ditch.

She had barely regained her seat, her fingers working frantically to rebundle her loosened braids, when the door slammed open. "Out! All out! Onto the roadside. No laggin', now!" A hard hand grasped her wrist and began to pull her out. "On yer feet, lad."

Serena stumbled out onto the road, still fumbling with her hair.

A ring of horsemen surrounded the stage, some of them holding lanterns. Her stout seatmates were being firmly decanted, sleepy, stunned, protesting. "This is an outrage," stormed the thin merchant. "You've no right—" They were shoved to the far side of the stage. More men dismounted. One had pulled the driver from his seat and was holding a pistol to his head.

The tallest of the horsemen now dismounted. Shoving the others aside, he came toward her, swinging his lantern high. Too late she saw the shadows of her breasts, revealed by the clinging of her rain-damp shirt.

"What have we here? A wee ewe in ram's pelt?"

Serena gasped. Mulliner!

"Well," he said softly. "the fair daughter of Weyford herself. And what be ye doin' on the road so far from home?"

He leaned closer. She backed away, bumping into the side of the coach. He reached out for her. She swung her head frantically from side to side, looking for some opening, some route of escape.

One of the men had found her bundle. He shook it out. Her clothes, her comb, her few belongings lay scattered on the muddy roadstead. Someone lunged after the few coins that rolled out. Another seized the gilt-framed miniature. One man picked up the comb and began running it through his hair, simpering for the benefit of his fellows. Her precious books lay open, their rain-dampened pages stirring in the wind, then tearing loose as thick boots trampled over them. "Oh—my books! At least leave me my books."

"Ye'll not be readin' 'em just now." Mulliner laughed. "That razor-tongued pirate won't be cheatin' me this time. I'll warrant he had a fine piece himself after he sent me packing." For an instant, his mirth distracted him. Serena darted past him as again he lurched toward her.

She ran. Her terror lent her momentum. She plowed through the knot of men, scrambled over the barrier, and raced down the road.

She heard the sound of hoofs. Oh dear Lord, she thought, I've no chance against the horse. Already she was tiring, her headlong pace perceptibly flagging.

The woods. He can't ride his horse among the trees. She veered off the road. The going was harder here. Branches whipped her face, snatched away her cap, tangled in her hair. Roots sprang up to trip her. Tree trunks leapt into her path. She dodged and swerved, clearing a fallen branch at the last moment before it sent her headlong.

Stop, she told herself. Listen. The hoofbeats had ceased. Was he pursuing her afoot? Hand pressed to her breast, she bade her heart slow down. Her breath tore at her throat, burning its way to her lungs. Her chest heaved convulsively as her heart pounded with effort and terror. Her breath was loud in her ears. Quiet! she told herself.

Yes! He was following—on foot. His steps crashed through the underbrush. She must set out again. But wait, she thought. Which way should I go? Can I follow the course of the trail while staying in the cover of the woods? How far were we from Lumberton? Are there cottages farther along the trail? Woodsmen or farmers who might lend me aid?

She started running, as quietly as she could, trying to keep just to the right of where the road might be. The footsteps were gaining. She speeded up again. The ground beneath her feet was uneven, humpy and hummocked. There—an opening between two trees. Run through it. Now, dodge that clump of bushes. A stump. Run around it. Another pause. Were the footsteps fainter? Was Mulliner's far greater bulk a hindrance in the close forest spaces?

She dared a look over her shoulder. The mist obscured her view, though the light seemed greyer now. She stumbled and crashed into a tree trunk, grazing her forehead on the rough bark. Whimpering with the pain of it, brushing aside a trickle of blood that snaked toward her eye, she blundered on, half-blinded. A vine twisted round her ankles, clutching and tearing. She wrenched herself free, scarcely feeling the pain as the thorns tore at her flesh.

Up ahead—the sky is lighter! She paused, gasping for breath, and tried to listen again. There was no sound. She crept forward, quietly, quietly. It seemed her tortured breathing must echo for miles. Still no sound behind her. Has he abandoned the pursuit? Perhaps he has gone back to direct the disposal of the coach and its passengers.

The woods ended abruptly. Open field lay ahead of her, scattered puddles gleaming faintly in the predawn light. The rich, mucky topsoil glistened wetly: She was no longer in the Barrens. Staying in the shelter of the trees, she reconnoitred. All seemed peaceful and still. And there, at the top of a slight rise was a faint orange glow that must be candle-light. Someone was abroad in this chill, dank dawn.

She took a deep breath and set out across the field. A half mile, perhaps less, to succour. Cross this field, skirt those clumps of trees, and—

Hoofbeats! He had guessed her intent and outflanked her. Now he was between her and the woods.

She began to run, her feet squelching in the mud that sucked and clung and tried to hold her fast. One shoe was gone. She limped, not daring to stop to remove the other. The horse was gaining, gaining, although a glance behind her showed her it, too, was floundering in the mud.

If she could gain that clump of trees, he would have to dismount to follow.

Spurring herself to one last effort, she staggered forward. When she saw her mistake, she was too close to change her course. The third-growth saplings clustered so tightly together none but the smallest child could squeeze between them. They would prevent Mulliner's passage—but hers was barred as well.

She heard the horse stop, Mulliner dismount.

She swerved to the right, zigzagging along the fringes of the copse.

Now he was behind her. Right behind her. She heard his panting
breath even above the rasp of her own. A hand seized her braids. She
was jerked to a halt. "Not this time, me fine lady. Not this time."

He seized her arm and whirled her about, his bulk shutting out air
and light. He pressed her against the spindly tree trunks, an arm on
either side of her. She tried to duck beneath them. He grabbed her hair
again and yanked her upright, pulling so hard her brows arched. She
winced with the pain of it and tried to bring up her knee.

He slapped her. Her teeth clattered together. She felt her lip swell, a
trickle of blood run down her chin.

"Not this time," he said again. He chanted the phrase as they struggled.
Then the incantation changed. "This time . . . this time . . . this time
ye'll spread yer legs fer me . . ."

He forced her to the ground. She felt pebbles and twigs tearing at her
back as his hands pressed her shoulders into the earth.

"No. Please, no."

He paid no attention. She struck at him with her fists. He caught her
hands and wrenched her arms brutally over her head, pinioning them
with one hand while the other tore at her clothes.

She felt the bosom of her shirt ripped wide. Twisting and struggling,
she tried to shield herself.

"What have we here?" The clumsy fingers searched between her
breasts. The back of her neck burned as he ripped off the thong that
held the deerskin pouch. "Gold, I'll warrant," he breathed, one hand
fingering the damp leather while the other held her fast. "I'll warrant I
know where ye got that—Brandon pays his doxies well."

He tossed it aside. "This night's work stands to pay *me* well." Then his
hands were on her breasts, mauling them. She felt his heated breath
upon her flesh as his mouth sought her nipples.

He let go of her momentarily as his hands fumbled at her breeches.
She rained futile blows on his back. He paid them no heed. The buttons
at her waist tore loose. She felt him tug and pull the breeches down
about her thighs. She twisted and fought. Cloth ripped. Her legs were
freed for an instant, but before she could kick he rained a series of savage
blows upon her thighs.

Her muscles would not obey her. Her thighs relaxed. Pain brought
tears to her eyes. He knelt, forcing his knees between her legs as he tore
at his own garments. She tried to roll aside, instinctively clenching her
knees together.

He tore them apart. His fingers dug into the tender flesh between her legs as he forced them apart, forced them up and back.

Then he thrust his maleness into her, thrusting, thrusting, against her resistant flesh.

The pain was a hugeness that filled her, burning, tearing, ripping her asunder. She screamed. He cuffed her again.

She saw his face above her in the brightening light, gleeful, triumphant. "This time," he gasped. "This time. This time."

In rhythm with his chant he thrust himself farther inside her. "This time. This time." Deeper. Deeper. Thrusting, twisting, widening the river of pain that coursed through her, engulfing her, choking her, dimming the light, roaring, roaring in her ears.

His hands were on her breasts again, brutally squeezing and twisting.

The roaring in her ears was louder. "This time," he gasped. His back arched, his whole body convulsed as he gathered himself for the final impalement. "This time." With a thrust so violent it seemed he must pierce to her heart, to her throat, to rend her in two, he reached his climax.

From far away she heard his hoarse cry as the river crested and drowned her.

❧　❧　❧

IT WAS FULL LIGHT, the grey, glaring light of a sky swathed in cloud. There was a buzzing in her ears, about her head. Gnats whined at her forehead, at her mouth, drawn by the blood that had caked there.

The light hurt her eyes. The whining of the gnats, the bites of mosquitoes were a torment. Feebly she tried to brush the insects away. Her hand fell back to the earth.

She lay there for some endless time longer—a minute? an hour? Every part of her ached and stung, her arms, her shoulders, her back—the individual sensations merging into one enormous pain that centred in her belly, grinding, twisting, cramping. Cramping!

Forcing herself to full consciousness, she tried to focus on her belly. The child. Has he hurt the child? Searing pain shot through her as she tried to move her legs. Her thighs felt sticky. Gingerly, she touched her inner thigh, then brought her finger into her line of vision. Blood.

She struggled to sit up. She could not. She rolled over onto her stomach, wincing as the movement tore open the scratches on her shoulders. She pushed herself to her hands and knees, her loosened hair hanging about her face, tangled and clumped with mud. Sweat poured from her forehead with the effort.

She hunched herself forward until her groping hands could grasp the trunk of a sapling. Hand over hand, her arms shaking with the effort, she pulled herself up, to her knees, to her feet. She stood, doubled over, black spots dancing before her eyes, advancing, receding, advancing again. The slim tree quivered with the tremours that shook her. Now the blood was sliding down her legs in slow, viscid waves that surged in rhythm with her pain.

I must . . . I must find help. Last night . . . the field, the hill, a house. I know there was a house. I saw a light. Now, which direction . . .

Gritting her teeth against the pain that seemed about to saw her in two, grasping the saplings for support, she made her way around the copse. How long was it? How many steps? How many pauses to rest, panting, sweating, conscious of the constant flow of blood? A little farther, just a little farther. She straightened, shielding her eyes against the light that jumped and dazzled.

There. The house was nearer than I imagined. How far did I run last night? She shuddered. Again the pain tore at her belly.

She set out across the field, up the slight slope toward the distant house, tottering and swaying, gasping for breath, tears and sweat tracing rivulets in the smudges on her bruised, swollen face. She was nearly naked, what little remained of her shirt flapping against her knees. Her bare feet sank into the soggy earth with each step.

"I must . . . I must . . .," she murmured. "I must find someone to help me . . . the child . . . I must." She concentrated on keeping herself moving, on walking, not falling, on getting to where she must go.

Now the house was before her, three stories of weathered wood, narrow-shouldered and prim, on its treeless plot atop the little hill. Tall, narrow windows, tall, narrow door, high front stoop, so high . . . I can't . . . I can't climb those stairs. "Help me," she called faintly. "Please, help me!"

No one answered. Nothing stirred.

She fell to her knees and began crawling up the worn, splintered steps, sobbing now with exhaustion and fear. Suppose there is no one home? "Help me, please," she called again. She sprawled for a moment across the warped boards of the stoop, panting. Then she crawled to the door-frame and pulled herself to her feet.

"Please, God," she sobbed. She knocked feebly on the cracked, weathered panels of the door. Were there sounds of someone stirring inside? She heard a roaring in her ears. A dark veil danced before her as she raised her hand to knock again. The door opened.

Serena fell across the threshold. A short, round figure moved to catch her followed by a second, tall and spare. "Please help me," she whispered. "Joe Mulliner—rape—baby—I can't—"

Someone lowered her gently to the floor. The last thing she saw as the dark veil enveloped her was two worried faces hovering over her. Both were black.

BOOK II

Doctor Will

CHAPTER ❧ 17

S OMEONE WAS MOANING . . . moaning and retching . . . retching and shuddering . . . struggling against . . . "No! No! Take your hands off me!"

"Quiet, child. Quiet. You do be hurtin' yourself."

"Gently, now. We will carry her into the parlour. We cannot risk the stairs."

Serena felt herself being lifted, carried—felt again the sting of cuts and scratches and, so constant now it seemed wholly a part of her, that grinding pain in her belly. "No!" she said once more, but feebly, hopelessly. The river of pain was sweeping her away again. She saw, but dimly, as though through water. She felt, but vaguely, sensations coming from some distance beyond her ken.

"Why, she be all over bruises. Look here. And here."

"Fetch warm water. And soak some sphagnum moss. We shall need it to stem the blood once I've cleansed her wounds."

Hands were stripping off the last shreds of her garments. She felt the sting as blood and dirt were laved gently from her body. The hands touched her thighs. Instinctively she clamped her legs together. "No!"

She felt a calm, cool touch on her forehead. "Look at me," a soft male voice said. She opened her eyes. The black face leaning over her was haloed with white hair. Dark eyes shone with concern. The face was elongated: prominent forehead, bushy white brows, a strong jaw beneath a neatly trimmed white beard. The nose was long and aquiline, almost Indian in its conformation. Although little lined, the face was not young. She had a sense of agelessness, of wisdom, of what she discerned instinctively as goodness.

"Who are you?" she asked, dismayed at how faint her voice sounded, how far away.

"Will Pond. Doctor Will, some call me. This is Charity, my sister."
Another face, black and shiny, plump as Doctor Will's was lean, bobbed
up at his shoulder. "Try to lie still now."

"A physician? Then you can—"

"Some call me doctor, as I said. And yes, I think I can save your child."

"The blood—"

"You have been assaulted. Viciously. Most of the blood is from your
wounds."

"Then, the baby . . .?" Her voice, her strength, were fading. "Please, . . ."
The river of pain was rising again, blurring her eyes, surging through her
ears, shutting out sound, shutting out thought.

"Drink this," said Doctor Will. She gasped and choked, fighting the
bitter potion that burned her throat and trickled down her chin. "Drink
it all. That's a good child."

"But wait. I must tell you how . . . who . . ."

"Later. Rest now. Rest quietly."

Serena lay back, panting. Now the river was supporting her and she
was borne atop its waters, the pain still present but somewhere far below,
beneath the current on which she drifted, with her but not of her, no
longer her concern. She stopped struggling, letting herself glide, glide
along the swirling waters, giving herself up to the flow . . . the darkness
. . . the peace . . .

❧　❧　❧

SHE AWOKE to a sense of return from a far journey, past sights and sounds
forever beyond recall. The pain was gone. She felt drained, blenched, as
though blood no longer coursed beneath her skin to give it colour and
life. She raised her hand to look at it. It was pale, almost transparent, the
fine blue veins clearly visible beneath the skin. Her body felt light yet
weighted, as though weariness pressed it down into the bed on which
she lay. The bed?

She raised her head and looked about her. She was lying in a small,
plain room, sparsely furnished: the bed, a simple chest, a chair. The tall,
narrow window was curtained against the light of what appeared to be a
brilliant day; the curtains were plain muslin. The rag rug on the floor,
the chipped ewer on the stand by the bed, bespoke hard wear. Yet everything was scrubbed and clean; the bed linen, soft with use, was snowy
white. The fireplace with its plain mantel stood cold and empty, swept
clean. Embossed on the fireback was the scrolled "W" of Weyford. Serena's
lips quivered. She lay back against the pillows, perspiring coldly, spent.

The door swung open. A little calico cat with a crooked black nose ran

in and sprang onto the bed. A short, plump black woman came hurrying
in after her. The woman was simply, even shabbily dressed: a skirt of
dark grey worsted, plain bodice, white apron. Her hair was tucked neatly
under a cap, and her brown eyes glowed with good humour. There was
a look of tidy compactness about her; her plumpness became her, seemed
natural to her aura of calm amplitude. The smooth, taut skin of her
face, of the rounded arms beneath her rolled-up sleeves, gleamed like
polished wood. "Git, cat!" she said, softly but firmly. "This lady be sick."

"Oh, let her stay!" Serena sat up shakily and stretched out a hand to
touch the little cat's head. Sure of welcome, the cat settled near the foot
of the cot and began to wash herself. "You are . . . Charity, was it? It's
hard to remember."

"Well!" Charity's brown eyes shone. "You be awake. Yes, I'm Charity
Pond—Doctor Will's little sister. Little!" She looked down at herself,
laughing softly. "How you be feelin'?"

"I'm not sure how I feel," said Serena, lying back dizzily against the
pillows. "Or where I am, or how I came to be here, or—" Memories
came rushing back. "The baby. Did the doctor—"

"Hush, now. Don't be frettin' yourself. That baby be born in its own
good time—wasn't no tellin' it different. When you be thinkin' it be
born? November? December?"

"Why, I suppose . . . November. I hadn't really thought."

"Well, November be comin' soon enough. Now, Doctor Will, he want
to talk to you. You be feelin' well enough?"

"Yes. Yes—I want to see him, to thank him—and you."

"Be no need to thank me for doin' my Christian duty. Here, let me
help you sit up." Charity fussed over Serena, piling some pillows behind
her back, tucking the coverlet about her. When she had bustled out,
Serena pulled the little cat toward her. "Do you have a name, puss?
Mietze Katze, that's what Mother always called cats. I'll call you Mitzi.
Does that suit you?" The cat began to purr.

"I see you have been befriended." Doctor Will had come into the room,
moving so quietly, for all his height, that she had not heard him enter.

Now Serena remembered that soft, deep voice, giving firm orders to
her, to Charity. "By Mitzi, you mean?" she said. "Yes, it seems so. But
what you have done for me—how can I thank you? You must have saved
my child, my life. I—"

"But that is my calling. And what I have most wanted to do in this
world. And it pleases me to see you recovering. Now, here—here is something I think will cheer you." Doctor Will extended a cloth-wrapped
package that Serena had not noticed.

"It's—*my books!* My books! Oh, how did you find them? How did you know?" Gently, Serena opened first one book and then the other. All had suffered damage. Pages of the Shakespeare stuck together. The calfskin cover of John Donne's works was water-spotted; the pages were curled and smelt slightly of damp; some were loose. The ink of Mistress Mansey's inscription had run. But does that matter, thought Serena, beside the joy of having the books in my hand again when I thought they were gone along with everything else? Then she paled, as full awareness of her position swept over her. Everything, she thought. My clothes, my picture of Mother. And the gold—the gold that meant my future.

Doctor Will was watching her closely. He marked the way she touched the books, her fingers gently caressing the pages, trying to smooth out the creases. Books are precious to her, he thought, as they are to me. For a moment his thoughts harked back to the effort it had cost him to accumulate his small library of medical texts, painfully purchased one by one in Philadelphia, painfully studied through many a weary night as he struggled with the unaccustomed terms, the formal language never heard in the shabby cottages where he had received his brief schooling. His attention returned to the girl before him. Something had upset her. "Best lie down," he said. "You are not yet strong."

"No," said Serena. "We must talk. Do you know who I am, how I came to be here? That I am penniless, lost, that I cannot repay you for what you have done for me? Indeed"—she stroked the soft folds of the faded nightdress she was wearing—"that I am indebted to you even for this gown to cover my nakedness?"

"Let us not talk of debts. No, child, I do not know who you are, nor how you came to be at my doorstep. Do you want to tell me?"

Serena thought for a moment. Anxiously, she scanned the concerned face, the kindly eyes. The urge to confide, to pour out her grief to this gentle man, was strong. She opened her mouth to speak, then shut it firmly. To speak of Stuart Brandon or Joe Mulliner, to recall her all too recent pain and terror would be to bring it to life again in the confines of this tranquil haven where she was finding the beginnings of peace. "No," she said. "That is, not how I came to be here. Perhaps later . . . but no, not now. My name is Serena Wainwright. And you—you are the man they call the Black Doctor of the Pines?"

Doctor Will gave no sign that he recognized her name. "Will Pond is my name, as I told you. And some say 'Doctor Will.' But I am not a physician. Men of my colour do not become physicians." He spoke quietly, without bitterness, yet his face contracted for an instant with a spasm, not of present pain, but of pain remembered.

"But even at Weyford you were called on for healing."

"Yes, the Lord has helped me do that. I will tell you more about it later, if you wish. But as for you, child—in a day or two you will be recovered from your wounds. Then you can go home."

Serena's eyes stung. Her lips began to tremble. She looked away from Doctor Will, her fingers absently stroking the cover of the book she still held. "No, I have no home to go to."

Doctor Will sat down on the chair by the bed. Silently he regarded the girl before him as she bit her lip and struggled against her tears. A beauty, he thought. Even now, her face pale and drawn, her eyes shadowed with fatigue and grief, her tawny hair twisted into a thick plait down her back, and her figure concealed by the voluminous nightdress—still, she was a beauty. And he knew who she was now, of course. The Wainwrights of Weyford were known far beyond the confines of the Barrens. And from time to time the ironworkers had come to him, with cuts, with burns, with fevers of the lung provoked by the fierce conditions of their trade.

Why can she not go home? The child she is carrying? And how did this sheltered girl come to be with child—to be wandering, barefoot and bleeding, through the fields? She had, he assumed, been a passenger in the coach that had been waylaid. That he had found her books, flung about by the roadstead, and then had brought them here had been mere happenstance—a guess, an intuition, that the "Serena Wainwright" of the inscriptions was the injured young woman in his home. She had been wearing the remains of lad's clothing. But why the disguise? From whom had she been running—even before the attack? Perhaps, he thought, she will tell me in time. For the moment she needs rest, rest and security.

"Let this be your home," he said. "Rest here. Recover your forces. You must rest, you know, and remain quiet in body and mind until your child is born. You could yet lose it."

Serena looked up. She glanced around the room, its shabby furnishings telling their own tale. "But I have nothing . . . nothing. Do you understand? I cannot pay for my keep. And, if you say I must rest, not work. . . . How can I repay you for what you have already done, let alone fling myself upon your charity?"

Doctor Will stood up. "My Charity will be only too glad to help take care of you," he said, smiling at his little joke. "And later, when you are stronger, perhaps you can help in preparing the herbs. Now, repay me by caring for yourself as I prescribe. Begin by eating—I see Charity coming with some soup." He left the room.

Serena sat up and took the mug that Charity proffered, cupping her hands around its comforting warmth. As she sipped at the steaming broth, Mitzi picked her way on finical feet across the bedclothes, sniffing and demanding her share.

C H A P T E R 🙠 1 8

F LAMES LICKED at the base of the cauldron, sending acrid smoke
into the stifling air. Serena let go the wooden paddle and stepped
back from the fire, lifting the damp coil of hair from her neck in hope of
attracting some vagrant breeze. The August air, fecund and moist,
refused to stir. Sticky sweat clung to Serena's body, running down her
face, between her breasts, along her sides. The sun, a pale yellow disk
swathed in heat haze, beat down upon the unprotected yard where the
trampled earth, scorched and grassless, lay flattened with exhaustion.

It was high noon. Not even the walls of the house offered shade. The
bubbling concoction of willow twigs, Doctor Will's sovereign remedy for
headache, sent up clouds of steam undispersed by the slightest breath
of air.

From the rear of the house came the sound of hammer and saw as
work progressed on the ell that would, when completed, provide living
quarters for Serena and her child behind a greatly enlarged kitchen for
the brewing of remedies. Doctor Will's practice was burgeoning, and the
deluge of patients coming from miles around had overflowed the pleasant
parlour and spilled into his private quarters.

Soon after Serena's arrival, Doctor Will had effected a cure that spread
his fame far and wide and vastly improved his fortunes. The daughter of
a Lumberton merchant had been brought to him, suffering from scrofula.
"The child is a pitiful sight," Doctor Will told Charity and Serena at supper that night. "A pitiful sight: There are ulcers all over her body. She
cannot lift her arms and can scarcely stand for the weakness. The physicians have tried blistering; now they counsel bleeding her. And bleeding
is highly thought of, that I know. But for all that Dr. Rush of Philadelphia
so highly recommends it, I cannot but feel there is something wrong in
draining the body of a sick person. I have brought her some salves and

teas. Tomorrow I go back to bring her nearer here, so that I may watch
her carefully."

After two weeks in the Black Doctor's care, the child had been well enough to comb her hair; soon she was up and about. The grateful father had spread word far and wide. Doctor Will's custom had been for the most part confined to the back trails and the cottages of Pineys and labourers. Now his homemade wagon was seen rumbling along the streets of Lumberton and Mount Holly, the old mule standing hitched before the fine homes of merchants and shippers.

As the War had moved southward and Jerseymen began rebuilding ruined farmhouses and reordering their lives into their accustomed rhythms, Doctor Will had roamed farther abroad, safe from British molestation. And now that clients were eager to pay him with more than just prayers of thanksgiving, he was able to begin the additions to his house of which he had long dreamed. With Doctor Will away on calls, Serena and Charity had been kept busy concocting the brews and funnelling them into the green glass flasks that Doctor Will ordered especially for his remedies.

Now the back door banged as Charity bustled into the yard. "Serena, child, put down that paddle! You be hurtin' yourself! Remember what Will told you about restin'."

Serena wiped her perspiring face on her sleeve. "It was boiling over."

"And so? Likely the ground could use some waterin'. Go—set you down. I'll stir this." Charity's voice was sharp with anxiety, but her eyes were kind. She peered at Serena's flushed face. "You be goin' inside, Serena—go on with you! There be some cool water in the kitchen. Take it and set in the parlour—don't you be climbin' up to that hot garret." Charity cast a practiced eye on the progress of the new construction. "They be months yet. Listen, child—take my room like I be tellin' you to. That heat's not good for you, nor yet the baby."

Serena smiled. "Thank you, Charity, but no, I would not dispossess you. I'm grateful enough for a place to lay my head—and the child's when it comes. And, you see, I like my little garret. It's high up. From the window at the far end I can look out and, sometimes, I can see all the way to—" She stopped. The Barrens—I almost said it. I can see the Barrens, the dark mass of pines, the tips of a few cedars, the monotonous miles. Home. But to say this was to admit to her longing, to suggest she was not happy here with Charity and Doctor Will, whose kindness had come between her and utter destitution. "Thank you," she said again, quietly, firmly, "but no."

She made her way into the house, moving heavily. Her feet and ankles were swollen, her belly seemed enormous, for all it was three months before the child would be born. She looked down at the bulge at her waist, straining the makeshift apron, the plain linen gown borrowed from plump Charity. Did I ever walk instead of waddling? Or run swiftly and easily without a care where I placed my feet? Wearily she sank down onto a bench near the kitchen door. The pitcher of water on a stand across the room seemed too remote to be reached.

As she sat in a daze of heat and discomfort, she became aware that, underlying the sounds of hammering, was a bustle and stir from the roadstead beyond the hill. Awkwardly, she mounted the garret stairs, seeking higher vantage. What is happening?

The heat in the garret took her breath away; the pungent odour of herbs hanging from the rafters smote her queasy stomach. She made her way to the dormer window that looked toward the road and knelt clumsily beside it.

Here, farther from the din of carpentry, the sounds were clearer. The jingle of harness, the creaking of wheels. Shouts . . . laughter . . . voices gaily calling. Clouds of dust rose from the roadstead, swirling about a lively caravan: Jersey wagons . . . a carriage or two . . . plodding farm horses weighed down with two riders — even, in one case, with three. Young people sat in the wagons, wedged together with baskets and bundles, barrels and jugs. Ear upon ear of freshly picked corn . . . peaches . . . the first apples of the season . . . cider aged and fresh.

Beneath an improvised canopy a fiddler sawed away, oblivious of the scrapes and squeals evoked by his rough passage. Children ran beside the wagons; dogs frisked and barked. One wagon held a bevy of young girls, white caps on their heads, crisp aprons about their waists, shrieking and giggling as they jolted to and fro, their hands busy with the weaving of a chain of black-eyed Susans. Some rosy-cheeked lads rode alongside, grinning, chaffing the girls and one another. A sturdy goodwife on the seat beside the driver cast a benevolent glance over her shoulder and then fixed her attention straight ahead.

The wagons were headed southeast. The sea! thought Serena. They are going to the sea! A similar procession had passed by in June, on its way to celebrating Big Sea Day. Then, still weak, still dazed, still lying most of the day on the sofa in the parlour, spent by her ordeal, Serena had scarcely noticed. Now she looked longingly after the wagons.

The sea. Oh! she thought, I know how it will be for them — that moment when they breast the last of the dunes and the strand lies before them, the waves sparkling in the sunlight, the pale foam running out smoothly at their feet. There . . . there by the sea would be a salt-laden breeze to lighten the sticky air, setting the dune grasses to rippling and fluttering the ribbons on the girls' summer frocks.

She could all but smell the salt, feel the crunch of broken shell beneath her feet, sense that delicious moment when the first flattening wave slid across her ankles and cool, wet sand oozed between her toes. The sandpipers would be running their eternal race with the waves, forward to snatch a choice tidbit, back, back, as the waves pursued them, then forward again as the water receded and foaming bubbles revealed where miniscule creatures hid beneath the sands. The gulls would be wheeling and screaming, laughers and herring gulls and terns, white and grey and black and immature brown. Sand crabs would be scuttling like pale ghosts above the waterline, poised almost invisibly on the tips of their delicate claws, stalked eyes alert for danger before they popped into their burrows.

And it would be cool . . . cool as only the seaside could be on an August afternoon like this one.

Cool . . . She lifted the heavy hair from her neck again and looked down at her swollen body. The mound of her belly was splotched and stained with the contents of the cauldron. Her faded dress was streaked with damp wherever it touched her. She felt clammy and unclean, careworn and old.

What have I done to myself? she thought, despite her resolution not to indulge in regrets. Last year at this time I too was by the sea, wading in the shallows, heedless and free. If only I had never gone to the White Stag, never met Stuart Brandon, never. . . . Tears mingled with the sweat on her face, splattering the swept boards of the rough pine garret floor.

❧   ❧   ❧

AT LONG LAST she became once more aware of her surroundings. Are those voices? Has a patient come to call? Is Charity still in the backyard — will she hear? Hastily tidying her garments, splashing her face with water, Serena made her way downstairs. Muffled voices were coming from the parlour, where Doctor Will was wont to hold impromptu consultations. A deep male rumble. A feminine treble. Had he come home then? Serena started back toward the kitchen, but something in that feminine voice made her pause. Her heart began to thump painfully. Despite herself, she listened.

"It is my father I wish you to see. But before we go, I . . . that is . . ."

"You wish to consult me yourself, madam?"

"Yes. No. I . . . it is about my husband."

"He is ill?"

"Not exactly. He . . . he has been severely injured, burned, you see, about . . . about the lower limbs."

"And you wish for something to alleviate his pain, then? I can suggest —"

"No. His burns have healed. That is, he is terribly scarred, and scarred about the face, also. But his scars give him no pain now, though they impede his movement."

"Then what do you require from me, Mistress Sawyer?"

"He cannot . . . he is unable . . . unable to . . ." There was silence.

Doctor Will spoke gently. "He is unable to perform his duties as a husband?"

"Yes." The voice was barely audible. "We have been married for over a month now, and he . . . he never . . ."

Doctor Will coughed. "Has he tried?"

Silence.

"He has not? Does not?"

"He, well, he becomes very angry. And once or twice he has asked . . . has asked me to do . . . things I could not do, could not dream of doing. But I thought . . ."

"Yes?"

"They say you brew potions. And I wanted to try, well, to try to . . ."

"To arouse his manhood?"

"Yes. For me. *Me*. Not . . . well . . . not someone by whom he was once obsessed."

"I see. I assume this is important to you because you want a child?"

"Not exactly. I mean, yes. It is most important that I conceive. And soon—before my father . . ."

"I understand. If your father is as ill as you say, you want him to take comfort in the knowledge that a grandchild is coming? Perhaps to inherit?"

"Yes."

"Well, my dear, I shall consult with your husband if you like, when I come to see your father."

"But that was not what I wanted. I mean . . ."

"You wanted some potion you could give him without his knowledge?" Doctor Will's tone was stern.

"Well, . . ."

"My dear lady, I am not a necromancer. I do not deal in magic or in potions. If there is some herbal I can give your husband that will strengthen his constitution, I will do what I can, and gladly. But what you ask smacks of charlatanry—even of witchcraft. I will have no part of such doings."

A soft cough. "I'll pay you well. I'll—"

"You do not understand. The Lord helps me heal. He has revealed many remedies to me. But it is not the Lord's work you are asking me to do—it is Satan's. And I will not do it. If that is all you seek here, you had best be on your way."

"No! Please. My father needs your help. He is weakening steadily, and his mind, well, at times he does not know us. He calls only for . . . he is not himself. Please, Doctor, please come and do what you can for him. And please, forget what I have asked you. I was mistaken."

"Of course I will come. But first I must arrange for my absence and gather some remedies that may be of use. Please, madam, seat yourself. I will send my sister in with a cool drink for you. And I'll not be long."

Doctor Will came into the narrow hallway, stopping short when he saw Serena. She stood with her back against the wall, hands braced at her sides. Her face was grey, her breathing shallow. Her forehead was beaded with sweat. "Serena, child," he said, "come, sit down. There is someone here whom I think you should—"

"Doctor!" came the voice from the parlor. "One moment. There's something else I must ask you." The voice came closer. Its owner stepped into the hall.

Doctor Will stepped in front of Serena, shielding her from the woman's sight.

Serena shook her head. Gently she motioned him aside. "Good afternoon, Prudence," she said.

CHAPTER ❧ 19

THE ROUGH WAGON Doctor Will had built for himself jounced and swayed on the sandy road. A cloud of dust hovered behind the wheels and smaller dust clouds kicked up by the mule's hoofs tickled the nostrils and parched the throat.

Doctor Will cast a worried glance at Serena, braced stolidly beside him, one hand gripping the edge of the wooden seat, the other arm curved to support the weight of the child in her womb. He had urged her to lie down in the back of the wagon, where fabric stretched over some salvaged barrel hoops cast a semi-shade. "Thank you, but no," she had said. "The motion will disturb me less if I can see where we are going."

"We will be driving all night," he had told her. "There is no time to lose. And it will be cooler by night." And again he had urged her to ride with her sister in the far more comfortable carriage. She had refused.

What lies between those two? he wondered. There was something there, some antipathy coursing years wide, blood deep, strong as only an enmity of the blood can be. Had Serena's beauty drawn her sister's envy? He had marked the resemblance between them, the resemblance that left Prudence wanting at every turn. Was it that? Was it the father's favour, the favour that now, in his extremity, the old man could not hide: calling for the daughter whom, Doctor Will guessed, he had banished?

❧ ❧ ❧

"SERENA!" PRUDENCE had said in answer to her sister's greeting. "You— here!" Even in the dimness of the hall he had seen her paling with shock— shock and fury. "Are we never to be quit of you?" And her eyes swept Serena's thickened figure.

He could see the effort with which Serena pushed herself free of the

supporting wall, stiffening her knees lest they buckle beneath her. He
had thought, on hearing "Mistress Sawyer's" errand and the name of
Samuel Wainwright, to go to Serena and warn her, prepare her gently
for the presence of her sister and the news of her father's illness. The
opportunity had eluded him. The sisters faced each other, the one so vivid
in her beauty even now, with her body misshapen and her clothes near
rags; the other an attenuated reflection; both oblivious to his presence.

"Father—" began Serena. Her voice faltered. She swallowed. "Father,"
she said again, "he's ill? He's . . . dying?"

Prudence gave no answer. She continued to stare at Serena, her hand
across her mouth.

Serena caught the glint of the ring on her sister's finger. Who? she
thought. And then: But of course; Doctor Will called her Mistress Sawyer.
"Caleb," she said, "you've married him?" When he couldn't have one
sister, he took another, she thought. And for all that, it was Weyford he
really wanted. Then she remembered what Prudence had told Doctor
Will. "He's injured?"

Realizing that Serena must have overheard the conversation, Prudence
became, if possible, paler. "So you've taken up eavesdropping? I'm not
surprised. It must seem a trifling offense beside fornication and bastardy."

Serena attempted no denial. "I was surprised to hear your voice," she
said. "I could not help listening."

"As you couldn't help lying with highwaymen?"

Doctor Will placed his hand protectively on Serena's arm. But she
scarcely noticed.

"Strong language for a dignified lady," began Serena. Then she clenched
her jaw. Taking a deep breath, she said, "Prue, please, let's not quarrel.
Not here. Not now. Please, tell me what's the matter with Father."

Prudence held silence for a moment, clearly thinking it over. What is
going through her mind? thought Will Pond. She's a schemer if ever I
saw one.

Prudence narrowed her eyes. "He's dying. The night of the fire he was
taken with apoplexy. Since then he's been seized twice more. He . . . he
can't seem to get his breath. We've had a physician from Philadelphia.
He's been bled several times. But he's no better. One of the furnace crew
suggested this man here"—she jerked her chin toward Doctor Will—"and
Mother insisted." Her manner made it clear she considered this black
man an incompetent, or worse yet, a fraud.

Doctor Will glanced at Serena. When the new Mistress Sawyer had
begged for a "potion" to cure her husband's infirmity, she had been humble
enough before him—Serena knew that as well as he. My blackness, I

suppose, lends my reputed powers an element of the exotic. Yes, a devious woman. And deviousness is always dangerous, even when it is as transparent as this. I know this child. For months she has been unflagging in her work for me. I see no sign of the depravity her sister is imputing to her. Have a care, child—this woman hates you. What's more, she fears you.

"You said—that is, you seemed to be saying—that Father has been asking for me."

"I didn't . . ." Prudence gave it up. Little as he knew of the Wainwrights' situation, Doctor Will could guess that someone's greed—clearly not Serena's—played a considerable part in it. Prudence, he surmised, was now pondering the advantage of confronting her father with his favourite, swollen with child. Had he known of Serena's condition when he banished her from his house? I assumed so, thought Doctor Will, but perhaps not. Then why . . .

"Yes," said Prudence reluctantly. "He has been asking for you. He doesn't remember the immediate past, the fire, or, well, your absence. He thinks . . . well, we're not certain what he thinks."

"And Mother?"

"She's not well herself. She does what she can for him."

"And Caleb?"

"He's been running the works." At the look on Serena's face, Prudence burst out, "And very successfully, too, now that he's able to get about. He was badly burned fighting the fire that old reprobate Buzby set— fighting the fire, while you ran away."

This thrust had evidently gone home. Serena looked down at her hands, folded together, resting on the shelf of her belly, and clenched them tightly. When she looked up there were tears in her eyes. "Perhaps Doctor Will can help Father. We must try. And I must go to him."

Again that pause as Prudence thought it over. "Very well. I'll go ahead and give Mother warning."

"Wait," said Doctor Will. "You've come in a carriage. Let Serena ride with you. In her condition she should not be riding in a springless wagon the thirty miles or more to Weyford."

Prudence stirred, about to object. Serena forestalled her. "Please, Doctor Will, I'd rather come with you."

❧   ❧   ❧

Now THEY RODE together in virtual silence. Serena felt very ill. The child within her kicked and squirmed as though objecting to the rigours of their journey. Half dazed with heat, Serena watched the road slide slowly

by, the same road she had travelled in the night, in the mist, months
ago. The verge was spangled with buttercups and frosted with Queen
Anne's lace, spilling the sweetness of honeysuckle into the breeze stirred
by their passage—all the drowsy beneficence of summer.

Then they entered the Pines, and the remembered sights and smells
clustered thickly about Serena. Hollies in the wetter spots, green berries
already ripening to red. Swamp waters reflecting the dark, noble spears
of the cedars. The frosted blue of the whortleberries, teased by the dappled sunlight into releasing their nectarous scent. The oily leaves in
which the oaks hoarded moisture glittering blindingly. And over all,
beneath all, the spiciness of pine.

Late in the day they passed through Atsion. Doctor Will's wagon was
known there, and idlers by the inn remarked its passage and speculated
upon the identity of the white woman with him. But no one recognized
Serena.

They plunged into the woods again. And now the ghosts danced ahead
of Serena, the ghost of her girlhood and the phantoms of the last night
she had stumbled along this trail, faint with weariness and sick with
apprehension. Had I known what would befall me, would I have continued? Or would I have run back to Weyford, done Father's bidding,
found myself now Caleb's wife?

But, she thought, that would all have been changed, perhaps. How
could I have foreseen Caleb's injury, Father's stroke? And is life with
Doctor Will and Charity really worse than a lifetime's bondage to Caleb
Sawyer? Well, whatever chance lay there—if chance it was—I've now
forfeited forever. He is husband to Prudence now.

Dusk settled down, and birds silenced by the heat of day sent their
liquid trills into the cooling air. The journeyers met no one, no laden
oxcarts, no travellers. Except for the creaking of the wagon and the slow
clopping of the mule's hoofs, bird song was the only sound. What faint
breeze had arisen at sunset soon died with the ebbing of the light. Heat
lightning fitfully outlined the massed tree trunks, startling the mule out
of its stride.

At least, thought Serena, it will be dark when we pass the White Stag:
dark, deep night when no one will be abroad, no one will see us, see me.
For the first time in many miles she spoke to her companion. "Doctor
Will," she asked timidly, "do you think you can help my father?"

"Now, child, how can I know until I see him? Though I must warn
you his condition sounds grave. Those I have seen with apoplexy—and
your sister said your father has been seized several times—usually continue to be seized again and again until . . ."

"Until they die." Serena supplied the words he hesitated to say to her.

"I know. And yet, an old woman who lived near Weyford—Mistress Hennings—was seized but once. She lived many years. She walked with a cane, and her right arm and leg were weak, but she seemed hale enough for all that."

"Well, child, we must see how it is with your father. 'Tis the difficulty in breathing that worries me. That, and his clouded mind. But, as I say, we cannot know until we see him."

They rode on in silence. Night thickened about them. Doctor Will lit a lantern, then extinguished it when he saw that swarms of insects were drawn by its light. The sand of the trail glowed faintly, sufficient to guide the wagon. The mule plodded stolidly, dragging the wheels in the course laid by ruts in the road. Once or twice at some fingerboard Doctor Will asked Serena for directions.

The night hours passed as they jogged along, drowsing. Bats swooped across the trail, intent on their own pursuits. Somewhere an owl hooted. The wheels rumbled hollowly across the Quaker bridge as lightning flicked over the dark waters of Weyford River. Not even a barking dog marked their passage by the White Stag. But seeing the familiar shape of the inn, Serena was suddenly wide awake.

With a nod of the head she directed Doctor Will onto the trail to Weyford village. She could not speak. She felt her insides twist into a knot of apprehension as the familiar turnings of the trail emerged grey in the light of the false dawn. Clip clop. Clip clop. Nearer and nearer. No light yet showed in the workers' settlement.

There—just ahead—was Wainwright House proud upon its knoll. The fire had not touched it. They rumbled over the bridge by the dam. She looked across the water, unconsciously seeking the cheering glow of the furnace fires. There was none. Had the furnace gone out of blast, then? Had the demand for arms slackened as the War moved on to distant fields of battle? Or were the darkness and silence signs of Caleb's incompetence?

She felt her face to be slick with sweat. "Wait, please," she said. Stiffly she slid down from the seat, Doctor Will moving swiftly to help her as soon as he guessed her intention. She moved awkwardly across the trail and, with the certainty of long accustom, felt her way down to the lakeside. Doctor Will picked his way behind her, reaching her in time to assist her to her knees. She dipped her hands into dark water, cedar-scented, soft and cool. She splashed it on her wrists, on her face. Then she dried her hands with her apron and shook droplets from her hair. She gave her hand to Doctor Will and he helped her to her feet. "I'm ready now," she said.

☙ ☙ ☙

"So you've come back." Caleb stood before her hunched and horrible in the flickering light of the candle in his hand. The right side of his face was puckered and shrivelled with a network of shiny red scars. His beard was gone; the scars twisted his lips into a sidewise grimace. He had lost most of his hair, and a cluster of shilling-sized scars formed shadowy craters on his bare scalp. He bent forward slightly, his legs spraddled, his torso twisted to compensate for his lameness.

He's monstrous, thought Serena. How can Prue . . .? The eyes were the same, downcast, devious, except that the scars pulled the right eye into a squint. For an instant he looked straight at her, and she knew he had neither forgotten nor forgiven their last meeting. Prudence stood slightly behind him, silent.

"I suppose," he said, "you think you see a corpse worth plucking. I warn you, Serena, your father may be daft, but he's not blind." He looked meaningfully at her figure. So far he had ignored Doctor Will, who now interceded.

"Mistress Wainwright has had a gruelling journey. She needs rest and sustenance. You, I presume, are Master Sawyer?"

Before Caleb could answer, Serena said, "Don't mind him, Doctor Will. He judges others' motives by his own." She turned back to Caleb. "Doctor Will has come to help Father. And I've come—you know why I've come, whatever you may pretend to your advantage."

A door opened down the passage. Shuffling footfalls came toward them. Serena started forward. "Mother!" She stopped. Was this Anna, this timid figure walking so hesitantly, clutching a wrapper about her shrunken frame?

"*Ach! Die Serena.*" Anna stopped several paces from the group by the door.

Prudence rushed toward her, clutching her sleeve. "Mother," she said, "the . . . that doctor is here to see Father. Is he awake?"

Anna looked doubtfully toward the tall black man. "Doctor?" she said vaguely.

"Doctor Will Pond. The Black Doctor," Prudence shook Anna's arm as though to rouse her. "Remember? You insisted he be sent for."

"The Serena—in this house? Has she not—away she has gone. *Das Feuer*—" The fire. Anna groped her way toward the drawing room and sat down on a chair by the door.

Serena could say nothing. Anna's vagueness was a shock. How could she have failed so in a few short months?

"Never mind about Serena," said Prudence. "There's no time to explain now. Is Father awake?"

"The Serena," Anna repeated. "The Serena he asks for. *Bitte*—please, I do not understand."

Doctor Will stepped forward. "Madam Wainwright," he said, slowly and gently. "I have come to examine your husband. I am a physician." No time now to mention his reservations about that title. "Serena lives with me now, she assists me. Please, where can I find your husband?"

Anna roused herself. "So fast they all talk," she muttered. "I understand not. *Ja, mein Mann*—my husband, the Serena he asks for. In our bed-chamber he is. Come, I show you." She rose and shuffled toward the stairs, her hand on Doctor Will's arm.

❧   ❧   ❧

CAN THIS BE Father? This shrivelled figure that barely mounds the counterpane?

Samuel Wainwright lay motionless and alone, propped up on pillows in the centre of the bedstead he had shared for thirty years with his wife. The massive carved bedposts seemed to dwarf him still further. The first light of day fell in silver slivers from the shuttered windows onto the pillow, tinting his sunken face a ghastly grey. The once massive jowls hung in papery folds at either side of his slack mouth. One side of his face sagged lower than the other. The fingers of one hand picked restlessly at the counterpane; the other lay in a stiff, useless claw. The rasp of his breath was loud in the still room.

Doctor Will started toward the bed, then glanced at Serena. Her face was completely drained of colour. She swayed on her feet, making vague motions with her hands as though to grope for support. Swiftly he pushed a chair beneath her, steadying her as she collapsed upon it, forcing her head down.

"Father," she said faintly.

"I know, child. It is the shock. When you last saw him he was well?"

Serena nodded, remembering her father striding from her room, blustering threats, demanding her obedience.

The gaunt figure on the bed stirred restlessly. Samuel opened his eyes, then closed them again. The rasping breaths came faster. "Sss—Sss—" Spittle ran from his mouth as he strove to speak.

Doctor Will went swiftly to the bed. "Sir— You are asking for Serena?" Samuel blinked assent. "She is here. Come, child." He helped Serena up and guided her to the bedstead, bringing the chair.

"Wait!" Caleb and Prudence were at the door. Anna huddled silent between them. They came toward the bed, tense and agitated.

Doctor Will fended them off. "Be still, you two—do you want to kill him at once?" They hesitated.

Serena heard nothing of this. "Father, it's me. It's Serena." Samuel's hand paused in its restless motion. She held it in both of hers. "Papa?" she said, as she had when she was little. The hand in hers stirred. The fingers, as soft and insubstantial as an empty, well-worn glove, lightly pressed her own. "Papa," she said again.

The hand in hers relaxed. The laboured breathing seemed to ease. Samuel's face slackened. In terror, Serena looked up at Doctor Will.

"He is resting. And now, so must you. Come, child. You have had a long, long night. I will see what I can do for him."

Stumbling with weariness, Serena allowed herself to be gently led from the room.

Chapter ❧ 20

"**F**OOL!" SNARLED CALEB. "Fool to have brought her here. Fool to leave her at his bedside for hours. Fool to have brought in that blackamoor imposter. Can't you see they're in league to cheat us?"

It was the night following Serena's return. In the testered bed that had once been Serena's, in the room where she once had lingered by the window to greet the promise of each dawn, Prudence cowered against the headboard, her slender fingers nervously plucking at the fine lawn of her high-necked nightdress.

It was hellish hot, the air a fetid exhalation of pent fevers of the day. No breeze stirred the hangings of the bed; no slightest breath of air disturbed the flames of the candles on the stand beside it. They hung motionless, suspended, except when Caleb's pacing set them to guttering. Their flickering light then made of his face a hideous mask. The scars glistened, blood-red and taut, while the muscles of the uninjured side twitched and writhed with his anger. His right eye, the slanted eye, was shut; his left bulged — bloodshot, white-rimmed. The thrusts of his fingers sent his sparse hair flying wildly about his face. The contractures in his legs had impaired Caleb's gait. As his rage impelled him about the room he lurched stiff-legged, catching hold of the bedposts, the chair-backs, the mantel, setting ornaments to teetering.

The room had been but little changed. The porcelain clock still ticked to itself on the mantel, its delicate chiming a reproach to the passions unleashed in its purview. Serena's bearskin was gone, an oval rag rug put down in its place. As Caleb rounded the corner of the bedstead for what must have been the twentieth time, he tripped on the rug's edge and kicked at it viciously. The tall windows that faced the lake had been swathed in heavy drapes. Caleb loathed the morning light, burrowing into the covers at each dawn and berating Prudence if the smallest ray penetrated the darkness he imposed.

Prudence was paralyzed with terror. These rages! Never would I have
believed him capable of such unrestraint. This is not the man I knew
before his injury: mild-mannered, soft-spoken, courteous and deferential.
Nor is it the man I married, the man, timid and grateful, whom I nursed
from the moment they brought him here, hideously burned, on the
morning after the fire. Now, just what has provoked this explosion?

"I did not know I would find her there," she said softly. "Mother has
been quite desperate for someone to help Father. You know the physicians have but worsened his condition."

"So? And if it worsens still further, what have we to lose by it?"

Prudence gasped. She knew her new husband to be ambitious, to
wish the works under his sole control. But until this moment she had
not suspected—had feared to suspect—the extent of his avarice, the
ferocity of his need to prove himself master of Weyford. Nor, in her
secret heart, did she truly believe him capable of running the works,
however she might protest Serena's doubts on this score. "You wish
Father dead?"

Caleb's silence made answer.

He continued his pacing, while Prudence slumped appalled. At last she
said timidly, "But he has asked for Serena. Asked again and again when
he could speak at all. And I thought if he saw her, saw that she is—"

"Pah! You think his addled wits are capable of grasping her condition—
and its cause? And if he does see that she is about to whelp, suppose he
turns teary-eyed at the prospect of a grandchild? We've given him no
such prospect." His wild eyes dared her to confront him with the reason.
"And what if that woolly-headed blackamoor stumbles upon some cure,
some palliative at least that renders the old man alert enough to reconsider his will?" He paused. "Not that it's likely. There's a charlatan if ever
I saw one."

"I'm not so sure of that. They say he—"

Caleb wrenched himself round to face her. The capering shadows set
his scars to dancing in crazed gavottes of their own. "You had better hope
he is a fraud," he said meaningfully. Abruptly he snuffed the candles,
and she heard him begin to undress. At long last he crawled in beside
her and both lay sleepless in the torpid night, together yet apart, backs
to each other, wrapped in imaginings that brought no rest but only
unquiet dreams.

⁂ ⁂ ⁂

ACROSS THE square hall with its carved chests and chairs, Serena lay
sleepless in the prim bed that had once been her sister's. Even in her

worry she found grim amusement in the thought of the newlyweds' dilemma. They can't well turn me out, she thought. For one thing, the neighbours might see me. Nor could they have put me in the tower room with Doctor Will—though I'm sure they thought of it. She chuckled bitterly at her sister's consternation in having to house a black man—not as servant but as a guest from whom, moreover, Anna at least had sought assistance.

She heaved herself to a new position, one hand pillowing her sweat-damp cheek, the other laid on her belly to feel the constant movement of the child within. "You're lively tonight," she whispered. "Can't you let your mother sleep?"

It had been a long day, an endless day after an endless night. Her limbs were still cramped and stiff from the gruelling journey. The long hours by her father's bedside had further tortured her muscles. Nor had she slept more than a few hours this morning when Doctor Will had insisted she rest.

Susan, silent but radiating sympathy, had found some of her clothes that had been bundled into the attic. Prudence had annexed the best gowns to her own wardrobe. Small good they'll do her, Serena thought, with her namby-pamby ways. And the simple gowns that were left had been made for the old Serena, the slim and carefree Serena who had left this house, never to return. Dressing wearily, her limbs leaden with exhaustion and heat, Serena had found that even with every seam let out, the indigo gown she had worn in the tower room—the loosest gown she owned—hiked up over her belly and cut into her armpits, straining and pinching, adding its martyrdom of pinpricks to the greater concerns that tormented her.

At once upon arising she had sought out Doctor Will and found him in the sickroom. Anna rocked in a corner, watching vaguely as the Black Doctor examined her husband. He seemed to be asleep. His good hand fell limply upon the counterpane when the doctor let go of it. His eyes were closed, his face was slack. Only his rasping breaths declared him alive.

Doctor Will concluded his examination by putting his ear to Samuel's chest. He listened for a long time, moving from spot to spot, frowning in concentration. Then he straightened the rucked coverlet and beckoned to Serena. He spoke in low tones that could not penetrate to the corner where Anna sat. "Your father is very ill, child, very ill. It is not just the apoplexy, though that accounts for his lapses of mind, his general weakness. Something is obstructing his lungs. He cannot breathe deeply as he should. And that in turn worsens his torpor."

"His lungs?" Serena thought back. A small, hacking cough, almost a clearing of the throat, had so long seemed natural to her father that no one mentioned it. Some mornings before prayers he would harrumph a bit; the habit became part of him, like his bluster and his furnace-blackened hands. "A bit of the blast," he would sometimes say absent-mindedly when stopping to cough. And indeed the sulphurous fumes and soot-heavy furnace smoke made coughs a constant presence among the ironworkers.

"Yes, child. I let him breathe some camphor vapours, but it seemed to do no good."

"But surely there is something you can do for him?"

Looking into her eyes, stretched wide with anxiety, reddened with sleeplessness, Doctor Will sighed. "I have made an infusion of foxglove; it should strengthen his heartbeat, perhaps make him more alert. Here." He showed her the flask, had her read the directions he had written. "I have given him one dose this morning. Give him two spoonfuls in a cup of wine three times a day. Stir it well. Spoon it into him if he cannot drink. And be careful. Write down when you've given it, and let no one else give it to him. Too much could be mortal."

"I understand."

"And this—" Doctor Will did not look at her. He handed her a stoppered jar. "It is a decoction of poppy seeds. Give it if he complains of pain. This—and strong red clover tea, strong as you can make it, all he can drink."

Serena paled. These were the remedies Doctor Will reserved for cancers. She looked up at him pleadingly. "Surely, no."

He looked at her steadily, his dark eyes glowing with compassion. "Yes, I fear it is a growth that impairs his breathing. I cannot tell you how I know. But there is something about his face, about the gauntness. And your mother tells me he does not eat, cannot swallow. If his illness be what I think, it will move very quickly. He will have pain, but he may sense little of it. And not for long."

"Is there nothing—?"

"Nothing, except to ease his end. And that falls, my child, to you. Your mother is weakening herself. I have seen swollen limbs like hers before. They speak ill of the condition of the heart. And your sister—" He forbore to finish his thought. The dying man could expect scant comfort from those two, wrapped in their plans and schemes. He saw that Serena understood him.

"I will leave these remedies with you. I say remedies—for this they are but palliatives. But they can make his hours easier. And if you can make him take in some food you may increase his strength: milk, egg caudles, a drop of applejack perhaps."

"You are leaving me alone here?"

"I have other patients, child. I can do no more to help him. He may linger in this way for weeks. Once I have seen a patient live some months. When the end is near, you will know. Send for me then."

"How will I know?"

He hesitated. "You will know. And I will come, I promise."

Serena gazed steadily at him. Something within her cried: But it's so far. There's no one to help me, no one I can depend upon. Please don't leave me here all alone. But she said nothing.

After a moment, Doctor Will patted her shoulder. Then he left the room. She stood for a time looking after him. Then she turned back to the still figure on the bed.

&   &   &

Now IT WAS NIGHT, and Susan was keeping watch. Serena tried to sleep. I must rest. I cannot endure what lies before me if I do not rest. She tried to stretch, to draw the tension from her limbs. I miss Mitzi, she thought, miss the feel of her soft fur, the rumble of her purring under my fingertips. Even in the heat it would be a comfort to have her beside me, my one familiar in this wilderness of strangeness that once I called my home.

She turned again, careful to keep her balance on the narrow bed. It is like them to have taken my room. Nothing could show more clearly how Prue itched to supplant me, obliterate my memory if she could, shame it if she could not. And Caleb? If I know Caleb, it gives him some twisted pleasure, some special satisfaction all his own, to be sleeping in the bed that had been mine.

She sighed, turned the damp pillow over, and tried again to sleep.

&   &   &

THE THUNDER woke Caleb, growling and muttering to itself in the distance. He lay awkwardly sprawled on the sweat-damp sheet beside his sleeping wife. His virgin wife. The fever in his brain had scarcely cooled. Is that tawny-eyed bitch to thwart me again?

His hand stole between his thighs, cupping his flaccid manhood idly, nursing it as he nursed his grievances. His arson had brought him nothing from the British; Weyford had not been harmed. Now that the War had moved southward, the payments he received for sabotaging the furnaces would cease. Did the men suspect why one mishap after another kept the furnace out of blast: a mistimed charge, a broken cog in the water wheel?

He thought not—though they were restless. Just this afternoon Mike McGuire had stopped him by the bridge. "When do we be puttin' the furnace into blast again, Master Sawyer?"

"I don't know. Soon."

"Seth said you'd not been fixin' the broken wheel. She'll no run without water to drive the bellows."

"I know. I know. Now be about your business."

"My business be the makin' of iron. And a small bit o' business I been doin' since the Old Man took to his bed. There's me wages ridin' on it. I be owin' a big bill on yer books."

"Have I dunned you for it?"

"No, ye haven't. But I'm not likin' to be owin'. And it be August. Soon enough it come winter and no iron to be poured." Mike backed off a bit, eyeing Caleb sidewise. "You do be wantin' the furnace in blast?"

"Of course."

"Then what you be doin' about the wheel?"

"*I don't know!* Now leave me alone. Don't bother me—understand? Don't bother me."

"It be yer business to be bothered, like as it's my business to pour iron. Ye be runnin' the works. If the Old Man be about, ye'd not see a wheel lie idle fer weeks."

"*Mind your tongue, man.* Or you'll find yourself without a position here."

"Without a position, mayhap. Without work I be already."

McGuire had spun on his heel, hurrying over to a knot of men gathered in front of the store. Animated talk began, and Caleb intercepted sharp glances in his direction.

≈ ≈ ≈

IF THEY SUSPECT something, he thought now, it is probably incompetence, not treason. And indeed he had taken so little note of the complexities of ironmaking that he was hard put to devise plausible accidents. But incompetence? Wait, he thought. Let them wait. And they'll see I'm worth two of Samuel Wainwright. We'll mortgage the land to buy more, and more. And we'll strip it clean. Iron's finished anyway, when the War ends. But there are trees to last my time, and a fortune in charcoal and cordwood to be had, more than enough for my. . . . Let that cursed heap of soot and stone crumble and fall. I'll dump the old woman somewhere — she's not long for this world by the look of her — and take Prudence to England. We'll live with civilized people, a sea's breadth away from this Godforsaken hole.

But first I must secure my hold on Weyford. Damn that bitch! How dare she come back here, parading her swollen belly before me, that belly filled by Stuart Brandon, forcing his way into one more place that ought to have been mine.

His hand worked busily. Beside him, Prudence uttered a little snore. She had refused him what he wanted on their wedding night, recoiling in simpering horror — "In my *mouth* . . . you want me to, to . . . to put *that* in . . ." Whatever she had expected of the mysterious demands of men, it was not the act he had asked of her. And if she had helped me, helped me just a little, I might at last have . . .

But Prudence was a poor stick of a thing in any case, a second best, a last resort, a grasp at Weyford, at the position that everlastingly eluded him. Her breasts under the voluminous nightdresses she affected were small, soft mounds of spiritless flesh, not like . . . not like . . .

His thoughts returned to Serena, crawling over her in lubricious speculation. The fecund amplitude of her body as it was now both fascinated and repelled him. He thought of her breasts, milk-swollen, pressing against the cloth of the too-tight gown as though surging with the eagerness of the life growing within her. They would be hot in my hands, firm as ripe peaches, and the nipples, the nipples, if I were to suck them . . .

For the first time since the fire he felt a stirring of his manhood, the slightest of swellings, an arising quiver.

He turned on his stomach, hands beneath him, imagining the hot bedclothes to be Serena's flesh. Still his manhood grew. And then he remembered the bulge of her belly. My God! I'd like to claw that wretched growth from her, tear it to pieces with my fingers. But no . . . no. I don't want to kill her. I want to punish her . . . punish her . . . punish her. Until she begs me to stop, cries and begs and pleads.

She will never be mine now, never tied to me as a wife obedient under law to whatever I desire of her. That, too, they have taken away. . . . Old Samuel . . . Stuart Brandon . . . and this woman by my side who ensnared me in my weakness.

He began to rock awkwardly in the bed, his mouth buried in the pillow as in Serena's breasts, his twisted lips writhing as though taking suck from her. And his manhood grew and grew. Punish her . . . punish her, said the voice within him. Grasp those turgid breasts and twist them,

force the forming milk from their nipples into his ravening mouth. And
then . . . and then . . . he thought again of the lash lying hidden among
his things. And of how he would lay it on her, and on that wretched,
that obscene growth protruding from her, that visible evidence of all he
had wanted, all he had lost. And she would struggle, and beg, and he
would lay it on the harder. And then . . .

His manhood was a hugeness in his hands. His thrashings shook the
bed. Prudence woke. "Caleb. What —"

He turned to her. He flung back the sheet. There was a growling in
his throat. "Punish her. Punish her." It was not Prudence beside him. It
was Serena. And this time she would not escape him. Fierce in a sudden
access of strength, he tore the nightdress down the length of his wife's
body. She gasped and struggled. He ignored her. The manhood so long
denied pulsed and throbbed. He flung himself upon her, forcing his
knee between her legs, seeking awkwardly, thrusting blindly. And then
he was in her and the world exploded with her squeal of pain and his cry
of triumph. A drumroll of thunder shook Wainwright House. And the
clouds released their rain.

CHAPTER ❧ 21

ACH MORNING the sun rose angry from the moulten Atlantic and seared the earth to silence that only the cicadas dared challenge. Its rays lay like red-hot bars across the August afternoons, and the nights were heavy with heat. The leaves of the giant sycamore hung limp, some yellowing, some scorched to brown.

The burnt leaves drifted lazily to the ground to rustle among the peeling strips of bark and crumble beneath Serena's feet, dustily resigned to autumn. They lay, she thought, like the papers on her father's desk, where requisitions . . . demands . . . pleas for iron, curling and yellowing in the heat, jostled in vain for Caleb's attention.

Once or twice since her return the furnace fires had been coaxed to a feeble glow—to little avail. A few heats had been poured, second-rate stuff that would have shamed Old Samuel, had he known on what cracking mixtures the once-proud "W" was being inscribed.

But always something halted the blast. Now the leather bellows had cracked. The new cylindrical bellows that should long have been installed lay rusting while Caleb ranted and screamed at the men who tried to patch the old one. One by one the seasoned hands had left in disgust, some going to Batsto, some to Aetna, some to the rebuilt works at Mount Holly. Mike McGuire remained, worry lines etched deeper each day into his soot-blackened face.

Caleb seemed unperturbed. Indeed, Serena imagined she detected a hint of triumph in the sidelong glance that followed her comings and goings into the sickroom. Beset with concern for her father—and for Anna, who daily sank deeper into dreams—Serena had not yet had heart to tax him with the mysterious quietude of the works.

On this hot morning Weyford Lake exuded a scent of cedar and decay. In the shallows the tepid water lay dark as amber, and as still. As Serena approached, a heron rose like a wraith and soared to the opposite shore, where he lowered himself in graceful spirals to the branches of a pine, folded his great wings, and became invisible. Mist hovered in swirls above the lake's centre where the avid sun drank the last of the night's small store of coolness.

Seeking a moment's respite from the gloom and miasmic odours of the sickroom, Serena wistfully traced the heron's flight. Then she bent, balancing awkwardly, to tug at the slippers that pinched her swollen feet. How she longed to feel the sun-warmed waters caressing her toes, to kick up droplets and watch them turn to rainbows as she had as a little girl.

A hand clutched her arm. She started, nearly falling, and came about to face Caleb. His good eye stared. His scars glistened. "Get into the house," he hissed. "Now—at once. How dare you flaunt your belly before the village in broad daylight?"

Serena wrenched her arm free. "Do you think there's a person in Weyford who does not know that I'm with child? And what does it matter beside what's happening to Father, to Mother, to the works you are destroying in your ignorance?"

"Silence!" He shot a glance behind him. No one was about. The loungers who frequented the store were still abed, and the village street lay empty. "Come into the house," he repeated in a milder tone, sensing that anger would but goad Serena into an outburst he did not want all Weyford to overhear. "Breakfast is ready."

Serena opened her mouth to speak, then thought better of it. Not here, not now, she thought. Slowly she dragged herself up the steps and into the house. Caleb offered her no aid.

੧   ੧   ੧

WHAT A TRAVESTY of former days these breakfasts are, thought Serena as she found her place. Caleb has not even the decency to wait for Father to die before usurping his chair. His chair, but not his place. Caleb is not the man to take Father's place; indeed, he's barely a man at all.

Almost as though he read her thoughts, Caleb sent her a venomous glance as she struggled into her seat. If he had his way, thought Serena, I'd be slopped with the hogs. I wonder why he allows me at table?

No grace was said. Anna, huddled in dreams, made no effort to serve, and Prudence pulled the silver porringer toward her with a peevish sigh. The food was much the same as always. The heavy embroidered cloth still lay on the table; the china still gleamed in the sunrays that poured through the windows. Only the accustomed eye would note the subtle differences: the tiny chip on the spout of the teapot, the faint film on the glassware, the smears on the windowpanes.

Everything is the same, thought Serena—and everything is changed. Without Father at its head, the table has no life, no spirit. She remembered the many times she had jousted with her father at this table, intent upon some small prize or other in the way of a gown or a privilege. And the last time we both sat at this table, I jousted and won and, not content with my prize, set out upon the folly that brought me to my present pass.

How could she reconcile the Samuel Wainwright she remembered with the shrunken figure mumbling to itself in the bed upstairs, diminished and pathetic, lost and confused? She recalled how on that January morning Weyford had been bustling, and the stillness now prevailing sounded a knell more disturbing than the lusty clamour of the works had ever been. Doesn't anyone else see it? she wondered. She looked around the table. Prudence was not eating. Anna was looking vaguely toward the head of the table as though wondering why Samuel was not there. Caleb spooned oatmeal, eyes fixed on his plate.

"Have you ordered new leather for the bellows?" asked Serena.

Caleb started. His eyelids flickered, but he did not look up. "No."

"But can they mend the old one? Will it bear the pressure if they do?"

"I don't know."

"Well, what do you propose to do if it doesn't?"

"I don't know."

"Can Mike McGuire put together the new cylinders?"

"I haven't asked him."

"Well, then—"

Caleb looked up at last. His fingers shook as he unconsciously twisted the napkin in his hand. "Don't bother about these matters, Serena. They are not your concern." He spoke softly, yet each word leapt across the table like a spring uncoiled.

"It *is* my concern. We have orders to fill—I know we do."

"And just how do you know? Who told you?" Caleb glanced down the table. Prudence sat staring at the tablecloth, heedless of the quarrel.

"Father's desk is littered with orders. To see them is to know what they are."

Caleb struck the edge of the table with his fist. The china rattled. A fork fell to the floor. "You've been spying. I won't have it. I won't have it, I say!" He struggled to his feet. "You're on sufferance here, Serena—can't you understand that? Because the old man asked for you. Because your sister was such a fool as to fetch you. But one more word about the works and I'll pack you off to your blackamoor before the day is out. The works

are not your concern—do you understand me? Not your concern *ever*
again. Now go upstairs or I'll have you thrown off now."

"No you won't," said Serena softly. "Not so long as Father wants me here."

Prudence looked up. Her face was white and frightened. "Do as he says, Serena. Please."

What's this? thought Serena. Even in her agitation she noticed the difference in Prue. But she dismissed it as unimportant for the moment. "Father wants me here," she repeated. "That is what matters now." She rose and walked out of the room.

Caleb watched her go, Prudence watched Caleb. From Anna's end of the table came a thready voice, singing to itself. *"Sah' ein Knab' ein Röslein stehn, Röslein auf der Heide . . ."*

☙ ☙ ☙

"GOOD MORNING, Father." Speaking as cheerfully as she could, Serena quietly crossed the room to the big bed. She had greeted Samuel thus for many mornings now. Sometimes a fleeting grimace signified that he had heard—but heard what? she wondered. Sometimes it seemed he heard someone else, not her. More often there was no response. Yet it seemed important that she greet him.

Susan rose stiffly from the chair by the bed and stood behind it, her features taut, her eyes fixed on Serena's face.

"Good morning, Susan. How is Father today?" Without waiting for an answer, Serena went to the bedside and took her father's flaccid hand in hers. Then she looked into his face.

Susan came swiftly toward Serena, grasping her elbows and steering her toward the chair for which she groped. Serena sat for a moment, her head bowed. Then she looked beseechingly at Susan. The last bit of colour drained from her cheeks as the dark, calm eyes stared into hers. She swallowed. "How can it be? Only last night he seemed the same as ever. . ." Her voice trailed off.

Susan nodded. "That be how it happen, Miz Serena. The sickness, it be all through him now."

Serena stared at her father. How quickly, she thought, she had become accustomed to the thin, quiet man in the bed, the shrunken ghost of her blustering father who lay, hour after hour, scarcely moving, meekly swallowing the infants' gruel she fed him, now and then uttering grunts she had come to recognize as requests for water, for the urinal, for someone to fan away the flies.

Now the white hair sprawling on the pillow framed a face she barely knew. Samuel's jaw hung open. His breath whistled past lips cracked with fever. His chest heaved in uneven spasms as his lungs fought for air. His fingers plucked at his nightshirt, at the sheets, pinching and releasing, pinching and releasing. He flung his head restlessly from side to side as though seeking the air the obstruction in his lungs denied him. And yet he still lived. Though it seemed each tortured breath must be his last, though his heart beat so wildly his thin chest pulsed with its struggles, he lived. The rheumy eyes opened. He looked up. "Sss— Sss—"

"I'm here, Father. I'm here."

She felt the weak pressure of the thin fingers curled trustfully about hers. Then they dropped away. Samuel's breathing seemed to lighten somewhat. His eyes closed, and the battle for air went on.

Gently, Serena eased her hand away. Her knees shook as she stood. "Stay with Father, Susan," she said. "Call me if . . . call me. I must ask Caleb to send for Doctor Will."

Susan watched mournfully as Serena made her way to the stairs. "That one no be sendin' for no doctor," she said. But Serena did not hear.

🐾   🐾   🐾

"HE's DYING—don't you understand? Dying. I don't see how he can live through the night—how he lives even now." Serena's voice shook.

"He's been dying for weeks now."

"But this is different. His face—it's like a skull. Go and see for yourself if you don't believe me."

Caleb's shudder was ill concealed. Not once in the past weeks had he visited the dying man. "Very well," he said indifferently. "If you say so."

"Then you'll send someone for Doctor Will?"

"Why? You said yourself it's hopeless. Your precious blackamoor himself said there was nothing to be done."

"To save him? No. But to relieve his pain? To bring him what ease we can? Of course there's something to be done."

Caleb did not reply. He seemed barely to hear. His gaze was turned inward. A slight smile hovered about his twisted mouth. Now it will all be mine, he thought. Mine. And she'll not take it from me. He looked straight at Serena and smiled openly.

Oh, my God, thought Serena. He's not thinking of Father. He's thinking of Weyford. Of how he will be master of it. Her own lips curled in contempt. "Caleb," she said, "Father is dying. Whatever it is you want,

he cannot deny it to you now. For God's sake, for mercy's sake if not for
mine, please fetch Doctor Will. Please, Caleb. I would go myself if I
could."

Caleb emerged from his trance. "But of course you can't," he said,
gaze fixed on the bulge at her waistline. His eyes narrowed. A spasm
crossed his face. He might still do it, he thought. The old man might foil
me yet—he and that pregnant bitch together. That Samuel was in effect
his prisoner, that no lawyer could reach Samuel without his knowledge,
he ignored. Only when the old man is dead, he thought, only when the
will is read, will I be safe. He did not consider that from fears such as his
no safety could ever be found.

"Please, Caleb."

Caleb nodded as though to himself.

"You'll send someone at once?"

There was a pause. "Yes. Yes, of course." But Caleb's eyes remained
fixed on the papers beneath his hands.

🙣 🙣 🙣

THE VILLAGE STREET lay deserted, parched and panting under a black sky
that held all the day's heat in its smothering folds. On both sides marched
the workers' houses—identical houses, identically spaced, two rooms
upstairs beneath the sloping rafters, two rooms down, tiny dooryards
neatly contained in their fences, tidy garden plots behind. Most were
dark, some deserted. Sweating beneath the cloak she wore in an effort
to conceal her bulk, Serena hurried along the dusty street. There. That
was Mike McGuire's house. The faces of tall hollyhocks shone whitely
in the dusk by the door. The bittersweet scent of flowering tobacco
weighted the motionless air.

Thank God, thought Serena, there is a light. Scuffles and giggles came
from within. By day this house boiled with children; they must still be
about, no doubt finding it too hot to sleep in their airless cubbyholes
beneath the roof. "Mike! Mike McGuire!"

The scufflings and giggles increased. The door was flung open. Behind
Mike, Serena caught a glimpse of bright eyes and copper curls. Mike's
two small daughters hid in their mother's skirts. "Miz Wainwright!"

"Mike—I need your help."

"Come ye inside, then."

"No. Please, no." Involuntarily, Serena looked down at herself. Even
in her agony for her father, she could not have brought herself to come

during the day. It had cost her something to come at all, and then only when she was sure that Caleb had not—and would not—send for Doctor Will.

Mike came out onto the stoop and shut the door behind him.

"Mike—you would know—has Master Sawyer sent for Doctor Will?"

"Your father be taken bad?"

"Yes! This morning. But somehow I feel that nothing has been done."

"He's not been sendin' fer anyone that I be knowin'. Seems there's no meanness that weasel-mouth won't try."

Serena was not surprised. She thought of her father's ravaged face and shook with fear and anger.

"Mike, will you go?"

"I can't go meself, Miz Wainwright. The furnace . . . but, look, now"—he shifted uncomfortably as he saw her lips quiver—"I'll send a boy to the White Stag. Nick Sooy, he be yer father's friend. He'll send word, like as not with a horse fer the doctor. How's that, now?"

"Of course. Master Sooy will do that. Oh, Mike, thank you. Thank you. But wait . . . here's a note for the doctor. I can't pay the messenger, but . . ."

"No need to pay," said Mike gruffly. "The Old Man—yer dad—he's been a good master of Weyford." His calloused hand touched her shoulder. "Ye be goin' back to the Big House. Sit by him. With luck and some fair ridin', the black doc'll be here tomorrer."

❧ ❧ ❧

SERENA KNELT by the bedside and prayed for her father to die.

"It's too much," she sobbed. "Too much. Oh, Doctor Will, why can't you let him go?"

"He'll go when he's ready," said Doctor Will sternly. "And when the Lord is ready to receive him." As Serena raised her tear-streaked face to plead with him, he added, "It cannot be long now." He bent back to his work.

From his many weeks of lying immobile, Old Samuel had bedsores, many gangrenous, each an arrow in his flesh. As Doctor Will tried to cleanse the rotting flesh and apply some salve, Samuel squirmed and flung his good arm about, uttering whimpers more heartrending than screams. "Ow! Ow! Ow!"

"Doctor Will!" Serena grasped his arm. "Stop now! What difference does it make for the few hours he has left? Why torture him?"

Doctor Will shook off her arm. "These sores must be cleansed. They will pain him less then, child. Hold him, if you would help him. His struggles increase his pain."

Serena went to the head of the bed. "Papa" she whispered. "Papa— can you hear me?" Still the whimpering continued. "Ow! Ow!" Serena took her father's hands in hers, holding them fast to subdue their wild flailing. "Papa" she implored, "please lie still. Please. It will be over soon . . . soon . . . and then you can rest. I'll bring you an egg caudle—you'll like that, won't you? And we'll put a fresh coverlet on. And after that, we'll . . ."

Serena babbled on, hardly heeding her own words, but keeping her voice as calm and soothing as she could. Tears splashed down on Samuel's face as she cradled his head against her. The harsh breath rasped on. Her father's body thrashed convulsively with each stroke of Doctor Will's hands.

"There, now. It's done." Doctor Will straightened up. He helped Serena lay her father on his back, pillows heaped beneath him. Gently, Serena laid her father's head back on the pillows. She sat down by his side, still holding his hand.

Samuel quieted. His eyes were half closed. Susan brought some wine weakened with water, and Serena raised her father's head and held the cup so he might drink. He swallowed a few mouthfuls, then his head dropped back. Doctor Will quietly seated himself in Anna's rocking chair.

The seconds ticked on into hours, their passage counted by the rise and fall, rise and fall of Samuel's breath. The afternoon wore on and faded into dusk. Serena's face, her back, her waistline were drenched with sweat. Her buttocks stuck to the chair; the rails of the chairback seemed imprinted, one by one, in deep red wheals on her flesh. Fat, drowsy flies buzzed about her head and the sick man's. She brushed them away.

Serena expected Doctor Will to order her to go and eat something, perhaps to rest, and she steeled herself to refuse. But he said nothing. At intervals he gave Old Samuel some poppyseed infusion and urged him in vain to drink the clover tea. Except for frequent trips to the commode, necessary now that her pregnancy was advanced, Serena remained by her father's side. From time to time she sipped some water, feeling ill at the very thought of food.

As the room darkened, Samuel seemed to grow more restless. Doctor Will brought some candles. "Where is Mother?" asked Serena. He shook his head. The sturdy door of the room, closed against intruders, muffled all sounds; they might have been alone in Wainwright House—she, and Doctor Will, and the dying man.

Samuel turned his head toward the light. His breathing quickened, coming in short, tortured gasps. Suddenly he tensed. His hand clutched Serena's with a hint of his old strength. His mouth worked. Then he spoke, loudly and clearly, in the commanding voice she had thought never to hear again. "The heat—it's time to pour the heat. Can't those numbskulls see it?" He began to struggle as though to rise. "The taphole," he cried. "Open the taphole. Do you want a breakout?"

"Calm yourself, Father. It's all right—it's all right. They're pouring now—don't you see?" Tears streamed down her face. Doctor Will came to help her as she eased Old Samuel down, holding his hand, stroking it, laying her cheek against it. Strange, she thought, I never touched Father when he was well. I can't remember him ever touching me.

"Pouring," Samuel echoed. "Yes . . . yes. A fine heat." He lay back, panting. Serena leaned over him, laying a wet cloth on his forehead.

Then Samuel Wainwright's eyes opened, blue and shining, alert as in the old days. He looked at Serena bending over him. Clearly he knew who she was now. He raised his arm. His palsied fingers stroked her hair. "You're a good girl," he said.

And then he died.

CHAPTER ❧ 2 2

THE PROCESSION SNAKED across the bridge and up the slight incline of the village street. When those at its head and the burden they bore had disappeared around the bend beyond the workers' houses, the last of the mourners were still waiting to cross the bridge. Mike McGuire and his sturdiest mates bore the coffin. They looked like strangers in their Sunday clothes, their faces scrubbed clean of soot, their hardened hands still bearing its traces.

Behind them paced the honorary pallbearers: Nicholas Sooy; the masters of Batsto and Atsion, come riding in haste to bid their colleague farewell; the owner of the Pleasant Mills; the Honorable Archibald Cranmer, Old Samuel's attorney. A small detachment of militia marched behind them, clad in homespun hunting garb and such polished oddments of military gear as could be scavenged for the occasion.

The weather had turned, and wind scented with char from the burnt-over acres whipped the crape on the hats of the men. Rain lashed at the coffin and its bearers, slicking the bridge's cedar planking so that the mourners had a care to watch their footing as they crossed. It beat upon the windows of the tower room where Serena stood watching the procession.

❧ ❧ ❧

ON THE EVENING of Samuel's death, while the candles burnt in his chamber and Anna, scarcely seeming to know where she was, sat beside her husband's body, Prudence had sought out Serena in her room. She had stood over the bed where Serena lay exhausted but sleepless, reddened eyes staring at the ceiling, and nervously wrung her hands.

"What is it, Prue?" But I already know, thought Serena. She motioned

Prudence away from the bed and rose awkwardly to her feet.

"The funeral . . ."

"Yes?"

"Well, we think . . . Caleb says . . ." Prudence looked down at the floor. For some reason, this was harder to say than she had expected. Serena's face, puffy with weariness and tears, the too-tight dress, perspiration-stained and pulling at the seams, bespoke the long hours when Serena had sat at Samuel's bedside, ministering to his needs without complaint, shouldering the unpleasant tasks that Anna could not do and Prudence shrank from doing.

Prudence swallowed. Where were the words with which Caleb had only this morning armed her? Words like "shame" and "disgrace" and "insult to Father's memory"—and worse, words like "whore" and "bastard" which she had never thought to hear him utter?

Why doesn't she come out with it? thought Serena. We know who's master of Weyford now. And she thought of Caleb, dressed in the fine black suit he must have had tailored in expectation of this day, playing lord of the manor to an audience of mourners. Her back ached from her hours of vigil by the bedside. Her head swam with tiredness. In her chest pain throbbed in rhythm with her heartbeat. Let us be done with this fencing, she thought, wanting only to lie down in the deepening dusk and mourn for her father alone.

"Caleb says," repeated Serena, irony weighting her words, "that he does not wish me at the funeral. Or rather, given his hypocrisy, that it would be best for me not to attend. Is that what you came here to tell me?"

Prudence nodded. She let the slur upon Caleb pass unremarked.

Surprised, Serena looked more closely at her sister. She recalled how at breakfast—how long ago that seemed!—Prudence had eaten nothing. Nor had she spoken except to beg Serena to heed Caleb's warning and leave the room. Now, in the deepening dusk, her face gleamed pale. Her eyes seemed shadowed with more than the coming of night. Something is amiss, thought Serena. Something new. But before she could speak, Prudence raised her head.

"Surely, Serena, you must know how it ill becomes us to have you—"

Serena drew a deep breath. "*Surely, Prudence,*" she interrupted, mimicking her sister's pious tones, "you must know me not at all if you think I would have so little respect for Father's wishes—*Father's*, not Caleb's, not yours—as to make a mockery of his funeral by appearing there like this? By making it an occasion for hissing and tattling, and not the tribute he deserves?"

Serena almost smiled at her sister's pained expression. "Don't you think I know that for each one who comes to mourn, two will come to gossip and pry? The goodwives round about Weyford have thought me a trollop for years. They are but waiting their chance to scorn me—and with me the Wainwright name. There can't be a person in Weyford who has not heard of my 'condition.' I know that. But to flaunt it openly, and at such a time, when I know how Father felt about it—"

Serena's voice broke. "I've said goodbye to Father. And he to me. I don't need public farewells that bid fair to become a Roman spectacle." She turned away, lest Prudence see the tears that now coursed unchecked down her face. Her shoulders heaved as she struggled for control.

"Serena—" Prudence swallowed hard. "I loved him too, you know."

"And so you found every excuse not to venture near his bedside. Did you think death was catching? Or were you afraid to soil your white hands?" Why does it ease my pain to say cutting things to Prue, who doubtless, as she says, loved Father too?

Prudence made no reply.

Serena turned around. "I'm sorry, Prue. It was hard for me to see him that way, so different, so . . . struck down. I suppose it was too hard for you to bear."

Prudence shook her head. "It was you he asked for. All of us could see that. And how do you think that made me feel? You again, when I thought you'd gone forever. It's been you he favoured, always you." Her eyes grew distant, gazing down the years. "No matter what I did—or you did—no matter how hard I tried to please him, it was you. Always you. Until . . . until you ran off."

Now it was Serena's turn to look back down the years, back to when she was small, to when the rivalries of young womanhood had not yet come between herself and Prue. She raised her hand to shield her eyes as the rays of the sinking sun glared through the dusty window. As she did so, the sun struck the scar of a burn on her wrist, turning it orange as though the fire still lingered there.

It was Prue that she had run to when the scrap of red-hot iron had flown into the nook where she was hiding and struck her arm with searing force. The fear of being discovered watching the work again when she had been repeatedly forbidden to do so had been greater even than her pain. What was I so afraid of? she thought now. Not that Father would whip me, threaten though he might. But the glare in his blue eyes when he was angry . . . the twitching muscle in his jaw . . . the throbbing vein in his forehead . . . that tremor in his voice—these things terrified me as the threat of blows could not. So Prue sneaked to the kitchen for grease, bound up my arm, helped me hide the burn beneath long sleeves.

And held me in the night when the wound throbbed and stung.

What happened, Prue? she almost asked aloud. But she knew the answer. It lay in a thousand small hurts, a hundred incidents in which Samuel had indulged Serena while ignoring the virtues Prue paraded. And it lay at last in the mind of Caleb Sawyer, whom Prue — for whatever reason — had apparently loved, and whom Prue now had as husband, and knew she did not have as mate.

For a moment Serena yearned to throw her arms about her sister, to offer what comfort she could for those losses large and small that she sensed lay behind the meanness of spirit that Prudence so often displayed. The impulse died, withered by the hot resentment shining in Prue's eyes. "You need not worry, Prue," Serena said gently. "I will keep myself well hidden until after the funeral." Her expression hardened. "And then," she said, "I will leave Wainwright House."

C H A P T E R ❧ 2 3

N OW SERENA STOOD watching from the tower room as Prudence, dressed in black, supported the stumbling figure of Anna, diminished by distance, huddled beneath a black shawl. The new minister, Pastor Estaugh, supported Anna on the other side. Behind them walked Caleb, in his new black cloak and tricorne, its cockade draggled and wet, carrying—I can scarcely believe it, thought Serena—Old Samuel's fine Malacca stick.

Unable to watch any longer, she turned to another window, concentrating on the orchard. The summer-burdened, apple-laden trees made reverence to the storm, their layered skirts silver-spangled where the wind tipped up the backs of the leaves. Beyond the neat rows, blackened spars sheathed in mist protruded from the charred forest floor. They sported whorls of new-green growth, recalling the promise Sam had made in another burnt woods so long ago.

I was right to leave Weyford, thought Serena as the last of the mourners trudged unnoticed out of sight. Right to seek a new life for the child and myself, however difficult that life may be now. There is nothing I can do to save Father's dream, nothing I can do to keep Weyford from dying as he did, so long as Caleb wields the power here. If only there were some way to break his hold! But for now I can see none—no way to keep him from destroying all Father's achievement with his ignorance and his greed. No way, unless . . . unless . . .

She shook her head to dispel the unadmitted hope that her father had left her some small share in Weyford's future. Yet why else had Caleb bade her stay to hear the reading of the will? Strange that he should do that.

She went to the head of the precipitous stairs and listened. Wainwright House was still. Even the servants had gone to attend the last rites for ❧ 165

their master. Now was the time to creep down and make ready for whatever she was about to hear.

❧ ❧ ❧

THE NORTHEASTER had brought with it a taste of fall. In Samuel's study, a
fire had been kindled. It burnt poorly, sputtering and smoking as the
wind beat down the chimney. The blue smoke made the room even
dimmer, swirling in layers around the candle flame that wavered in the
draught, and veiling the expressions of those ranged about the polished
oak table.

Anna was absent — fittingly, thought Caleb. The old woman is no
longer with us, whether physically present or not.

Prudence sat with her head bowed, her hands folded upon the table
edge as though in prayer. Serena sat rigidly, her chair pushed back from
the table to make room for the child she carried, her hands quietly folded
upon the bulge of her belly. Was she perhaps recalling their conversation
of yesterday?

She had confronted Caleb in this very room. He had marked the twitch
of annoyance in her face at finding him seated behind Samuel Wainwright's desk. At her entrance he shoved the papers he was holding into
a drawer and slammed it shut, catching his fingers. The sharp pain that
shot through his hand did little to improve his disposition. He sat back
in the heavy carved chair that had been Old Samuel's throne and waited
for her to speak. The gleaming expanse of mahogany that separated
them, the graceful curve of the desk edge he traced with his finger,
reminded him that he was master now, she supplicant. He warmed with
pleasure — and saw that she sensed not only his gratification but its
source.

He expected her to remonstrate, but she did not. "What are your
plans for the works, Caleb?" Before he could cut her off, she plunged on.
"The War has departed Jersey. It may go on some time longer, but it
will go elsewhere if the reports we hear are true. If the Patriots lose —
unlikely though it now seems — the British may well confiscate Weyford,
or destroy it, and I suppose in such a case there's little we can do?"

She watched Caleb closely as she said this. He felt sweat forming
beneath his stiff new garments. Does she know? Does she merely suspect? He could not tell. Her face remained inscrutable except for the
amber eyes, which burned into his. She can't know, he thought. Then
he took heart. And what does it matter if she does? He waited to see
what else she had to say.

"With the War over, or at least passed," said Serena, "the orders for armaments will fall off. What will you be making in their stead?"

"Why should you care?" Caleb spoke meaningly. "I've told you often enough it's no concern of yours. What's more, you're a woman. What do you know of such matters?"

"More than you know, I'll warrant. And I know there's work to be had. Not at the pace we've been smelting, I'll grant you, but work nonetheless. Just replacing all the fences that were melted down for shot will bring some pretty orders. I've heard the fence round the State House in Philadelphia will be replaced as soon as it's deemed safe from remelting. And the rebuilding of Mount Holly will consume a great deal of iron, too. Have you gone about securing those commissions? With Father dead, you can be sure his competitors will waste no time in promoting the superiority of their iron to yours—nor, from what I can see, will they need to lie to do so. No heat of iron worthy of the Weyford name has been poured since Father took sick."

"Enough!" Caleb sat as upright as his twisted form allowed. "I've let you run on, making every allowance for your supposed grief—but that's enough. Now listen to me, Serena: *The works are not your concern.*"

"Of course they're my concern. Father gave years of his life to build them. He lost his life trying to save them. Am I to let them be lost forever because he is not here to protest?"

"Serena, you forget yourself. You had your opportunity to save yourself, to save that precious soot pile you think so much of—your opportunity to be my wife. We both know how you chose to avail yourself of it." He felt his face burning as though her spittle still clung to it. "And we both know what your father thought of the choice you made. Don't we?"

"Do we? The will's not yet been read." Serena bit her lip. A fool I am indeed to so betray my hopes.

Caleb smiled. "Quite so. The will has not been read. I'm sure you will wish to be present on that occasion."

ta   ta   ta

AND NOW here she was. Caleb could see that her obvious pregnancy flustered Archibald Cranmer nearly to incoherence. The fat attorney's bald head was glistening with sweat, his plump cheeks were puffed with indignation, and the two corkscrew curls on each side of his face quivered. The shame of it! he was clearly thinking. Pregnant women did not appear in public, even on such an occasion as this, and a woman both pregnant and unwed. . . . Now he understood the will in his hands. This was as brazen a trollop as he'd ever met, notwithstanding his clandestine journeys to a certain house in Philadelphia.

Cranmer unfolded the document and cleared his throat. Serena's gaze was fixed on his face; she looked at neither Caleb nor her sister as the lawyer began to read.

"'The last will and testament of Samuel Richard Wainwright, of the County of Gloucester, State of New Jersey, United States of America . . .'"—Samuel, patriot that he was, would insert in his will no cavilling provision that doubted the new nation's future—"'being of sound mind and constitution, do make the following provisions for the disposal of my Estate . . .'"

Bequests to the church at Pleasant Mills, to Susan and various other servants; a bequest to be used "for the additional outfitting, as necessity dictates, of the Fifth Troop, New Jersey Militia."

A provision that "my wife, Anna Wilhelmina, née Meissner," receive her legally decreed third share and lifetime tenancy of "the structure known as Wainwright House, with all privileges thereof, including such personal necessities as she may require, to be paid from the income of the Estate . . ."

A provision that "my daughter, Anna Prudence," receive "for her sole use and disposal, an annual allowance of two hundred pounds sterling or its equivalent in gold"—prudent Samuel had foreseen the debasement of the Continental currency—"to be paid from the income of the Estate . . ."

Caleb saw the worried glance Serena sent Prudence. She's thinking the estate will be worthless if I manage it, he thought. She'll see. She'll see soon enough. And then she'll be punished. His hand stole to his lap.

Archibald Cranmer paused for breath. He took a sip of neat brandy from the glass at his elbow. He, too, looked at Serena as he resumed his measured reading. "'And of my erstwhile daughter, Serena Katherine,'"—Serena flinched. Caleb tensed. Now, he thought: now—"'who has most grievously disappointed my hopes in word and deed, tarnished my good name and dragged the Wainwright reputation in the dust, . . .'"

Even in the dim light Caleb could see the painful flush that spread from Serena's throat to her cheeks and forehead as the lawyer continued, his tones as sonorous as he could make them, for he, too, felt the gravity of this moment: "'with her whorish behaviour and insolent flouting of all decencies and her continued defiance of my wishes . . .'" Serena flinched each time the lawyer paused portentuously, eyeing her over the tops of his spectacles and clearly relishing his part in her ordeal— flinched as though he laid a lash across her back.

Caleb's excitement grew. His manhood stirred with each involuntary shiver of Serena's. Yes! Yes! Go on, man—go on! Now she's being punished!

"'. . . I say only that she is my daughter no longer, that I repudiate her utterly and irrevocably. . . . '"

Serena stared before her, her eyes glazed. With an effort she squared her shoulders and held her head high.

Bend, thought Caleb. Bend that stiff neck, slut. Now it's your precious father who's laying on the lash for me.

"'. . . and direct that she have no share in the Estate, nor in any of its appurtenances, nor in its income . . .'"

Bend, damn you! Caleb's excitement rose higher as he saw Serena's face blanch, but for two burning spots of colour on her cheeks. Her gaze was now fixed upon her hands, which sought each other's comfort below the table's edge. She seemed not to breathe.

"'. . . direct or indirect. And I further direct that none who shall inherit under this testament employ any of their inheritance on her behalf, lest my wrath come from beyond the grave to punish them for their flouting of my wishes . . .'"

Now Serena looked up and straight at Caleb, her eyes burning coals, her face drawn tight, her lips set, deep lines springing out at their corners.

Wait, thought Caleb. Wait. He could scarcely sit still in his excitement, as his recovered manhood pulsed and throbbed beneath his hand.

"'And I further direct that she be banished from the premises of Weyford, its properties, appurtenances'"—the lawyer droned through all the legal variations of the words—"'in perpetuity, and I set upon my heirs and assigns the responsibility of enforcing her banishment.'"

Serena huddled in her chair, her eyes tightly closed, swallowing convulsively, one hand clamped to her lips.

Look up! Look up! thought Caleb. I want to see your eyes. I want you to feel the knout laid on by your precious father's hand. But Serena did not look up.

Now, thought Caleb. I want you to hear what's coming now.

The lawyer drew a deep breath and took another sip of brandy. "'And to Caleb Archibald Sawyer, who has managed my furnaces and who has, furthermore, stood faithfully by me as a son by his father, I give, devise, and bequeath a two-thirds share and sole control of the property known as Weyford'"—again the legal descriptions—"'on the sole condition that he marry Anna Prudence, my daughter, within one year.'"

Prudence gave a little squeak and crumpled forward onto the table. Serena came out of her frozen trance. She stirred to go to her sister's aid. But her legs would not support her. She slumped back into her place.

Caleb took no notice. A pulsating explosion of his manhood beneath the table absorbed all his attention.

ᴥ ᴥ ᴥ

WAINWRIGHT HOUSE was still. The last mourners had taken their departure; Archibald Cranmer had bustled away, flown with brandy and self-importance, in pursuit of the fine dinner and soft bed that his tale of this afternoon's scandals was certain to procure for him. Prudence slept exhausted and alone in the big testered bed; Anna snored in hers. In the tower room where Caleb sent her, Serena spent her last night in Wainwright House.

When the lawyer had stammered his farewells, when a shuddering Prudence had been assisted from the room, Serena had risen shakily from her chair. Leaning heavily on the table, supported by her trembling arms, she looked at Caleb at last. "I shall be leaving in the morning," she had said very quietly. "Doctor Will is coming for me then. Unless you insist that I leave now, on foot?"

Exhausted by his own passions, Caleb looked up at her. "That will not be necessary. I trust your father's ghost will be content if you depart on the morrow."

"My father's ghost is, I hope, in some far place, at rest. For if it is not, he must be weeping to see what he did in his anger and his shame."

"But it's done, just the same."

"Perhaps." Serena had left the room.

Now Caleb stood again by Samuel's desk. Spatters of rain hit the uncurtained panes. Their blank surface reflected the glow of the fire and the flame of the candle in his hand. He put it down and went to assure himself again that no one was about. The shadowy hall stretched empty toward the stairs. A single candle sputtered in a wall sconce.

Caleb shut the door and threw the bolt. Then he drew out the papers he had secreted in the desk drawer this morning. He scanned them again in the flickering candlelight.

The words were penned in Samuel Wainwright's hand.

> In return for the advance of the sum of two thousand pounds to be used at my discretion for the improvement and enlargement of the property known as Weyford ironworks, most particularly including, but not restricted to, the furnace and forge together with their machinery and other appurtenances, but including also the stores, bog iron operations, and collieries, and not excepting expansion of

the real property by purchase or hire, I hereby deed to Captain Stuart Brandon, in perpetuity, a two-thirds claim upon said property and the income therefrom, saving only that a salary, to be agreed upon between us, shall accrue to me and my designated heirs for the management of said works for so long as they shall remain profitable, and that tenancy of the proposed residence, to be known as Wainwright House, shall remain mine so long as I shall serve as manager of the works, and shall devolve upon my heirs and assigns, so long as they shall be related to me by blood and shall participate in the profitable management of Weyford ironworks. This agreement, which shall be confidential between myself and Stuart Brandon, shall be binding upon my heirs and assigns, and shall have a claim of precedence upon my Estate.

To the foregoing in its entirety we set our hands and seals on this fifteenth day of April in the Year of Our Lord seventeen hundred and sixty-seven.

> — Samuel Wainwright
> — Stuart Brandon

The document was sealed but not witnessed.

As it had earlier, Caleb's hand shook as he contemplated the paper. He stared out the window and encountered his own reflection, shadowed and misshapen.

"Bah!" he said aloud. "He'll never come back. Never. Since he eluded the British at Barnegat there's a price upon his head. He wouldn't dare. And if the British lose the war? Well then, how can he prove this document ever existed?"

He tore the paper to bits and cast them into the fire.

CHAPTER ☙ 24

SERENA STOOD BY her father's grave. On this first morning of September, the storm might never have been. The sky arched illimitable over the Barrens, white puffs of cloud playing at tag across its field of purest blue. The air, dry and crisp, hinted of autumn, and the feathery grasses of the little churchyard rippled in a breeze that tasted of the sea.

On Samuel's grave the orange clods of earth lay moist and still slick with the rains of yesterday. To his left lay the graves of his infant sons, their iron markers tipsy in the sodden ground. To his right lay young Sam, the soil mounded upon his coffin already green with growth and sinking to the level of the enfolding earth. Can it be but four months since Sam died? Serena wondered. Four months seems so little time to encompass all that has happened. From the crest of the rise where the graveyard lay, Serena could see all of Weyford, cleansed and polished, the waters of its lake a mirror of the sky. Wainwright House stood proud and solid, sheltered by the massive arms of its guardian sycamore. Beyond the house lay Anna's flower garden, the individual blossoms indistinguishable, the whole a tapestry of red and orange, green and gold.

By the little church that watched over the graveyard, Doctor Will waited with the wagon to take Serena home. Home, Serena thought. How strange to think of home as any place but Weyford. Is that my home, then, the little house where kind people gave me shelter? Do I belong there — or anywhere, now that Weyford is no longer mine?

She looked back toward the church. Shadows were retreating beneath its stone foundations, pursued by the ascendant sun. It is getting near noon, thought Serena. I must go. Yet she lingered.

☙ ☙ ☙

SHE HAD LEFT Wainwright House soon after dawn, hoping to get away before anyone was stirring. But as she took Doctor Will's arm to climb into the wagon, the great front door opened and Prudence slipped out. She was carrying a large, awkward bundle.

Prudence, too, looked exhausted by yesterday's revelations. Wisps of hair straggled beneath the lace edge of her cap, and the bodice of her gown was buttoned crookedly. "Wait, Serena," she called softly, looking nervously over her shoulder. She hurried to the wagon. "Wait," she said again.

"What is it, Prue?"

Prudence proffered her burden. "Your clothes," she said. "I . . . I've packed the gowns you loved the best. The apricot silk and . . . well, you'll see. And some undergarments . . . a cloak." Seeing that Serena was not going to reach for it, Prudence passed the bundle to Doctor Will, who stowed it away in the wagon.

What use have I for ball gowns where I'm going? Serena almost said. But something in her sister's expression held her back. She swallowed her angry retort. "Thank you, Prue."

Prudence looked back toward the house again. She seemed more nervous than before. "And there is this." She drew a small parcel wrapped in calico from the folds of her gown and extended it hesitantly toward Serena. "Open it after . . . when . . ." She blushed. "It's for the little one."

Serena's bitterness rose in her throat. What makes you think I'd accept gifts from you? But she could neither speak nor take the package. Her hands were clammy. Her knees shook, and she clung to Doctor Will's arm.

"Here," said Prudence sharply. She thrust the parcel at Serena so hard that she took it instinctively. Then she clutched Serena's free hand, pressing some coins into her palm. "It's not much," she stammered. "I don't have . . . Caleb doesn't give me . . . But it may help sometime." She whirled and ran back toward the house, her hips swaying awkwardly, her skirts tangling about her knees. The door shut silently behind her.

Serena stared after her, the muscles of her arm tense with the impulse to hurl the coins to the ground. I don't want it, she opened her mouth to say. I want nothing from you, from any of you. Not now. Not ever. But again the words stuck in her throat.

Gently, Doctor Will pried her fingers loose from the parcel, which he put in his pocket. Taking her arm, he urged her into the wagon. "Come, child," he said. "We must be going."

Serena swallowed hard. "The grave," she said faintly. "Before we go, I want to see my father's grave."

Doctor Will nodded. He clucked to the mule and they set off.

Now, AT THE GRAVESIDE, Serena unclenched her fist and looked at the coins. Her palm was scored red where their rims had dug into it. Two gold coins, a few silver. She looked back at the mound of raw, new earth and beyond it, back to Weyford. There it stood like a brightly lit miniature, the lost kingdom of her youth, tantalizingly close, heartbreakingly remote, snatched from her by her father's own hand.

She felt again his touch upon her head, heard his struggle for breath as his hoarse voice croaked, "You're a good girl." Her heart twisted within her. Tears spurted from her eyes. "Which were you, Father?" she whispered. "The man who spoke those last words, who looked his last into my face with love? Or the man who wrote that will to banish me from home forever—no, not merely to banish me but to humiliate and scorn me, to brand me always before all who heard your words? Which, Father? Which?"

From deep within her, the measured voice of reason answered her anguished plea. When Father bade me that last farewell he was ill, struck down, beside himself, dying. Did he even know who I was? Or do I but wish he did?

Only now did she let herself know how much she had hoped that Old Samuel's will would offer her reconciliation, that her departure from Wainwright House while the fire raged had not been a final parting. For a moment she bowed her head.

Then she looked up. Anger kindled her eyes. Her chin rose. Her lips set in grim lines. "When you wrote that will, Father," she said aloud, "you knew what you were doing. You were in full command that day, fully yourself, fully alive. And you cast me out on the word of a man whose evil you refused to let yourself see, all the while he persuaded you of mine. Did you need a son that badly? A man to run the works? For of course," she finished bitterly, "only a man would do."

She felt the sobs rise again in her throat. Her temples throbbed, her vision blurred. She looked a last time toward Weyford. The sunrays shattered the mirror that was the lake into shards that stabbed her tired eyes. She drew a deep breath, then another. Pain tore through her shoulder as she hurled the coins with all her strength at Samuel's grave.

"Be damned to you, then!" she cried. "Be damned to you all, every one of you. I'll not crawl to you again, begging mercy, begging forgiveness. I'll make my own way—and the child's way. Somewhere, somehow, I'll do it. I'll not look to you for help, nor for pity, nor for love. I'll look ahead, not behind. But I'll come back, Caleb Sawyer. Someday I'll come back.

And I'll destroy you somehow, if it takes the rest of my life. When next I set foot in Wainwright House, Weyford will be mine!"

Turning her back on the grave and the vista beyond it, Serena started toward the church and the waiting wagon. "Be damned to you," she muttered again. "Be damned—" She stumbled, choking on her tears. She wrapped her arms around herself and bent her head. Rent by the pain of her spirit's parturition, she shook with sobs.

Doctor Will saw her falter. He ran to her, lifted her, and carried her back to the wagon, where he laid her gently down upon some quilts. They set off on the trail away from Weyford.

C H A P T E R ❧ 2 5

"Röslein, röslein, *Röslein rot, Röslein auf der Heide.*" Still singing softly, Serena gently loosed the tiny fingers encircling her own and laid Melissa in her improvised crib. She tucked the coverlet snugly in and arranged the crude hangings to fend off the creeping chill. She lingered for a moment, stroking the tiny head, smoothing the silky black hair already curling about Melissa's ears.

For an instant the baby opened her amber eyes, fringed with thick black lashes, and gazed up at Serena. Two lines sprang up between her brows in a frown that was twin to Stuart Brandon's. Then her face relaxed. She gave a faint sigh and settled into sleep. Her fists were curled beside her head, her eyes squeezed tightly shut, as though sleeping were work and she determined to do it properly.

Still bending to avoid the sloping rafters, Serena backed quietly away. When she could stand at her full height she tiptoed along the bare, creaking boards to the window at one end of the garret. "Come, Mitzi," she whispered to the little calico cat who pattered along beside her, rubbing against her cold ankles. As Serena settled in the rocker by the window, Mitzi sprang lightly onto her lap and began her ritual of tamping and purring, purring and circling, until she curled into a tight fur ball wrapped by a tail that flicked gently, gently, against Serena's hand.

Doctor Will himself had brought the rocker up to the garret. "Rockers go with babies," he had said, his high forehead creased with kindly concern. "This was my mother's—her one bit of good furniture." The rocker was simple enough, of hickory and oak with ladder back and rush seat. Now, as in those long months when she had been awaiting Melissa's birth, Serena found comfort in its motion. To and fro, to and fro. Rest . . . don't think now . . . don't feel . . . just rest and wait.

She buried her fingers in the white softness of Mitzi's frill, absently

stroking the velvet paws, the silky tail. The little cat had befriended her
from the first, easing the ache of loneliness as its warm body now eased
the chill of the garret, the melancholy of the waning light.

The windowpane was smudged with the tears of the dying year, some
liquid, some frozen. They slithered down the glass in erratic trails, meeting and merging, parting and rejoining. Like lives, thought Serena. Like
my life and Stuart Brandon's. We met, we parted, and the rejoining is
that small life in the crib there. Melissa is all that is left to me of that
meeting, that passionate joining that changed my life. And his? Did it not
change his? Would he have come back to me? Now I will never know.

She sighed. Her breath fogged the cold pane, and idly she traced
designs upon the glass. The curlicued "W" of Weyford. An "S." A "B."
Impatient with herself, she swept the letters away with her palm, wiping
off the moisture on the coarse fabric of her apron. The abrupt motion
disturbed Mitzi, who stretched and dug her claws into Serena's sleeve
before settling down again.

"Why can't I forget him?" Serena whispered. "Why, Mitzi? Why?"
And why can I not shake off this mood, as disconsolate as the rain and
sleet, as bleak as the wintry fields? I should go downstairs, help Charity
brew the infusions, do about the kitchen, anything to be in motion. She
rocked on, contemplating the ebbing of the day.

Already the garret was in shadow except for the pale smear of light
from the window at the farther end. Bunches of herbs hung to dry —
mint, yarrow, chamomile — and strings of onions swayed in the draft.
Baskets of roots became eerie shadows under the slanting rafters. Even
in the chill, the air was freighted with a medley of scents, some sweet,
some pungent, some faintly musky or overlaid with mold, mingling with
the cedar of the shingles on the roof. In the summer the scents had
been overpowering, thickening the air heated all day by the blazing sun
until it seemed she could not draw it into her lungs.

Now sleet was slapping the roof and Serena's breath showed faintly
on the air. She leaned forward, calming Mitzi with one hand, to look out
across the raw shingles on the newly built ell below. The field she had
stumbled across so many months ago lay deserted, the grasses bleached
by last week's frost. The little stand of sassafras was denuded, its splendid
cloak of pinks and reds, purples and golds flung carelessly down to lie
sodden and faded upon the earth. She could not look at that stand of
trees without shuddering. Now they were blurred by descending darkness
and her own tears.

To and fro she rocked, seized by the pain of loss. Mother. Father.
Weyford. The girl I was, the freedom I had not recognized as such: free-

dom to roam the Barrens, to learn the secrets of that brooding vastness on whose fringes I now must live, cut off from its moods and seasons. And Stuart Brandon—always Stuart Brandon.

She remembered one morning when they had lain together, warm and replete with the aftermath of passion. His habitual reticence had dropped from him like a cloak unneeded in the warmth of her presence. He had told her, then, something of himself as a child, solitary and shunted aside by a mother humiliated by his mere existence, thrown upon the mercies of servants, many indifferent, a few kindly, a few cruel.

He had feared the dark stairwell leading down to the cellars with the unreasoning fear of a small boy before terrors inexplicable to adults, sure that something—a ghastly something—lurked waiting for him at the curve of that stair. "She sent me down there—my mother," he told Serena. "She told me there was nothing to fear, and that I must 'be a little man' and prove this to myself, lest I grow up not merely a bastard but a coward into the bargain. Her maid—Charlotte—was in league with her. And when I reached the curve of the staircase—the darkest place, the place I most feared—Charlotte sprang from the shadows, shrieking, and blew my candle out. I can remember it still—my pounding heart, her bony fingers clutching my shoulder, her cackle and my scream echoing from the stone walls. That—and my mother's laughter."

Serena had seen the muscles jumping at the corners of his clenched jaw. She felt his body shaking with anger on behalf of that betrayed small boy. And she sensed, without words to shape the thought, that the boy still dwelt within the armour of irony affected by the man at her side.

Was that the bond between us? she asked herself now. Those glimpses, small and few, of his struggles and his pain? Could it be that he cast me aside because I pried into his secrets and could see what he sought to hide? But I could have sworn it was for this he came to love me—I *know* he loved me. Or do I? Did I see only what I chose to see, and love him because I could talk to him as I could to no one before, as I can talk to no one now? Of my love for the making of iron, and for the sea . . . and of my yearning for the wide world beyond the Barrens that he knew and I did not?

She forced herself to sit up, gently to put the little cat down, to rise and walk toward the stairway. By Melissa's crib she paused. The infant stirred, uttered the softest of sounds, then went on with the business of sleeping. "You don't know," said Serena softly, "what having you has cost me. And I swear by all that's dearest to me that I'll do everything in my power to see that you never know—that you grow up to laugh and to learn, to be free in a way I could not." But how? How?

Serena started down the stairs, looking back to where the rocker still swayed gently to and fro. How fortunate I have been withall, she thought, to have found such kind people, to have stumbled blindly to the one place, perhaps, where Melissa could safely stay with me.

"Serena! Will be wantin' you."

"I'm just coming down." Serena ran down the last of the stairs with all her old accustomed grace. Mitzi scampered at her heels. She shook her head to break loose from memory's clinging strands. That moment when I stood at Father's grave, that painful expulsion from the womb of childhood, was the real moment of birth: that moment when I stopped believing that Mother and Father would make the world right for me. The birth of Melissa, asleep now in the garret behind her, seemed by comparison a half-forgotten dream.

ᴥ   ᴥ   ᴥ

DOCTOR WILL beckoned to her from the passage to the newly constructed ell. His face was lit by the grave smile that Serena had come to love. The door, hitherto locked, stood ajar. Curious, Serena tried to see past Doctor Will's tall form. For some months now, the ell had been forbidden territory. Doctor Will nodded. "Go ahead, child. Now you may enter." He stood aside to let Serena precede him into the short hall.

The wide boards had been painted and a small braided rug put down. Entering the large room to her left, Serena gasped with surprise and appreciation. "I didn't realize how large it was!" Mitzi slipped ahead of her and began inspecting the new territory, sniffing at corners, slipping behind crates.

Open shelves lined the walls. Crockery jars and corked bottles of green-blue glass ranged along them, some full, some waiting to be filled. From the beamed ceiling hung bunches of herbs like those in the garret. Pegs had been installed for the hanging of many more. Tucked under some waist-high ledges were baskets of wild cherry bark and sassafras root. Here, too, there was space for many additions. The floor was scrubbed brick.

At the far end of the room stood an Atsion stove, its square cast-iron sides shining with blacking, the slits in its door revealing the cheerful fire within. Open kettles, one steaming, stood upon it. Mitzi, done with her inspection, curled up on a rag rug near its warmth.

Serena moved lightly about the room, touching now this, now that. Paddles for stirring, funnels for infusions, pottery bowls large and small. Several mortars and pestles. And, on a small shelf above the work space near the dry sink, *The Herbalist* and some books of formulae.

"Oh, Doctor Will, working here will be a joy. So much space. And—oh look!" she cried, as though he, too, were seeing this for the first time, "Water laid on!" The builder had contrived a system by which water pumped into a cistern might be drawn as needed into the wooden sink.

Amused, Doctor Will watched as Serena made another circuit of the room, exclaiming upon this or that. "Very well," he said. "But this is the workroom. There is yet more for you to see."

Looking back over her shoulder as though she could hardly bear to leave, Serena followed him out into the passage and through the door at its end. This time she said nothing. Instead, she reached out and took her mentor's hand.

Her new quarters had windows on three sides, their crane-berry-dyed curtains drawn now against the deepening dusk. Between two windows at the far end was a fireplace; here, too, glowing logs brought warmth and light. A comfortable bed heaped with quilts . . . a chest of drawers. Near the fireplace, on an oval rug, stood a cradle. "There is a place there for your rocker," said Doctor Will, nodding toward the cozy spot.

Serena stood rooted to her place, tears in her eyes. "How did you do all this without my knowing?"

"Oh, we have our ways. Babies take time and attention." Doctor Will chuckled, then peered at her more closely. "No tears, now, Serena. You will need clear eyes—come, look at this."

At the window opposite the bedstead stood a writing table, clearly new. The precisely turned legs, brass drawer pulls, and satin finish bespoke the work of a master cabinetmaker. "This looks like the work of Master Randolph," said Serena. "But how—?" She paused, not wishing to insult Doctor Will by asking how he could afford such a treasure.

"I have made some calls at Speedwell from time to time," said Doctor Will. "And Benjamin Randolph, like everyone else in these times, has recourse to barter." With the Continental currency more a subject of jest than a medium of exchange, and gold and silver coin daily more scarce, Doctor Will had indeed been paid in odder currency than this desk: a brace of fowl, baskets of sassafras root, even a porcelain chamber pot.

Thinking of the hours of work, the solitary journeys through wild terrain, the writing table represented, Serena could find no words. "I can't accept this—"

"You shall take it," Doctor Will interrupted. "You will have ample opportunity to earn it. Look at these." He went to the desk and picked up some books, handing them to Serena. Her wrists sagged with the weight of them.

Serena held the books near the brass lamp to read their titles. John Wesley's *Primitive Physick*. A treatise by Benjamin Rush on the care of wounds and camp diseases. Culpeper's *English Physician*. A translation from the French of the work of Ambroise Paré. Pamphlets and herbals. She looked up at Doctor Will in surprise.

"These are your textbooks?"

"Yes."

"You wish that I study them?"

"I do indeed." He motioned her to sit in the desk chair and pulled up a stool for himself. "I have watched you, Serena. You have a good mind and a keen eye. You've a talent for the work of healing. Neither you nor I can ever be licensed physicians—you, because you are a woman; I, because I am black. But we can help. We can heal. At least, until they stop us."

"Stop us? Who? How?"

"So long as I confined my work to the Barrens and to the poor, to places where few physicians care to go, they took no notice of me. And then, the War has preoccupied not a few of them. I have never presented myself as a physician, nor as a surgeon, never asked a fee—only payment for my herbals. I have not run afoul of the Act." An "Act to Regulate the Practice of Physick and Surgery" had been passed by the colonial legislature in 1772. "But who knows? My work has attracted attention. It has brought me a comfortable living. Attention and money draw envy. We shall see."

Doctor Will looked up from his musings into Serena's worried face. He forced a laugh. "Do not fret, child. What lies in the future—who can say? For the present, read the books. Study them. With some of what you read, you will agree. With some, you may differ. As you know, I do not hold with bleeding, with blistering, or with any reputed cures that do harm in themselves. Others use them freely. So, read and learn. Observe those who use my remedies. Think about what they need and what I do for them—and what God and their own bodies do to cure them. You will be of great help to me. You already have been."

"And Charity?"

"Charity is both kind and wise. But she will not be with me always—surely you've seen she has a suitor? And learning of this nature does not interest her. Perhaps you did not know, but Charity cannot read."

"Nor did I know. Not read—and she your sister?"

"By the time Charity was born, I was near to leaving home. My father"—Doctor Will paused—"Father was a great believer in the Bible. In one verse of the Bible, the verse that reads 'He that spareth his rod hateth his son: but he that loveth him chasteneth him betimes.' By his lights, Father loved me dearly. By mine—well, I left home at the earliest opportunity."

"To go where?"

"Many places, some good, some bad. But in time, with the help of a kind clergyman, I learned to read. And from the time I was small, I had been intent upon learning medicine. I would innoculate my playmates with glass and spittle. And bring fallen nestlings home. I was a man grown before it was brought home to me that men of my colour do not become physicians." He forbore to say how it had been brought home.

Serena studied the kindly face with its aureole of white hair. "And these books?"

"I earned them. With heavy labour and small errands. I have taken my turn at an iron furnace, pushing the ore barrows. And at cutting cordwood, and hauling it, too. And when spare coppers came into my hands, I put them aside until I could get to Philadelphia by whatever means, walking, working my passage on Samuel Cooper's ferry. And there, in a shop on Market Street, a kind Quaker gentleman helped me choose my books. In time, I puzzled out the terms. The Pineys, and some of the Lenape at Brotherton Mission, taught me about herbs and simples. I have learned from many people: from my patients, and from the evidence of my own eyes. And now"—Doctor Will forced his gaze back to the present; he smiled at Serena—"they call me the Black Doctor. And the Lord helps me heal them. Shall you help me, too?"

I asked how to help myself, how to earn my way, thought Serena. This is my answer. "Yes, Doctor Will. I will study. I will learn. And I will help you." They clasped hands.

CHAPTER ✣ 2 6

"I DON'T BELIEVE IT. It makes no sense!" Serena's vehemence startled Melissa in her crib. Her words pursued one another through the stillness of the firelit room. On the writing table, lamplight fell on the open book. A detailed engraving of the veins of the human body, indicating which to puncture to what purpose, lay exposed. With Latinate pomposity the text extolled the theory that "humours," the cause of every ailment known to humankind, must be purged from the body by bleeding, and by "puke and physick."

"Pah!" said Serena. Startled, Mitzi catapulted from her lap and slid to the floor in a scrabble of claws. "It makes no sense," Serena repeated more quietly, rubbing her thigh where Mitzi's claws had dug into her flesh. "Bleed this vein for one 'humour,' that vein for another. Here lancets, there leeches. And purge the patient with salts and senna all the while. When men bleed in battle they sicken and die. Why then drain the blood from sick people? Don't physicians ever look at patients' faces?"

She slammed the book shut with a force that raised dust from the pages, then, repentant, gently smoothed it, knowing how Doctor Will treasured his texts, however he might contest some of their contents. The sound woke Melissa in earnest, and she began to wail.

Serena went to the cradle and set it to rocking. How big Melissa was getting. Soon this cradle would be too small. She knelt beside it, laughing a little at her own ill humour, chanting to a tune of her own: "They never look, never look, never look. Do they? Do they? Do they?" With each repetition she butted her head gently into Melissa's plump stomach. The baby chortled and laughed, pleased with this new game. Then she remembered her earlier grievance. She was hungry. Her lower lip trembled. Tears began again.

Serena set about changing the baby's wet garments, then sat down in the rocker and opened her bodice. Melissa nursed contentedly, pausing from time to time to make soft cooing sounds. Absently, Serena smiled down at her and guided the small pink mouth back to the nipple.

The faces, she mused. The faces of the well, the sick, the dying. How much they have taught me in the few months since Doctor Will and I embarked upon this collaboration! As his reputation spread, more sufferers had crowded the little parlour, waiting—some patient, some peevish—for him to return from his calls. No doctor's shingle marked the narrow house on its hill, set apart still from Lumberton village. But people found it anyway.

Now that spring had come there were fewer coughs and wheezes. But the pace did not slacken. Soon there would be the fevers of summer, the infants with bloody flux, ironworkers overcome by heat, women with swollen, painful feet, dropsical with pregnancy.

The faces tell so much, thought Serena. The drawn, enduring look of women aged before their time by work and childbirth, their faces eroded by tears and furrowed by pain, their mouths toothless and sunken more often than not. The shadowed look of fatigue about the eyes that marks the chronically ill . . . the gaunt look of the cancerous . . . the blackness of pupils stretched wide by pain . . . the pinched look about the nose that heralds death . . . and, worst of all, the pathetic, hopeless gaze of dying children.

And the bodies, too, have their tales to tell: The rigid contortion of muscles braced to meet pain . . . the eloquent curve of arms wrapped about an aching belly, containing the agony within . . . the shuffle of infirmity . . . the twisted limbs of the rheumatic . . . the moist bloom of healthy skin and the flaccid pallor of the dying.

As if by instinct—but in truth, she knew, in response to those myriad signs he seemed to absorb through the tips of his sensitive fingers— Doctor Will diagnosed and suggested, always with humility, with caution and care, with knowledge that the body itself was his best ally, if he could but understand its message. No dosing with senna for a body already weakened. No blistering except, from time to time, a chest plaster for a patient with a cough. And no bleeding.

I agree with Doctor Will, thought Serena. It makes no sense. And yet there are patients who feel cheated: patients who expect "puke and physick" to be part of their cure. And it is those patients who seldom respond to the gentler measures Doctor Will prescribes for them.

"Finished, little one?" Serena asked her daughter. Melissa smiled, crowed, and grabbed a strand of Serena's hair. "Ow! Aren't we lively for this time of night!" Serena perched Melissa on her knee and began to jog her gently. *"Hop! Hop! Hop! Pferdchen geht gallop!"* Playing with Melissa in the moments she could spare from work and study had brought back Serena's German, the verses and stories dimly recalled from long ago.

Someone tapped softly on the door. Then Charity came in.

"My, she be gettin' big!"

"Oh, yes! Look!" Serena offered the baby her fingers. Melissa pulled herself up, bouncing on sturdy legs and laughing.

"That dress soon be too small for her."

"Yes . . ." Serena's face clouded. Some time after Melissa's birth, Doctor Will had given her Prue's parcel. It contained a tiny dress of soft linen, daintily embroidered with flowers and love knots, trimmed with ribbon and edged with lace.

"Could be this a new one." Charity held up a package. "A boy brought it — just left it and ran away."

Serena held up one hand to fend the package off. "You open it."

Charity's strong fingers worked at the knots. The wrapping fell away. She held up a nightgown and cap of finest nainsook. "Look now — that be pretty!" Charity searched through the wrappings, but there was no card. None was needed. Both women knew whence the garments had come.

"Serena," began Charity, ignoring the stony look, "your sister must be lovin' you some — else why she be makin' these baby clothes?"

Serena did not reply. She looked down at the child in her lap. Melissa squirmed, perhaps feeling tension in her mother's grasp. Mechanically, Serena rose and put the baby back in her cradle, handing her a favourite toy. The bunch of wooden rings on a wooden hoop had been made by Expectation Jones, the carpenter who had built the ell.

"Then why you be keepin' the things, lettin' 'Lissa wear them?"

Again, Serena gave no answer. Instead, she bent over the writing table, her back to Charity, affecting to fiddle with the lamp. The flame sputtered as a single teardrop struck it, then another. Still Serena did not turn. She leaned forward, arms braced on the table edge, head bowed.

Charity sat down heavily on the chair by the bed, legs spread, hands on her plump knees. Her soft brown eyes misted with concern. This was no time to tell Serena her news. And yet, she must be told soon.

"You still be wantin' to go back? That be it?" Charity asked softly.

No answer.

"You been't happy here? We s'posed you were, Will and me."

Serena swallowed. Charity and Doctor Will have been kindness itself, she thought. They have offered me a haven, a way of life, a way of earning a living. How can I tell Charity how I feel when I don't know myself? How can I speak of the lonely nights when I know my body awake and clamourous, when I remember each word, each touch, of those hours with Stuart Brandon that will never come again?

How can I tell these people who have made a home for me, sacrificed their comfort for mine — for I know well what this room has cost them in comforts of their own — that I'm sick with longing for Weyford, for the breeze riffling the leaves of the sycamore outside my window, for the smell of pine, the soft splash of a heron wading in the lake, the excitement of a blowout, the sense of distance and trails yet unexplored? How can I say I feel caged, pent, smothered by this life that holds the only hope I can see for myself and Melissa? That I am desperately lonely for someone to talk with about what still means most to me — the making of iron? How can I say that I feel my life is over when it had barely begun? Can I tell Charity that these parcels from Prudence — tempted though I am to send the garments back in shreds — are yet a link, a tie, a sign that Weyford is still there, waiting for me, for the day when I find a way to return to it, the day I am its mistress?

I have never spoken of Stuart Brandon, not to anyone. Nor of Weyford and what its loss has meant to me. Doctor Will has some suspicion, some glimpse. But no one else . . . no one.

Serena's heart was thumping wildly, as though pounding on the walls of the body that contained it, seeking release of its pent-up grief. And suddenly she could contain it no longer. She looked at Charity. The black woman sat stolidly, watching her turmoil with quiet compassion. Now the dark eyes looked straight into Serena's. Charity held out her arms. "Come. Be tellin' me," she said.

Serena flung herself to her knees, burying her head in Charity's lap. Charity stroked her hair. "Let it out . . . Let it out." Serena's tears came in torrents, bursting the dam erected by her pride, shaking both their bodies as the two women clung together, tears and more tears, flowing and streaming, laving her bruised spirit, bringing release.

❧　❧　❧

FAR INTO THE NIGHT, Charity listened as Serena talked and talked, pausing to tend to Melissa's needs, then resuming her tale. She herself said little.

She don't be needin' me to butt in. She be needin' me to listen. Only once did she interrupt, when Serena recounted how she had heard of her unnamed lover's death.

"You sure he be dead? That Caleb person—he be a liar, you said so yourself. And so's your sister—sometimes anyways." Serena was silent for a moment or two, her clasped hands wrestling each other as she fought the battle within. "Yes," she said at last. "I'm sure. Caleb was so vicious in his satisfaction as he told me."

Caleb might not be knowin' for sure himself, thought Charity. But she said nothing. Suppose the man be alive? What good be he to Serena?

As though reading Charity's thought, Serena said bitterly, "What hope have I of him, alive or dead? Oh, yes, in my desperation I thought to go to him. But I've thought often since what a fool I was. Was he to welcome news of another bastard? He more than likely has one at every port of call."

And yet . . . and yet . . . How could he see Melissa and not love her? She's so like him. So like him I cannot look at her without remembering. "He's dead," she insisted as though to assure herself. "I know he's dead." She quelled the stubborn hope that she was mistaken.

For a moment the two women sat silent. Then Serena lifted her head and gazed unseeingly across the room. "And then I left Weyford," she said, wanting to conclude her tale now that she had begun it. "It was during the fire . . ."

At last the tale was done. Drained by the telling, Serena sat motionless while Charity renewed the fire and brewed some chamomile tea, going to the workroom for honey and ginger to stir into it. "Drink this," she said. Serena took the mug, wrapped in a linen towel, and began to sip. "I'll look after the baby," said Charity. "Good that it be Sunday—no patients likely to be wantin' you. Rest. Sleep a while. You'll feel better now, now that you've let it out. But before you be goin'—she came to stand before Serena, hands clasped before her, smiling shyly—"let me be tellin' you *my* news: I'm goin' to be married. Maybe have one of those"—she nodded toward the sleeping infant—"for my own self."

"Oh, Charity!" Tired as she was, Serena responded to the glow in her friend's face. "Is it—of course, it must be—Expectation Jones. The man who built the ell?"

Charity nodded. "Not much of a secret, I guess. Will, he been teasin' me for months now. Yes. It be 'Tate."

"I am glad for you, Charity. He is a skilled man—a good man, I'm sure." Serena concealed a flash of amusement at the thought of buxom Charity sharing the pleasures of intimacy with the wiry, taciturn carpenter. "Will you be living here?"

"Oh, no. I be leavin' Will to you. We find you a girl to do the chores, and you tend the medicine makin'. 'Tate has found a good place—work that's like to last for years."

"Here in Lumberton?"

"No. But near enough. You be hearing about the doin's of that Yankee newcomer Jonas? He be buildin' a flock of works—settin' up his own town, they say. 'Tate and me, we be movin' to Jonasville."

Serena reached out and squeezed her friend's hand. "I'll miss you, Charity," she said.

C H A P T E R 　 ❧ 　 2 7

"COME, MY GOOD DOCTOR. You must let me compensate you for your services."

"Thank you, sir, but no. I am not a physician."

"But I insist." Fishing about in a bulging purse, the stranger extracted a gold piece and extended it to Doctor Will. "Please, let me express my gratitude."

Serena paused by the doorway, behind the "Master Smythe" whom neither she nor the Black Doctor had seen before. Though surely, she thought, there is that about the cast of those shoulders that is familiar. And that blond, greying hair, lying in a queue on the fine black broadcloth coat, that too I feel I have seen before. Her eyes flashed the warning: Don't trust this man.

Doctor Will's expression did not change. Only Serena could detect that he acknowledged her signal: acknowledged it and concurred. "You are kind, sir, and I thank you—but no. If you wish to purchase some simples, very well. But I charge no fee for the knowledge the good Lord imparts to me. And as I said, I am not a physician."

Reluctantly, the stranger returned the coin to the fine leather purse in his manicured hand. Even in the dim light of the antechamber, the sumptuousness of his garments was apparent: the velvet trim, the silver buttons on his waistcoat, the good cordovan leather of his carriage boots. "Very well, then," he said, a trace of petulance in the high-pitched voice, "let me purchase a stock of what you recommend."

"Mistress Wainwright"—before patients and strangers Doctor Will was unfailingly formal—"fetch some flasks of my tonic." Passing Doctor Will on her way to the workroom, her head turned away from the stranger, Serena answered Will's quizzical smile with one of her own. The tonic—a mixture of hard cider, honey, juniper berries, garlic, and some precious grains of cayenne—was Doctor Will's standby for ailments he suspected to be spurious. "It cannot hurt and may help," he had explained to her. "The taste is just good enough to make it palatable—and bad enough to make it creditable."

Returning with her arms full of flasks, Serena drew back, startled. Smythe stood in the doorway of the workroom, contemptuous of Doctor Will's silent disapproval. Not for this man the respectful timidity that held most patients back from exploring the workroom's mysteries. The cold blue eyes deep-set beneath the high, narrow forehead darted everywhere, noting the shelves, the utensils, the work spread out upon the counter. The narrow nostrils of the high, beaked nose twitched, appraising the mingled scents of herb and spice and steam.

The man stepped back to let Serena pass. She felt the chill of his glance striking her flesh as he peered down the neckline of her simple blue gingham gown. Serena set the flasks upon a table near the door and retreated toward the kitchen.

"These should serve you for several months," said Doctor Will. "Take two spoonfuls in some hot water on arising: You will find it clears both the head and the bowels." He smiled faintly. "I can discern nothing amiss to account for the difficulties you have recounted, but I have found this tonic helpful to many with your complaints."

Smythe went to the front door and signalled. A short, dour servant entered, collected the flasks at Smythe's gesture, and departed without a word.

"Now"—Smythe drew out his purse again—"how much?"

"A shilling a flask—if you can spare it."

The thin lips curled in a narrow smile. "A bargain, to be sure, for a remedy of such powers." Smythe flung some coins upon the table and was gone before Doctor Will could reply.

When Serena came back into the room, the Black Doctor was staring blankly at his palm. "Look!" He showed her the gold coins. "Far too much." He went to the front door and looked out, but the stranger's coach was gone.

"What do you make of this, Serena?"

"Nothing that bodes well for us. His coming here at all is strange enough." Both of them knew that a man of such apparent wealth was unlikely to come calling. Such men did not seek help; they summoned it.

"Yes," mused Doctor Will. "And 'Smythe'? That is not a Lumberton name. Perhaps there are Smythes in Mount Holly of whom I do not know. But, Serena, I can affirm that 'Master Smythe' was not ill. He spoke of 'lassitude and debility.' But his colour was good. His strength was not impaired. And his eyes were bright and alert."

"Too alert. I'll swear he read the label on every flask. Well—" Serena turned. "I've work to do to prepare for tonight. We may know soon enough what he intends."

"And I've calls to make. Master Pettigru is laid up again with gout."

"Wear your shawl, Doctor Will—please." For all its blue sky and brilliant sunshine, the October day was chill.

ða   ða   ða

THADDEUS PETTIGRU winced as Doctor Will gently palpated his gouty toe. "Have a care, man." The foot resting on the velvet stool was swollen, the great toe a shiny, angry red and twice its normal size.

"I've something new for you to try," said Doctor Will. He poured from an earthenware jug into one of the lawyer's crystal goblets. "Look." Doctor Will held the goblet up to the firelight. The liquid within it glowed ruby red, clear and vibrant. "An infusion of crane-berries. We gathered a fine crop from the marshes this autumn. They grow in Massachusetts, too, you know, and a colleague from Boston writes me that his patients with gout have been much relieved by this liquid."

"Give it here, then. I've a mind to try almost anything." Pettigru winced again as he leaned forward to take the goblet. He sipped, grimaced, and sputtered. "So beautiful to look at, so sour on the tongue, Will! Like some women, what?" He pursed his lips, then swallowed the draught in three gulps. "Better than leeches, I suppose."

"You might try eating less meat and drinking less wine."

"I might. But then again I might not. How much of your brew must I swallow? And what do I owe you for it?"

Doctor Will explained the course of treatment. "As for what you owe me—I'll count it paid if you will render me some advice."

"Done. That is"—the jowly face with its fringe of curls grew shrewd; the small blue eyes peered sharply up at the Black Doctor—"if I need not be too long about the law books."

"I think you need not. Tell me: Do you think me in danger of being charged with impersonating a physician?"

Pettigru leaned forward, eyeing the other man more intently. "Has someone threatened you?"

"No—no, I merely wish to be informed."

The lawyer looked dubious. "If someone is threatening you, it's best I be forewarned." It was less a statement than a question.

"There have been no threats," said Doctor Will, suppressing his uneasiness about "Master Smythe" and his possible intentions.

Pettigru rubbed his chin and gazed into the fire. "To be honest, Will, I cannot speak with any assurance. While this war continues—who knows what's law? British law? Colonial law? If we win, will the acts of the colonial legislature be honoured? If the British win—curse them, they still might—who knows what edicts will fall upon us? We who've supported the Patriot cause will have more to worry about than suits for malpractice. It will be our necks they're after—not you, Will, but me and many others. Until we know the outcome of this struggle, who can say what the law is? And who will care?"

That is what I wonder, thought Doctor Will. Who might care enough to send a spy to my home? "But under the 1772 Act? What is my position?"

"You don't call yourself a physician? Oh, I know well the title by which others speak of you. But you yourself?"

"Oh, no. I am not a physician and would not call myself one."

"And you do not charge for your examinations, or your calls?"

"Never. Only for the tonics, the simples, any herbs or salves I may use. And then only what the patient wishes to pay."

Pettigru pondered. "I will read the Act again, Will. But I am certain you are safe—not from persecution, perhaps, if some of the resident pomposities in Mount Holly or Burlington take umbrage at your treatments being more effective than theirs. But safe from prosecution probably. And certainly from conviction in any court that gives you a fair hearing. More than that I cannot say for now."

Doctor Will nodded thoughtfully. "I shall take my chances," he said.

◆　◆　◆

SERENA BUSTLED ABOUT the kitchen, beating and stirring, testing the heat in the hearth's cast-iron oven. Eggs, whipped to a froth. Butter newly churned. Sugar—a precious loaf, that. She hummed a little tune of her own making, laughing at Melissa, who sat watching on Clara's knee. "An egg . . . and two . . . and three. Butter for you and me . . . Sugar for my sweet . . . Molasses . . . there's a treat." Melissa, her black curls a tangle, her amber eyes alight, laughed back.

Serena handed Clara a wooden spoon for Melissa to lick. "How wise of you, Melissa, not to have waited for November to be born. Look at that sunshine!" The blue of the October sky filled the kitchen windows; the colours of the distant trees cast a glow on the whitewashed walls. "Done!" Serena poured the cake batter into the pans, tested the oven one last time, and thrust the pans inside. "Now we wait." She paused.

"Did you hear that, Clara? There is someone about the parlour. Tend the fire for me, please."

Wiping her hands on her apron, Serena entered the parlor. Poised in the centre of the room as though on tiptoe, an air about him that curiously mingled diffidence and command, was a man she had not seen before.

"Were you seeking Doctor Will, sir? He is making calls today." This was the second visitor of the day apparently oblivious to the Black Doctor's schedule. With so many coming to the house, he had found it best to set Mondays and Fridays as his days for making outside calls—except, of course, for those cries for help that admitted of no delay. His regular patients knew this, and did not come on those days.

"My apologies. I was in the vicinity and thought to— Well, no matter. You are Mistress Wainwright?"

"Yes. You have the advantage of me, sir. May I ask your name?"

"Bless me. Here is one person who does not know me by sight! I am Hiram Jonas . . . of Jonasville."

"Oh." For all that she seldom ventured into town, preferring to avoid the curious stares that singed her flesh, Serena was well aware that Hiram Jonas and his doings had been the talk of the town since long before Charity and 'Tate had departed for Jonasville. The newcomer—a Yankee, it was said, and a shrewd one—had purchased a defunct sawmill and a vast acreage surrounding it. Tales of what was abuilding there had preoccupied village gossips for months.

He's scarcely as fearsome as he's been painted, thought Serena. Rotund, balding, no taller than she, he stood lightly on the balls of his surprisingly small feet, hands clasped behind him, returning her scrutiny look for look. Hair almost white, in a tousled fringe around his pate. A forehead scarcely wrinkled, broad and high. Plump cheeks, pursed lips, a cherubic look about the face belied by the bristling eyebrows over wide blue eyes that missed nothing of her face or figure. He was dressed in black— breeches, waistcoat, gaiters—all of finest worsted, innocent of trim. His tucked white linen shirt was mussed, its frill slightly stained.

He smiled, laugh lines fanning out from the corners of his eyes. "Do I warrant such scrutiny, Madame?"

Serena blushed. I *have* been staring rudely. But then, so has he.

Before either could speak, a commotion arose behind them. Melissa, wobbling on unsteady legs, toddled into the room, Clara in pursuit. Jonas saw her first. "What have we here—a runaway?"

He has a warm smile, thought Serena. "Melissa!" She took her daughter in her arms. "You know you are not permitted in here!" Sensing disapproval, Melissa put her fingers in her mouth and gazed at her mother wide-eyed.

Jonas laughed. He leaned over and extended his hand. "How do you do, Mistress Melissa?" The child took a finger in both of her hands and shook it vigorously. "A little beauty," said Jonas. Freeing his hand, he straightened. "And her mother's daughter, for all she has hair as black as night." He opened his mouth, then closed it tightly, perhaps thinking better of some question that might prove embarrassing. His eyes narrowed. He regarded Serena shrewdly for a moment. "How old is she?"

"A year old today."

"A birthday child! Well, well—so important an event deserves commemoration." Jonas dug into the pocket of his waistcoat and extracted a shiny silver coin. He extended it to Melissa, who grabbed it and put it into her mouth. "That's right. Bite it. See that it's a sound one, mind!"

Serena laughed with Jonas, then handed her daughter back to Clara. Her brow creased with annoyance. Charity, she thought, would never have let Melissa escape her like that. This woman does her tasks so grudgingly; she brings nothing of herself to her work. How I miss Charity and the good cheer she brought to every undertaking.

"If you want to see Doctor Will," she said to Jonas, "you had best come back another day. He seldom returns from his calls before nightfall." Why is he staring at me again? He seems so bouncing and good-hearted, and so friendly to Melissa. Why then does he make me uneasy? "Unless I can be of assistance to you?"

To her surprise, Jonas flushed. "You are kind—but no," he said after a pause. "I wish to consult Master Pond upon a private matter. I shall return another day."

"He makes calls on Mondays and Fridays. On other days he is generally here—unless, of course, he's needed urgently."

Hiram Jonas bowed slightly, acknowledging the information, then turned and bounded lightly toward the door. "Good day, Mistress Wainwright," he said. "I shall be seeing you again."

Serena stood for a moment, looking after him. Then the odour of burning molasses sent her down the kitchen passage at a run.

❧　❧　❧

"Oh, 'tate—it's beautiful! That cunning tray! I've not seen another like it. Let's set her in it right now!" The high chair was made of smoothly sanded pine, its legs and the rungs that braced them decoratively turned,

the high back carved with the image of a kitten. A tray fastened with
pegged dowels that allowed it to be lifted made the chair complete. The
wood had been stained dark and varnished.

Charity held the tray up while Serena hoisted Melissa into her new
perch. Expectation Jones stood by, smiling slightly, silent as usual.

For this occasion, Serena had put on a gown of peach-coloured silk. It
lent a glow to her complexion as the lamplight shone on her bronze hair,
freed this night from the braided coil in which she now habitually wore
it. Eyes thoughtful, she looked around at the faces of these kind friends.
Can it really be a year?

The gate-leg table, both its leaves raised, was spread with an embroidered cloth and set for four. At the centre stood Serena's cake, rich with
raisins and dried apples, a bit lopsided but festive for all that. Some
parcels were heaped beside it. Charity started to add another, then
hesitated, looking at Serena. "Can she open it now?"

"Can't you wait?"

"Not another minute." Charity laughed. The baby twisted and turned
the parcel in her hands, pulling at the cloth wrappings. "Here, let me."
Lower lip wobbling, Melissa watched doubtfully as Charity took the
parcel back and unwrapped it. "There!" A silver spoon emerged. The
baby snatched at it and began banging it on the tray, chortling wildly.

"Well!" said Serena. "Your gift is a success." She put her arms around
her friend. "The chair would have been quite enough. Thank you,
Charity—'Tate, too. Thank you."

"Master Jonas been openin' a store for us workers. He be givin' us a
special price when I said it's for you. Now! What's in the other parcels?"

"One is a scarf I've made. The other . . ." Serena's voice trailed off.

"Be it from *them?*"

"Yes."

"Want me to open it? Or should we be waitin' for Will?"

"He sent word he'd be late. When he comes in, he'll be wanting his
supper."

"Let me open it, then. See, 'Lissa? For you, birthday child." Charity
shook the package in front of the baby, who looked up for a minute,
dropping the spoon. 'Tate retrieved it from the floor, and she resumed
her banging. "Oh, look!" Charity shook out a dress of ivory batiste, tucked
and smocked, the skirt embroidered with M's intertwined. "Your sister,
she worked hours on this," said Charity, fingering the delicate folds.
"Should I be puttin' it on her?"

"Go ahead," motioned Serena, her thoughts far away. Prue knows the baby's name. And her size — when she's no child of her own from which to guess it. How closely are they watching me, those at Weyford? And why?

The sound of the front door opening interrupted her musings. Doctor Will came into the kitchen, still wearing his shawl. There was a strange look on his face, at once joyous and solemn. "I've news," he said. "Lord Cornwallis has surrendered at Yorktown. The War is almost over."

Before they could take this in, he turned to Serena. "I've other news, too. Joe Mulliner has been captured and tried. He's to be hanged at Woodlington, Saturday next."

CHAPTER ✿ 28

WITH THE THRONG jostling her from all sides, Serena fought to keep her balance as she struggled up the steep hill past the Friends' meeting house. The little town of Woodlington on its bluff overlooking the creek lay bathed in golden sunshine oddly at variance with the sombre purpose of this day.

Not that those around her appeared to find it so. A spirit of holiday prevailed. Behind her the High Street was fair crowded with the curious—on horseback, in carriages, and not a few afoot—and up ahead, nearer the Court House, the way seemed already barred by the press of bodies thickly packed. Customers streamed in and out of the beckoning tavern doors. If notoriety had been the Pine Robber's aim, he had achieved it on this, his day of execution.

On the green grass of the meeting house lawn, beneath the tall beeches that were scattering their leaves like gold coins upon the ground, families were encamped amongst the tombstones with their baskets of pasties and ale, preparing to make a day of it. Small boys scampered about beneath the giant horse chestnuts, pelting one another with their prickly fallen fruit. Along the High Street, where the solid brick houses of the wealthier citizens drew back in tightly curtained disapproval, loiterers lounged about the prim slate stoops, some touting points of vantage that were not theirs to sell.

"Are you certain you wish to attend this?" His face drawn in concern, Doctor Will had helped Serena from the wagon.

"I'm not certain I wish to attend—but I'm certain I must." Serena's face had been pinched and grim. Joe Mulliner was the beginning, she thought—the wayward spark kindling the blaze that swept away life as I had known it. I am not certain why I feel so, yet I know I must be witness to his snuffing out. "I shall be all right. Please, Doctor Will, don't concern yourself with me. I know you have no wish to be there."

"I've no stomach for killing," said Doctor Will. "Nor for crowds that glory in it, however deserved this ruffian's fate may be."

"Nor I—but in this case . . ."

"Is it vengeance that impells you here?"

Serena's face had grown thoughtful. "No, not vengeance. Some need for . . . I can't express it. Completion, perhaps. Completion that will allow me to live unhaunted by the past."

The Black Doctor had patted her shoulder and climbed back into the wagon. "I think I understand, child. I'll be off. I've a wish for a word with some of the merchants. While I am there, I shall pick up a load of provisions, if"—he smiled his gentle smile—"they have not all run off to the spectacle. Shall I meet you here at dusk?"

Serena gave him a tremulous smile. "Please." She waved him away.

❧ ❧ ❧

Now she wished she had not come. Somehow she had not expected the crowd, well aware though she was that hangings were popular sport. In picturing Mulliner's end, she had seen it as a tableau of but two figures, herself and Mulliner—except for the ghost of Stuart Brandon, which hovered everywhere. Had he told her the truth of his connection with this blustering outlaw? Now she would never know.

Her thoughts had brought her nearly to the Court House. Its mellow brick walls and quadruple chimneys dominated the small square. The white limestone lintels above the front windows sparkled in the sunlight. The raw yellow wood of the gallows and its platform, hastily erected for the occasion, was a stark intrusion upon the normally peaceful scene.

Hawkers moved among the crowd, crying their wares. Muffins and pasties. Cider and ale. Wooden miniatures of the gallows. In the lee of the crowd, by a horse trough, some children were crouched, playing at hangman, jerking the mechanism of the toy gallows again and again, shouting with glee as the tiny black figure attached to the raffia noose swung to and fro in crude imitation of death.

Serena turned from the grisly spectacle and found herself face to face with a vendor. "Two shillings only," he cried, brandishing some pamphlets. Large-lettered headlines swam before her eyes, the ink still damp, smudged and smearing. "Read the Dancing Desperado's confessions. Proceeds to his widow and orphan child."

If Mulliner had a wife and child, no one knew it till now, thought Serena. But somehow she found herself pushing through the crowd to a relatively quiet corner, a pamphlet in her hand. "Being the Confessions of the Notorious Bandit and Pine Robber, Joseph Mulliner, Composed in Woodlington Gaol at the Behest of His Priest and Confessor." Hands shaking — What am I afraid of? — Serena leafed through the pages. Every line bespoke the printer's haste: letters leaping wildly above the type line, lines repeated, letters missing.

Even in her agitation, Serena laughed. The hand of the unnamed "confessor" lay heavily on every page. Whatever revelations — about herself? about Brandon? — Serena had feared, they would not be found in this mawkish *culpa* for sins as horrendous as they were unspecified. Had Mulliner even seen it? Neither the debonair bandit of their first encounter nor the frenzied attacker of their last could be glimpsed in the pious repentances and premonitions of hellfire that crowded the smeared foolscap pages.

The crowd was growing restless. Neither Mulliner nor the officiating worthies had yet appeared. "Bring 'im on!" one burly man shouted. "Let's see 'im dance to the hangman's lay!" called another. The crowd took up the chant. "Mulliner! Mulliner! On with it!" The door of the Court House opened. A small detachment of militia, led by Major Stapleford, marched out into the sunshine. In a dashing raid Stapleford, forewarned, some said, by a defecting Pine Robber, had effected Mulliner's capture during yet another tavern sortie.

The militiamen formed a rough semicircle at the foot of the gallows, laying elbows and rifle stocks about them to force back the jostling crowd. A blustering of Freeholders emerged from the shadowed portico to take favoured places as official observers. For a moment the doorway stood empty. Then Mulliner appeared, hands tied at his back, his massive form filling the doorway, shoulders brushing the jamb, as two armed guards behind him hustled him rudely forward.

The onlookers surged toward the platform, pressing against the human barrier that blocked their way. For a time the seething mass shifted and swayed as each fought for a point of vantage and the militiamen fought to contain the crowd. Serena, buffeted by the sweating bodies all about her, struggled to keep her feet. Elbows dug into her ribs. A stout goodwife, screaming "Kill him! Kill him! Hang the dirty thief!" thrust her body in front of Serena, stepping on her instep as she did so.

Serena's temper snapped. "Damn you — I've a right to see, too!" Before she quite knew what she was about, she had dived into a gap that opened suddenly between two yelling men. Elbowing, kicking, squirming her slight form into every available space, she fought her way forward until a sudden shifting of the mob catapulted her onto the cobblestoned space before the gallows—face smudged, hair undone, struggling to catch her breath. A militiaman grasped her shoulder and shoved her none too gently back into the ragged ring of bodies that lined the cleared space.

Mulliner, meanwhile, had mounted the steps onto the platform. An official stepped forward to read the indictment against him: This farmstead plundered, that set afire. The Tuckerton stage robbed, its passengers beaten, the coach overturned into a creek. Familiar names rang out above the now-silent crowd as the list of victims grew longer. The widow Bullock and all her children tied to trees while their homestead was burned before their eyes. The Laceys, man and wife, shot and killed as they tried to defend their property. On and on went the litany of crimes.

Mulliner paid no heed. He stood lightly at the edge of the platform, his black velvet suit rumpled and stained but his swagger unimpaired. He raked the crowd with his glance as impudently as he had at the White Stag, as though he sought a partner for this, his last dance. His eyes met Serena's. Her breath caught in her throat. Dark waters roared once again in her ears. She saw those eyes as she had last seen them, burning into hers, heard his incantation—"This time. This time."

Mulliner gave a slight shrug of recognition. He barely paused in his survey of the crowd. Serena fought for equanimity, scarcely able to believe that this encounter meant nothing to him. To me, she thought, Mulliner is Nemesis, the destroyer of all my hopes, the despoiler of some inner refuge where I can never again rest unafraid. To him, I am but one of many victims, insignificant, forgotten once his plunder is complete. Only Stuart's thwarting of his initial intention had etched my identity briefly into his brain. It is I, not he, who will live forever scarred by our encounter.

The official finished his reading and looked straight at the prisoner. "Joseph Mulliner, for these heinous crimes and others unmentioned you are sentenced to hang by the neck until you are dead. Thereafter, may you burn in eternal hellfire. State, if you will, your final request."

Mulliner tossed his head. "Untie me. I've no mind to meet me Maker trussed like fowl fit for roastin'."

The militiamen tensed. The official hesitated. Then he nodded assent. A fumbling turnkey untied the Pine Robber's bonds.

Hands on his hips, Mulliner once again surveyed the crowd. His glance swept past Serena to the far end of the semicircle where two blowzy women, dressed alike in cheap purple silk, hugged each other, weeping. "Grace . . . Honour." Thinking the words the first of a repentant oration, the crowd settled back for a wallow in self-satisfied virtue. The two women darted forward. Before the guards could stop them, each had thrust a pouch into Mulliner's hands.

Dodging free of those reaching to subdue him, Mulliner tore open the drawstrings and hurled both pouches high above the crowd. Coins rained down, pelting the bystanders, rolling on the cobbles of the square. "There ye be, good folk," cried Mulliner above the sudden din. "Be havin' a drink on me!"

He roared with laughter at the scramble that ensued, laughing still as the guards wrestled his hands once more behind his back, laughing as the hangman, teetering on tiptoe, dropped the hood over his head.

Serena had been thrown forward as the crowd fought viciously for the coins. From the sidelines she watched as the guards, wasting no more time, frog-marched the prisoner to a position above the trap door and adjusted the noose about his neck. The hangman threw a lever. The trap door opened. The massive form of Joe Mulliner dropped, jerked, kicked convulsively for some moments, then was still.

By tossing the coins into their midst, Joe Mulliner had cheated the crowd of the spectacle they had come so far and waited so avidly to see. His mocking laughter, silenced forever, seemed yet to echo above the Court House square.

*　*　*

THE CROWD, realizing at last that the hanging was over, howled with frustration. The mob teetered and swayed on the brink of riot. "Militia! Present arms!" called Major Stapleford. Sensing the threat of the muskets all about them, the onlookers shuffled, muttered, turned away. Its spirits dampened by a sense of anticlimax, the crowd dispersed, breaking into groups of two, three, a dozen. Women shooed their youngsters ahead of them. Men drifted toward the taverns. A few stragglers lingered, watching the platform where the body was being cut down and the coroner waited to declare it dead.

Serena threaded her way through the crowd, seeking some quiet place where she might rest until her trembling ceased. She felt drained. Even as she fought not to vomit, a fierce thirst assailed her as dust rose from the cobbles to tickle her throat.

She mounted the stoop of a shuttered house to one side of the square. Perhaps I can rest on this railing, she thought. Is there a hawker selling cider anywhere about? She turned to scan the thinning crowd from this higher point of vantage.

Her heart stopped, then began to race. Framed by a narrow alleyway was the tall, cloaked figure of a man, walking with the feline grace that still haunted her night after night. Barely aware that she had even left the stoop, she was pelting across the square, bumping into bodies that stubbornly refused to yield. "Out of my way!" she muttered fiercely. "Please—out of my way!" The pulse in her throat was pounding so wildly she feared that she would choke.

A hand clutched her shoulder. She gasped and stumbled, her headlong dash checked.

"Miz Serena!"

"Let me go! Let me go!" She squirmed to shake off the hand, arching her neck, straining to see over the intervening heads to the alleyway. The tall figure had vanished.

The grip on her tightened. "Miz Serena—wait."

The voice was familiar. She turned and confronted Jake Buzby. Another ghost. Was this to be a day of haunting by all the ghosts of her past? Had that been a ghost, too, that glimpse of Stuart Brandon—a phantom conjured by hopes and dreams she kept secret even from herself? She twisted frantically around, trying once more to see the spot where Brandon—was it Brandon?—had disappeared. No one was there.

"Miz Serena." Jake—surely it was Jake—tried again to capture her attention. "Bide a moment. I be needin' to talk to ye."

"Jake—" The rumpled figure with its many layers of clothing, all charcoal-stained and tattered, its aura of applejack and tobacco, stood solid and familiar on the stones of the cobbled square—no ghost, surely. "I thought you were dead, killed in the fire you . . . the fire that . . ."

"Say it, Miz Serena. The fire I set."

"Well, didn't you? If not by intention, then by neglect? That fire killed my father, Jake, as certainly as if he had been burned to death. But they said you had been caught in it yourself."

"I hear't the Old Man be dead. That be a bad day, Miz Serena. He was a fair good man. But me? No. Me woman was kilt, as was stayin' in me hut. And me dog was kilt, as was guardin' it—little Cinders, you remember? Harmless a mutt as ever lived. But I been't kilt. Though it's sure that devil meant to kill me—kill me and brand me with the blame fer it all."

"What devil?" A burning in the pit of her stomach told Serena who that had been. Yes, of course. But Caleb burning Weyford? What dark motive, what lust to avenge himself, would prompt him to destroy the prize he had pursued so relentlessly?

Jake Buzby was watching her intently, squinting against the sunlight, the better to see her face. He nodded.

"Yep—him. Prissypuss Sawyer hisself. I tripped over Cinders as I was comin' back with some fresh jugs. Dead, he be. Poisoned. And there be Master Caleb, puttin' a light to the turpentine he'd splashed all over. Shack went up like a torch. Woods was alight in a minute. And there he be—caperin' and dancin' like the Leeds Devil hisself, laughin' and shoutin' and followin' the flames. Saw there was no savin' me woman—I was like to burn up me own self if I'd tried. Lit out for the branch, I did—back behind the fire line."

"Then Caleb—he wasn't burned fighting the fire as he claimed?"

"He *set* the fire. An' he got burnt with his crazy dancin' and caperin'. Lost his way, I reckon. Must'a found the branch, though, else he'd a'burnt to a crisp. Better fer Weyford if that bin the end o' him."

"But, Jake, if Caleb set the fire he should have been caught—punished. Why did you run away instead of bringing him to justice?"

Jake squinted at her as though she were daft. He chuckled mirthlessly, a rusty sound from deep in his massive chest. "Look, Miz Serena, that devil I saw—speak out against him and me life don't be worth nothin'. And"—he spat on the cobbles for emphasis—"who be believin' me against him? Folk do be thinkin' I set the fire. They be after me, not Master Caleb. No—me, I lit out. I been coalin' somewheres else—that's a big Barrens with lots of room to hide. I'd not be in Woodlington but for the hangin'. Like to see that thievin' Mulliner get his comeuppance."

Serena tried to collect her scattered wits. Half her mind, abstracted, still puzzled over the cloaked figure she had seen. Had it been Brandon? Or had her unvoiced yearning betrayed her eyes into deceiving her? The other half grappled with Jake's revelations. Caleb, she thought. He, not Mulliner, is Nemesis. Jake is right: *He* killed my father—albeit without direct intention. Clearly, though, he had no qualms about killing Jake. And that poor little dog. She recalled Cinders' soft brown eyes, his tailwagging attempts to please. She shuddered.

"Jake," she said, "you're right to stay away from Weyford, right to give Caleb no hint that you're alive. But if I should need you, need the evidence of your eyes . . ." She faltered. No, Jake would no more tell her his burrow than a fox would tell a bloodhound. Already his eyes darted about the square, seeking out whoever might have seen them.

"Well, then, if *you* need anything . . ." She stopped. How foolish I sound. What is this soot-stained reprobate, wise in the ways of the woods, likely to need from me? "You know where I live?"

"Yep. With the Black Doctor."

How quickly gossip travels. "Well, then, if you need me—"

Jake chuckled and spat again. "I takes care of m'self. But you, Miz

Serena—have a care. That devil—he'd not be stoppin' at murder, havin' done it once. I be watchin' you since you was little. You be a better iron-master than Sawyer—and he be knowin' it. He be knowin' those works be his in name only. He'll not rest safe with you about the Barrens, I be thinkin'. Have a care. Now, goodbye. I only been bidin' here to warn you." He patted her shoulder clumsily and turned to go.

"Thank you, Jake. Goodbye, then."

Serena did not watch his departure. She whirled instead and ran to the alleyway where the tall, cloaked figure had vanished. She ran along its narrow downhill passage between blank brick walls, ran along the curving trail to which the alley led, a trail through thick woods behind the houses. The beaten earth kept its secrets—she saw no footprints. Soon the trail became a footpath, dropping steeply along the bluffs toward the creek.

At last she stood panting at the water's edge, shielding her eyes from its glare. Wavelets slapped gently against the pilings of a quay. But of the phantom she had pursued there she saw no trace.

CHAPTER 🌢 29

S HRIEKING WITH LAUGHTER, Melissa played tag with the waves. A
crimson sash tucked up her skirts. The ocean, autumn-blue, its
tide full-moon high, calmly bowled its combers at the shore. As each
flattening wave sent foam hissing duneward, Melissa led the way, her
sturdy legs churning. Then, as the sea sucked back each breaker in a
swirl of sand and shell, she whirled about and pursued it. Her dark curls,
escaping the ribbon that bound them, were sleeked from her brow by
the sea wind. "Back! Back!" she shouted, entranced by this newly met
playmate. Water blue as the sky slowly filled the winged footprints behind her.

At the base of a dune, Serena and Charity basked in the mellowed
sunlight, watching her play. All about them, in baskets of split oak and
willow, lay the fruits of their day's labours. Bayberries dusted with pow-
dery wax . . . juniper berries, coolly blue . . . the glossy red hips of the
beach roses. Where the dunes behind them rose and fell like the waves
of a second, dark-green sea, bayberry bushes fluttered with the blossoms
of autumn: orange-and-black butterflies, hundreds to each shrub, pausing
in the migratory journey that brought them to this littoral. Flights of
swallows dipped and wheeled across the marshland as one being, contending for the succulent berries with which the bushes were laden.

"Look, Charity—" Serena pointed, laughing. A glossy grey-black swallow waddled toward them, its cleft tail draggling in the sand. Vainly it
flapped its wings. "Greedy!" teased Serena. "You're so stuffed you can't
fly! Mitzi would make short work of you—it's as well for you she's safely
in Lumberton."

In companionable silence, the two women went on with their sorting,
glancing now and then toward the tide line where Melissa still flirted
with the breakers. At last the child settled down to hunting shells, scooping 🌢 205

her finds into her skirts, running up to Serena now and then in a skitter of sand. "Look, Mama!" Mussel shells, slick and wet, purple and blue . . . "mermaids' purses" holding skates' eggs . . . razor shells and clam shells . . . the feather of a gull . . . strings of coin-sized pouches encasing nascent whelks. With a swirl of muddy skirts, Melissa raced away in search of still more treasures.

"That dress be ruined." Her supple brown fingers sorting berries, her eyes squeezed half shut against the glare, Charity looked fondly after the small, busy figure.

"No matter. Let her enjoy this freedom. It is fortunate she does not want to play with the other children. And the dress is near outgrown anyway."

"Yes — she be gettin' big. I scarce can believe she's 'most three." Charity gave Serena a shrewd look. "They be shunnin' her?"

Serena sighed. Shading her eyes, she looked southward down the beach to where women were silhouetted against the sky, crouching and stooping, wielding clam rakes, filling baskets, distance lending their movements the grace of a dance set to the rhythm of the waves upon the strand. On the dunes women bent to gather bayberries. This journey to pick the grey-blue pellets was an annual affair; candles made from their fragrant wax were highly prized for their clear light. Some few of the goodwives gathered juniper berries or rose hips to make home remedies, but most left the gnarled, dark-needled trees and the sprawling thorny beach roses to Serena and Charity.

This year it seemed the women kept their distance more pointedly than before. What has changed? Serena gathered the fine silver sand and let it sift through her fingers into small, sliding heaps. "Yes —" She faced her friend. "They shun her. And me — me perhaps even more. You know I seldom go into the village?"

Charity nodded. Serena's avoidance of Lumberton, her dislike of the gauntlet of eyes she must run when passing the idlers at the shop doors, had been obvious to Charity long before her move to Jonasville.

"Well, since you've gone, I've had to go sometimes — Clara does not market the way you did. The merchants take advantage of her ignorance. And when I do go . . . well, it seems the women turn away from me. They huddle together and gossip. And their eyes . . . there is something about their eyes that is new. A look of speculation — and accusation." Serena's fingers tensed momentarily. She dropped her gaze. Fearing to alarm her friend, Serena did not say that on her last trip to the village, some urchins had pelted her with stones.

"But Will's practice? You do be helpin' him?"

"Not as I'd hoped, or as he had. Oh, Charity—" Serena clutched her friend's arm, "I've worked so hard, and learned so much! I could help them. I know it. And Will—he knows it, too. There's twice as much work as he can do alone. At least"—she paused thoughtfully—"there was." She let the sand run through her fingers again, feeling its heat, its fineness, sorting the sun-warmed, sea-smoothed pebbles from among the finer grains as she sorted thoughts in her mind. "He'd even planned to buy a second wagon to send me about the rounds. When people sent for him of a sudden, and the parlour was full of waiting patients, he thought to send me in his stead."

"And?"

"And—well, some will have none of me. Mistress Worrell even shut the door in my face. And others—their faces close up, their bodies tighten. Small children, sometimes, will confide in me. But the others . . ."

The others, thought Serena, are hostile. The women would eye her figure and purse their lips in disapproval, their glance flicking from her shining hair that seemed always about to burst from its net to her swelling breasts and trim waist that the sober dark garments she wore for these calls could not conceal. And the men . . . ill though some of them were, they had yet breath to whisper indecent proposals the moment their wives' backs were turned.

"They have forgiven Doctor Will, perhaps, for being black, but not me for being mother of a bastard. Perhaps if I were an old crone, bent and shuffling, with a wart upon my nose, they would accept me as a healer. But as I am?" She shook her head, looking down at the sands trickling through her slender fingers.

Charity nodded. "And when Will be with you?"

"Oh, they tolerate me then—as his handmaiden." She laughed bitterly. "If they only knew that the remedies they swallow so eagerly come from my hands—that I alone brew most of them and have concocted the formulae for many. Doctor Will has given over the herb room almost entirely to me. I've enlarged the herb garden, started a hedge of sassafras. And next spring—" She broke off. Will there be a next spring?

The two women sat silent for a moment. The wind shifted southward, bringing a drift of pine smoke from the cooking fires by the shore. "I must go see whether I can help with the meal," said Serena. "And I must fetch Melissa away from the water before she catches a chill. Will you watch her? There are dry clothes for her in that bundle." She set off across the sand.

❧ ❧ ❧

IT SEEMED TO HER that the women about the fires drew together at her approach. Their congenial chatter ceased; they watched her in silence. Serena's palms felt suddenly clammy. Swallowing hard, she addressed the goodwife nearest her. "Mistress Littleton, I fear I've been remiss. How can I help you with the supper?"

For a moment Serena feared the woman would not answer. The pause lengthened, measured by the booming of the surf. Mistress Littleton's face was a study in circles: round eyes, round pursed lips, round puffed cheeks. The circles converged, drawing tightly in upon themselves as she eyed Serena. She stepped back, closer to her watching companions. "We've no need of help from the likes of you," she snapped. Turning her back, she flounced away to join her sisters.

For a moment Serena stood still. Her cheeks burned as though the woman had slapped her. She blinked rapidly, breathing fast, wanting to curse them aloud, to grab one of them by her colourless hair and pull, to spit into the kettle of chowder and let them make what they would of that. She glanced back to where Charity was gently combing Melissa's tangled hair. Even at this distance she could feel the other's concern. Charity had seen. Charity knew.

"A pox on the bitches," muttered Serena, the vulgarity tartly satisfying on her tongue. "Let them stew in their own bile — I shan't give them the pleasure of seeing how they've hurt me." And yet, she thought, and yet . . . I cannot bide here even one moment more.

Then she was stumbling down the beach, lurching and slipping in the soft sand above the tide line, then running, running on the tide-packed strand, spattering water at each footfall. The wind plastered her clothes to her body, tangling her skirts about her ankles, slowing her down. On she walked, splashing in the shallows, with no thought but to put distance between herself and those women and their purse-lipped disapproval. Charity had seen. She would attend to Melissa, see that the fruits of their picking were stowed in the boat to be ferried across the bay.

The day was ending. Beyond the dunes, to the west, the sun had nearly set. Already the sky above the ocean was darkening, but for a luminescence where the full moon was about to rise. Serena paused for breath, looking out to sea. A single ship was visible, its full sails tinted pink by the last rays of the sinking sun.

There was that about the set of its masts that looked familiar. The *Audacious!* breathed Serena. Then she chided herself. Fool! Since that day in Woodlington any ship would seem the *Audacious* to you, every tall stranger Stuart Brandon. What sign has there been, in all these months since the hanging, that he is even alive?

Still she lingered, her spirit yearning toward the horizon where the ship appeared to hover motionless on the sea. The slight haze above the water made of it a dream ship. She recalled that moment of exaltation atop the mast of the *Audacious*. Then the whole wide vista of my world stretched before me, revealed for the first time to my sight. Now I stand becalmed, like that ship out there, my feet mired in dailiness, my hands fettered by obligations—to Doctor Will, to the calling he has tried to open to me. And to Melissa—Melissa most of all. Somehow my daughter must be freed from the life in which my passions have imprisoned me.

Resolutely, Serena strode again along the beach. But a few moments more, she thought, of peace in which to think. Then I'll turn back. She lifted her chin and looked ahead once more. Then she hesitated. While she had stood dreaming in the shallows the solitude of the beach had been shattered. As the distant shapes of men drew nearer she saw that these were some of the gang of youths who had helped row the longboats across the bay. Louts, all of them, she thought, recalling the lewd remarks of Jed, their leader. I've no wish to run afoul of them now.

Looking over her shoulder, she saw that she had come much farther than she thought. She could barely see the glow of the beach fires behind her, and the dusk was thickening rapidly. To her right was the surf, not far to her left the soft sand above the tide line. Should she need to run, either would slow her down.

Louts, she thought again, I'm not afraid of you. Or, she amended, if I am—for there were five of them, swaying drunkenly, slack-jawed but tough-muscled—I must not let you know it. She straightened her shoulders, fixed her gaze on the horizon, and walked directly at them. They fanned out just enough to block all passage on either side. Coarse laughter blew toward her on the wind. Jed, a pimply youth of eighteen or so with lank, unkempt hair and prominent bad teeth, stopped ten paces in front of her, his hands on his hips. "Look. It's the black man's doxy out to take the air." The others edged closer to their leader.

Serena drew a deep breath. I could turn and run, even now. But though I've the fleeter foot, they've no skirts to trip them. Unwonted, her flight from Joe Mulliner flashed before her. No—oh, no. I cannot endure that again.

She feared even to look behind her, to see who might hear her, should she call. One sign that I am afraid and they will be upon me. Am I too far away for those about the cookfires to see what is happening? Suppose they did see—who amongst them is likely to come to my aid?

I may hope someone will. But I dare not depend on it. The best course is to brazen it out.

She tightened her lips into a sneer as contemptuous as she could make it. "Let me pass." Firmly she walked into their midst.

For a moment it seemed the ploy would succeed. Two of them moved aside slightly. She brushed past them, her throat closing at the rank smell of sweat that hung about them. Now she was almost in the clear.

One jerked at her skirts and made her stumble. "Not so fast, whore." She wrenched her skirts free and tried to run. A filthy hand seized her and spun her about. "We've a mind to talk to you." A vicious push sent her toppling against Jed, who pushed her away in his turn.

Forming a rough circle about her, they jerked and shoved and whirled her from one to another, always catching her before she could find her footing and hurling her on, laughing, clutching roughly at her buttocks, her breasts, her hair, mocking her fright, taunting her with coarse jests. Tiring at last of this sport, they flung her into Jed's arms. He pulled her against him, forcing her arms behind her back, clamping her thighs between his. She tried to kick free, but her feet could find no purchase. His breath was foul in her face as he bent toward her. She felt him pressing his manhood against her body, swivelling his hips and thrusting them forward in crude pantomime of possession.

The others laughed coarsely. He thrust a hand into her bodice, pulling her breasts free. "Look! What fine paps that bastard brat takes suck of—and, like as not, that black potion-peddlar, too." She felt his fingers, rough with filth, squeezing viciously. Then the heel of his hand sent her sprawling. At once the others pounced upon her, one at each wrist, two holding her ankles so tightly the pain shot to her knees.

She squirmed and twisted against the cruel grip. "Help me! Someone . . . please . . . help me!" The wind snatched her words away.

Her body tensed, she tried again to twist away. The circle of faces pressing upon her blurred and shifted as the grip on her tightened. Then the leader was standing between her pinioned legs, his breeches open, his manhood in his hands, flaunting it at her and laughing.

"Pull up her skirts." She felt the chill touch of the night wind on her flesh as they complied. It was nearly dark.

"Help!" she screamed again. Her captors loosened their grip. One let go. "Have a care, Jed," he said uneasily. "Someone might see."

"And what of it?" Abruptly, Jed knelt over her. He seized her hair with one hand, thrusting himself at her face with the other. "Look at that, bitch. You think I'd dip that where a black man's been tuppin' you?"

"Feared it'll turn black, Jed?" Someone snickered.

"Pah! There's clean white meat enough for the takin'. I'd not dirty myself on his leavin's."

He backed off. She could breathe. "Make tracks, lads! Leave her filthy cunt for her master."

In a moment all five of them were splattering down the strand. The sound died away. The full moon shone upon an empty beach, silent but for the mutter of the surf and Serena's sobbing.

After a time she struggled to her feet. She brushed the sand from her garments and tidied herself as best she could. Then she started back down the beach to where her friend and her daughter would be waiting.

ə ə ə

THE MOON PAINTED A PATH for the laden boats across the calm black bay. Serena sat in the bow, her arms clasped tightly about the sleeping Melissa, Charity silent at her side. The dour farmer in charge of their boat rowed stolidly, a pipe clenched in his teeth. Around them were the shadows of other boats, some rowed by Serena's tormentors.

When the group had gathered for the crossing, all had ignored her. That the women knew of the attack, she was certain. So, too, was she certain that they tacitly supported the attackers.

In silence they landed on the bay shore. In silence they disembarked. No one helped Serena and Charity load their waiting wagon; none offered to hold the sleeping child.

"I'll drive," whispered Charity. "You be restin' in the back."

"No. You have done most of the work. Nor could I rest. Here, Charity— lie here with Melissa on these quilts. I've thinking to do."

Charity peered into Serena's eyes, burning coals in her moonlight-pale face. Should I be puttin' my arms 'round Serena? Should I be comfortin' her, makin' her rest? No. If I be doin' that she be breakin' down, cryin' for all them to see. "All right. You be drivin'." She climbed in and Serena took the reins. Soon the white trail was unwinding before them.

The wagons crawled homeward, laden with gatherers and their finds. Some dozed, some sang, some chaffed one another about small incidents of the day. Whispers, too, spread from wagon to wagon. Serena took no notice, and no one spoke to her. Hands clenched round the reins, shoulders rigid, she stared ahead unseeing as the horse trudged patiently along.

So that is what they are thinking? That Doctor Will and I— How could they think such a thing? How could they so misjudge not me, perhaps, but him? The wagon rumbled on. How proud I was of this new wagon, how pleased with the horse to draw it instead of that balky mule. How proud, too, of the trust Will placed in me, of the wooden case he gave me to hold my special remedies, of the healing I've learned to do. Is this refuge I've found, this work I've learned to love, to be taken from me, too? Today they shun Melissa. How soon will they attack her as they did me? Is she to be marked as a bastard all her days, her pain the price of my folly? And Doctor Will? Is he to pay, too, with his reputation, his practice, his livelihood? Where will this end? How can I fight them?

The brooding Pines gave no answer.

CHAPTER ❧ 30

T HEY LAY ON THE DECK of the *Audacious*, bathed in sunlight, their bodies fused. Up in the shrouds, the sea gulls mewled and squabbled. Serena thrust her fingers into Brandon's hair, ran her palms along the sweat-slick muscles of his shoulders. Stuart Brandon's hands were possessing her, his weight was upon her, his maleness inside her. His voice was hoarse in his throat. "Serena! Serena!"

She arched her body to meet the thrusts of his. The gulls shrieked louder. Now the cries of the gulls were drowning out Brandon's, his voice and theirs become one. His body drew away from Serena's, taking flight with the gulls, swooping among the masts, soaring toward the topmost sails. Where his warm lips had pressed against her skin she felt the kiss of the sea wind, austere and cold.

She half woke, her breasts clamourous, her loins moist with yearning. She had thrown off her quilts, and the midnight chill sheathed her body in ice, holding it rigid, entrapped.

"Serena! Serena!" I cannot move, she tried to answer. But she could not speak, could not obey, could not climb the mast to meet him up there in the crows' nest, could not . . . His voice died away. But the gulls were still shrieking . . . shrieking.

Between sleep and waking, she forced her eyes open, still caught in the web of her dream. Here was her familiar room, black with shadow, white with the moonlight that lay cold upon the bedclothes, the chairs, the scattered papers upon the writing table where she had sat so late, struggling with Doctor Will's accounts. The cipherings scrawled on the foolscap sheets were visible, so bright was the moon. Beside her slept Melissa, undisturbed. There was no Brandon, no *Audacious*. No, but the gulls . . .

The last filaments of sleep loosed their hold. Her dream drifted away. From outside came a fierce caterwauling.

"Mitzi!" Serena looked toward the foot of the bed. The little cat was not curled in her usual spot. The yowling outside became louder. Shivering as her bare feet touched the cold boards, Serena padded to the window. The fields stretched silent and empty toward the dark bulk of the distant trees. There was nothing to be seen from this vantage. The yowling came again. Was it fainter?

First tucking the quilt about Melissa, Serena felt her way through the hall to the kitchen door. She flung back the bolt and tugged the door open. Moonlight and frost had sifted mother of pearl over every leaf in the garden. Each dried, spiky stem, each coiled tendril of vine had become a jeweller's work in filigree.

"Mitzi!" Serena called softly. In the field beyond the garden silvered weeds trembled with the force of some conflict whose course she could trace by their swaying. Serena heard chittering and thrashing. The weeds shook convulsively. Then Mitzi emerged into the dooryard. Ears flat, eyes glazed, her tail a stiff brush behind her, she streaked past Serena to safety, the dark bulk of some pursuer close behind. At sight of Serena the intruder faltered, fell back, then scuttled to the shelter of the rustling weeds. A raccoon? Another cat? The blurred shadow had seemed larger than Mitzi.

Serena barred the door and tiptoed back to her quarters. Mitzi had taken refuge beneath the bed: Her phosphorescent eyes, their pupils mere slits, were all that could be seen of her. "Mitzi, are you hurt?" Serena whispered. She reached under the bed to caress her pet. "Come, Mitzi. Let me help you." Her hand brushed Mitzi's head and came away wet. "Mitzi!" whispered Serena more urgently. The cat hissed, backing yet farther into her refuge. "Very well—lick your wounds, then." Serena rose and went to the window. She looked at her hand. Blood lay upon it, black in the cold moon's light—black as the ink on the scattered papers that rustled in the draught that swept the room.

❧ ❧ ❧

"DOCTOR WILL," said Serena some days later, "we cannot go on in this fashion." With the crow quill she used for ciphering, Serena gestured at the buckram-bound ledger. The scattered, crumpled papers had been tidied away, the scrawled notations upon them translated to neat columns of figures, to names enscribed in the copperplate hand that Mistress Mansey had praised so long ago. Sleet tapped at the window, demanding entrance for winter.

Doctor Will sighed, shrugging into the folds of the shawl she had

draped about him to fend off the chill. The rocker in which he sat was
too low for his tall frame; it creaked as he shifted uneasily, his long legs
jackknifed. The fire sulked and sputtered, barely alight. The muttering
of the wind in the chimney, the incessant patter of the sleet, made the
room seem colder.

He looks older . . . looks old, thought Serena. Those new spectacles
give him an owlish mien, and there's a dusky tinge to his skin I've not
seen before. Or is it a trick of the light? She shifted the candle stand to
throw more light on the ledger and saw how his breeches, stretched tight
over his bony knees, had grown shiny with wear. As though guessing her
thought, he moved his fine, slender hands to cover the worn spots. There
was the faintest touch of a tremor about his fingers. "Cannot go on, child?
But of course we must go on. What can you mean?"

Serena sighed in her turn. I must make him see, must convince him
that his vagueness about money, his reluctance to acknowledge what is
happening, are placing us all in jeopardy—and threatening, too, those
few faithful patients who still come here. "Look." She pushed the heavy
book toward him and leafed rapidly back through the pages. "Here are
the accounts from last year. See how many pages there are, how many
names. And now this." She turned back to the accounts she had been
writing. "You see? The October accounts cover barely a page. There are
fewer names upon them with every passing month. And were it not for
Hiram Jonas—"

The rocker protested as Doctor Will drew back, back into the shadows
beyond the range of the lamp.

Serena looked up. What is it? she started to ask. But she said nothing,
appearing to look away, watching Doctor Will from beneath the screen
of her lashes. He seemed to have fallen into a reverie. There is something,
she thought, something about Jonas' visits that disturbs him. I've thought
so before, and now I am certain. But what? Putting the thought aside,
she went on with the task of explanation she had set herself.

"Master Jonas, at least, pays—and pays in gold. But the others . . .
Doctor Will, please listen. The others barely pay at all. The ones I know
you've called upon, I mean, for I swear you do not write down half your
calls. And when they do pay, it is with no regularity, no order. A sack of
crane-berries, a few sticks of firewood, a sack of weevily meal eked out
with sawdust more likely than not. Or, worse yet, they pay in Continentals." The Continental currency, never well accepted, had become the
butt of tavern jests; "not worth a Continental" was understood by all to
mean "worth nothing—or perhaps even less."

Doctor Will rose abruptly. The rocker swayed wildly behind him.

"Serena," he said, in a tone more stern than she had ever heard from him, "these people are at wit's end. Specie? I know not where Hiram Jonas finds specie these days—and he is a wealthy man. The others, many of them, have lost all they have. Their barns have been burned. Their livestock has been stolen by first one army, then the other. What little they can raise must go to feed their children. Am I to refuse them assistance or to beggar them by asking for the little they have managed to salvage? I will not."

"But many of them—"

"Child," said Doctor Will more gently, "I understand that you are troubled. But now the War is ended, better times will come. And when they do, our patients will pay us again. Bear with me, I beg you." He bent over her, stroking her hair with gentle fingers, steady now, and warm. "We will endure. And take heart," he chuckled softly, glancing toward the discarded papers she had set aside to smooth and use again. "I shall keep better accounts for you, and write down my calls more faithfully, as you ask." He transferred the shawl from his shoulders to hers and left the room.

Serena hunched over in her chair, twisting her hands together, fighting the tears that had welled up at the touch of his hand on her head. It's no use. He will wear himself out and never see, never want to see, that the patients we have left are those who will never pay, those who fail to pay not for lack of something to pay with—salt, which is as good as money these days, or a jug of the applejack that's brewed in the woods just as always—but because they take advantage of his kind heart. And what will I do, what will become of Melissa, when there's not enough to feed us all?

Instinctively, she sought to bury her chilblained hands in Mitzi's fur. But there was no warm, living muff on her lap. For days now the little cat had huddled in her retreat beneath the bed, refusing food, drinking but little, spurning all entreaties and hissing and scratching at any attempt to remove her.

"Hiram Jonas," Serena muttered to herself, returning to her earlier line of thought. What does he want here? Why does he so often forget Will's calling hours? And what, for that matter, is his complaint? Neither of them will tell me. Well, why should it matter? She rose briskly, shivering with the sudden movement, and closed the ledger. At least his money's good. Charity tells me there are great doings at Jonasville. And we can ill spare a patient. Looking down at the writing table, she shrugged. Did I really expect to persuade Will Pond of what he does not want to know? Hearing the knocker on the front door strike, she hurried from the room.

☙ ☙ ☙

"MASTER SMYTHE —" Now what can he want? Serena wondered, striving to conceal her distaste. His bold glance raked her figure. The entryway where they stood seemed too small, too crowded. "Pray be seated in the parlour while I seek out Master Pond." Before this insinuating stranger she would not say "Doctor Will."

"It is not the Black Doctor I've come to see, Mistress Wainwright. It is you." Smythe laid his tricorne on the settle and flung his silver-headed stick into the stand by the door. He shook his head as Clara came to take his cloak. "There's a chill about this place. Has your . . . patron's custom declined so far that a few sticks of firewood strain the contents of his purse?" With exaggerated shudders Smythe clutched the cloak about his meagre chest.

"Clara," said Serena, "light the fire in the parlour and show Master Smythe to a seat. And then come to my quarters. I've some orders to give you about supper." She turned to Smythe. "If you wish to speak to me, I fear I must ask you to wait a few moments. I've business to complete with Clara first."

Smythe's pursed his thin lips more tightly as he sent her a shrewd glance. I see through your ruse, said his narrowed eyes. But he merely bowed slightly and followed Clara into the parlour.

"Clara!" said Serena when the girl entered her chamber, "you must hurry. The Doctor was going to the Simmins' first. Mistress Simmins is about to make a muster. Find him and bid him come back here."

Clara made no move to obey but stolidly kept her place. Her round, somewhat vacant blue eyes, set a whit too close together above her plump red cheeks, were mutinous. "It be cold out there, Mistress. It be sleetin'—look." She waved her sturdy arm toward the window, then thrust both hands back beneath her soiled apron.

"Indeed," said Serena. "And if Doctor Will at his age can go out into the sleet, so can you. Wear my cloak. But for heaven's sake, hurry!"

The girl still stood gazing out the window. Serena lost her patience. "Hurry, I said!" Grasping the plump shoulders, she spun the girl toward the door, longing to plant her foot on the ample buttocks. "Go! Now!" Oh, if Charity were only here! I'd not need even to tell her to get Doctor Will—she'd have been off at first sight of that weasel face.

Serena watched through the window until Clara was visible on the road. Her idling gait guaranteed her a soaking before she had gone twenty paces.

"That wench is all but useless," muttered Serena. "At that rate Mistress Simmins' infant will be a grandsire itself before she gets there. Well, . . ." She squared her shoulders and started down the hall.

At the door of the parlour she stopped short. Smythe had seated himself at the round parlour table, his back to her. Head down, he was staring down at nothing. The posture of his body, the set of his narrow shoulders beneath the cloak, sent a tingle of recognition through Serena. The years between rolled away, and she was back at a White Stag ablaze with festive light, the fiddles squealing, tankards clattering upon the trestles, and Enoch, beside her, whispering unheard into her ear as her stomach clenched and her hands grew clammy. By a sheltered table stood Caleb Sawyer, and at that table . . . at that table was this man, sitting in just this way, the two of them intent upon something on the table before them. And that something had been the paper she had picked up and that Brandon had later tossed into the fire. The paper that branded Caleb Sawyer a Tory spy—yes, and this man his contact.

She took a deep breath, clenched her fists, and moved into the parlour. "Now, Master Smythe, pray, what business do you have with me?"

Smythe squirmed round to face her and arranged his features into a smile. "I come as a friend, to give you warning. Will you not be seated?"

"I prefer to stand." Fearing that her face would reveal her shock, Serena walked with what steadiness she could muster to stand across the table from him, the fire at her back. From here she could watch both his face and the doorway, but her own face would be in shadow. "Warning?"

Let him tell me, she thought, sparring for time to collect her wits. Though I can well guess what he's about. It is something about Will's practice. That was his reason for snooping round here before. But—her mind was awhirl with recollection and surmise—can Caleb somehow be back of this, too? If the pair of them connived at spying, what else might they be about, now that the British have been defeated? Then she recalled Jake Buzby's warning, forgotten since Mulliner's hanging: "Ye're a better ironmaster than Sawyer, fer all ye're a woman—he'll not rest as long as ye're about."

She swallowed hard and willed herself to stand calmly, her hands loosely clasped before her, glad there was no beggar look about her. To put herself in good spirits for her talk with Doctor Will she had dressed in a gown from her Wainwright House days. Conscious of the touch of fine worsted on her shoulders, the lace frill about her throat and wrists, she held herself proudly. Her chill receded. Warm blood coursed through her veins, and with it resolution.

Smythe hitched his chair back from the table and folded his arms

across his chest. Leaning back at his ease, his long legs in their shining
boots crossed negligently at the ankles, he tilted his head and set his
cold, grey gaze to roaming once more the length of her body. "I think
you must know," he said, "that the days of your . . . patron"—again that
pause, that meaning look—"are numbered."

"If you mean Will Pond, he is not my patron but my colleague. And
why should he be threatened? He . . . we have done nothing to warrant
persecution."

"Colleague, eh? Well, perhaps one might so describe your . . . associa-
tion, if one were charitably inclined." He fixed his glance upon the swell
of her breasts, and his balding forehead reddened slightly. Abruptly he
sat bolt upright in his chair. "But, Mistress Wainwright, the charity of
your neighbours has long been exhausted. Your cohabitation with this
blackamoor is a scandal, your bastard brat the talk of the countryside.
And as for that black charlatan," he struck the table lightly with the flat
of his palm, emphasizing each word, "his 'cures' shall be exposed for the
fakery they are—fakery, if not worse. Witchcraft is not too strong a word
for some of them."

He leaned forward, his glance holding hers. "Do you think the legitimate physicians of this town will close their eyes forever to the black
arts going on here?" He gestured toward the herb room.

Serena clenched her fists. "Legitimate physicians—pah!" Anger for
Melissa's sake, for Doctor Will's, consumed her caution, setting her
temper alight. "The legitimate physicians, the ones who know how to
heal, have been serving with the Army. Those lie-abeds in Mount Holly
are the real charlatans. You know it—and so do they. Why, Doctor Elmer
himself sent patients here before he joined the troops as surgeon. Doctor Will . . . Master Pond told me so."

She took a deep breath. "And as for your other slurs upon my charac-
ter—and worse, Master Pond's—they are beneath contempt. And what's
more, I think you know it. You're too clever a man to be taken in by the
gossip of goodwives and tavern loungers. If that's the nature of your warning, I'll listen to no more of it." She waved her hand as though to brush
him away. "Be gone. I've enough of your threats and filthy accusations."

Smythe leaned back in the chair again. "You are quite the firebrand,
Mistress Wainwright." He licked his thin lips. "No doubt that fire serves
you well beneath the quilts. You must make that black he-goat feel young
again. Have a care, though, lest there be yellow kids gambolling about
the dooryard. That *would* bring an end to your neighbours' patience."

"Enough!" cried Serena, her face flaming. She clenched her hands hard
together lest she strike him. He is goading me, she thought, watching

him watching her, his eyes narrowed and intent. But to what purpose? "Sit here if you like, since I'd not touch you, even to evict you. But you'll sit alone." She brushed past him. *I must get out of here before I forget myself.* As she passed, he seized her wrist in a painful grip.

"Sit down!" He rose with a swiftness that surprised her. Pulling out a chair, he forced her into it. The pain in her wrist was excruciating, momentarily wiping out all thought. When he was certain she would not rise, he released her. "Listen to me, Mistress Wainwright, and spare me your outraged virtue. Your bastard daughter speaks more loudly of your morals than any words you might say. And more truly. And the events of recent weeks"—he looked at her meaningfully—"must have made you aware that your neighbours have had their fill of you."

He knows. Somehow he knows of what happened on the beach. Serena sat still and said nothing, rubbing her wrist.

Smythe settled back in his chair again, still watching her. "How many patients has your protector lost? Or, more to the point, how many has he left?"

She did not reply.

"No answer? I know you keep his accounts. How many has he left, Mistress Wainwright? Twenty? A dozen? Were it not for that Jonasville upstart, how long would you survive?"

Still she said nothing. Her mind raced behind the brow she strove with all her might to keep smooth. *Someone has been spying—spying intensely—for Smythe to know such details.*

"Does he have a dozen patients, Mistress Wainwright? Or is it fewer?"

It is *me—it is all because of me. The other physicians? They have no legal charge to bring against him, for if they had, they would long since have employed it. I know their jealousy, their petty malice, their resentment of his cures. But in me they have found their weapon.*

"A dozen if that. And scarce any that pay, leaving Jonas aside. Yet there were hundreds, were there not?"

Yes, hundreds, in the Barrens and of late in the towns. And some of them near to worshipped him. What has set them against him, against me? They accepted me at first—some of them. I'd some cures to match his. Is it only Melissa? Or is it these rumours about Doctor Will and me?

"You don't answer, Mistress Wainwright. But surely you take my point?"

Who could have started these rumours? Who has seduced the townsfolk into believing this filth about the Black Doctor, whom they knew to be the soul of probity? A few spiteful women? How credible are they— how credulous those to whom they spin their tales? No. There is some-

thing more back of this—something sinister. Caleb? Caleb and this man together? Are there no bounds to his malice? Even here, am I still within its reach?

Rousing herself, she looked straight at her tormentor. "Just what is your point, Master Smythe?"

Smythe leaned forward. Once again he contrived a smile. "I told you at the outset—I come as a friend. Surely you see that your continued presence here does the Black Doctor nothing but harm. You must go. But arrangements can be made . . ." His lubricious smile melted into a look more ingratiating and less persuasive. "I am not a heartless man. Nor am I unaware of your charms, as you must have perceived. With me as your protector, you would be safe from—"

He broke off. Serena was not listening. She was looking beyond him, toward the doorway, her eyes puzzled and intent.

Mitzi was coming into the room—slowly, haltingly, with staggering steps and a weaving gait. Her fur was matted, her eyes seemed glazed and dull. One ear draggled, torn and crusted, giving her a rakish look. She paused, swayed, then started toward Smythe, her lustreless eyes fixed upon his face, her lips drawn back in a soundless snarl. There were flecks of spittle about her mouth.

Forever after, when Serena tried to recall them, the next few moments were a blur. Doctor Will appeared in the doorway, still in his cloak. His eyes were fixed on Mitzi.

"Mitzi— What—?" Serena stretched out her hand toward her pet.

"No!" Doctor Will leapt toward her and struck her hand aside.

Smythe, too, saw the cat. "Is this your familiar, perhaps?" he began, extending a bony hand. "Here, Puss."

"No!" cried Doctor Will again.

Too late. With a snarl, Mitzi launched herself into space. She landed on Smythe's knees, biting at his arms as he instinctively drew them up to shield his face. Her claws raked his wrists, bringing blood. He flinched. For an instant he dropped his guard. Mitzi hurled herself at his face, mewling and whimpering. Her teeth flashed as she sank them into his cheek, into his ear.

Smythe's long arms flailed as he tried to drive her off, cursing, tipping back in his chair. With a throaty yowl, Mitzi fastened her jaws upon his Adam's apple.

Smythe recovered his wits. He grasped Mitzi about the neck. Ignoring the claws raking along his forearms, he wrenched her away from his throat. His hands tightened about her neck. Then he seized her jaw and forced her neck back . . . back.

There was a sickening crack. Mitzi's legs twitched spasmodically, then hung limp. Smythe raised her high above his head and hurled her from him. She hit the wall with a thud and slid to the floor, where she lay still, a huddle of blood and fur.

"Mitzi!" Serena rushed forward.

"Stop! Don't touch her!" Doctor Will seized Serena's shoulders and pulled her back. "Don't touch her, child."

"But she—"

"She is dead, Serena. You cannot help her. As you value your life, do not touch her. Come, child." Serena was shaking with the effort to contain her sobs before this hostile stranger. "Come—sit down. Try to calm yourself." Doctor Will eased Serena into a chair and turned his attention to Smythe.

The man slumped motionless, his legs sprawled before him, his eyes glazed with shock. Blood oozed from deep scratches on his face and hands. It dripped from his torn earlobe and stood in rounded droplets where Mitzi's teeth had pierced his throat. Sensing Doctor Will's glance upon him, he glared feebly and began dabbing at his wounds with the torn frill of his shirt.

"Wait," said Doctor Will. "Do not touch your wounds until I cleanse them." When Smythe paid no attention, Doctor Will struck his hand away.

"How dare you—?"

"Do you not understand? The cat was rabid. If you are not to die of the water sickness, those wounds must be cleansed with spirits."

"Rabid—" Smythe sank back into his chair. His hands fell limply into his lap.

Pausing only to pat Serena's shoulder and whisper, "Don't touch Mitzi, Serena," Doctor Will sped to the herb room, returning in seconds with cotton wool and a flask of the pure spirits he used in making tinctures. Ignoring the feeble motions Smythe made to repel him, he forced the man's head back and poured spirits into the punctures in his throat. Soaking the cotton wool, he applied it to Smythe's ear.

The man bucked and twitched at the sting of the alcohol in his raw wounds. Doctor Will ignored Smythe's struggles as he ignored the foul oaths that poured from him. Again and again he sluiced the cuts, mopping up the blood-tinged flow with lint that Serena, recovering herself, brought him from the dispensary.

"There," he said at last. "It may not spare you, but I have done what I can."

Smythe pushed him away and stood up, wobbling at the knees, clutching his cloak about himself once more. He stumped into the hall and snatched up his hat and stick. As he pulled the door open he turned, glaring malevolently. "You blackamoor bastard," he snarled, "you'll pay for this. And you as well, bitch—you as well."

Serena did not reply. Doctor Will had already turned away. The door slammed.

Doctor Will fetched a piece of sacking and dropped it over the corpse of the little cat. Careful not to touch Mitzi, he wrapped her in the sacking and started to carry her away.

"Doctor Will!" called Serena. He turned. Serena swallowed hard. The bundle he held seemed pathetically small, so much smaller than the living Mitzi.

Serena's lips shook so that she could hardly speak. "Please," she began. She cleared her throat. "Please—mark her grave so I can find it." He nodded and went out. When the last of his footfalls had faded, Serena allowed herself to cry.

CHAPTER ✿ 31

"SERENA, I AM GOING in to Lumberton. I must seek the home of that poor wretch and ascertain what has become of him."

Serena nodded dully. She was about the weekly baking. Melissa sat quietly in a corner near the fire, playing a game of her own devising with acorns and the shells she had gathered on the shore. Clara had taken flight minutes after the bloodstained Smythe had left the house, leaving Serena with all the household duties as well as her work in the herb room. Struggling with a recalcitrant flue, her face smudged and her eyes stinging from the smoke, Serena scarcely saw Doctor Will leave.

When she heard the creak and rumble of the horse and buggy, she looked up, half-surprised. Doctor Will's intentions impressed themselves for the first time upon her mind. "No! Better that he stay away." But when she rushed out the door to call him back, he was too far along the road to hear her. Her throat tightened as she saw how stooped he had become. He sat bowed over the reins, swaying slightly as the wheels jounced over the ruts. Soon he was lost from sight as the autumn mists swirled about him.

Serena returned to the kitchen and resumed her struggles with the flue.

✿ ✿ ✿

LOST IN REVERIE, Doctor Will was oblivious to the drizzle. Smythe . . . Smythe, he pondered. Surely the name is false, false as the fellow's smiles. A well-monied man, to be sure. His garments . . . and that gold piece. Well-known, then, he must be. And I've no call to be certain that Lumberton is his home. Most of the townspeople are known to me, and he is not among them. But I've a mind to try Lumberton first. If indeed he's contracted the water sickness, news will have got about.

Sadly, Doctor Will shook his head. Poor wretch, if that be his fate, his wiles will avail him nothing. He pulled a crumpled paper from his waistcoat and peered again at the spidery writing: "Come quickly. Smythe has need of your assistance." No signature. And no directions. Strange, he mused. Then he smiled slightly. Serena would not have let me come, had she seen this.

He was roused by the rumble of his buggy wheels rolling across the plank bridge. The waters of the branch ran nearly black, sullen and ominous. As the horse rounded the curve and trotted into the High Street, Doctor Will peered along its muddy length, then down a lane that skirted the wooded bluff. Below, he knew, lay the broad Rancocas Creek; still farther beyond was the complex of wharves where cordwood and lumber were loaded. Here on the bluff were the town's few stately dwellings. He drew rein. Some bustle and stir attracted his notice. People were milling about the street. As he watched, a lad pelted by.

"Boy! What goes on there?" The lad gave Doctor Will a half-frightened glance. For a moment it seemed he would not answer.

"It be Master Lipcote," he said at last. "They be about to douse him." He ran off to join the crowd.

Dousing: the ancient cure for rabies. Then this Lipcote must be "Smythe." "But it will do no good," said Doctor Will to the empty air. "Here, I must stop this." He guided the horse into the narrow lane and as close to the crowd as he dared.

It was a goodly throng, for all the mist and drizzle—men from the wharves in leather leggings and aprons; goodwives with baskets upon their arms; lads and dogs tearing in and out, the lads shrieking, the dogs yelping. To one side stood a cluster of richly garbed men whose tall hats, gold watch chains, and gold-topped canes contrasted sharply with the worn garments of the townspeople. Physicians, thought Doctor Will, noting their canes and a certain pomposity of bearing.

The house before which they gathered was stately enough, a square brick structure in the Georgian style, with white trim and shutters and a broad marble stoop. The panelled double doors stood open, their brass fittings reflecting what little light the sullen sky could muster. Through their side windows came the light of many candles, lit against the gloom. Some men stood about the stoop, watching the doorway. One furtive cloaked figure seemed familiar.

When the man turned to scan the crowd, Doctor Will caught a glimpse of the twisted scars upon his face. But that is Caleb Sawyer! Serena's brother-in-law! What is he doing here? Their eyes met across the crowd. Without greeting the Black Doctor, Caleb huddled more deeply into his cloak and turned back to face Lipcote's house. All thought of the reason for his presence left Doctor Will's mind as a strange procession trooped through the doorway.

Four men, servants by the look of them, struggled with a litter. Upon it, tightly bound with canvas strappings, was "Smythe." One of the watching physicians stepped forward, motioning toward a garden path that led down the bluff to the Rancocas. He stepped into the lead, his fellow physicians clustering round him.

Doctor Will pushed forward through the crowd, forgetting courtesy in his haste, not noticing the black looks and whispers, nor the way the crowd drew back lest he touch them. "Here, wait!" he called. "What are you about?" Seeing who called, the bearers stopped with a jerk. The physicians piled into them, nearly losing their footing. The litter swayed. But for his bonds, its occupant might have toppled onto the ground.

"Wait," said Doctor Will again. He came abreast of the litter, then drew back in horror. Smythe—Lipcote—was barely to be recognized. Cuts and scratches still covered his face and throat: unhealed, swollen and pustular, crusted with tarry ointments. The face was drawn into a grimace wracked by spasms, jerking and twitching. The scanty hair, matted and filthy, stuck up wildly. There were bloody patches on Lipcote's scalp where he had torn his hair out by the fistful. Spittle frothed from his mouth and oozed down his unshaven chin, wetting his nightshirt.

"What are you about?" Doctor Will repeated his question, addressing the physician with the largest paunch. As the man drew himself up to answer, his fellows clustered about the sick man as if to shield him.

But Lipcote had seen Doctor Will—or perhaps recognized his voice. A howl but half human arose from the litter. Beyond the screen of bodies Doctor Will could see Lipcote's form twisting convulsively against the restraints. His throat muscles worked, straining, standing out in cords. His face glistened with sweat and with the spittle that poured in ever more copious amounts from his distorted mouth. The wet lips writhed as he tried to form words, gasping for breath all the while. But no words came—only that hoarse howl.

"Stand back," said the portly physician, waving his cane at Doctor Will. "I am Doctor Burkette, Master Lipcote's chief physician. Stand back, you charlatan. Can you not see that your presence disturbs the patient?"

"He is more than disturbed," said Doctor Will quietly. "He is in extremis. Why is he out here in the cold and the wet, and not safe in his bed with whatever succour you can offer him?"

"Shhh!" The physician looked nervously about. The crowd had pressed forward, weaving and darting in efforts to see. The servants had laid the

litter upon the ground and were trying to push back the crowd. The other
physicians were clutching their hats, trying to keep their feet. "Did you
have but a modicum of medical knowledge," said Doctor Burkette, "you
would not need to ask what we are doing. The patient has hydrophobia.
The water sickness as laymen call it—and as you should know. He will
not drink. His body is possessed by an aversion to water: At mere sight
of a flagon he goes into fits."

"I know," said Doctor Will. "And his body is perishing for lack of water."

Doctor Burkette cleared his throat. "Precisely. We have bled him to
expel the vicious humours that possess him. We tried blistering, but he
flings himself about so that the poultices are thrown off. But he will not
drink. There is naught left but to douse him, and—" He blinked. *Why
am I speaking to this imposter as to a colleague?*

"But it will do no good."

"Nonsense. The shock of the cold water will cure him."

"It will do no good," repeated Doctor Will to the physician's back. "It
will merely weaken him more if it does not kill him outright." Here, he
thought, *I cannot permit this to continue.*

The crowd had been distracted by the argument. Unnoticed, the litter
bearers had picked up their burden and begun edging their way down
the bluff. The physicians followed, picking their way carefully down the
muddy path.

Doctor Will made his way down behind them. *How can I stop them? I
do not know—but I must try.* Reaching the waterside, he tried once
more to press through the crowd watching ropes being tied to the litter
handles. "Mind you bind him tightly to the litter," ordered Doctor Burkette.

At sight of the water, Lipcote had begun to howl again, flinging himself
against his bonds until the muscles stood out like ropes upon his arms
and legs, twisting and knotting with spasm.

At length, litter and bearers struggled up a small quay. "No!" cried
Doctor Will. But as he started forward, two burly men blocked his path.

As the little group on the quay neared the deep end, the howls of the
patient rose in pitch, becoming shrieks that reverberated over the water
and echoed back from the sides of the bluffs. Then the sound was abruptly
choked off.

"Keep him down . . . wait . . . now!" There was splashing and thrashing
about, then a choking gurgle. Doctor Will could see the bearers shift
and stumble as they raised the dripping litter. Then Lipcote's howling
sounded again, mixed with coughing and spluttering and frantic jerkings
of the ropes that held the litter. "Again," came the voice of the chief
physician. "Longer this time."

The process was repeated. It seemed to Doctor Will that hours passed, measured only by the hoarse breathing of the now silent watchers.

This time there was no outcry as the litter was raised—only silence. The watchers backed off as the litter, streaming water, was laid upon the quay. The sodden figure upon it lay limp and still.

"Now—you see? His fits have been cured. The ill humours have been drowned." The chief physician was smiling.

"Looks to me like Master Lipcote be drownt," someone called.

"Nonsense." But one of the other physicians knelt beside the litter, his ear to the patient's chest. He caught Doctor Burkette's eye and shook his head ever so slightly. "Nonsense," said the chief physician again. He pulled at one of his gold chains and drew forth a small mirror. Bending over Lipcote, he held it to the patient's lips. After some moments he straightened, consternation upon his face.

"You've killed him," said Doctor Will.

The crowd took up the cry.

"Killed him!"

"Murderers!"

"Drownt him dead."

Then a figure limped out of the shadows and scrambled stiffly up onto the quay. "Fools!" cried Caleb Sawyer. "Look about you! There's your murderer—that blackamoor sorcerer! Was it not in his den that this poor man was set upon? Was it not the blackamoor's cat—the sorcerer's familiar—that set upon him?"

The crowd stirred uneasily, muttering amongst themselves. There was that about Caleb's distorted face, its scars purple in the fading light, that did not inspire confidence.

Doctor Will gave Caleb a pitying look not untinged with contempt. With a last sad glance toward the tableau on the quay, he turned to go.

"You fools!" cried Caleb. "Don't let him escape you!" All at once the crowd shifted, then surged toward the Black Doctor.

CHAPTER ❧ 32

W HEN SHE HEARD the mob coming, Serena was in the herb room. Hoofs were pounding along the road. Muffled shrieks and catcalls penetrated the walls. Without thinking, she snatched up Melissa and hustled her to the stairs. "Quickly! Go up to the garret. Wait there till Mama comes for you!"

Melissa hesitated, her eyes wide, her lower lip trembling. "Mama, come with me."

"I can't." With an anguished glance toward the entryway, Serena swung the child up several steps. None too gently, she gave her a push. "Go! Do as Mama tells you. You'll be all right. But hurry!" With a light slap on the bottom she nudged Melissa upward.

Feet pounded on the path, then on the stoop. The yells and catcalls were louder. "Go!" shouted Serena. With a last tearful look behind her, Melissa scrambled up the stairs and out of sight.

Serena darted toward the door. In despair she saw that she had forgotten to shoot the bolt. Is the back door bolted? Yes. I have not been outside today. She flung herself against the front door. But she was too late. It burst open with a force that threw her to the floor. Someone cuffed her aside as she struggled to rise. Burly figures poured through the doorway. "This way. To the back!" someone shouted.

Serena recognized the voice. It was Jed. Pushing and shoving, the intruders trampled through the hall. A picture fell, the glass shattering. From the parlour came crashing and thumping as furniture was overturned. Serena scrambled to her feet. Seizing a heavy candlestick, she started down the hall toward the herb room.

❧ ❧ ❧

SERENA . . . I MUST WARN SERENA. She is all alone with the child. Doctor Will forced himself to his knees. He patted the damp earth, groping for his spectacles. His body felt bruised and stiff. The mob had not truly attacked him but merely trampled him in their haste to reach his horse and wagon. "Get his medicine case!" someone shouted. "Cut the horse loose!"

Stray kicks and cuffs had struck him as he strove to rise. One hooligan had paused long enough to grind the fallen spectacles under his heel. Then they were gone, scrambling up the bluff. He heard shouts, then hoofbeats. The startled physicians clustered on the quay, making no effort to assist him. How long had he lain there, but half-conscious? All had departed the scene. A preternatural stillness reigned over the creekside, broken only by the murmur of the water. The Black Doctor's groping fingers closed about the wire spectacle frame. Both lenses were smashed, the frames distorted. Doctor Will's fingers shook as he stowed the useless remnants in his waistcoat. A wave of dizziness swept over him as he gained his feet. He swayed slightly, then took a deep breath. Holding on to bushes and tree trunks, he made his way up the bluff.

The street before Lipcote's mansion lay empty.

🙶 🙶 🙶

FROM THE HERB ROOM came the sound of crockery smashing against the brick floor. The room was aboil with figures darting to and fro, pulling jars and flasks from the shelves, kicking over stools and workbenches. The fire flared through the open door of the stove as it consumed the bunches of herbs someone fed to it.

"Stop!" Serena hurled herself into the fray, laying about her with the candlestick. Broken glass crunched under her feet. She felt a savage pleasure as the candlestick struck flesh and bone, provoking startled yowls. For a moment the fury of her onslaught forced the intruders back. "Seize her!" The voice was familiar. As her eyes met Caleb Sawyer's, someone struck her from behind. A swirl of sparks streaked past her eyes. Then she fell.

🙶 🙶 🙶

DOCTOR WILL LIMPED toward home. It is but a few miles, he told himself. Best take a back trail. At the sound of hoofs he looked about dazedly, seeking a place to hide. The hoofbeats came nearer. He moved off the

road. Perhaps I can hide in that ditch. "Wait, friend! Master Pond! Wait!"
Doctor Will turned. Jouncing along in his upholstered carriage was Hiram
Jonas.

𝄞 𝄞 𝄞

MULLINER'S CLOAK was smothering her, choking off her breath. I must
get free! I must get away! Thrashing and struggling, she sat upright. Her
head cleared, but a black haze still hung in the air. Smoke!

Someone had scattered the burning coals from the stove and tossed
the last of the dried herbs on them as kindling. Flames were licking at
the shattered furniture piled in the centre of the room. Coughing, Serena
scrambled to her feet. She swayed dizzily but kept her footing. Her inti-
mate knowledge of the room came to her aid. She made for the sink,
first yanking at the piled debris to scatter it, giving the flames less of a
foothold.

Thank God! They had not damaged the cistern. Ignorant clods that
they were, they had doubtless failed to grasp its purpose. Filling a bucket
with water, she emptied it on the flames. The fire sputtered, then flared
anew. Another bucket. Another. Still another. Her arms ached from the
weight of the wooden pail.

There! A trail of flame was snaking toward the door, fed by the litter
on the floor. Even in her frenzied haste, she gave thanks for Doctor
Will's foresight. Had the floor been wood, it would be ablaze by now,
and she with it. Another bucket of water.

Dashing over the scattered embers, she seized a rag rug from the entryway and carried it to the sink. Scarcely feeling the pull on her strained
shoulder muscles, she swung the wet rug again and again.

𝄞 𝄞 𝄞

"WAIT HERE, if you please, Master Jonas." Doctor Will alighted stiffly from
the carriage. A faint smell of smoke hung in the air. The tall, narrow
house loomed lightless in the gathering dusk. There was no sign of life.

"Is something amiss? I'll go with you." Hiram Jonas beckoned to the
coachman.

"I don't know. Please — wait."

A quizzical look on his cherubic face, Jonas hesitated. Then he subsided doubtfully to the edge of the carriage seat.

⪭ ⪭ ⪭

"SERENA, CHILD!" Serena met Doctor Will in the entryway. Her eyes glistened in her smudged face, barely visible in the gloom. "Are you all right?"

"What does it matter about me? Oh, Doctor Will! What has befallen you? And because of me." The sight of the kindly face, bent toward her in love and concern, was too much for Serena. Flinging her arms about Doctor Will's neck, she cried bitterly.

Doctor Will let her cry for a few moments. Then he held her away from him. "What have they done?"

Serena could not speak. Taking his hand, she led him to the back of the house.

The herb room lay in ruins. Broken pieces of the work tables lay about the room, still smouldering. Serena found a candle and lighted it. Shards of glass upon the floor glittered like eyes winking in malicious triumph. Serena's books had been torn and scattered about; charred pages rustled on the hearthstone as a slight draught stirred them. A pungent smell arose from the floor where tinctures and infusions had been spilt.

"Child—" Doctor Will paused. Serena's head was flung back in an attitude of listening. Then he heard it, too: a faint whimpering.

"Melissa!" Brushing past the Black Doctor, Serena rushed toward the stairway and started up.

"Mama! Mama!" The voice came from outside. "Mama!"

Serena rushed out, Doctor Will close behind.

Melissa was scrambling up the high stoop, sobbing. Her curls were in disarray, her dress torn and stained. Blood trickled from a cut on her forehead.

"Melissa!" Serena fell to her knees and took the child into her arms, hugging her close, stroking the tangled hair. At her mother's touch, Melissa began to sob hysterically. "It's all right . . . Mama's here . . . What happened, darling?"

"Stone!" Melissa hiccoughed and began to cry more quietly.

"They threw a stone at you?"

Melissa nodded, burying her face in her mother's neck. Serena hugged the child, her own face grey.

"I'll get some water." Doctor Will returned with a bowl and a dampened cloth. Gently, he took the child from Serena and began to cleanse the gravel and blood from her forehead.

Melissa quieted, stoically bearing the sting. Then she looked up at Serena. "Mama, what is a bastard?"

Serena gasped. Then she said quietly, "I'll tell you later, Melissa. Come, now, it's time you were abed." She gathered the child into her arms. Melissa began to cry again. Holding her daughter tightly, soothing and rocking her, Serena looked up at Doctor Will.

"You see?" Tears streamed down her face. "This is what I have brought her—and you. If I stay here to help you rebuild, I shall most likely destroy you. And I shall surely destroy Melissa."

Her control broke. Her hand still mechanically stroking Melissa's back, she cried out the words she had not yet asked of anyone but herself. "Oh, my God, where shall I go? What can I do?"

The sound of footfalls startled them both. Serena looked up. Hiram Jonas stood there, his hands clasped under his coattails, his short, round figure rocking on his small feet. "May I make a suggestion?" he inquired.

BOOK III

❧

Jonas of Jonasville

CHAPTER ❧ 3 3

S UNLIGHT POURED through the leaded panes of the bay window, caressing Serena's shoulders and striking sparks of gold from the loosened hair that tumbled to her waist. She sat upon a velvet-cushioned bench, naked but for a drapery of silk that lightly traced the curves of her body from breast to hips, then spilled in gleaming folds onto the richly coloured carpet.

"Is this how you wish me to sit?"

"Yes, but . . . your right hand. Lift your hair from the back of your neck . . . no! Your arm must be higher. It must lift your breast . . . so." The swarthy young man with the intent dark eyes leapt cat-like to her side. He tugged her arm upward and tilted her head, shaping, arranging, until her hair spilled in silken ribbons over her breasts. "So," he repeated, satisfied.

He returned to his easel in the centre of the room and sketched busily, in bold, sweeping strokes. "Yes." He nodded, his eyes intent upon her form, seeing every pore of her skin, seeing her not at all. "First the draw-ing—you see? Then the clay. And after, long after, the marble."

Serena sighed. Ever so slightly, her lifted arm began to droop.

"No! No!" At once he was at her side. None too gently, he thrust her arm back into the position he had set. "You must stay still! Still! Until I finish drawing. And later, too. Still!"

Serena sighed. The posture was tiring, yet not tiring enough. It allowed her to think. How many hours must I sit here? How many days?

At the far end of the room, a panelled door opened. Hiram Jonas entered, his gold-rimmed spectacles and some foolscap sheets in one hand.

"How are you faring, Master Pietro? And you, my dear?"

Crossing and recrossing the bars of sunlight that striped the Persian rugs and waxed parquet, he bounced jauntily toward them. At the easel he paused, hands behind him, rocking from heel to toe as was his wont when pondering something. "The face is very fine, but the pose . . ." He hesitated. "Hmmmm . . . No. That is not what I wanted." He tapped lightly on the sketch pad with his spectacles. "Here. And here. This must be removed."

The young man hesitated. "The drapery? You wish that her breasts be undraped?"

"Indeed I do. They are very beautiful, are they not?"

Serena felt herself blushing. But the sculptor seemed undismayed. "Very beautiful, *si!* But did you not tell me the statue, it is to be for your garden?"

"And so it is." Hiram Jonas put on his spectacles. His blue eyes, wide and guileless, peered over their rims, first at Serena, then at the sculptor. "So it is." He waited.

"But . . ."

Jonas did not answer. He held the sculptor's eye until the young man shifted his glance, first to the sketch, then to Serena. His eyes kindled. Once more he bounded to Serena's side. "*Si!* The pose it shall be the same. But the drapery . . ." Skillfully he redraped the silken folds. "Perhaps a bit of subtlety to balance the revelation?" Now one end of the drape curved around Serena's shoulders, the other lightly caressed her left breast and spilled across her lap to the floor. Her right breast and her legs were laid bare. Pietro sent Jonas a questioning glance.

"Excellent — most subtle. To conceal the one is to reveal the other. You are indeed a master of your art." Jonas bowed toward the sculptor, who returned to his place by the easel.

"Hiram —" A plea in her eyes, Serena looked at Jonas, avoiding the eye of the sculptor, whose lips twisted cynically as he took in the scene. "Please . . . must I do this?"

Jonas shifted his gaze from her breasts to her face. His blue eyes narrowed, his plump cheeks firmed, lines sprang out at the corners of his eyes as his lower lip thrust forward. "Yes, you must." He turned to Master Pietro. "I shall arrange a place for you to work undisturbed on the modelling." He turned on his heel and left the room.

❧   ❧   ❧

"Oh, CHARITY, I *can't!* He means to put it into the garden for everyone to see! And that Italian — hearing it all! I cannot do this. I —" She broke off. What other deeds have I now done with a cloak of darkness for concealment?

Charity said nothing but continued brushing Serena's hair in long, soothing strokes. When Serena had arrived in Jonasville, Hiram Jonas had transferred Charity and 'Tate into quarters attached to Jonas House, blithely ignoring the mutterings this unwonted arrangement evoked from his servants and workers. 'Tate had become his foreman, Charity his housekeeper.

Serena pulled the velvet wrapper more closely about her body, tightening the sash with a jerk. "I won't!" she said. "There must be some end to what he can ask of me." She blushed, remembering the previous night, and other nights, too, a succession of nights whose sum was this interminable year. Why does this seem so much worse? Because there is someone else to hear and to see? Someone else to know—not to speculate upon, but to know—the nature of the relation between Hiram Jonas and me?

Charity laid the ivory-backed brush upon the polished mahogany stand. In the cheval glass with its carved oval frame, each of two sombre women met the other's reflected gaze. Serena's eyes fell first. "I know. I know what you are going to say. I made a bargain—and he has kept his part of it." If only I could write to Melissa. Does she miss me, there in New York? Does she remember me at all? Or Charity and 'Tate? Or the Black Doctor? Or has she already begun to forget?

ș● ș● ș●

No sooner had he ensconced Serena and Melissa at Jonasville, than Hiram Jonas began the search for Mistress Mansey. "She is in New York," he told Serena within a matter of weeks. "She is mistress of a girls' school there. I shall take ship at once, and—"

"No! No, Hiram. I shall see her myself, and explain to her—"

At once came that thrust of the lower lip of which Serena had already learned to be wary. Genial as he had seemed at Doctor Will's, Hiram Jonas brooked no interference with his plans, however whimsical. "Have you so soon forgotten the terms of our agreement?"

Not likely, thought Serena, since to protect all I hold dear I must relinquish it. "No, of course I have not forgotten."

"Well then, my dear, the sooner Melissa departs, the sooner she will forget that she has ever been here. And the sooner she ceases to call you 'Mama'—"

"—the sooner she forgets me. I know." Serena swallowed hard. She turned aside, looking fixedly through the window and forcing herself to concentrate on the progress of the men who were building a brick wall around the gardens.

When she could control her voice, she turned back to Jonas. She straightened her shoulders and looked directly into his eyes. "I will do as you ask, Hiram. As I have already done in other matters." She felt her face turn crimson. "But this you must grant me: that I see Mistress Mansey myself and explain to her. That I myself hear what she suggests for Melissa. Otherwise"—she raised her hands in supplication, then let them fall, clenched, to her sides—"otherwise, there is no bargain." And where will I go then? How will I find shelter for Melissa? How will I protect her from being stoned as a bastard again?

She held firm against the onslaught of questions that besieged her. Awareness of her quandary only strengthened her resolve to win this contest. Quite consciously, she drew a deep breath that pressed her breasts against the silken fabric of her bodice. She dropped her lashes to screen her eyes. "Have you not been pleased with your bargain so far? Have I not given full measure?"

The slight tremor in her voice went unnoticed. A faint flush travelled up from Jonas' brow and lost itself in the white curls that fringed his pate. He cleared his throat. "Yes, indeed you have."

"Then trust me with this errand, Hiram. Let me satisfy myself that Melissa will have a safe haven, one where she can be happy." Happy—and educated, as I was not. Prepared to face the world, as I was not. That is what I must arrange with Mistress Mansey.

Jonas rocked back and forth, stroking his chin. "This Mistress Mansey, can we be assured of her discretion? If she tattles the story all about, as old maids will—"

"Did she talk indiscreetly, she'd not be mistress of a girls' school," said Serena tartly. "Mine will not be the first secret she has kept."

Hiram Jonas smiled and nodded. "Well put, my dear. Well put."

ᴂ   ᴂ   ᴂ

SERENA SET her teacup down. Clasping her hands in her lap, she leaned forward. "That is the bargain I have made, Mistress Mansey. And a shameful bargain you may think it to be. But Hiram Jonas has money and power. I have neither. By myself I cannot protect Melissa, nor give her what she will need to protect herself when she is older. As Hiram Jonas' mistress I can do these things."

"And at what cost to yourself, Serena?"

"That no longer matters." Serena watched Mistress Mansey's face. It had changed but little. The high, intelligent brow, the sensitive mouth with the slight droop at its corners, held neither surprise nor condemnation. Only the heightened lustre of the soft brown eyes betrayed a hint of sympathy. With the quiet calm Serena remembered, Mistress Mansey studied her former pupil.

"The child is very young to leave her home."

"She is near to four." Serena's voice quavered, then steadied. "But she is wise beyond her years. And her very youth will help her to forget . . . forget me." Serena looked down at her hands, clasped tightly in her lap. "If there is some loving home where she could go until she is old enough for your school—"

"I know of none that would be suitable." With a slight wave of her hand, Mistress Mansey silenced Serena. "No one," she went on, "of whose discretion I could be sure. But . . ." She paused, fingering the eyeglass case that hung on a gold chain about her neck. "Would you entrust her here? To me?"

Serena's lips trembled in a half-smile. "To you? Oh, Mistress Mansey, there is no one to whom I would rather trust her. But you . . . and a small child? How would you find the time for her?"

"I will find it." That subject was closed. "You say the child is intelligent?"

"Oh, yes! Already she knows the alphabet. She can count. She is clever with her slate, drawing pictures."

"Then let her stay with me. I'll not say I have no motive of my own, Serena. Too long I've heard it said that women have no head for learning. I have suffered from that prejudice, as you have." The schoolmistress looked Serena full in the eye. "I have some hint, Serena, of what you might have been, had you had the opportunities your brother wasted, and the schooling."

Serena sighed lightly. "I had hoped once to be a teacher, like you." She thought of her flight on the night of the fire, of how she had sought to reach Mistress Mansey and beg her for assistance.

"Had you? Or is that the most you thought yourself allowed to hope for?"

For some moments there was silence between them. The fire crackled in the small grate, and snowflakes played a glassy tune upon the windowpane.

What dreams did *you* have? wondered Serena, watching the calm face across from her. But she dared not ask. Impulsively, she rose from her chair and sank to her knees at Mistress Mansey's side. She clasped the cool, slender hand between her own, then pressed it to her forehead. "I will send Melissa to you. Together we will decide what to tell her . . . and what not to tell her. But teach her—oh, please, Mistress Mansey, teach her, not as though she were to be a 'young lady,' not stitching and sketching and nonsense. Not 'womanly arts'—or not those arts alone. Teach her of the world as men learn of the world. Teach her mathe-

242 ❧ matics, and what science you can. Set her loose among books. Teach her"—Serena swallowed hard—"teach her what you would have taught me, if it were not too late." She laid her head upon her teacher's knee.

Softly, Mistress Mansey stroked her hair. "I will teach her, Serena."

❧ ❧ ❧

HIRAM JONAS SNORED, exhausted by his strivings. In the light of the full May moon, his bulk cast a black shadow upon Serena. She lay wide-eyed and sleepless in the massive, tumbled bed, her nerves stretched taut. Always it was the same. Like a voracious infant's, his mouth took her breasts, suckling, it seemed, for hours. But his manhood, scarcely larger than a child's, and barely turgid, could but rake at the coals of his desire, never bringing the release of flame except when, whimpering, he bade her press it to her lips as he had taught her. Then he had done, and quickly. Immediately, he slept, while she lay wakeful, and the silver disc that was the moon rolled silent down the arc that was the sky.

Now I know, she thought. Now I know for what complaint he sought Doctor Will's assistance. She leaned upon her elbow, studying Jonas' face in the moonlight. In repose it looked more child-like than by day. Should I despise him? Or be grateful to him? There seems no malice in him. Then why make a prisoner of me? Why bind me by my love for Melissa? It seems unlike him in a way. Why did he not ask me to marry him? I'd be his prisoner in law then, not by mere promise. Wives have no rights—or few enough.

She lay down again, turning her back to him, her body curled upon itself, seeking repose. Still it clamoured for the release that night after night was denied it. Forced by her will to submit to his attentions, her body played traitor, tormenting her with sensations she recalled but too well. Her breasts throbbed. Deep, deep within, a remembered fire refused to be put out. Her hand stole between her thighs to bring her what surcease it could.

CHAPTER ❧ 3 4

A DROP OF SWEAT trickled down Serena's face. It itched intolerably. She tossed her head to shake it off, then resumed her pose. The heated air scarcely stirred the moist curls about her brow. The breeze carried a hint of pine, barely perceptible beneath the nearer scents of hay and moistened earth. From this vantage in the loft she could see the men working about the grounds, labouring beneath the weight of the oaken buckets which they emptied at the base of newly planted trees. Beyond the high brick wall that now enclosed the garden she could see the glitter of the mill pond. The rush of the spillway and the creak of the water wheels at Jonas' manufactory drifted to her ears, borne lightly upon the vapours of the somnolent afternoon.

She felt her eyelids drooping with a languor that went beyond weariness. The heat, the scent of pine, lay upon her skin like a caress. Almost she could feel herself a child again, drowsing by some Barrens stream, teasing herself by putting off the moment when she would strip off her shoes and stockings and dabble her feet in its fragrant cedar waters.

"Your arm."

"What?" Was it drowsiness that lent the sculptor's voice its husky note?

"Lift your arm."

"Oh." Her glance met his across the bare boards of the floor. The clay model was progressing. He had worked for some weeks alone up here, coming only today to ask her to pose as he modelled some details. He had shed his shirt, and his leather breeches hung low about his hips. His powerful shoulders gleamed with sweat. The appraising glance to which she had become so accustomed—the glance that encompassed every pore of her skin yet ignored her person—was gone. Today he saw her. In the instant that both of them knew it, he turned away.

He dipped his hands into a bucket of water, then into the deep barrel of clay. The spatter of drops upon the floor seemed loud in the breathless stillness as he rolled a bit of clay between his palms. All at once she was conscious of his hands.

They were large in proportion to his compact, muscled body—large but well shaped, with long, spatulate fingers, deeply tanned. Droplets of water glistened in the black, wiry hairs on his knuckles. He kneaded the pliant clay with a touch firm yet sensual, then applied it to the model. She could see only its back, but from the angle at which he was working, she could tell that he was sculpting her bared breast. The ball of clay he had been rolling between his fingers—was that to form the nipple?

The heat in the room seemed more intense, pressing down upon them, thick and sultry, scented by the cedar shingles in the roof high above their heads and the salt hay in the haymow behind her. By the window, dust motes danced in the sunrays, yet thunder hung in the air.

Once more he dipped his hands into the bucket. His eyes never leaving her face, he stroked and smoothed. The muscles of his forearms rippled beneath his glistening skin. In the dark hair of his chest hung beads of sweat, trembling ever faster with the motion of his breath.

Serena felt her own breath quicken. As though her eyes had assumed the power to translate sight to touch, she felt his hands moving, sensed the intimacy of his knowledge of her body and its secrets. He had never touched her . . . he had touched her again and again, this stranger with whom she had exchanged in words but the barest of civilities.

Dusk settled upon the room like smoke. Still he worked on. Alert as he was to every nuance of her flesh, he saw, she knew, how her nipples had lifted and tightened, as she saw, with preternatural keenness, the quiver of his lips, the tremor of his perspiring hands as he thrust them into the cooling water.

Now he breathed as though he were running.

Her lips parted. Her throat felt dry, parched by the flames that swept through her body—the body she had so long denied. She felt their warmth in her loins, in her belly. She was dimly aware of an ache in her shoulder and realized that her arm was still raised as the pose demanded. Its muscles twitched with weariness. She lowered it to her side, expecting the barked reprimand with which he greeted any such flagging.

He said nothing. His hands still rested upon the model, but his arms were still. She could see little of his face, only his eyes and the fire at their centres. Nothing but the sound of their breathing disturbed the twilit stillness of the chamber.

Without turning her head to look, Serena was acutely conscious of the soft hay piled behind her. Thunder rumbled again, more loudly now,

its sound intensifying the silence of the room. A faint breeze trailed cool
fingers down Serena's heated skin.

The yearning of the lonely years, the tension of a hundred nights spent tossing in Hiram Jonas' bed, sleepless and unfulfilled, coalesced into moulten fire pooling at the centre of her body. She could withstand it no longer. Suddenly, with a smile of defiance, she raised her arm once more, lifting the mass of heavy hair from her neck with a smooth motion, squaring her shoulders and thrusting out her breasts. She licked her dry lips.

He tensed. Then, in the instant's pause before he leapt to her, he stopped short, poised in an attitude of listening.

She heard it too, then: the sound of quiet footfalls on the floor below. The loft floor trembled faintly as someone mounted the ladder.

"Good evening," said Hiram Jonas. "Can it be that you are working in the dark?"

Neither answered. The silence grew. Why do I feel he has been watching us? Why does it seem that he knows — knows exactly what was about to happen?

It seemed a long time before Jonas spoke. "Can you have forgotten, my dear? It is time for you to dress. Tonight we inaugurate my theatre."

❧   ❧   ❧

THE LIGHT of a hundred candles was shattered to rainbows in the prisms of the great chandelier. Then, one by one, they were snuffed out. Along the curved apron of the stage, whale-oil footlights burned on, the crimson velvet curtains glowing in their light.

Damask panels framed in gilt lined the walls. Rows of chairs ranged back from the footlights, their cushions crimson like the curtains. They were empty. As the curtains swept apart, the footlights flickered, then steadied. The liveried musicians upon the stage lifted their instruments and began to play. The lilting notes of Haydn skipped into the hall.

High above the players, Serena sat with Hiram Jonas in the shelter of a gilt-and-velvet box. As she sighed her pleasure at the music, the jewels at her throat and breast shimmered as though they had extinguished the candles by capturing their light. Her bronze taffeta gown rustled with the movement of her breath. Jonas, too, wore full evening dress. They sat entirely alone.

The quartet ended. As Jonas and Serena applauded, the musicians shifted in their chairs, adjusting sheets of music, straightening the candles upon their music stands. There was a pause. Then the footlights flickered again as a woman swept onto the stage, her long train swirling behind her as she turned to face the footlights. So short was she, so buxom, so mincing was her gait, that Serena stifled a giggle. "She looks like a pouter pigeon," she whispered. Jonas frowned and shifted in his seat.

The soloist signalled the musicians. One picked up a flute and put it to his lips. A cadenza recalling, thought Serena, the sound of a wood thrush at twilight, issued from the instrument. Then the singer began. The two voices, woodwind and human, together wove a cadence so exquisite they seemed as one. Floating upon the music, her spirit drifting with the notes, Serena forgot singer and stage. Ever upward soared the melody, high and still higher, to the ceiling, to the sky. Then it wafted downward at last, as gently as a leaf on its autumn journey toward earth. The music ceased.

The singer bowed, her bejewelled hand clasping a fan before her bosom, her whitened wig with its piled-up curls in peril of falling, as her powdered bosom threatened to spill from her gown. Serena sat in a trance, forgetting to applaud, forgetting even where she was and who was with her. Never have I heard such music — never, indeed, any music but Mother's playing or the scrapings of some Barrens fiddler.

Jonas nudged her. Coming out of her dream, she clapped her hands as hard as she could. "Again," she breathed. "Oh, please — again."

As though she had heard, the singer beckoned her accompanists once more. This time all joined in the music, a cascade of variations so intricate Serena could scarce attend them. Up, down, and around, voice and instruments gamboled and frolicked, now joining, now parting, now in harmony, now in counterpoint, not one melody but two or three. Trying to follow, Serena felt she was trying to grasp at sunbeams. "Oh, what is it?" she whispered.

"Mozart — Wolfgang Amadeus Mozart," Jonas answered softly. "Madame Constanza has sung in his court operas. Under his personal direction."

"Mozart —" murmured Serena to herself. The name meant nothing. But the music . . . I had not known, she thought. She turned to look at Hiram Jonas. But for this man I might never have known. For once she smiled at him with her whole heart. Sensing, perhaps, something of her gratitude and pleasure, he smiled back and patted her hand.

The remainder of the performance floated past. When the curtains swept together for a final time, Serena sat in a daze, barely noticing that Jonas had left his seat. She frowned slightly, intent upon the echoes that lingered in her mind.

She started as a hand touched her shoulder. Jonas had returned. Behind him in the narrow entrance to their box stood 'Tate Jones. Serena blinked as the candles in the wall sconces were rekindled. Jonas, she saw, had a scrap of paper in his hand. Even at some distance, she could smell the heavy scent that pervaded it.

"Serena," said Jonas, "it appears that Madame Constanza will not be able to join me at supper. She writes"—he squinted at the paper, which was covered with writing in a flamboyant hand—"that she is 'indisposed' and will return at once to her chambers. Damn!" he said petulantly. "I had most particularly desired her present. Perhaps I had forgotten to tell you—"

Serena steeled herself. This expression often presaged news that Hiram Jonas had purposely been keeping to himself. Still half bemused by the music, she waited.

"A business associate—a specially important connection—is coming to join me for late supper."

Serena had had an inkling that some meeting of consequence was afoot. It was unlike Hiram Jonas to eschew her company at supper on such an occasion as this: The first performance in his private theatre was an event he had anticipated for months now. Yet tonight he had said not a word about her presence at table, even as he took Charity aside to give her elaborate orders. Serena waited while Jonas pondered, blinking and pulling at his lower lip. At last he turned to 'Tate. "Jones, stay here with Mistress Wainwright. When I send word—and not a moment before—escort her to the drawing room. I wish her to join us for supper."

"But Hiram, there is no need for 'Tate to wait with me. I can sit here quietly and think of the music—the lovely music," she added, giving him a smile, "until you call for me. It's but a step through the garden to Jonas House."

"You are not to wander about in the dark alone. Stay with her, Jones." And he was gone.

ᴥ ᴥ ᴥ

"Oh, stop here a moment, 'Tate. The night is so beautiful." Serena lingered outside the scrolled iron gate that led into the gardens. The gilt eagles that poised, wings outstretched, upon the tall gateposts gleamed faintly in the dark.

'Tate paused obediently. It be a bad night for me, do the Master catch us bidin'.

A shower at sunset had laid the dust and cooled the air. From Serena's flower garden came the heady scent of stock, the pungence of rosemary. The leaves of the horse chestnut trees that guarded the walkway rustled faintly, spattering the bricks with some last drops of rain. Then the moonlight pierced the dispersing clouds. A silver haze arose as cool air struck the sunwarmed bricks, bringing with it the musky smell of earth.

Serena breathed deeply. Beyond the garden walls, the treetops tossed restlessly. A bird gave a sleepy trill reminiscent of the music that had so enchanted her — as the music had been reminiscent of birdsong. Oh, to stay here in the garden, she thought, while the night conceals its raw newness, to rest upon a wall and drink in the savour of the night until the last lovely notes fade to memories.

"Miz Serena," whispered 'Tate.

She caught his urgency. She nodded. He unlocked the gate and threw it back, stepping aside that she might enter.

Light from the manor house spilled upon the path. The tall windows, their shutters thrown open, glowed hospitably. The chandelier in the hall was lit, and the candle flames trembled in the wall sconces as Serena and 'Tate passed through the great entrance door.

At the end of the hall, the carved double doors of the drawing room stood open. Serena caught a glimpse of the supper table with its heavy damask cover, its tall vases filled with flowers, its silver candelabra ablaze with light. Male voices drifted toward her: Jonas' light tenor and another voice, deeper, more resonant.

A pulse began to beat in her throat. "I can go by myself, 'Tate," she heard herself say. As in a dream she drifted toward the open door.

"Ah, there you are, my dear," carolled Jonas. "Serena, may I present —"

She heard no more. Transfixed, she stood in the doorway, praying not to fall.

Towering over his rotund host, one hand upon his shirt frill as he prepared to bow, the faintest of smiles hovering about his lips, stood Stuart Brandon.

C H A P T E R ✺ 3 5

S HE HAS CHANGED, thought Stuart Brandon. I remembered a child. He had remembered disconcertingly often. But this was a woman. For a long moment he watched her, still standing in the doorway, struggling to regain her poise. The hand with which she gripped the moulding bore a splendid emerald ringed with diamonds. Diamonds shimmered in her hair like raindrops reluctant to fall. The jewels upon her breast sparkled in the light of the room's many candles, flashing in cadence with her efforts to catch her breath.

His glance swept the length of her body, marking the bronze iridescence of the gown that complimented her eyes, the waist more slender than he remembered, the curve of hips and breasts more womanly. Her eyes, dazed, were fixed upon his face. The shadows beneath them were new. Her face was thinner, her cheekbones more prominent; no trace of childish roundness remained. My God, what a beauty. I had forgotten.

As he watched, colour swept back into her face. She drew a deep breath and moved toward him, hand extended. He felt the quiver of the icy fingers she proffered. He bowed. "Good evening, Mistress Wainwright. You seem distressed." His lips brushed her skin.

Serena swayed slightly. She felt crushed, flattened, as though she had pitched forward upon the ground from some great height. Is it happenstance that he should greet me with the first words he ever addressed to me? No. He had spoken, she saw, in full knowledge of his words' significance. His blue eyes glinted; the fine lines at their corners deepened as he raised one brow.

Damn him! She fought to force air into her lungs past the strangling obstruction in her throat. Damn him — I'll not faint before him like some vapouring virgin. I'm mistress of Jonasville now, or near enough. The cold touch of the jewels upon her throat renewed her courage, reminding her of her changed position. Yet the voice of Hiram Jonas seemed to come from some great distance.

"Serena," he whispered urgently, "are you quite well? Whatever is the matter, my dear?" His small plump hand gripped her arm.

She forced her gaze away from Brandon. "Nothing is the matter, Hiram." She touched Jonas' hand with hers, on which the shape of Brandon's lips seemed limned by fire. Gently she freed herself. "I merely felt faint for a moment. So many candles . . . in this heat . . ." Her voice trailed off. Indeed, the candle flames were dancing before her eyes like so many rockets. She turned to Brandon once more.

"Good evening, Captain Brandon. What accounts for your presence amongst us, now that there are no British merchantmen to plunder?" Alone, she thought. I must talk with him alone. I must tell him about Melissa.

Hiram Jonas continued to fuss. "You do not seem yourself, my dear. Captain Brandon, would you be so good as to assist Mistress Wainwright to a chair?" He gestured toward the supper table. "She'll be the better for some food. I'll have them serve us at once." He bustled away.

Brandon's lips curved in a faint smile. "My apologies," he said, "for the impetuosity of my late companion." He bowed slightly and extended his arm.

Serena placed her fingertips lightly upon it, feeling the hard muscles beneath the fine blue broadcloth of his coat. Her vision cleared, and she saw him fully for the first time. Silver buttons trimmed the revers of his coat; his waistcoat was brocade, his linen immaculate. Chamois breeches stressed the long lines of his thighs, supple boots his muscular calves. His dark hair was neatly dressed in a club; his face was deeply tanned. As she touched him, something quivered within her—some renascence of the feelings of the sultry afternoon.

"I—I thought you were dead," she blurted. "All these years when I—" She hesitated.

"Dead?" He looked down into her face, his brows once again arched sardonically. He began moving toward the supper table with the lithe grace she remembered so well.

"Captured and hanged by the British. When they ran you aground at Barnegat."

"*They* ran *me* aground? And at Barnegat? You grant me little credit as a seaman, Mistress Wainwright. I would have credited you with a wit too sharp to give credence to such a tale." He pulled out one of the heavy carved chairs. With the barest excess of solicitude, he seated her. Then he took the chair opposite. Facing her across the snowy damask, he threw back his head and laughed. "That fat popinjay of a British captain would be happy enough, were it true. Now Mistress Wainwright — surely you know as well as I that all but the channel of Barnegat Bay has five feet of draught or less. Would I be likely to run afoul of it? That man-o-war may even now be grounded in the muck."

"But Caleb said—" She recalled the stifling air of the tower room, the jolt in the pit of her belly, Caleb's malevolent triumph. "Then that, too, was a lie," she said softly. "Oh, if I had known . . . What a fool I was to believe him."

"Are you suggesting, Mistress Wainwright, that the thought of my demise has disturbed you? Considering the terms upon which we parted, you have a spirit more forgiving than I would have dared suppose." He broke off.

Hiram Jonas had seated himself in the armchair at the head of the table. A silent manservant began proffering silver servers. "Try that casserole of crab, Brandon." Jonas helped himself to a gargantuan portion. "A specialty of Jonas House."

For some minutes there was silence as each addressed his meal. Jonas attacked the food with gusto, swallowing oysters one upon the other, draining each rough, crinkled shell with noisy sips, oblivious of the juice running down his wrists and forearms, soaking the frills of his shirt cuffs. "Sample that venison, Brandon." He waved his arm toward the burdened sideboard. "Help the Captain to some of the joint."

Serena pushed food about on the plate with her heavy silver fork: succulent crab in creamy sauce rich with cheese and buttered crumbs, new peas freshly green. My favourite, she thought. And I've not eaten since morning. She could not swallow one morsel. She reached for a cut-glass goblet and forced some wine past her dry throat. If only Hiram Jonas would not notice her lack of appetite. And yet — a hint of an idea came to her. She looked up, startled. Brandon was speaking.

"How delightful — and how surprising, Mistress Wainwright — to come upon you here, so far from home." A faint twitch of his lips acknowledged the triteness of his comment.

Jonas looked from one to the other. "You have met before?" He pursed his lips, then smiled broadly. "Ah, yes — yes, of course. You would have met at Wainwright House when Captain Brandon was working with your father. A fine ironmaster, Samuel Wainwright, not like that unprincipled nincompoop who married your sister."

Despite her preoccupation, Serena giggled. How well he has pegged Caleb Sawyer. Though Hiram underestimates him. When his malice drives him, he's shrewd enough. She shivered.

Jonas threw her an anxious glance.

Brandon's brows rose slightly. "Caleb Sawyer? Is he master of Weyford now?"

He knows this already, thought Serena. I'm sure of it. He is merely sounding Hiram out. A glance at Brandon, whose expression subtly mocked his tone of polite inquiry, confirmed her thought.

Hiram Jonas looked surprised. "You did not know? But of course you've been in Europe these past two years." He mopped at his face, then his hands and wrists, with the damask napkin. "You may bring the sweet," he told the manservant, watching attentively as crystal dishes of rich custard and plump raspberries were handed round.

"Yes," he continued, spooning custard, "Caleb Sawyer is in charge of Weyford. And he is running it into the ground. Business is slack since the War, to be sure, with no more cannon or shot to be made. But there's new business to be had, were he to look for it. New iron business, I mean. Atsion is in blast again and doing well with cauldrons for the new salt-works—and Franklin stoves, too. Sawyer could have made a fair sum supplying Jonasville alone. I'm using iron by the ton." This was true enough, thought Serena. Jonas had an intense fear of fire, and all possible parts of his buildings were made of iron rather than wood.

"But Sawyer's stuff's not worth the buying." Jonas signalled the manservant to bring him another dish of custard. "A cracking mixture, the lot of it, when it's poured at all. The furnace is out of blast for weeks at a time. And I doubt he makes a half-ton a day when he does pour. But"— he broke off—"this talk of iron must be tedious for Serena. Shall we repair to the drawing room?" Without waiting for an answer he pushed back his chair.

Brandon rose at once and bowed to Serena. "May I?" He offered his arm. Serena stood up, glad to be done with the pretense of eating. But she hung back, letting Jonas go ahead of them. Now, she thought. She took a deep breath. "I must see you alone," she said softly.

"Indeed?" He looked at her quizzically. "And how, pray, is that to be arranged without offending your . . . protector?"

"Serena!" Jonas' tone held a hint of the querulous. "Come along and pour our coffee." He squinted up at her as she hastened to do his bidding. "Are you quite well?" She is paler than was her wont, he thought. What could be the matter with her?

"Yes, of course," said Serena. But she put her hand to her brow for an instant, watching Jonas intently from beneath it. Then she poured coffee from the silver service the manservant had set on a low table before silently departing from the room. When both men had been served, she took a cup for herself and sat down in a velvet-covered armchair.

Brandon sipped coffee from a porcelain cup, gold, blue, and translucent white—Chinese, and one of Jonas' treasures. "Excellent. Now, pray tell us, Mistress Wainwright, since you find ironmaking tedious, what pursuits occupy your time?"

Serena stirred restlessly. But I don't find it tedious, she wanted to protest. Nor, she thought, does Hiram believe that I should. He is being unwontedly conventional tonight. I wonder why? Then her thoughts returned to Brandon and the meeting she so urgently desired. How long will he be here? How much time have I?

"Serena is most interested in the progress of the gardens," Jonas interposed when she made no reply. "She has planned much of the work there."

"Indeed? Perhaps you will be so good as to show them to me tomorrow. Or"—he looked directly at Serena—"are they seen to best advantage by moonlight?" He watched the play of the candlelight on her throat and breast as she breathed more quickly, seizing the opening he had given her. His breath, too, was quickening.

"Night conceals many flaws," she said, "and reveals many secrets. Especially at midnight." The barest narrowing of his eyes acknowledged her message. Giving him no time to reply, she turned to Jonas, who seemed to be puzzling over her last remark. She put her hand once more to her brow. "Hiram, I must beg your indulgence—and Captain Brandon's. You were right to think me unwell. I had best retire and leave you and the Captain to your business." She rose and walked unsteadily to the door.

Jonas bounced up to accompany her. Brandon stood politely. "It's time we were all abed," said Jonas. He patted her arm. "Sleep in your own chamber tonight, my dear," he murmured. "I'll not disturb you. Shall I send Charity to you?"

"No . . . no, I shall not need her. It is sleep I need, only that. See to your guest." Serena paused in the doorway. "Good night, Captain Brandon."

"Jonas," said Brandon, "I quite understand you'll wish to see Mistress Wainwright safely to bed. You've shown me my chambers, after all." His eyes sought Serena's. "I suspect that a solitary stroll in Mistress Wainwright's gardens will serve to clear my head." He bowed to them both. "Jonas, it has been a most illuminating evening. We can discuss our business tomorrow. Good night, Mistress Wainwright. I trust your indisposition will vanish as swiftly as it appeared." He bowed again and turned away.

CHAPTER ❧ 3 6

THE SCENT OF HONEYSUCKLE lay heavy on the air—honeysuckle and what else? A scent more cloying, less natural, teasingly familiar. Serena paused in the shadows. The door of the barn stood open. She sensed more than saw a movement within. Near the ladder to the loft a figure in white moved stealthily.

Frozen to the spot, Serena wondered what to do. Who besides myself is abroad in the night? Then she heard two voices—a man's and a woman's—softly murmuring. She could not hear their words, but the cadences were those of a language not her own. She heard scufflings and the creaking of the ladder, then the woman's laugh, low in her throat, muffled yet exultant.

Madame Constanza, she thought. The singer. Was it only tonight I thrilled to her music? That scent—her note to Hiram was drenched in it. But of course: the singer and the sculptor. They share a common language, and who knows what else? Uneasily she laughed, her hand across her lips to stifle the sound. So this is her "indisposition." This is how it came about that I, not she, was Stuart Brandon's partner at supper. How alike we are in our subterfuges.

Whispers and rustlings now came from the loft. Unbidden, memories of the afternoon flashed through Serena's mind. Again she saw those supple brown fingers, smoothing and stroking the clay. Are they now taking measure of the singer's ample curves? Is her pouter-pigeon bosom pressed against that muscled chest?

The rustlings from the loft assumed a rhythm that she could not mistake. Its pace increased.

Serena felt her own breasts harden, her own loins ache with tension unreleased. Hastily, she moved away, quelling her awareness that it was not the sculptor's image that had kindled the fire at her core, the fever that had kept her pacing in her room for an hour in nightdress and wrapper, every sense alert to measure the quality of the silence, to assure herself that the household was indeed asleep.

She crept quietly along the garden wall, scanning the shadows for some sign of Brandon's presence. How different the garden looks in moonlight, she thought. The footings dug for the brick walks might be chasms, so black do they appear. Where is Stuart Brandon? There, behind the shadowy mounds of boxwood so tediously hauled from Mount Holly? In the orchard? Behind the stillhouse? Has he come at all?

The rustle of her silk wrapper seemed thunderous in the moon-drenched stillness. Cautiously, she approached the cedar hedge that enclosed the nook where Jonas planned to place her statue. She slipped round the hedge and stopped, her hand upon her throat, feeling its pulse surging in time with the roaring in her ears.

In the centre of the enclosure stood Stuart Brandon, a sculpture moulded in shadow and silver light. He had removed his coat and cravat. His shirt stood open. His face was obscured; only his eyes caught the light. Are they really blue as sapphires in the moonlight, or do I only remember them that way? They seemed to grow darker as he watched her approach. For a moment neither spoke, neither moved.

Then their bodies came together at the centre of the nook, colliding with a force that made them gasp. Her arms were about him, she was straining against him, her breasts and hips and thighs pressed urgently to his body, her hands thrust into his hair, pulling his mouth down to hers. She felt the taut muscles of his thighs, the eager surge of his maleness, his arms holding her, hurting her, pulling her yet more tightly against him.

Then they were lying in the soft scented clover, his body half on hers. Her hands tore at his shirt, that she might run her palms along his shoulders. Her lips sought the hollow at the base of his throat that her fingers had traced so often in dreams. She did not hear her wrapper tearing, did not know that she herself was clawing at the bodice of her nightdress, sensing it only as an impediment to feeling his naked flesh against her skin.

Then his mouth was at her breast, teeth and tongue questing voraciously, and she could not tell whether the low growling moan that filled her ears came from his throat or hers. With her eyes closed, her head flung back, she arched her body against his, oblivious to all but the sensations tearing through her—her breasts, her belly, her legs, her loins. His hands moved and hers helped him, tearing the last of her garments away. Dimly she sensed the cool, moist touch of the clover upon her naked back, the spiciness of the crushed blossoms.

His body left hers. She whimpered, reaching for him blindly. When she opened her eyes he towered above her, his naked body silver in the moonlight, taut and ready as she remembered it.

"Now?" His voice was hoarse and urgent.

"Yes!" she cried. "Oh, yes—now." And she felt herself impaled upon his body, his maleness touching the tension at her core. She seized his buttocks and urged him deeper, ever deeper, meeting each thrust of his body with a wild thrust of her own, feeling the coil of tension within her wind tighter, tighter, still tighter, until, released by the force of his ultimate thrust, it sprang free, its pent force surging through her in spasm upon spasm, wave upon wave of pleasure, pulsing and quivering to the tips of her fingers, suffusing her with light.

Faintly she heard him cry her name. Then his mouth was on hers as his maleness convulsed again and again within her until at last she felt the weight of his whole body, heavy upon her, exhausted and still.

                         ❧ ❧ ❧

How LONG they lay there she was never to know. The moon had sunk below the horizon and the last stars illumined Stuart Brandon's face as he lay looking down at her, his head propped on one arm, one hand stroking her body as though reclaiming it by touch. How light her body felt, as though it floated in a sea of warm air, yet her arm as she raised it felt heavy, boneless and slack.

Her fingers traced the line between his brows, brushed lightly over his nose and lips, then trailed along his collarbone, lingering in the hollow at the base of his throat, twining idly in the wiry hairs on his chest. His hand stopped moving. She smiled lazily up at him. With her free hand she grasped his fingers and cupped them around her breast. At their touch a quiver deep within her faintly echoed the tremors that had so recently shaken her whole being.

Her eyes, accustomed now to the darkness, searched his face. He was looking down at her with a tenderness she could not mistake, a softness about his mouth that she had seen but once before, on the bank of a Barrens stream swift with spring. In her eagerness she forgot how that episode had ended. Now, she thought—now I can tell him. And it will be over, all the nightmare, the servitude to Hiram Jonas, the necessity that imprisons me here. Melissa, she thought, and her mouth curved in a smile. His daughter. How can he help but love her?

Deep in reverie, she failed to see the change in his expression. It was tense, almost frightened, as though he contemplated with dismay the depth of his response to her. He snatched his hand away. He sat up, and his profile in the starlight was harsh and austere. "So, Mistress Wainwright, we meet again." His tone was cold as the dead moon. "But we meet at Jonasville and not at Wainwright House. And you are Jonas' mistress." He stood up and began gathering his scattered garments.

Taken aback, she sat up as he began to dress. "Did I not predict," he said, "that you would find a new protector? A poor prize Weyford must have seemed in comparison to Hiram Jonas' wealth. Your father's trade must shine with faint lustre compared with the gold you can earn on your back. You had beguiled me, Mistress Wainwright, with your prattle of managing Weyford. Ironmaking's hard work, after all. I congratulate you upon your choice — and upon your talents. You've lost not one whit of your skill. Hiram Jonas must find it worth every penny he pays for it, and by the look of those baubles you wore at supper he pays a pretty price. Well, he can afford it. As you no doubt assured before you sold yourself to him."

What am I saying? he asked himself. The very words taste bitter upon my tongue. I hate them. I hate the scenes they conjure yet I must look, must see her as she is — like all the others. "Didn't you?" All at once he was kneeling beside her, gripping her shoulder, jerking her around to face him. "Didn't you?" he repeated, shaking her with each word. "How long had you left my bed when you tumbled into his?"

Serena winced, her mind in tumult. But you left me, she screamed in her mind — left me without warning, with naught but the cruelest of farewells, with not a care for what should become of me. What do you know of those hot, haunted nights in the tower room, of Caleb's jibes, of the fire and my flight, of Joe Mulliner's vengeance and my despair when I found myself penniless, robbed of the gold that was all you had left me with for all our time together.

As she stared at Stuart Brandon, swallowing, trying to force words past her closed throat, she relived the steps of the course that had brought her, first to Lumberton, then to Jonasville: the agony of Melissa's birth, the endless drudging hours tending steaming cauldrons in the August heat, her back and legs aching, her hands blistered and raw — and then later, the sleepless nights made hideous by fear as she saw herself about to lose what little safety she had gained, saw that her hard-won skill at healing availed her naught, that she was placing her loved mentor in greater jeopardy with every hour she remained at his side.

She remembered her searing anxiety about Melissa's future, her terror lest the stones of the villagers find a target in Melissa instead of herself —

and her despair when she found that they had, when she cradled Melissa's tear-stained, bleeding face to her breast and surveyed the wreckage of the herb room, knowing Doctor Will's house to be a haven no longer, the only work she knew no source of security, no support for her child. *Why can I not protest—scourge him as he deserves?* A strange lassitude had settled upon her, she felt weighted down by the day's strain, paralyzed with frustration at his insistence on thinking the worst of her.

"It seems those we love, we trust least of all." *Who had said that? He had—of her father. Oh, Stuart, does this mean that you love me? And if this is how you show it—as Father showed it—what hope is there for me?*

"How long was it? A week, a month?"

She did not see his tortured expression. Her mind seethed at his injustice. *What can I say? What weapon I forge can penetrate his closed mind? How can I tell him about Melissa now? Will he even believe she is his?*

"Stuart, you don't understand—"

So abruptly that she reeled, he let go of her. "I understand but too well. There's never but one explanation when a woman like you crawls into bed with a man thrice her age. Money. That's what you want. It's what they all want. They'll spread their legs for it—sell their souls for it, so fast it makes one's head spin. No simpering coyness then. No lover's plea has the ardent ring of the clink and jingle of coin."

"Was it money that kept me with you?" Serena spoke quietly, though her voice shook.

"We all have our moments of weakness. Even I." The curl of his lip, the sweep of his contemptuous glance encompassed her, himself, and the moments of passion just past.

He turned away, refusing to see her expression, her face white in the starlight, her shadowed eyes immense, forbidding himself to feel the qualms it aroused in him. *I'll not let her beguile me with lying looks.* "Why should you look so wounded? Women are all whores, some more talented than their sisters. Why not accept my compliments upon your skill?"

Her head came up. Her eyes blazed. She opened her mouth to protest. He swept on, oblivious. Within him the rage he refused to acknowledge as jealousy contended with the love he refused to acknowledge at all, lest it bind him inextricably to her.

Still she knelt there, not looking at him now, fighting to master her rage sufficiently to speak. He walked over to stand just behind her. For a long moment his hand hovered near her head, almost touching the silken hair.

Then he pictured her in Hiram Jonas' bed, heard her laughing deep in

her throat as her body quickened and her hands moved with intuitive
skill. Perversely, his own body stirred, but he ignored it. This was not
Serena before him. It was his mother. It was Margaret. He turned away.

Serena leapt to her feet. Heedless of her nakedness she pulled him
round to face her—her eyes ablaze, her body quivering with rage and
pain. "You're a fool, Stuart Brandon! You *don't* understand. You don't
want to understand. If I've become Hiram Jonas' mistress—and yes, I
am that, and I'm not ashamed of it—it's because I had to. Because there
was no other way to support—" Abruptly she was silent, her hand clapped
to her mouth.

If I tell him, I put Melissa in his hands. And how will that serve her?
What will it gain her? A loving father? How deluded can I be? And more:
Dare I place Melissa at the mercy of his whims? Subject her to his love,
half-offered, then withdrawn? Subject her to his hatred of women? For,
whatever his reasons, he despises us all. No! I cannot. Far better to
leave her where she is. At least she is safe there. Perhaps he can still
ensnare me by means of the love I can't seem to relinquish. But he shall
not torment Melissa. Nor shall I crawl before him with explanations he'll
not let himself believe.

She turned aside. "You don't want to know," she repeated dully. The
words dragged with her weariness. "Be damned to you, then." She stooped
to pick up her ruined wrapper.

He seized her and looked into her eyes. "The gold is not enough for
you, though, is it?" he said in a strange, strangled tone. "That's why you
arranged to meet me here. I'll wager the old man cannot satisfy you.
Can he?" His fingers dug into her shoulders, forcing her once more to
the ground. She cried out, but he choked her off, his mouth crushing
hers with bruising force. She struggled, but he held her fast.

He drew back once. His eyes glittered. "He's not enough for you, is he?"

He was upon her, then inside her. She gasped, held immobile in a
steely grip that conveyed no tenderness, her body jolted by fierce thrusts
that were like blows—blows meant to punish, yet also to possess. Fragments of thought, hints of his true purpose—to wipe out his rival, to
obliterate the pain that the thought of that rival engendered—floated at
the fringes of her consciousness, then swirled away.

She twisted away from him, struggling to breathe. He seized her hair
and forced her mouth to his. Despite her, her body responded, each
shudder of his evoking a shudder of her own until at last his cry and hers
cut the night at the same instant. Still shaken by reverberating tremors,
she felt the chill dawn air where his body had rested but a moment before.
He was gone.

C H A P T E R ❧ 3 7

"**D**O YOU SEE the possibilities, Jonas?" Drawings littered the library table. Peering through his gold-rimmed spectacles, Hiram Jonas leaned closer, watching Stuart Brandon trace an intricate design upon the topmost sheet. "With but a few minor changes you can triple your output without increasing the flow at the dam head—with all the power you need and not a single labourer added to your shop." Brandon rolled the plans up tightly. "Have you a place to conceal these?"

"I'll lock them up." Pressing a hidden spring behind a row of leather-bound volumes, Hiram Jonas swung one bookcase outward, disclosing a panelled wall. This he opened in turn to reveal a shallow cupboard. Taking the plans from Brandon, he stowed them carefully away, closing panel and shelf upon them before he spoke. The shelf was now indistinguishable from the others lining the library walls.

"'Tate Jones built this to my plans," he said. "No one else knows of it. A splendid workman, 'Tate—and loyal. Appreciative of his place here, and his wife's. Not everyone would confer upon a black man the place I've given 'Tate. But then, of course, his wife, Charity, is devoted to Mistress Wainwright."

Stuart Brandon smiled grimly but said nothing. He took the wing chair Jonas indicated while his host settled comfortably in its mate, his hands folded upon his ample belly.

"Did you have much difficulty obtaining the plans?" Jonas nodded toward the hidden cupboard. Shortly after the Peace of Paris had been signed, certain British merchants, fearing competition from the erstwhile colonies, had sought protection from Parliament to replace that once afforded them by colonial restrictions. To choke off the new nation's burgeoning industries, a law had been enacted forbidding export of British machine tools and leasing of patents abroad. The sale of industrial plans to an American had become, under British law, a crime.

"Very little, in all truth," said Brandon. "Between the followers of Adam Smith, who think the legal restraints sheer folly, and men of no principles but a keen regard for their purses, it's not that difficult for a man both cautious and discreet to be privy to any plans he asks for. Provided, of course, a judicious display of specie accompanies the asking. The Crown would have done better to license patents, collect its fees, and set its minions to hunting other game. But then, is it not against woodenheadedness of precisely this nature that you Americans fought the war?"

"True enough," said Jonas. "But I'd not care to have some erstwhile Tories get wind of what we're about. I'd not put it past them to alert the British authorities for spite. Which puts me to mind of Caleb Sawyer. I've said little to Serena, but there's no doubt in my mind he'll be the ruin of Weyford. He's selling off cordwood and charcoal at a great rate—far too fast, though Samuel Wainwright's acreage was larger than anyone's. You'd not recognize the place if you saw it. Acres of stumps—miles of them. And no attempt to thin the new growth. Serena would be most upset. And for all he's not pouring a half-ton a day he's digging limonite far faster than is wise. I'd guess the twenty-year cycle the ironmasters count on is illusory in any case, and Sawyer's handling the ore beds so badly they'll not renew themselves in twenty years—or fifty. Well, enough of that." He grimaced.

"Some brandy?" Without awaiting an answer he seized a crystal decanter from a nearby stand and poured two generous tots of amber liquid. "There's a cedar swamp I've a mind to mine. A portion of it touches Weyford property—perhaps even overlaps it." He handed Brandon one of the square-cut crystal tumblers and raised his own exuberantly. "To our joint enterprise." Brandy splashed over his fingers. He drained his glass and wiped his hand absent-mindedly on his shirt frill.

Brandon sipped judiciously and nodded. "Enterprises," he amended with an unpleasant smile. "Is Mistress Wainwright joining us at luncheon?"

The apparent inconsequence of the question made Hiram Jonas blink. "No—as a matter of fact, she is not well. I am most concerned about her." His brow creased in a puzzled frown as he pulled at his pursed lower lip. Then he shook his head as if to clear it and poured himself a second brandy. "Another? Aged applejack—my own. You'll not find its like outside Jonasville."

"Thank you, but no. A single glass is potent enough. A Barrens specialty, I understand. Jersey Lightning—and aptly named. Storms, it appears, are typical of the region." He drained his glass and set it down upon the tray. The ironical smile hovered again about his lips.

Now what does he mean by that? thought Hiram Jonas. Why does a second meaning seem to lurk beneath every word he speaks? A clever man and a good ally—far better as ally than as enemy, I'll warrant. But a world too subtle for my taste.

He downed his second glass as quickly as the first, then cleared his throat. "Enterprises—yes, of course. I've another venture or two afoot. You might be interested to see"—he pulled his gold watch from his waistcoat—"yes, there's time. Come with me." He bounced up and led the way out of the library.

⠦ ⠦ ⠦

THE CLAMOUR MADE CONVERSATION FUTILE. The saw blade shrieked as it bit into a cedar log a full three feet in girth. Chains rattled, the mill wheel groaned, the floorboards shook. The air was pungent with the sharp-edged sweetness of cedar, hazy with sawdust gilded by the sunlight pouring through the wide-open doors. The dust settled thickly upon every surface, upon hair, upon clothing. The burly men who tended the saw looked like mummies swaddled in gravebands of dust, only their eyes alive.

Hiram Jonas flung a hand toward the shed-like interior that stretched dim and silent beyond the clatter. He tried to speak, cupping his hands to his mouth and shouting, impatient to explain. Brandon shook his head. Jonas semaphored some orders to the workman in charge and led Brandon deeper into the gloom. At intervals in the turpentine-scented shadows workmen bent to their tasks. 'Tate Jones prowled among them, shouting in the ear of one, gesturing to another. Wood shavings littered the floor. At length Jonas opened a door outlined by light on the farthest wall. The two men stood blinking on a plank bridge spanning the mill-race, watching the darkling waters spill glassily over the dam.

"You saw the thickness of that cedar log?" asked Jonas. "We've our work cut out, mining those logs from the swamp bottom. The Lord knows how long they have lain there; today's trees are kindling compared with them. And durable? The roof of the State House—Independence Hall they're calling it now—is shingled with Barrens swamp cedar." He snatched a silvery weathered shingle from the ground and rapped his knuckles against it. The sound rang clear and resonant, a tone or two beneath the high-pitched clatter behind them. "Hear that? Sound as iron. It will out-last the Hall's bricks, I've little doubt."

"That is your plan then—lumbering?"

"Part of my plan—a small part only." Jonas stared out over the mill-pond, placid and still, blue with the sky's reflection, crimson at the water's edge where tupelos resplendant in fall livery bent to admire their images. "September," said Hiram Jonas, waving toward the glossy-leaved trees. "Autumn's coming. Yet see the flow of the water? We've not much fall to the land here, but Barrens streams run swift and deep. And reliably. They may ice over, but they never run dry. Their power's not great, but it's certain."

Jonas gestured back toward the shops. "Did you see the work as we passed through?" Brandon nodded. "What plans for wood lathes can you find for me? Not for work such as Benjamin Randolph does: There's but a limited market for fine furniture like his. What I've in mind is solid stuff, for husbandmen and shopkeepers who've neither time nor skill to build their own. I've plans for production on a mass scale."

"I see that, and I've no doubt you've come upon something there. But there are limits to water power."

Jonas pulled a bandanna from his waistcoat and mopped at his brow and crimson pate. "That's something else I want you to find out for me. That Scots tinkerer Watt has patented a steam engine. I've done some work with steam myself"—he squinted up at Brandon—"this is in confidence, mind you. I've no doubt, no doubt at all, that steam power will replace water power, and in not too long a time. Well, then, we've ample fuel here. And ample space. The plans I've made . . ." He mopped his brow again. "Infernally hot, this sun, eh? And I think I hear"—he cocked his head in the direction of Jonas House—"yes, I do. It's the bell for luncheon. Come . . . come." He took Brandon's arm and propelled him toward the house.

🕭　🕭　🕭

THE MEAL WAS A SILENT ONE. Serena was absent. Hiram Jonas bent to his plate. Madame Constanza had joined them for luncheon, but she spoke little English or none. Her dark eyes had kindled with interest as Stuart Brandon bent over her hand. Now she watched contemplatively as he, too, ate in silence.

Hiram Jonas, thought Brandon. Is he a visionary fool? Or is there merit to his plans? An empire of varied manufactories far from the city? Built not only upon iron but on lumber, on furnishings, on glass, on pure water and air? I wonder. How much should I invest in his schemes? How much is he making here?

"Cities are stinking warrens," Jonas had said on their way back to the house. "People cheek by jowl, choking in their own filth, the middens alone are bound to overwhelm them. Look at Philadelphia. More to the point, look at London. Americans are accustomed to space about them. They'll not long tolerate such a crush. But here?"

The sweep of his arm encompassed Jonasville and the Barrens beyond. "Smell that air. Taste the water. Incomparable. We've the waterways and the sea for transport—raw materials in, finished goods out. Plentiful lumber for housing—I'll show you the plan for the workers' quarters. Serena has taken a great interest in those. And pure water—as I say, water's to become important one day."

"You've an empire a-building here," Stuart Brandon had agreed. "And a profitable one," he added, nodding toward Jonas House: the gilded eagles at the gate, the vast walled garden, and the construction fanning out in all directions from the central core of the mansion.

"Profitable, yes, so far as it goes. But all this"—Jonas waved his hand— "it's far from self-supporting now. I've sunk thousands into it. I'll sink thousands more before I've done." He halted abruptly. Short legs spread, thumbs hooked into his waistcoat pockets, he stared earnestly up at his tall companion, his blue infant's eyes half closed against the glare.

"I've many thousands to spend," he said. "But they are not of my own making. I inherited them, and an obligation with them, for the money was made transporting slaves." Jonas cupped his hand to his ear, then gestured toward the sheds they had just left, as though to call Stuart Brandon's attention to the clamour of industry drifting toward them upon the hot midday wind. "Machines—," he had said, "we're at the beginning. It's machines that will eradicate slavery from the earth. And I'm in the thick of it, here. Jonasville will be a model for the future. And it will make my fortune—an earned fortune—the while."

I wonder, thought Stuart Brandon at luncheon, dimly aware of the singer's efforts to penetrate his abstraction. His nostrils flared as a wave of her scent drifted to him. Sandalwood, was it? And ambergris. Heavily underscored by musk. Yet the whole of it not entirely disguising the acrid sharpness of stale sweat. For the first time he looked at her closely.

Sensing his scrutiny, she drew a deep breath that thrust her breasts just perceptibly in his direction. She smiled. Her large eyes, lined with kohl, widened. The pupils darkened. At her décolletage, her jewel-encrusted brooch, too ornate to be properly worn by day, flashed in time with the exaggerated quickening of her breath. Overripe, he thought, but succulent still, I've no doubt.

Hiram Jonas pushed his plate away. Rising, he bobbed a bow in the singer's general direction. "If you will excuse us, Madame? We'll take our coffee in the library," he added to the servant. "Brandon? Madame will await us in the drawing room, perhaps?"

At his host's glance, Stuart Brandon rose. Bowing punctiliously, he moved to pull back the singer's chair. As she rose, she glanced meaningfully over her shoulder. Her pink tongue flicked across her full red lips; her blackened lashes drooped, hiding her eyes. She turned to leave, gazing meaningfully into his eyes, all but panting, fluttering her fan.

He bowed again. Her face, he saw, was heavily powdered. A rim of powder stained the satin neckline of her gown. At this close range, her perfume was overpowering. For a moment he closed his eyes. The image of Serena rose before him, her fine white skin, innocent of cosmetics, the clean lustre of her hair, scented ever so faintly with verbena. He bowed Madame Constanza through the panelled double doors and followed his host to the library.

❧ ❧ ❧

"So," SAID STUART BRANDON WHEN THEY had settled once more into the wing chairs, "Master Caleb is in the saddle at Weyford. And married to Serena's sister. How did he get round the old man? The son was killed in the War, I take it?" Hiram Jonas nodded. "And the sister was the eldest," Brandon went on in musing tones. "Quite so. But Serena was the old man's pet." Be still, you fool, he admonished himself. Yet he went on. "Strange he should cut her out of Weyford. Or did he?"

Jonas did not answer. Head down, hands folded upon his belly in his pose of accustom, he gazed up at Stuart Brandon, his blue eyes guileless.

"But then," continued Brandon, a sour ache at the pit of his stomach goading him on, "Jonasville clearly had more to offer her." Be still, he told himself again. Do you want him to suspect — suspect what, exactly? That Serena was your lover before she was his? That she is your lover now? And is she? Did you not swear to yourself you had done with her?

Hiram Jonas straightened in his chair. His hands clenched the chair arms as he leant forward. "Captain Brandon, you judge Mistress Wainwright wrongly."

"No doubt it is her affection for you that keeps her in her anomalous position." Enough! he told himself. "I beg your pardon, Jonas. These matters are none of my concern." He made as though to rise, but Jonas waved him back into his seat.

"Indeed, they are not your concern, Captain Brandon, but I've cause to know you're but speaking aloud what others whisper in corners. There's little I can do to protect her from the scandalmongers, but —"

"Little," burst out Brandon, "but to marry her." He snapped his mouth shut and rose from his chair.

"She would refuse," said Jonas, looking down at his feet. "And in any case, I'm not really—" He broke off and arose in his turn. Placing a hand on Brandon's arm, he looked earnestly up into his face.

"Believe me, Captain Brandon, I'm well aware of what our little world must think of Mistress Wainwright's alliance with myself—and of how they must judge her. True enough, there's little about me but my wealth to attract such a woman as she. I know that. But I also know that had she not been desperate, and more than that, had she not been desperate for—" Jonas stopped. *The story of Melissa is not mine to tell. Moreover, to reveal her existence would ill serve my cause with Serena.* "Sit down. No—please."

Reluctantly, Brandon seated himself at the very edge of the chair. He remained there, tensely poised, while Hiram Jonas related what he knew of Serena's life with Doctor Will, of the rumours that had pursued her, of the grisly death of Lipcote, the threat to the Black Doctor's practice, and the part he suspected Caleb Sawyer to have played in the tragic dénouement—omitting only Melissa's part in the events.

"She was without friends there, solitary and brave. I watched her for some years. Perhaps no one suspected how lonely she was. When I arrived to drive her here, I found her at the grave of her little cat, weeping desolately. Yet even then, she would not have come with me, were it not for the threat her continued presence there posed to her—that is, to Master Pond."

Both men sat silent for a moment. Then Hiram Jonas jumped up. "Well—enough of that. Madame Constanza is embarking from Tuckerton today; she sails to New York on the evening tide. May I ask you to escort her to the wharf? Her manager is to meet her there."

For a moment Stuart Brandon did not answer. Indeed, it seemed to Hiram Jonas that Brandon had not heard. Then he, too, rose abruptly. His lips twisting ironically, he bowed to his host and smiled. "Of course. My pleasure." He led the way out of the library.

CHAPTER ❧ 3 8

"ÖSLEIN, RÖSLEIN, *Röslein rot*—" Oh, be still! Serena slumped over her writing table. The quill dropped from her fingers, leaving a blot upon the page. Restlessly, she rose and paced the room, pausing before the cheval glass to examine her face. Her lips were puffy, her eyes shadowed. Her breasts felt swollen and sore, sensitive to the lightest touch of her silk nightdress. To Serena, the history of the past night seemed writ large upon her face, yet Hiram Jonas' expression this morning had revealed only concern for her.

"Rest—rest." Anxiously he had patted her shoulder. "Perhaps you've a touch of the fever." He fussed about, plumping pillows, making sure that the bowl of iced water he had ordered was still cold. He urged her to the bedstead, dipped and wrung a linen towel, and laid it tenderly on her forehead. "Rest, sweet," he said again. Then, as though embarrassed by the endearment, he had tiptoed away, closing the door quietly behind him.

Serena reseated herself at the writing table but rose almost at once. The room was stifling. Yet when she flung the window open, the faint breeze that stirred the curtains was hotter still. The day sparkled and dazzled. The sun set heat waves to shimmering on the slate roof of the bay window below her and struck golden rays from the eagles guarding the gate.

She left the window open. Better hot air that was alive than the suffocating closeness of this room. "*Röslein, Röslein, Röslein rot* . . ." Again the refrain echoed through her mind's stunned stillness, bringing the sting of tears to her eyes. Resolutely, she returned to her desk, found a fresh sheet of foolscap, and began to write.

Dearest Melissa,

How I wish that I could really write you, or better yet, see your
dear face. Mistress Mansey writes that you do so well at your alphabet that I'd not be surprised could you read this letter. But since I
cannot be with you for an unknown span of time—I cannot countenance the word "never"—I have resolved to write these letters
and keep them so that someday, when you are older and can understand, you will know your Mama thought of you every day you
were away.

And when will that be? On what fine day can I greet my child with
the tidings of her bastardy, the knowledge that her father . . . her father
. . . What a fool I was! Did I think, perhaps, that Stuart Brandon would
settle me in a cottage somewhere, with flowers about the door, mayhap,
and his child gambolling about us, happy and free? Or even—since no
folly seems beyond me—that he would make me his wife? What but a
wish to believe against all experience could make me think Stuart Brandon
would welcome the role of father, or even believe Melissa his? What terrible lies our necessities compel us to tell ourselves!
With a sigh she resumed her letter, writing for some time.

. . . Do you remember Charity and 'Tate, or the high chair that
'Tate made for you? Charity is here at Jonasville, too, and Hiram
Jonas has placed 'Tate in charge of the carpentry works. Charity
runs the house and takes care of me when she can . . .

And as well as I let her. "So that be him," Charity had said after supper
last night when Serena stumbled back to her room. Serena did not ask
how Charity knew. In telling her secrets so long ago at Doctor Will's, she
had been careful not to mention Stuart Brandon's name. She probably
guessed from my face, thought Serena now, for what else could so have
shocked me after what she and I have endured together?
"Have a care," Charity had said last night. "Have a care, Serena."
And well I might have, thought Serena. The sound of the luncheon
bell pealed faintly through the closed door. She went once more to the
window but drew back into the shadows. Brandon and Hiram Jonas were
approaching the gate, Jonas gesticulating as he talked, Brandon pacing
gravely at his side, nodding slightly from time to time. From her vantage,
Jonas' stumpy figure seemed even more rotund. The men passed through

the gate. Soon the bulk of the house obscured them from her view. She went back to her desk and picked up her pen.

&#x0B; &#x0B; &#x0B;

CALEB SAWYER POUNDED HIS FIST on the desk that had been Samuel Wainwright's. "I won't stand for it!" His voice rose perilously near a shriek. The papers piled upon the desk rustled and shifted. Mike McGuire gazed tactfully at the window as though he could see through the shutters that closed out the sunlit afternoon. He knew enough to avert his glance from his employer's face, the scars now a glistening white, the unmarred tissue crimson.

"I won't stand for it," Caleb repeated. "Look at this!" Scrabbling about amongst the documents, he seized a letter and thrust it at Mike's face. The paper fluttered in his shaking hand so that Mike could read but scattered phrases. "Not of the quality of the previous . . . one cracked upon receipt, the other when exposed to the fire . . . albeit the moulds for the cipher will not match, will order from Batsto hereafter . . . " The flowing signature was plainly to be read: "G. Washington."

Mike drew a deep breath and faced his employer squarely. "I did be warnin' ye, Master Sawyer. Them firebacks been't fit to ship. They should've been recast. Sure, the shipment be late, but—"

"Exactly. It was late. Half a year late. We had to ship the order or lose the commission."

"We be losin' it anyways."

"Enough of your impudence! I'll not have it, I tell you. Nor are these all the ill tidings that came by the last coach." He shuffled again through the papers, then stood hunched over the desk, breathing heavily, while Mike read.

One paper was a page torn from the *Pennsylvania Gazette*, yellowed and brittle. It bore an advertisement for Weyford pig iron, "the Quality of which is so well known as to require no Description," signed by Samuel Wainwright. The writer of the accompanying letter—a major customer— suggested that the "W" no longer be debossed upon the pigs, since "the quality of Same is so well Known" that all chance of selling them was lost, so long as they bore Weyford's mark.

"I'll not stand for further calumny of this kind. This is the end—understand? The end of it!" Mike drew back a step as Caleb's cane flew by him and crashed against the mantel.

"Be it, now?"

"The end—the *end*, you fool, can't you understand? There's no money to be made in ironmaking, the whole business is plagued with ill luck."

Mike looked around the room, his gaze resting on its vestiges of luxury as if to underscore the fortune Samuel Wainright had made in this same trade. There been't no such runs of bad luck when the Old Man was alive, he wanted to say. Not when repairs be timely made. The dams be kept up then. The water wheels be kept runnin'. The bellows be mended before the leather hung in shreds. At sight of Caleb's face he thought better of it. What purpose would it serve—what harm might it do? Caleb's fingers drummed upon the desk; his white-rimmed eyes fixed upon Mike's as though daring him utter one word of what he was thinking.

Mike remained silent, resolving to take the post at Batsto that the Richards family had offered him time and again. What except loyalty to the memory of the Old Man—and Serena—kept him here in bootless struggle against Caleb Sawyer's ignorance and neglect?

The silence lengthened, broken only by the faraway din of the forge. "I be quittin'." Mike had opened his mouth to say the words at last, but Caleb forestalled him. "Shut the furnace down. The forge too. Let the fires go out."

"Now, Master Sawyer? In the middle of the charge?"

"Now!" Caleb's voice rose again to that unnerving near shriek. "And the forge fires, too. Tell the men to come to the counting-house when they've done. I'll choose those I'll permit to remain in my employ—those who can work with the lumbering crews. And a few for the cedar mining, perhaps. The others can pack their goods and go."

"But their women and children—them who lives here?"

"That's their concern. They've no rights to those cottages beyond what I allow. And the upkeep's a damnable expense. Let them pay rent from their wages if they wish to remain there."

Mike's eyes blazed. "Those be their homes! Some of 'em be livin' here for years."

"That is their misfortune. Had they produced better iron and kept the furnaces going, they'd not be in this fix. Let Richards take care to them, if he's so eager to take over our custom. Now go!"

Mike hesitated. "Ye be givin' those orders, ye be givin' 'em yer own self." He laid the papers back on the desk and walked heavily out of the room.

Caleb limped over to the fireplace and retrieved his cane. The orders could wait. He seated himself once more at the desk, slipping a letter out of the centre drawer. It was signed by one of his contacts from the days of spying for the British, and it concluded: ". . . have found a faint trail of the man Jonas. It leads to New England and it smells of subterfuge. I suspect that Jonas is not his real name, though the Philadelphia banks have his gold under that signature. It may take some time, but I believe we will ultimately be successful in tracing him. I await your instructions."

Caleb Sawyer smiled and drew the bronze inkstand toward him.

৯৫ ৯৫ ৯৫

SERENA WROTE STEADILY for some hours, pouring out her love and longing to a Melissa wrought by her imagination, a Melissa grown adult and compassionate, tolerant and wise. Sometimes she stopped for long moments and pondered, fingering the shells she had saved from that long-ago day at the seaside, humming softly, "*Röslein, Röslein, Röslein rot . . .*," scarcely aware that she did so.

Finally she sanded the last sheet. Rolling the papers up, she tied them with a bit of ribbon and hid them at the bottom of her wardrobe. The sound of wheels and horses' hoofs drew her back to the window.

Hiram's coachman was stowing away a valise and some bundles. Three figures clustered beside the coach: Hiram Jonas, Stuart Brandon, and a woman she recognized as Madame Constanza. Jonas bustled about, giving orders to the coachman, patting the sleek necks of the horses. Then the coachman took his place at the reins. Hiram Jonas flung open the coach door and Stuart Brandon bowed, offering his arm to the singer.

As Madame Constanza prepared to mount the small step, her plump breasts brushed Brandon's arm in a movement as casual as, Serena knew, it was contrived. The singer settled herself in a flurry of skirts, revealing more than a glimpse of silken ankles and plump calves. Brandon bowed once to Jonas, climbed in beside the singer, and shut the door upon them. He leaned toward his fellow passenger as the coach pulled away.

"Damn him! Damn him! Damn him!" Serena cast wildly about her for something to throw, something to smash as she longed to smash his face. Fearing to alert the household, she flung herself upon the bed, muffling her cries in the pillows. She felt the cords stand out in her neck as she beat upon the mattress with her fists. "Damn him! May he rot in hell. I never want to see him again!" Again and again she beat upon the bedding until at last, exhausted, she lay still.

Dusk hazed the room when she awakened. Arising dizzily, she splashed some cool water on her face. The silver-blue light of waning day had pooled in the cheval glass. Serena went to stand before it, addressing the shadowy form that was herself. "Well, are you ready now to give up your idle dreams? To count yourself fortunate to have found a man who, for all his strange demands and petulant childishness, is kind to you? A man willing to assume the burden of your child, to give her the future you could not?"

As she stood there, staring blankly at the wraith in the mirror, she heard a light tap at the door. "Serena? Sweet? Are you well enough to take some supper with me?" She took a deep breath and squared her shoulders. Then she unlocked the door and bade Hiram Jonas come in.

CHAPTER ❧ 39

"**PUT THOSE BARRELS** over there." Serena pointed this way and that, directing the sweating workmen. The sun was warm, for all it was October, suffusing the garden with its mellow amber light. Beyond the walls, almost completed now, butter-golden tulip poplars towered against the sky. The persistent green of the oil-glossed oak leaves had a newly reddish cast.

She picked up her skirts and started toward the workmen. Then she paused, head tilted, eyes wistful, as a flight of wild geese arrowed their way southward, gabbling to one another as the point birds in each trailing vee fell back to let others breast the wind. As one flight passed, another took its place, then another, the birds' long, pliant necks stretched tautly forward, wide grey wings beating, beating, down-covered breasts gleaming, white as the snows the geese fled. Soon their formations were black checkmarks enscribed on the cloud-piled horizon. Their voices drifted behind them on the wind, baying and yelping like some species of sky-borne hound.

"Here, Mistress?" Serena sighed lightly. She snatched up her rolled-up plans and leapt nimbly across some scattered bricks. The walks were progressing, but slowly, their herringbone pattern requiring time and care to lay. Beckoning the most likely of the workmen to her, she knelt and unrolled the plans upon the ground, weighting the corners with bricks.

"Look, Thomas," she said, pointing. "You see? The iris are to go by the wall . . . here, the lighter-coloured in the foreground, the darker behind them. The sacks are tagged with the shades of colour. These other bulbs are to go in the flower beds along the walk."

The man glanced apprehensively from the plan to the barrels. Of course, Serena thought. He cannot read, for all he's clever at his work. ❧ 273

She smiled at him encouragingly. "I'll set them out for you—then you've but to plant them. Mind you cover only the roots of the iris deeply; the tops of the tubers must be near-exposed, else they'll not bloom. The other bulbs go this deep"—she measured an eight-inch span with her hands.

❧ ❧ ❧

SHRUGGING TO RELIEVE the ache in her shoulders, Serena approached the last barrel and sorted through the straw and sacking. The bulbs were not as firm as she would like; the short-cut, fan-like leaves of the iris had yellowed. The same storm that had polished the sky and swept in this sun-splashed day had delayed the ship that carried this long-awaited order. How long ago had she sent to Williamsburg for it? Months! Now she chafed to get the iris into the ground without delay. But as luck would have it, some plants for the herb garden, sent by Doctor Will, had arrived this very morning.

Some hours later, she straightened, rubbing her back. Already the shadows of the distant trees had climbed the garden walls and were creeping across the ground. She glanced along the length of the flower beds that lined two sides of the garden. The workmen could manage alone now. She hastened to the site of her herb garden. It was to form the focal point of one of the walks whose axis was the statue enclosure.

Here, in the garden's sunniest corner, a checquerboard pattern of brick and slate enclosed chamomile and bee balm, lavender and thyme. Two species of mint, carefully restrained by brick coping, flourished in a shadier spot where a hidden spring kept the ground moist. The coarse leaves of rhubarb had been relegated to a less conspicuous spot. Upon the sandy earth stood two split-oak baskets carefully packed with moist sphagnum to preserve the tender slips and roots of plants best set out in the autumn. How like Doctor Will to do this for her—to send her this bit of her own lost garden, tended so carefully during her years with him. These plants she would set in herself.

When she had done, she ached in every bone. You don't work as you used to, she admonished herself. Her dress, a faded gingham salvaged from the rag bag for this purpose, was stained with earth and splashed with water. She looked with satisfaction upon the withered-looking leaves and spiky twigs set out in precise patterns amid the brick and stone. They will take hold, she thought. And when the sundial Hiram has promised me is placed, this part of the garden will look as I have planned it.

The workmen had finished with the iris beds; they lay in shadow now.

The east wall, however, still caught the rays of the westering sun, and the tall hollyhocks that grew there glowed translucent in its light. Stiffly, Serena walked over to them. Some late bumblebees, their fuzzy bodies coated with bright-yellow pollen, still burrowed greedily into the cup-shaped flowers that clung to the tops of the plants. Round pods of seeds marched steadily up the stalks in pursuit of these last blooms. Serena plucked a handful of the pods and thrust all but one into the pocket of her apron. She squeezed the remaining pod until it popped open, scattering seeds upon her palm.

With one finger she stirred the flat, round seeds with their slightly frilled edges, arranging them in patterns. Mother! she thought, remembering the rows of hollyhocks in the garden at Weyford and herself toddling after Anna, clutching seeds just like these in her moist palm. Mother — Is she still alive? Surely Prue would have sent word to me if Mother were ill? Or would she? Remembering her banishment from Weyford and the haunted look with which Prudence had thrust the coins into her hand, Serena shuddered. Am I quit of Caleb now? Somehow I doubt it. She put the thought away from her and started toward Jonas House.

Hurrying past the enclosure where, this coming spring, the statue would be placed, she looked toward the gate that led to the kitchen garden. She stopped abruptly, her heart thumping. Coming toward her was Stuart Brandon. He carried a small wooden crate. Her impulse to turn and run was instantly quelled, for Hiram Jonas stumped just behind him, beaming.

ಇ   ಇ   ಇ

"STILL AT WORK, my dear?" The two men came up to Serena, who stood tensely watching their approach. "Your industry speaks well of you," Jonas continued, "but mind you're not late for the performance. We've a guest tonight, as you can see." She wondered at Hiram's good humour, for ordinarily he would have been angry at both her tardiness and her attire. His pride in his theatre was inordinate, his suspicion of visitors considerable. Performances were strictly on time, and those few guests who were allowed to meet her at all, saw her only in the most formal of attire.

"Good evening, Mistress Wainwright. How does your garden grow?" Encumbered as he was by the crate he carried, Stuart Brandon yet managed a courteous bow. But although his glance took in every detail of her dishevellment, the stains and splashes upon her gown, her torn apron, the smudges on her face and the strand of hair that hung over her eyes, the sarcastic jibe she expected was not forthcoming.

"Good evening, Captain Brandon. I take it you are joining us for supper? If you'll excuse me, gentlemen, I'll —" At that moment a curious sound emerged from Brandon's crate: a plaintive cry like that of a querulous infant. Startled, Serena looked more closely at the crate and saw that holes had been bored into the wood. Now whatever creature was inside it clawed at the box and wailed more loudly.

"May I?" Brandon looked at Hiram Jonas, who nodded, smiling so broadly that his eyes were mere slits.

"Mistress Wainwright —" Brandon knelt and pried off the top of the crate. A half-grown kitten emerged, shook itself, and sat down upon the walk, washing its paws to keep itself in countenance. But this was a kitten like none Serena had known: its sleek body, all bone and sinew, a creamy tan; its wise narrow muzzle, alert ears, and slender paws a rich dark brown. As it stood up and moved curiously toward her, she saw that its tail was also brown, slender and proudly upright but for a kink near its tip. Its large eyes, slightly slanted, were blue.

"Oh!" she cried softly. Slowly, so as not to alarm this strange creature, she knelt and extended her hand. The kitten backed off, appraising her gravely. Then it uttered a short, hoarse meow and came forward, nosing into her hand until her fingers found the angle of its jaw and began stroking. Then it purred loudly, arching its slim neck to keep its chin in contact with her hand. Still moving slowly, Serena picked it up, marvelling at the lightness of its lithe body. She rose. It commented again, but without alarm, and settled in the crook of her elbow.

She looked up to find Brandon watching her, his eyes dark and inscrutable. Hiram Jonas looked pleased. "His name is Sundar," said Brandon. "His parents are ship's cats on the *Audacious*. They were palace cats in the Orient. Did you see that kink in his tail? It's said to be a badge of rank, for the women of the seraglio wear many rings, and the cats are privileged to carry them. There's as much truth in that as in most legends, I suppose." He smiled somewhat tentatively, still watching her face.

"He's beautiful," said Serena. "He's almost not like a cat at all — more like . . . oh, I don't know . . . like an impression, an essence, of what a cat can be."

Brandon looked at her sharply. A spark gleamed in his eyes for a moment, then was gone.

To avoid his piercing look, Serena buried her face in Sundar's fur. It was short, far shorter than Mitzi's, and very soft, light as goosedown. He

began to lick her ear, and she laughed lightly, for his rough tongue was
as much like any other cat's as everything else about him was different.
"Is he for me?" Both men nodded. "Oh, thank you! Hiram, is this your
doing?"

Hiram Jonas chuckled, pleased by her pleasure. "No, it's Captain
Brandon's. He brought the beast. I knew nothing of it until he walked in
with it today. And he's had a time convincing me I should allow you to
keep it in the house. I suppose he thought of it when I told him about" —
he stopped and cleared his throat — "well, about . . . Mitzi, wasn't it?"

"You told him that?" Serena looked at Brandon again. She could not
fathom his expression, and for once he could not sustain her glance.
Somewhat self-consciously, he reached out and patted Sundar's head.
His hand brushed her arm as he did so, and Serena jerked it away. Then
she looked at Hiram Jonas, for surely these gestures had given them
both away. His expression gave no hint of what he was thinking.

Suddenly flustered, Serena recalled her attire. "Thank you, Captain
Brandon," she said stiffly. "It is a most thoughtful gift." Feeling the sting
of tears in her eyes, she brushed abruptly past the two men and made
for the house. Sundar, startled by the sudden movement, squirmed to
her shoulder and clung there, steadied by her hand, as she broke into a
run. Hiram Jonas and Stuart Brandon stood side by side, watching, as
Serena disappeared into the kitchen garden. Faintly they heard her calling as she opened the rear door — "Charity! Charity! Oh, come see!"
Together, they turned toward Jonas House.

❨ ❨ ❨

FOR ONCE Serena paid the music no attention. Flanked by Jonas and
Brandon, she stared straight ahead as though enthralled by the musicians,
who might have been playing behind a wall of thick glass for all she heard
a note of their endeavours. The hall was empty except for the three of
them, the velvet chairs ranged unoccupied below. The light cast by the
unextinguished chandelier shimmered in Serena's necklace of rubies,
diamonds, and pearls and in the matching clips that caught up her high-
piled hair.

She was clad in a low-cut gown of taffeta whose play of dark and bright,
light and shadow recalled the fiery leaves — scarlet and crimson and
deepest vermillion — of the tupelos by the lake. When she saw Stuart
Brandon's face as he bent over her hand Serena knew him to be struck
by the memory she had intended to recall to him. For the colour of her
dress was that of the claret wool she had worn at Weyford's Christmas

long ago—and worn at the White Stag frolicking that had brought her to Mulliner's notice, and thus to Brandon's bed. Had he also perceived what she had meant him to remark: the contrast between that occasion and this, between the ignorant girl of that fateful night and the superbly gowned woman who sat poised by his side?

But how different am I? she thought, sensing heat where his arm brushed hers, preternaturally aware, though she never met his eyes, of every shift of his expression—aware, too, of Hiram Jonas to her right, seemingly absorbed in the music, beating time with his foot and humming under his breath like a giant bumblebee. What does he know? What does he guess? Hiram is no fool, though I've seen him take a fool's part to deceive.

Brandon appeared as intent upon the music as she, though she suspected he heard as little. Absent-mindedly she watched the flautist, a scrawny man whose elaborate wig sat askew, twirling his fingers affectedly. The violinist who was also the leader glared at the other fiddler, and she sensed the culprit was out of time or tune. Now both sawed away in unison again, with a vigour that portended a climax to the piece. Yet when Hiram Jonas burst into loud applause, she started.

Stuart Brandon clapped neatly, hand upon hand, then sank into renewed reverie as the musicians began again. Serena eyed him sidewise, thinking of the afternoon, and of Sundar. She had left the cat curled upon her satin quilt, replete with cream and a dinner of chicken scraps that Charity had found for him. Stuart Brandon would never beg my pardon, she thought. Yet what is this gift but an apology? Is this his way of acknowledging such of my struggles as Hiram recounted?

Brandon stirred, folding his arms. And in the next instant she was aware of his fingertips stroking the soft skin in the crook of her arm. She tensed, ready to jerk away. But any sudden move would alert Hiram Jonas. Willing herself to ease her arm away, she sat motionless instead as softly, softly, Stuart Brandon caressed the sensitive flesh, seeking its pulse and, she knew, feeling that pulse leap beneath his fingers.

She tucked her right hand in Jonas' arm, as though seeking protection. He patted her hand and returned his attention to the music. Beneath his concealing arm, Brandon's fingers continued their exploration, stroking the tender skin inside her upper arm, his knuckles barely grazing her breast. And then she felt her free hand move without volition to lie upon the velvet edge of his seat cushion, palm up, fingers curled, its side pressed against his muscled thigh. His fingers found the sensitive centre of her palm and circled, circled, as the rushing blood hummed in her ears and both of them stared at the stage, seeing nothing, while the music swirled about them, unattended.

C H A P T E R ❧ 4 0

S TUART BRANDON ROWED in smooth strokes, sending the heavy boat
swiftly on its course. The bow clove the waters cleanly. They
parted like basalt before a chisel to reveal the blackness beneath the
slick surface painted white, blue, and crimson by clouds, sky, and the
ripening crane-berries floating in the shallows.

Brandon's linen shirt was open at the neck; its sleeves were rolled
carelessly above his elbows. Serena sat in the stern, hands braced upon
the gunwales, watching the play of muscle in his tanned forearms with
each stroke of the oars. The warmth of the sun made his shirt cling to
his shoulders. He paused, shipping the oars neatly, and wiped his forehead on his arm. Twin runnels of sweat coursed along his neck. Serena
watched them, mesmerized, as they joined in the hollow at the base of
his throat and trickled downward.

She forced herself to look him in the face. He was watching her, his
eyes blue and bright as the Indian-summer sky. For a moment he held
her glance, then he laughed and picked up the oars again, his slim fingers
curving around their leather grips. Once more the boat skimmed across
the swamp waters, so bright on the surface, so black underneath.

❧ ❧ ❧

WHY DID HIRAM despatch us here? True, he had pleaded his need to await
an expected shipment. "Serena, my dear," he had said at their late supper,
"Captain Brandon has expressed a wish to see the cedar works. Would
you serve as guide? You've a good grasp of the work there."

He turned to Brandon. "You'll not think me remiss as a host, Brandon?
The property abuts Weyford, as I believe I mentioned, and I've little
doubt Serena knows the lay of the land better than I. You'd best go by
water, the way we float the logs. That particular spong lies near the Flats;

you'd be days traversing them on foot, if you did not get lost entirely."

Brandon's brows drew together. "Spong?"

Serena laughed lightly. "Hiram forgets you are not native to the Barrens—but then, neither is he. A spong is a kind of bog, one where water lies year-round. Some are large, some small, but this particular one is immense. Not all of it's been explored, but it appears to border most of the Flats. And they, of course, have barely been explored at all."

She shuddered a bit, thinking how easy it would be to enter the Flats and wander confused until one starved to death or went mad: mile upon mile of white sand covered with stunted pine and oak, barely head high but so dense that a man might pass unheard and unseen within ten feet of another, or encounter a deer within arm's reach, swishing through the tight-packed branches.

"Thank you for your instruction, Mistress Wainwright. Had you thought, perhaps, to be a schoolmistress?" One eyebrow slightly lifted, Brandon smiled at her, unperturbed by her angry stare.

You didn't know, damn you, and now you do, and I'm made the fool for telling you. When will I learn? The silence grew and spread, pulsing with the tension between them, until Hiram Jonas broke it, slapping the damask cloth lightly with his palm and smiling at each of them in turn. "It's settled, then? I'll order the kitchen to put up provisions for you. If you leave at dawn you'll not be back till long past sundown."

Brandon half-bowed in Jonas' direction, his narrowed eyes fixed upon Serena. "My pleasure," he said.

THE BANKS OF THE STREAM slipped dreamily by. At intervals of their long passage upstream, black-eyed daisies and loosestrife splashed gold and magenta upon the water. Elsewhere the trees hung over the stream, their roots gnarled toes groping for purchase on the banks, their branches arching to form a leafy tunnel that the light could barely penetrate: oak and cedar and the silver-leaved swamp magnolia. Here the waters revealed their true darkness, rich with the residue of cedars long since dead.

Even the birds seemed reluctant to break the silence, but when at last Serena and Brandon reached the broad, slick waters of the spong, the clang of adzes and the shouts of men drifted to them, guiding them to the cedar-mining site. The tall slim shapes of the living trees stood watch over the proceedings, but these lordly white cedars, mast-straight and a hundred feet high, seemed upstart children beside the corpses of their ancestors which the men now struggled to exhume.

And struggle it was, fraught with dangers. The nearly flat-bottomed Durham boats, adapted for this purpose, rocked and swayed perilously as sweating, swearing men fought with pulleys and grapples to break the swamp's clutch upon the victims it would surrender but reluctantly. As Serena and Brandon neared, a drowned log burst free, the grip that held it to the swamp bottom grudgingly relinquished. With a splash and a sucking sound it broke the surface, surprising the men who tugged upon the chain and sending the smaller of them pitching overboard.

Serena watched in horror as the man thrashed about, frantic to grasp the boat, lest he sink to his death in the limitless muck beneath the shallow water. Two of his fellows grasped his wrists and pulled, but the swamp, as though seeking a new victim to replace the one that had been wrested from it, held tight. The boat rocked as victim and rescuers struggled to maintain their hold upon each other.

"Hold on!" shouted Brandon, sending his boat lurching across the water with powerful strokes, the corded tendons of his neck revealing the effort that his arms transmitted to the oars. The small boat shot up to the larger one and those aboard reached down to steady Serena as Brandon leapt onto the deck and joined the rescuers. "Trim the boat," he gasped. "Trim the boat, or we'll all be over." Yanking Serena along with them, the men hastened to obey, for the boat was tipping dangerously, threatening to pitch one and all into the bog's mortal clutch.

Brandon joined the rescuers. "On the count," he cried, leaning far overboard to grasp the flailing man beneath the armpits, the cloth of his shirt tearing with the strain on the muscles of his shoulders and back. "Rock with the count, men — with the count now. One . . . two . . . one . . . two." They pulled in time with his seaman's cadence, the boat rocking with their rhythm. On the third count the man popped free, sprawling upon the deck, breathing in gasps, his legs from the hips down coated with black slime.

Now all of them laughed immoderately, slapping Stuart Brandon's bared back and chaffing with the erstwhile victim. "Jersey Lightnin' all 'round," called the man in charge, and they passed the flask from hand to hand, drinking deeply, until one of them thrust it at Serena, then drew back with a sheepish grin. "No, thank you!" She, too, laughed in relief.

With a bustle and a stir they now set about restoring normalcy, making fast the painter of Brandon's boat, fumbling in the small cabin for dry clothes, leading their somewhat dazed fellow to a secluded corner where he might shed his drenched, filthy garments.

Brandon ripped off his ruined shirt, flexing his shoulders, bending and twisting to ease his cramping muscles. Serena felt a jolt at the pit of her stomach. Her fingers tingled with the desire to clasp his slim waist where the tanned flesh met his breeches. She realized that her heart was pounding and that she had been holding her breath. She breathed deeply of the heated air heavy with the sulphurous scent of decaying vegetation. His look leapt the distance between them—eyes narrowed, lids drooping at the corners, weighted by remembrance and desire.

❧   ❧   ❧

"THOSE LOGS! Have you ever seen trees so immense? Whatever could have felled them? How long do you suppose they have lain there?" Serena felt herself babbling, her voice artificial and high, skipping lightly over the water to echo back from the mist-hazed shore. Yet her interest in the topic was not feigned; the dead forest giant—wet with primeval ooze, suspended dripping and defeated while men hacked at its roots to trim it to smoothness for its journey to final dissolution—exerted a strange fascination.

Stuart Brandon did not reply. He plied the oars with concentration, keeping to the centre current, scanning the banks of the stream for sheltered mooring where they might have their supper. The speed of their downstream course betold the strength of the current hidden beneath the deceptive calm of the winding stream's dark surface.

The creek widened and split to embrace a small, swampy island, and, taking the starboard course, they came upon a tributary that neither had noticed during their upstream passage. Soon Brandon had moored their boat beside a small quay, weathered to silver, mossy and crumbling: remnant, Serena wondered, of what long-dead woodsman's bootless venture into commerce?

At the prodding of some vagrant memory she looked about her apprehensively. "I think we're on Weyford lands now." She felt constrained to whisper.

"And what of it?" Beneath the casual tone she sensed the arrogance that made his slightest whim a matter, to him, of compelling necessity. "Are you not the heiress to Weyford?"

How much does he know? And how much does he guess? What has Hiram told him? And for all that, how little Hiram knows. She tossed her head and did not answer, occupying herself with the bundles of provender so that she might avoid his searching look. In the deepening shadows of approaching night, his face was difficult to see.

He sat silent, making no move to disembark. Without words they ate and drank while the last chitterings of birds died down in the trees and the rustle of night creatures began. When both had done, neither moved to depart. At last she looked at him, unable any longer to endure the heavy silence. As the evening cooled he had put on a borrowed shirt, too tight for his broad shoulders, rolled above his strong wrists and open at his throat to ease the strain upon the linen. His signet ring, slung about his neck on a thong for safety as he rowed, glinted in the dark hairs curling on his chest.

They stared at one another, their eyes, in shadowed sockets, reflecting the gleam of the red harvest moon that had risen stealthily beyond the trees. And then, in a sinuous movement, she flung herself from her seat to kneel before him, her hands upon his lean hips, her throbbing breasts crushed against him, her body held fast by the hard muscles of his thighs. Her mouth clung to his, ardently questing. Soon the boat floated free at the end of its mooring, and rounds of ripple, ringed with light, surged outward from it, one upon the other, faster and faster, to lap unheard against the pilings of the little quay.

❧   ❧   ❧

NEITHER SAW the furtive figure edging closer, crab-like, behind the shelter of the brush, nor saw his nod of satisfaction when the brightening moon revealed their faces to him. Neither saw his body tremble, then sway in rhythm with the rhythm of their own, nor, when the woman's shadow knelt above the man's, head flung back in the ecstasy of her impalement, did either hear the foliage rustle with the hidden watcher's spasm of release.

Later, when the shadows merged, the woman's shadow collapsed upon the man's, his arms about her, and the light-ringed ripples moved ever more languidly with the gradually diminishing rocking of the boat, the watcher stole away unseen.

Much later, when the moon hung low on the opposite horizon and the boat, floating easily, barely guided, had long since reached its destination, Caleb Sawyer quietly entered Weyford's countinghouse, lighted a shuttered lantern, and picked up his pen.

C H A P T E R ❧ 4 1

T HE RAIN HAD DIMINISHED, but the wind still paced the garden,
trampling the brave pennants of the iris, beating the drenched
daffodils to the ground. Big-bellied clouds lay on the horizon, gravid
with yet more rains to swell the streams now in spate with ten days'
unprecedented downpour. Even the porous soil of the Barrens had long
since reached saturation point, and for the first time Serena could recall,
men spoke of flooding and looked anxiously to the state of their dams
and water wheels.

Now, at midday, the watery light from the windows was scarcely sufficient to write by, the weak April sun was so deeply swathed in cloud.

My dearest Melissa,

I am so pleased to hear of your progress. Mistress Mansey keeps
me well informed, but I do so wish I could hear you tell me what
you think of your lessons. Perhaps you will be a woman grown
before you can read of my joy and pride in you . . .

She wrote on, listing and praising Melissa's accomplishments one by
one, pausing from time to time to consult with Sundar. Full-grown now,
slender and sleek, he lay upon her writing table with his forepaws curled
under him, blue eyes slanted shut in a half-sleep, an eyeblink away from
full alertness.

Doctor Will continues well and his practice prospers with sufficient
patients to occupy his energies, now that he is growing old.

Serena reached out to fondle Sundar's ears. He tolerated her attentions
with the merest flick of his dark brown tail to suggest that the time was
not of his choosing. Serena laughed but continued to stroke his warm

body for the comfort it gave her. Doctor Will, when she last saw him, had seemed almost frail, though as gentle and kindly as ever. To the question she put to him he gave thoughtful answer; as she had suspected, the trauma of Melissa's difficult birth made another pregnancy unlikely.

The garden has done splendidly, at least until these rains. Forking in middens as your Grandmama did seems effective in promoting growth. The iris made a fine display, though the squirrels wrought havoc among the bulbs.

She went to the window as was her wont when thinking. The chalky smell of wet slate crept in beneath the sash on strands of mist, but the crackling fire kept the room cosily warm. Remembering her struggles at Doctor Will's and the pressing need to conserve firewood, Serena snuggled contentedly into her gown of rose-red challis and fingered her shawl of softest merino. Life *is* better now, she thought, and there's so much here for me to do.

Master Jonas has let me oversee the building of the new workers' quarters and himself is busy with some scheme for piping water to their dooryards. The manufactories continue to grow, and on every voyage Captain Brandon —

She crumpled the sheet and pushed it from her, then, on second thought, rose and cast it into the fire, watching until the last charred flake crumbled to ash. Better not to write of Stuart Brandon's visits, better that Melissa never hear that name, even in these letters that I never expect to post.

For, after all, what should I tell her? Serena mused with a soft, bitter laugh. That he's her father but doesn't know she exists? That I no longer long for him to acknowledge her but pray that she be forever spared the pain of his love that is now proffered, now denied? That I know him now for what he is, yet during his absences grow fevered with the need of him, of his voice in the quiet conversations in which I can speak as I can with no one else: of the work here and my thoughts concerning it, of what I would have done at Weyford, were it mine. And the need, too, of his body and his hands? How can I tell his daughter that my passion for Stuart Brandon imprisons me in a net of subterfuge and betrayal?

Since his return they had met anywhere, everywhere, seldom able to withstand for long the fire that each kindled in the other: met in the loft, in sawdust-littered, half-constructed cottages, even, a few times under cover of darkness, in Brandon's rooms at the Red Lion, for a certain scrupulosity prevented him from accepting the hospitality of Jonas House. So long as the winter continued mild the woods had offered them shelter; the fur robes that Brandon brought to spread upon the pine-needled ground were soon flung off as the heat of passion enveloped them.

Hiram makes it so simple, thought Serena. As winter chill crept into his aging joints he spent more and more time in the library, huddled over his plans and drawings with a tankard of hot cider at hand, or tinkering in his private workshed with this or that invention.

With the plans Brandon had smuggled out of England for him, he had managed to build a small steam engine, and his blue eyes were brilliant with schemes for harnessing its power to the sawmill, to the water pumps, even to his carriage — though so far he had failed even in small models to transfer sufficient power from the pistons to a drive shaft of some kind. Only Serena and Brandon were in his confidence concerning his wild hopes; these two alone he seemed to view as allies where all others might think him mad.

Soon Jonasville was accustomed to seeing the two of them together, Brandon as explorer, Serena as guide. And as they lay together in the warmth of passion's ebbtide, Brandon too had come to confide in Serena perhaps more than he knew, of his plans for his fleet of which the *Audacious* had been the start; of the conditions in England and its developing system of manufactories; of his investments throughout the former colonies. But always there came the moment when he withdrew into his fastnesses, slashing the bond between them with some sharp jibe, like as not on the subject of her relation to Hiram Jonas.

Yet Jonas made fewer and fewer demands on her, seeming to content himself to sleep beside her, body curved to hers, his hand cupped to her breast, snoring heavily yet waking upon the instant if she attempted to leave the bed. Such powers as he had were fast waning, and he appeared not to regret their diminution, clinging to her instead in a fashion at once fatherly and child-like. So long as she maintained a certain docility, a confiding air of humble gratitude, he appeared to pose no threat and harbour no suspicion.

Yet she wondered. Hiram, she cautioned herself often, is no fool, however it may suit him to play the genial cuckold, easily duped. Sometimes she caught him watching her when they sat at table alone, his plump cheeks set with unaccustomed grimness beneath the quizzical blue eyes.

What would she do if discovered, perhaps cast out? Brandon she knew, better than before, to offer no hope of shelter or quietude: The scars of his past still bound his heart closed. Her life and Melissa's remained at

the mercy of Hiram Jonas' good will. For all the luxury in which she lived,
she had almost no money of her own; when she was not wearing them,
Jonas kept her jewels locked away. Yet whenever Brandon appeared,
always unheralded, her qualms, her hard-won caution, and such loyalty
as she felt for Hiram Jonas melted away in the passion that consumed
her at a meaning look, a touch so apparently accidental as to deceive
any onlooker but herself. Well aware of the quicksands on which she
trod, she was yet unable to repair to safer ground.

She laid her head down on her now completed letter. Where will this
end? she asked herself. No answer came. Instead, someone tapped at
her door.

"Serena?" It was Hiram Jonas. "Come with me. I have a surprise for
you."

৯ ৯ ৯

THE BRICK GARDEN WALKS were slick with moisture, the beds on either
side of them puddled and muddy. Hiram Jonas held Serena's arm, lest
she slip. Serena half hung back, for by now she had some intuition of
where they might be going. But Jonas bustled along with his rolling gait,
the strands of his white hair whipping in the wind. Serena hugged her
shawl more closely about her while her skirts flapped behind her like sails.

As they entered the hedged enclosure, the foliage of the cedars showered droplets upon them, the branches springing free as they shed their
burden of moisture. Jonas squelched across the slate flags with which
the enclosure had recently been paved. "Look!" He waved at the canvas-
shrouded object that dominated the centre of the space, its covering
tightly lashed.

I was right. It's come at last, though I hoped somehow it never would.
With all the ships that founder on the Barnegat Shoals why was this
cursed statue not consigned to the bottom of the sea?

Hiram Jonas was beaming at her, rocking heel-to-toe, hands clasped
behind him. "No one has seen it — nor have I. Shall we unveil it?"

Serena nodded with what grace she could, determined not to be sullen
about what, after all, she could not prevent. Jonas attacked the wrappings, picking impatiently at the moist knots, while she scanned the sky,
hoping for the respite of a cloudburst.

"Ah! Cover your eyes!" She heard a flapping as Jonas tore the canvas
away. "Now, look, my dear — no, no, wait — keep your eyes covered." Jonas
gripped her shoulders and maneuvered her about, childishly eager that
her first view should be the most telling one. "Now!" he said finally. He
stepped away.

Serena dropped her hands and gazed at her likeness. The thick mist had condensed upon the cold marble; the stone was filmed with moisture like living, perspiring flesh. Her face aflame, Serena looked from Jonas to the statue. Does he see what I see—what Master Pietro saw and, with merciless fidelity, translated into curve and line and textured plane?

The sensuous thrust of the upraised arm, the turgid expectancy of the single naked breast, the urgent demand in every line of the body drawn taut by the tension that precedes fulfillment, the fine lines of longing about the mouth, and, about the eyes, a hint of shadowed sadness not to be explained by the apparent simplicity of the manner in which they were chiselled: She had been rendered naked to an extent far beyond her expectation, with a completeness as masterful as it was insupportable. Oh, dear God! She looked wildly about as though to fling the discarded canvas over the statue and somehow keep it concealed.

Hiram Jonas was watching her closely, his recently acquired look of speculative calculation deepening the creases at the corners of his eyes. His face firmed. His lower lip protruded. "An excellent likeness, is it not? Perhaps we should show it to Captain Brandon on his next visit? Would he appreciate it, do you think?" And as she paled, not knowing where to look, he jerked his head, bidding her follow him, and started at a brisk pace toward Jonas House. As she picked up her muddy skirts to follow him, the wind sailed toward her on a slanting wave of rain.

❧ ❧ ❧

JONAS HOUSE seemed unnaturally silent. Not a servant was to be seen, although the wall sconces had been lit against the gloom. Without shedding his sodden cloak, Hiram Jonas stumped into the library. Serena followed. Opening the hidden cupboard, Jonas extracted a paper. Seating himself with his massive desk between them, he waved her to a chair. She shook her head and remained standing.

Wordlessly, he thrust the paper at her. She held it to the shaded desk lamp and felt her knees buckle beneath her. Now she did sit down, still holding the paper in her shaking hand. No need to read this, she thought, the handwriting upon it is enough—that spiky scrawl, trailing down the paper: Caleb Sawyer. Damn him! Damn him! Must he hound me from every shelter I find? Her fury overrode her fear.

She looked up at Hiram Jonas. He was watching her closely with what she thought of as his "trader's look," the blue eyes appraising, the face carefully blank. There was no trace in it of an aging man's chagrin at being cuckolded by a younger rival: no trace of anger, nor of mercy, nor

of the bashful kindliness he had heretofore displayed. What, then, made
her feel the aching pressure of tears in her throat?

"I'm sorry, Hiram."

"It's true, then?"

She stood to face him more directly. "I'll not insult you with a lie. I have not read the specific accusation. But I saw the name of Captain Brandon and so"—she swallowed—"it is true in its essence if not in its particulars."

"Look at the date."

Reluctantly, she glanced again at the paper. It fluttered to the floor. "You've known all this time?"

He nodded.

"Since last October? And said nothing?"

He nodded again, his large head drooping heavily.

"You have been watching us all this time? Toying with us?"

He shook his head. "No—not watching you in the sense you mean. Nor toying with you." Now he looked up at her. The stern lines of his face collapsed. It seemed heavier, older, sagging at the jowls; at the corners of his eyes, the lines that had always fanned upward drooped even as she watched. His brows drew together, carving furrows in the centre of his forehead. "I thought it would stop." Now the blue eyes gazing up at her were shiny, and for a moment he turned aside.

He cleared his throat. "I thought it would stop. I knew you were young, beautiful, full of life, that nothing held you to me but money—not for yourself," he added hastily, "I knew that, too. But for Melissa."

He stared down at his desk. Serena stretched out her hand, then withdrew it without touching him. "Not only money, Hiram. At first, perhaps, but not now."

"And I thought that your concern for Melissa would bring you to your senses before long."

She could not answer.

"And then"—he sighed—"there was Brandon's reputation. I have had that investigated. That singer . . . others, many others. No woman has held him long. But this . . . you . . . this has not been like his other affairs. There's something . . . something different, that has brought him back here again and again." He looked up, his piercing eyes—his "trader's" eyes—boring into hers. "He is Melissa's father, is he not?"

Still she said nothing.

"You needn't answer, Serena. The resemblance is so plain even I cannot mistake it, fool though you think me to be."

She leaned over the desk, clutching its edge, her knuckles no whiter than her stricken face. "Don't tell him about Melissa, Hiram! I beg you. Don't tell him!" She looked down at him, her eyes searching his in mute entreaty.

He held her gaze for a moment. Then he nodded coldly. So abruptly that she staggered he pushed back his chair and rose to his feet. "We made a bargain, Serena. I have given full measure. You have not."

He rounded the desk to stand before her, gripping her shoulders with a strength of which she would not have thought him capable. "You will keep it from now on. Do you understand?" Without waiting for an answer, he turned on his heel and left the room.

When she was sure he would not return, she picked up her skirts and raced for the stairs. She closed her door and turned the heavy brass key. Then she flung open her wardrobe and searched frantically among her clothes for the breeches she wore for riding.

CHAPTER ❧ 42

WIND TORE AT HER GARMENTS and rain pelted her face as Serena cantered wildly through the darkening afternoon. She barely noticed, intent upon a single goal: to confront Caleb Sawyer and . . . what then? To kill him. It was not a thought expressed in words: It was a throbbing tension driving her onward, heedless of the branches that slashed at her, the slippery trail beneath the horse's hoofs, the intensifying storm and the gathering night. To kill him if she must, or—she sensed the ultimate purpose that lay beneath his relentless pursuit, his destruction of each haven she had found—to be killed by him. There must be an end to this, once and for all.

The horse shied as it approached the Quaker bridge, its eyes rolling. With difficulty she kept the frightened animal on its course, for water bubbled angrily through the cracks between the planks. The banks of Weyford River lay already submerged, and a tangle of snags and driftwood pressed against the bridge's pilings, threatening at any moment to send the whole structure careering down the angry stream. The roar of the water submerged all other sound; she felt but did not hear the horse's hoofs striking the planks.

Then they were across the bridge and spattering through the puddles—the water, in boggy spots, rising to the horse's knees, slowing and endangering their passage. How far had they come? The White Stag and other landmarks had whipped by unnoticed, but she sensed they were nearing Weyford. By now the land should look familiar, but it did not, and she had travelled another mile before she realized that the trees that had always lined this trail had been cut down. Only stumps remained, and straggles of cinnamon fern and whortleberry, already being strangled by contending seedling pines. Was she lost? This stark wasteland, swathed in mist, gave no clue.

But no—there was Weyford Lake, silver in the fading light, its surface pocked by raindrops. And there—there was Wainwright House upon its rise, the light of a single lamp gilding the drawing-room window.

Her approach had been heard. A 'prentice, hooded and hunched against the rain, ran out to take charge of the tired horse. He led it off, its flanks steaming. Barely aware of having thrown him a coin and some hasty orders, Serena mounted the steps. The doors were barred. Suddenly frantic, she pounded upon them with both fists. "Let me in! Let me in!"

One door opened slowly with a rasp of unoiled hinges. Prudence stood there, a diminished, haggard Prudence, the stump of a candle sputtering in a cracked saucer in her hand. "Serena!" The hand wavered. The candle went out. Prue cast a terrified look behind her.

"Let me in, Prue. Where is he? Where is Caleb?"

Prudence backed away, flapping a hand to fend Serena off. "At—at the forge. The water wheel . . . the flood."

Serena whirled, her wet cloak flying.

"Wait! Serena—no—wait!"

But Serena was already gone.

❧   ❧   ❧

THE ROAR OF THE WATERS drowned out her approach. When Caleb Sawyer turned she had stopped a few paces from him, appalled by what she saw. Though the furnace had long been idle the gates were still drawn, and water boiled through the narrow millrace, overflowing its walls. It seemed Caleb had managed to disconnect the furnace machinery, for the huge wheel spun free, its shaft shrieking protest at its pace. The wheel shuddered alarmingly, sending bits of wood and iron hurtling through the air.

Caleb stood on the small walkway that gave access to the works of the wheel. At sight of her his face contorted with a fury matching the storm's. "Bitch!" His lips shaped the word, but the storm snatched it away. He lurched toward her. "You've no right here! Go away! Go away!" Now she could hear his insane shriek, pitched high above the water's roar.

She stood firm. He darted past her, to higher ground, where the hulk of the cold furnace lent a sinister cast to the night. She ran after him. They faced one another by the ruins of the casting shed, water dripping upon them from its sagging eaves, circling warily like wrestlers seeking an advantage, each waiting for the other to speak first. The roaring of the swollen waters was diminished here, a low, throbbing counterpoint to whatever they might say.

Caleb's face was a phosphorescent mask of malevolence, the eyes deeply shadowed, the mouth a black slit.

"So, Caleb Sawyer, we meet again. You did not think to see me here, did you? You thought you could hide here forever, safely plotting to destroy me, behind the edict you had foisted upon my father. "Father—!" Her voice slipped the leash she had kept upon her anger, so fierce he backed away, circling, circling, Serena following, until she faced the path that led back to Wainwright House, he the turbulent stream.

"Father—" she said again. "You killed him, Caleb Sawyer. Oh, not with knife or pistol. That suited a coward like you not at all. A man twice your age might fight back! But you killed him nonetheless. You set that fire. Don't deny it—you were seen." She thought she saw him flinch. Then he began creeping toward her.

"You're mad, Serena. The old man died of the cancer."

"In the end, perhaps. But he really died before that, when he lost his powers and ceded Weyford to you. And I'm glad"—she choked—"glad he's dead, and cannot see the ruin you have made of his life's work."

The black shadows twisted on the white mask that was his face, so fearful in their writhings that she backed off in her turn.

"What makes you think I set that fire?" Now his voice was sinister, low and insinuating, barely audible in the tempest all about them.

"I told you—you were seen. No"—she shook her head, retreating despite herself before his crab-like advance—"you needn't think I'd endanger my informant by giving his name to you. But the authorities shall have it"—now she prayed that Jake Buzby could be found, that he would talk—"and evidence of your spying, too. It's not long since you placed those men's lives in jeopardy. They'll not have forgotten or forgiven. And then, Caleb Sawyer, they'll have you shot. Or you'll hang like Joe Mulliner, from the gallows in Woodlington square."

He came toward her in a sudden rush. She stepped back and lost her footing. She felt her ankle give beneath her. She was falling, rolling over and over down the muddy slope toward the stream and the wildly flailing wheel. The railing stopped her, though it shuddered with the impact of her body.

As she scrambled to her feet he came up to her, stumbling and sliding on the mud-slick slope. Then his fingers were about her throat, squeezing, squeezing, and she clawed frantically at his hands as a red mist blurred her sight and the roar of the waters receded before the rushing of her own blood in her ears.

☙ ☙ ☙

CALEB SAWYER felt his breath rasping in his throat, felt his manhood quickening as Serena's arteries pulsed beneath his fingers. He did not feel her nails digging into his hands, did not hear the threatening creak of the railing against which he pressed her.

"Now! Now!" sang the throbbing in his fingertips, and he knew that this was what he had always wanted: to touch that flesh she had flaunted and forbidden him, to extinguish those eyes that had flared with proud scorn, eluding him, defeating him, again and again, refusing to give in, refusing to submit . . . to submit.

"Now! Now you'll do as I say!" The thought was a fiery arrow through his brain, cutting off all sense of danger, all sense of time or place, leaving nothing but the red-hot lust to conquer, to kill, to feel the life ebbing from her beneath his hands—hands competent at last, competent for this—and then to possess her body in death as he had never been able to in life: to possess it completely, absolutely, to feel it lose its living warmth, cooling and stiffening around him in final, irrevocable surrender.

He felt her beginning to go limp. He closed his hands still more tightly about her throat, dimly sensing the painful throb of his manhood demanding release. Now!

Something, someone, fell upon him from behind, grasping his collar, tearing at his coat, kicking at the backs of his legs, the shock of it so complete that his hands lost their hold. Serena, choking, summoned a last burst of strength. She wrenched herself aside as he pitched forward. Then the rotten railing gave. He lurched into the headrace.

Clutching at bushes, at roots, fighting not to fall, Serena did not see him sucked by the greedy current into the path of the madly turning wheel. As hands grasped her wrists to pull her to safety, Weyford River claimed him, snatching him from sight. Then the wheel twisted from its mooring. It tottered, then half-fell, half-flew along the course of the raging stream. A blob of white that was his body bobbed to the surface, then whirled away, swept by the torrent, pursued by a froth of bubbles black with blood.

Serena sagged onto the bank, dazed and shaking. Prudence bent over her, shaking too, her eyes wild. "He's drowned!" she cried. "He's dead! We've killed him! Oh, Serena, thank God! Thank God!"

CHAPTER ❧ 43

O NCE MORE A funeral procession trudged forlornly up the hill to the small churchyard. This time there was no train of weeping mourners: Caleb Sawyer's coffin swayed uneasily upon the shoulders of men paid to carry it. Serena and Prudence trudged after it, pale and silent, each immersed in her own thoughts. Nor, when the procession straggled to a halt, was it the Wainwright markers beside which they paused. The grave had been dug in a solitary spot close by the encroaching woodland.

❧ ❧ ❧

"I'LL NOT HAVE HIM buried by Father," Serena had burst out in the Wainwright House drawing room two nights before. She and Prudence huddled by the fire, holding out their sodden garments to its warmth.

"Nor I," said Prudence quietly, her bodiless voice surprisingly firm. "I hope he is swept out to sea."

Serena looked up in surprise, studying her sister for the first time that night, fully aware, as her shock ebbed away, that it was Prudence to whom she owed her life. But for Prue's sudden appearance—did she follow me there?—it might have been I whose body Weyford River bore on its journey to the Atlantic.

Prue was staring into the fire, shivering slightly, her pale face drawn. The silence between them grew, broken only by the sound of the rain hammering with renewed force upon the windowpanes and the hiss of the fire as it spat out the damp in the wood. Then there came a sound of shuffling from the hall.

Serena's frayed nerves threw ghastly images onto the screen of her half-closed eyes. Caleb Sawyer, come back to avenge himself upon her?

She glanced at Prudence. But Prudence seemed not to heed the sound; she remained in her reverie. The shuffling came nearer. A light flickered in the shadows of the hall. Then Anna Wainwright entered, a candlestick wavering precariously in her hand. Prudence started. She rose and guided her mother into a chair.

"*Wer ist das?*" Anna quavered. Who is that? "*Warum sitzt Ihr hier so späht?*" Why are you sitting here so late?

Prudence sent Serena a bleak glance, then turned to her mother. "*Es ist die Serena,*" she said in her halting German. It is Serena. She gave her mother's shoulder a gentle shake. "*Die Serena,*" she repeated. She beckoned Serena to approach.

"*Die Serena?*" Anna's voice was querulous. "*Ist sie doch nicht tot?*" Is she not dead after all? She extended her hand as though groping.

Serena knelt before her, unable for a moment to speak. This shrunken figure, lost in its voluminous nightgown, a flannel cap perched askew on her head—can this be Mother?

"*Kindchen?*" Anna groped again with the pathetic undirection of the nearly blind.

"She kept asking for you," whispered Prudence. "Caleb told her you were dead, but she never remembered from one day to the next. Perhaps she didn't believe it."

Serena caught the withered hand and pressed it to her cheek. "*Nein, Mama. Ich bin nicht tot.*" No, Mama. I am not dead.

Anna's lips worked. "*Nicht tot.*" She nodded, vaguely at first, then more vigorously. "*Das wusste ich doch. Ja—ich wusste das.*" I knew that. Yes—I knew it. Her free hand found Serena's face. She explored it with her fingers, lightly touching Serena's lips, her cheek, resting finally upon her hair. "*Kindchen.*" Tears seeped from the blurred brown eyes. Unheeding, she continued patting Serena's head. "This have I known. I have known it."

Prudence gasped faintly. "She had lost all her English," she whispered.

Serena folded her mother into her arms. How frail she was, how birdlike her small bones. "I'm home, Mama." She rocked Anna gently. "I'm home." Anna's cap fell off. Serena laid her cheek against her mother's head, her tears soaking the sparse grey braids.

Suddenly Anna tore away from Serena's embrace. Her head turned from side to side; she peered blindly around the room. Her mouth trembled. "*Wo ist er?*" Where is he?

Prudence patted her, soothing, reassuring. "Caleb is not here. Serena has come. Caleb is gone, Mama—gone forever. He will never come to Wainwright House again."

No, NEVER AGAIN, thought Serena now, watching the coffin being lowered into the ground. Caleb's body had been found the next morning, caught in a mass of twisted snags below the dam. Never again. She barely heard the minister's final blessing. As the first clods fell upon the coffin she raised her eyes to meet her sister's. The look she found there matched her own: a blaze, barely suppressed, of triumphant exultation.

C H A P T E R 🐦 4 4

O N THE WAY BACK from the graveyard, Serena heeded her surroundings for the first time. A fringe of trees still encircled the grounds,
but in the gaps between them she could see the devastation beyond,
black and cheerless. The sombre half-light of the Barrens had been sup-
planted by the glare of acre upon acre of cut-over ground. Wainwright
House, built to last, still stood, four-square and solid, but daylight revealed
the toll exacted by neglect.

Untrimmed, unrestrained, the Virginia creeper had grown wild. A
few ground-floor windows stared, blank and blind. The rest had been
engulfed, their closed shutters held fast in the embrace of the rampant
vines. The green paint was peeling from the shutters, the once-white
window frames were grey. Rust from the iron sills had trickled down to
stain the brick. Tall weeds thrust their insolent heads through the cracks
in the iron-flagged walk.

A huge branch had been torn from the giant sycamore, and a scabrous
orange growth bloomed in the unhealed wound. No one was about. In
the clearing once dominated by the workaday din of the forge, only the
rush of the slowly ebbing waters disturbed the Sabbath stillness.

Prudence passed Serena, then paused by the verandah stairs, waiting.
Serena awoke from her sorrowful trance and hurried up to join her.
Unswept grit crunched beneath their feet as they mounted the crumbling
steps. Together the sisters entered the silent house. Two new sets of
iron bolts, clumsily wrought, had been fastened inside the doorframe
with a careless haste that splintered the wood. But Prudence did not bar
the door.

🐦 🐦 🐦

WHEN PRUDENCE SOUGHT her out, Serena was sitting at her father's desk. She had forced open the shutters, pushing and straining against the stubborn vines, enough to admit the first timid sunrays. A moth, released from its prison, fluttered against the smeared pane; the sun gilded the filaments of broken spider webs. To Serena it seemed that Caleb's presence was all but palpable.

What is that rite of the Papists, she thought, by which they banish evil spirits? Could a priest with bell, book, and candle expunge Caleb from this sadly changed room? She shook her head. No. No more than it could bring back her father, pondering his accounts, looking up as she entered, his shaggy brows rushing together at the interruption, then the craggy face lighting with his smile.

She roused herself briskly, shrugging her shoulders to shake off her melancholy. Only I can do it, she said to herself; only I can banish Caleb Sawyer once and for all. Looking around as though for a place to start, she noticed Prudence standing in the doorway, twisting her hands in her apron.

"Come in, Prue. Sit down." The years fell away, and again it was Serena who was in charge, though the younger of the two.

Prudence sat tensely on the edge of a carved chair, still twisting her hands together. How changed she is, thought Serena. She was an old woman even as a girl—now she *is* old, old before thirty, with lines upon her forehead and shadowed, frightened eyes. What can her life here have been?

"Serena," began Prudence timidly, "how is she—the little girl? Melissa?"

Serena remembered the gowns for Melissa, masterpieces of delicate stitching, always the right size, the exquisite needlework their only signature. They had arrived regularly at Doctor Will's—fine woolens in the winter; in the spring fragile muslins and batistes, trimmed with hand-crocheted lace fine as cobwebs. But none had come to Jonas House. Did Prudence not know where I was? Or, knowing, did she know also that Melissa had been sent away?

Prudence must have guessed the progress of her thoughts. "I couldn't," she whispered, her stiff lips barely forming the words. "He caught me at it one day, and—" She buried her face in her hands. "He tore the dress to shreds and flung it into the fire."

"Prue—" Serena came around the desk and laid her hand on her sister's shaking shoulder. "He has abused you? Is that why you were frightened?"

Prue looked up. "Not with blows," she said hoarsely, "at least not usually. Only with silence—days and days of silence while I tried to guess what had angered him. And even when he was not angry, he wouldn't talk to me, he wouldn't look at me. And Mother—"

Serena's eyes kindled. "He abused Mother? Oh, Prue, no!"

"Not exactly. It was more that he paid her no mind. And Mother . . . she sensed somehow that he wanted her gone, wanted her"—she stared straight at the great desk, shuddering, as though she, too, felt that he still lurked behind it—"wanted her dead, if necessary, but gone, above all. All of us—he wanted all of us gone."

Prudence paused. "I've seen you looking at the house, at the filth and disrepair. But, you see, all the servants had left, he had dismissed them or hounded them until they fled, all of them except Black Susan—she's not afraid of him somehow—and she takes care of Mother, there's little time for anything else." She looked toward the windows with their half-opened shutters. "He wanted to be left alone. He said"—she shuddered again—"he said he wanted privacy. Those bolts on the doors, the new locks? He had the only key. Lately he would lock us in when he went away, or even if he was here. He would bar the counting-house door"—Serena had noticed the new bolts here, too—"and sit here for hours alone."

"Prue," Serena whispered, "what was he afraid of?"

"Of everything. Of nothing. Of"—Prudence stared at the window as though the rays of the sinking sun held a secret she had not guessed before—"of you. He was afraid of you. That was why . . . why . . ." Her face looked so haunted that Serena dared not speak.

"He left me alone, except when . . . except when he—" Her face turned crimson. "Then it was your name he would call out, while he—" She paused, swallowing painfully, her chest beginning to heave with sobs. "He seemed to want to *rend* me." She choked out the words. "As though—as though he were *punishing* me. Not his—not he, himself. An . . . instrument, an ivory model of—oh, I can't tell you. And he would say your name with each—over and over again."

Her head fell forward and she sobbed uncontrollably. After a time she looked up, her face splotched and tear-streaked. "Last night, while you and mother were asleep, I took that evil thing and threw it into the river." Again she wept.

Serena knelt and put her arms around her sister, holding her tightly, stroking her hair. "It's over, Prue. It's over." Gradually Prue's weeping subsided. Serena pulled up a chair and sat quietly, holding Prue's icy hand in both of hers. They sat there, saying nothing, until the last light had ebbed from the room.

"SERENA, WOULD YOU come back here—back to Weyford?" They sat in the drawing room now, beside a cheerful fire. Anna rocked in a corner. Every lamp, every candle in the room was lit. Prudence did not ask why Serena went from wick to wick with lighted taper. Both sensed that Caleb had not finished with them yet. His malediction hung upon the air like some black mist.

"Caleb left Weyford to me," said Prudence. "I suppose," she went on ruefully, "he had no one else to leave it to. Mother had life tenancy, of course, under the terms of Father's will. I suppose that was why Caleb dared not send her back to her relatives in Pennsylvania. Some of Father's old friends, Nicholas Sooy, perhaps, might have grasped his intention and intruded upon his 'privacy.' But apart from that the place is mine.

"Serena," Prudence bent forward in her urgency, "you know what to do. I don't. Caleb has all but ruined Weyford with his greed—even I can see that. I don't know whether the furnace can ever smelt bog ore again. There's little money left, I'd guess from his pinchpenny ways, and little custom. Before Mike McGuire left he told me about the firebacks. General Washington was only one of many who refused our wares." Her cold, bony hand gripped Serena's wrist. "If you don't come back, Weyford will have to be sold—and who's to buy it, with half or more of the timber gone and the works in disrepair? Father would not have wanted it to go out of the family . . . Serena?"

Serena looked round the room, so familiar, so strange. She did not answer.

"Please, Serena. I'll gladly deed you what's mine. I know you'll take care of me and Mother." She folded her hands in her lap, then clenched them tightly. "Serena"—she kept her gaze fixed on her hands—"I know I had a part in your leaving here—in what Father did. I was . . . I was envious of you. I grudged you Father's favour. I grudged you your beauty, grudged you everything. And because Caleb wanted you, I . . . I'm sorry, Serena."

"I know, Prue. I know. It's not that. I'd like to come back. I could"—her eyes lighted; she raised her chin combatively—"I could bring Weyford back; I'm sure I could." She stared into the fire for a moment, her face alight with plans. Then the glow faded. "But I have other obligations."

"Melissa? But she could live here, too. They'd soon forget her origin, those who haven't forgotten already. After all"—and now it was Prudence who lifted her chin—"she is a Wainwright."

"Melissa? Yes, I suppose she could live here." Could she? Would she be accepted as a Wainwright? Perhaps. And Melissa's father? Forget her father. He need not know. And if he does, if he finds her here when he returns from England, and sees me in my rightful place again, Weyford returned to its former glory, the furnace in blast, the forge working, the new growth tamed and thinned—and how swiftly the Barrens grow back—might he accept me then, and her with me? The demon of false hope, the demon she had sought again and again to vanquish, whispered once more its terrible lies.

Then she thought, for the first time in three days, of Hiram Jonas. In what mood had he received her scribbled note? How would he greet her when she returned, as it had promised? She remembered his face as she last had seen him, as he summoned his mask of shrewdness to conceal the naked pleading in his eyes. Her throat throbbed with that remembered ache. Do I not owe him something, too? Damn you, Caleb Sawyer—may you roast in Hell! For had Hiram not known, had I not seen his pain, would there be the slightest question of my choice now?

She took Prue's cold hand in hers. "No, Prue, not Melissa. Someone else. I must return to Jonasville tomorrow." Seeing the tears in her sister's eyes, she gave Prue's hand a squeeze. "Believe me, Prue, you're forgiven. If suffering's any payment—and I don't believe it is—then surely you've paid for any harm you did me. I thank you for your offer. I want to come back." Her voice firmed. "I will come back. But first there is something I must do." And if Hiram pleads with me? If he insists that I stay—that I owe him this in payment for my betrayal?

I can't decide here—not here in Weyford. The pull of memory is too strong. "Go to bed, Prue. You look exhausted. I'll come back somehow, I promise. But I must leave tomorrow—at dawn."

Serena rang for Black Susan to tend to their mother. Then she helped her sister to her feet and led her off to bed.

CHAPTER ❧ 45

SERENA STOLE THROUGH the rear garden of Jonas House and moved cautiously across the lawn. Her eyes fixed upon the house, alert for any watcher, she stumbled over an object on the grass. She looked down. The object that had tripped her was the head of her statue.

Pieces of the statue were scattered on the turf—a finger, a hand, a whole arm. The head itself had been defaced, the nose obliterated, the lips smashed, the planes of the cheeks chipped and cracked. Forgetting all caution, she rushed inside the enclosure. More bits of limbs and drapery lay upon the flags. Only the torso had defeated the vandal. Chipped and battered, it still stood. A large sledge lay beside it as though flung there in disgust.

Serena felt sick. "Hiram?" she whispered. But surely, no matter how angry, Hiram Jonas would not have done this. She leaned against the pediment for some moments, fighting her nausea. Then she made for the house. This time she ran.

Charity met her at the rear entrance door. "What has happened?" cried Serena. Charity shook her head helplessly, gesturing toward the front of Jonas House. The glossy brown of her plump face was tinged with grey. "Hiram?" asked Serena.

Charity shook her head more vigorously. Then she found her voice. "No, not Master Jonas. A . . . a lady. A lady and a young man. They be comin' in a coach—two coaches. One be full of trunks and boxes."

"I'll go see about this." Charity tried to hold her back, but Serena flung off the restraining arm.

"Have a care, Serena," said Charity. It was what she had said each time she had known Serena was meeting Stuart Brandon.

WHEN SHE RAN into the wide hall, Serena nearly tripped again. Something on the floor wrapped itself about her legs. It was one of her gowns. Gowns lay all over the curving stair—gowns and petticoats and nightdresses, flung one upon the other. As she made her way to the foot of the stairs another drifted down. Then a voice shrilled, "There she is! Stay where you are, you trollop!"

Glaring down upon her from the landing was a buxom woman of uncertain age. Her lace cap rode uneasily atop a bushy fringe of hair whose strident red was surely the work of the dyepot. As the stranger and Serena strove to stare each other down, Hiram Jonas appeared at the woman's shoulder. He had come up so quietly that she failed to notice. There was something diminished about him. His shoulders slumped, his small hands twiddled aimlessly with the frills of his shirt cuffs.

As Serena stared, he mouthed two words. She grasped them at once, perhaps because she had already guessed their meaning: "My wife." Perhaps she had also guessed what would follow, for these words she grasped instantly, too: "Caleb Sawyer."

Of course. So that was Hiram's secret—the reason he did not offer me marriage. This is his wife. And the young man Charity spoke of is no doubt his son. Caleb Sawyer tracked them down wherever they were—in all likelihood Boston; Hiram mentioned Boston from time to time—and informed them of Hiram's whereabouts.

Who wouldn't flee? thought Serena, sensing in her opponent the born shrew's domineering ways. I'll wager he had never a moment's peace.

Then her amusement vanished in a blast of anger. Caleb Sawyer! Striking at me as though from beyond the grave. Was this the cause of my uneasiness, my sense that I had not yet done with him?

Espying the change on Serena's face, Mistress Jonas whirled about. "Samson!" The rasp of her voice sent shivers along the spine. "Tell this strumpet to leave our house."

Hiram Jonas quailed. His wife stamped her foot. "Now!" Her voice rose yet another note.

"But, Martha—"

"No 'but'! 'But' is all I hear from you. 'But, Martha this. But, Martha that.' I'm your wife. This is *my* home." She gazed avidly round the splendid hall, marking the mahogany stair rail, gleaming with beeswax, the paintings, the carpets, the massive chandelier. "*Mine*," she repeated on a note the chandelier echoed with a single ping. "She's not to defile it an instant more."

Hiram Jonas shrugged his shoulders. Turning, he pretended to study a painting—a bucolic scene totally at variance with the atmosphere of the hall—as though he were appraising its worth.

"Hiram," said Serena, "surely you cannot countenance what she is doing."

He kept his back turned.

"I'll leave, of course, Mistress Jonas," she said at last. "But all my things are here, my clothes, and—"

Her opponent uttered a strained laugh. "Your clothes, indeed! And who paid for them?"

Hiram Jonas turned around. With more spirit than he had heretofore shown, he eyed his wife up and down. "Had you thought to wear them, Martha?"

Her florid face turned purple. "Take them then!" She pounded down the hall, returning in a few seconds with an armful of garments. "Take them!" She flung each over the railing with all her strength. A petticoat wrapped itself around her arm. She yanked and clawed at it as though a living creature had entrapped her. "Take your whorish fripperies. But begone from this house, or I'll have my son take a horsewhip to you!"

Serena turned to Hiram Jonas. He kept his head down and did not look at her. "You'd best go, sweet." He sighed. "Can you go back to Weyford? Good. Charity will bring your things."

He scuttled back down the hall, his wife in pursuit. Her yammering echoed behind her until a far-off door slammed upon it.

For a long moment Serena stood as though paralyzed. Then she burst into laughter, peal upon peal, echoing in its turn through the now-silent hall. "Caleb Sawyer, may you hear of this in Hell! It's your plotting that has set me free!"

CHAPTER ❧ 46

O NCE MORE SERENA SAT in the countinghouse. She had had Samuel Wainwright's desk removed. In its place was the Randolph writing table Doctor Will had given her so long ago. She had had it placed so that the light came from behind her, and sunlight streaming through the newly polished windowpanes made an aureole of her piled-up hair. Oblivious to the room, to the refulgent day behind her, she stared down at the paper Stuart Brandon had laid upon the desk.

"So it was you," she said hoarsely. She coughed and began again, trying to force words through a throat tight with shock. "It was you behind that sudden spurt of growth here—you who lent my father the money to build Weyford up so quickly. Two thousand pounds . . ." Her voice trailed away.

Stuart Brandon nodded, his eyes bright with amusement and blue with the reflection of the clear November sky. He was watching her closely. "Yes, Mistress Wainwright, it was I. With war certain to come, what better investment than an ironworks? Except, perhaps, for a privateer's fleet. And as safe as privateering is perilous. Less amusing, of course, for that very reason. But your father was a born ironmaster. He needed only capital. With him in charge here I could have my amusement and a safe berth, too."

Serena's eyes flashed. "Yes—you have a propensity for arrangements of that kind."

"Why, Mistress Wainwright, whatever can you mean?"

She refused to be baited. Indeed, she scarcely heard his reply, for she was puzzling over the riddle of her father's will. Why had he bequeathed his property as he had, knowing, as he must, that it was not fully his to devise? Had he been that befuddled at the end? "Caleb Sawyer," she said, as though to herself, "did he know?"

Stuart Brandon laughed. "Caleb the plotter? I told you, did I not, that
I had a score to settle with him? Doubtless he destroyed your father's
copy of our bargain." His lip curled, though laughter lingered in his eyes.
"The worthy Caleb was ever one to underestimate his opponents. Surely
he should have guessed that I would take the precaution of retaining a
copy, duly sworn.

"Well"—and he all but laughed aloud—"it seems you have disposed of
Caleb for me." She looked up quickly. "Drowned by misadventure, Mistress Wainwright? Keep that tale for those more readily gulled. There
are enough fools willing to be so, I've no doubt. With his crony Lipcote
dead—by cleverness or good fortune you have cut quite a swath through
the ranks of your enemies—it's unlikely that anyone will inquire too
closely into how he came to fall beneath that wheel."

Still smiling, he folded his arms across his chest. "Tell the truth, now,
Mistress Wainwright: Did a single mourner follow his coffin to its grave?"

Despite her preoccupation, she giggled. "I was there. And my sister."

"And no doubt you were both prostrate with grief. Well—to business." The smile left his face. "You are indebted to me for two thousand
pounds—that is, if you wish to own Weyford. Can you pay it?"

"You know I cannot. Least of all now, when Caleb has all but ruined
us." Her voice quickened. "Why, by all that's holy, did you not press your
claim before he had made it worthless?"

"I had other matters to attend to."

She sat fuming. He stood quietly watching while anger and frustration
pursued one another across her face. Then he threw back his head and
laughed. "It seems that you are in my employ. You've nowhere to go
now that Jonas has thrown you out at the behest of his resident virago.
And I've no hope of finding another manager. Caleb has made the name
of Weyford a scorn and a hissing, not only among customers but ironmasters too."

He picked up his cloak from the chair and donned his tricorne with a
flourish. "Be of good cheer, Mistress Wainwright. How often have I
listened to complaints that your sex had kept you from the work you
were born for? If you're the ironmaster you think you are, you'll earn
enough to buy it back. If, that is, I'll sell it to you. Mind you take good
care of my investment."

In the instant before the bronze inkstand crashed against it, the door
closed behind him.

BOOK IV

❧

Serena

CHAPTER ❧ 4 7

THE SUNLIGHT OF yet another spring lay in scattered patches on the mellow wood of the writing table, the newly painted walls, the polished floor. In the centre of one of the patches, Sundar lay sleeping. At the writing table, Serena wrote hastily, her quill fairly skipping across the page, then scratching, stopping, dry. She jabbed it into the inkstand. Too full, it splattered the page.

"Calm yourself," she murmured. She sniffed appreciatively at the warming air that bellied the curtains, a curious admixture of apple blossom, pine, and soot. She resumed her writing, dimly conscious all the while of a quickening tempo in the din of the stampers, the blows of the forge hammers, the accelerating creak and groan, clatter and rumble that meant that a blast was nearing its conclusion.

Weyford lives again, she thought, without exultation—with, instead, the deepening satisfaction of a task well begun. Soon she must go to watch them pour the heat, to learn what she could about texture and temperature, to try to hone the sixth sense bred into every ironmaster— the sixth sense that overrode every written formula, the convergence of sight and smell and feel that said "Now!" Now it is time to add ore or charcoal or flux, to tap the furnace, to watch for a breakout or the variance in temperature that can ruin a half-ton of castings.

She knew a little now. Some of the lore she had seemed to know always, some had been picked up in her childhood ventures to the furnace, some had been taught her since. But it was not yet enough to make her master of Weyford as she believed herself capable of being.

Mike McGuire had taught her much. Others too: Many of the old crew had drifted back, the skilled hands she needed. But it was Mike who guided and led them, who silenced their mutterings about "petticoat rule." The renascence of Weyford might be faster in coming had she hired an ironmaster away from her competitors. But that was not the renascence she wanted. Better this slow, steady start with a Wainwright placed where a Wainwright always had been: as master of Weyford.

But now these accomplishments could not hold her attention. She wrote, reaching out from time to time to touch two papers that lay beside her, to stroke them reverently, hesitantly, almost fearfully lest they somehow disintegrate before her eyes. One was heavy parchment—a draft drawn in her name upon a bank in London to the sum of two thousand pounds sterling. The other was a letter from a London solicitor, referring to "my client, Samson Peabody, known to you as Hiram Jonas." Attached to it was a scrap apparently torn from a ledger upon which was scrawled: "For Melissa's future. H."

She smoothed the bank draft for perhaps the hundredth time and wrote:

> . . . and so, dear Mistress Mansey, tell Melissa whatever you think best. Tell her also that she will be coming back to you shortly, for she must complete her schooling. But put her on the earliest ship, and when you know what it's to be, send word to me by courier. With one of your servants she should travel quite safely. I shall journey to Tuckerton well in advance, to be there when she disembarks.

She studied these instructions for a moment, then impulsively added, "What joy! And however can I thank you!"

She added a few more instructions, then put the letter in its envelope aside and began another, far briefer. It was addressed to the New York offices of Stuart Brandon's shipping firm:

> Come to Weyford. I have urgent business to discuss.

This, too, she folded and enclosed. Then she dripped sealing wax upon them both—a blob of brilliant vermillion. When the wax had hardened slightly, she stamped it firmly with her seal, the flowing "W" of Weyford.

CHAPTER ❧ 4 8

"MAKE WAY! Hie! You there! Make way!" Puffing, its bearers maneuvered a sedan chair through the jostling, shouting crowd. The coastal schooner *Endeavour* was about to embark. From her deck, Stuart Brandon watched the chair's progress, the fire in his eyes dwindling to a spark of pure amusement. At his side the portly master, breathing heavily, sweating profusely, awaited the return of his employer's attention.

Reaching the gangplank, the bearers set the sedan chair down, the leader mopping his brow with a filthy rag. As the curtains parted he proffered one hand to decant a plump figure from the chair, while, with dexterity born of experience, he extended his free hand for his tip. With a grand gesture, Madame Constanza laid a coin in his palm. Then she sallied up the gangplank, her skirts billowing in the Hudson River breeze. The chair-man bowed, then looked more closely at the coin and swore, loudly and volubly.

"Madame Constanza," said Stuart Brandon. "An enchanting surprise, to be sure. And where will you next be singing?"

"Pheeleedelpheea," she answered, catching but a few of his words.

"Well, then, we shall be fellow voyagers for a portion of the journey." He snapped his fingers at a hovering cabin boy. "Escort Madame to the passenger quarters."

The singer fluttered her lashes and her fan, bestowing a languishing glance on Stuart Brandon. "Later?"

"Perhaps."

She gave him a look heavy with promise, then followed the boy, her ample curves swaying.

Stuart Brandon looked after her for a moment, his lip curled in distaste. Despite the breeze off the river, the scent of her lingered, heavy and cloying. She will find her berth a whit lonely, he thought. Then he forgot her. What urgent business might Serena have with me? She has never summoned me before.

"Captain Brandon." With the singer out of sight, the ship's master spoke with new urgency. "I beg you, heed these warnings I've received. The flags of several incoming vessels signal heavy weather."

"I am as capable of reading signal flags as you," said Stuart Brandon coldly. "These are likely the ditherings of alarmists. Still more likely they fly at the behest of captains who have something to gain by delaying the *Endeavour*. Prepare to set sail."

The short, stout master, his stockiness stressed by his old-fashioned petticoat trousers, squinted up at Stuart Brandon, choleric in his urgency. "Captain Symes is no alarmist and no ditherer. What's more, he knows the waters of the Jersey coast better than any of us; he's plied them nigh onto thirty years with but two wrecks, an enviable record. It is not the squalls alone that concern him; it is the full moon and the spring tide, and, of course, the wind out of the east—a dangerous combination. And the Shoals. For you to disembark at Tuckerton as you planned we may well have to cross them in darkness."

Better than any of us? How dare this fat fool cast aspersions on my seamanship? Stuart Brandon silenced the doubts that had nearly made him capitulate. "Enough!" His eyes steel, a knot of muscle jumping in his jaw, he faced down the worried master.

"I've some slight acquaintance with the Barnegat waters. And I say these are vapourings. What's more, the *Endeavour* is my ship—*mine*—and by your contract I'm chief officer whenever I'm aboard. If you feel yourself incapable of navigating the Shoals, you may disembark now and call at my offices for your pay. I'll sail her to Tuckerton myself. There, I've no doubt, I'll find a master with bowels enough to sail her the rest of the way." He tapped his foot, his nostrils flaring. "Well?"

"I'll sail her," said the master at last.

"Very well then. Take in the gangplank at once. I'll not allow your vapourings to make us lose the tide." Brandon stalked some distance away to lean on the rail, breathing hard. The master gave the order to draw the gangplank in.

⮞ ⮞ ⮞

THE WHARF with its colourful crowd began to move slowly away from them in a rising and falling motion set to the chanting of the seamen. Stuart Brandon became aware of someone at his side. He looked down. A girl-child of some five years clung to the rail beside him, teetering on the very tips of her polished black boots, taking little hops from time to time that she might see better, then turning to look up at the shrouds aswarm with men. A stolid, matronly woman, a servant by her dress, stood watchfully by her side.

The child was warmly covered by a thick cloak of dark blue wool from which peeped a short gown of flowered challis looped over a linen petticoat. Her felt bonnet perched precariously upon a mass of glossy black curls bunched up with a velvet ribbon. As she looked up at Brandon, he saw that her eyes were amber, flecked with specks of green and blue that reflected the sky and the river.

He felt a clutching sense of recognition but dismissed it; surely he had never seen this child before. Indeed, he took little interest in children. All the more surprising, then, that he should feel compelled to respond when she threw him a dazzling smile.

"Isn't it grand?"

"The ship?"

"Oh, yes—the ship. The way it rolls. And the sailors, climbing up there. And the gulls screaming."

"Is this your first sail?"

"Oh, no. But before, you see, I was little."

"And now you are big?"

"Well . . . bigger anyway." Surefooted as a veteran sailor, she suddenly let go the rail and pirouetted rapturously. "Oh, I do love this ship!"

"And where are you bound?" The child's companion looked at him suspiciously, but apparently decided that he posed no threat to her charge. .

"To Tuckerton," the child said. "My mother is to meet me there. And that is grander still." With an apprehensive glance at the servant, she beckoned him to bend down, fluttering her lashes like an accomplished coquette. "I thought she had gone away, far away across the sea. They said she would never come back. But I thought—I knew—she would. Or else I would look for her."

She dug into the pocket of her cloak and produced some shells: a scallop and some miniature whelks. "Look! I remember sand, and waves, and berries in baskets. My mother was there with me—my mother and a black lady. I knew I could find her. But I thought I'd have to wait till I grew up. I prayed and prayed. And she's come back, and she's sent for me."

"I see." The tale sounded fantastical, but then, this child plainly had a lively imagination. "And what is your name?"

"Melissa."

"Well, Melissa, I am Captain Brandon. I am owner of the *Endeavour* — and other ships as well. Later, perhaps, you can visit the helm with me and help steer. But now I must go to my cabin. We'll be in open water soon. Mind you don't get seasick."

"Oh, I won't be seasick. I love it when the ship rolls and the sails make that cracking sound—like rifles. I hope it's rough—very rough—I hope there's a big, big storm with big, big waves." She whirled round and round again, arms outstretched to welcome the storm she envisioned.

Laughing, he took his departure. As he rounded the curve of the deck he turned and waved to her. She waved back, her scrap of a handerchief fluttering in the freshening breeze.

❧ ❧ ❧

WITH A TREMENDOUS GROAN the ship heeled over, sending pewter tankards clattering across the deck to bounce off the bulkhead and roll beneath Brandon's bunk. The red globe of the lantern swung wildly, gyrating within its brass cradle. Instantly alert, jarred out of his cat-like doze, Stuart Brandon came to his feet. Bare to the waist, he rushed out onto the deck.

"Ship agrooooound!" The winds snatched the lookout's words away. The *Endeavour* struck the sandbar with a grinding jolt that set all her timbers to shuddering.

Brandon, slipping and sliding on his way to the helm, cupped his hands to his lips. "Lower sail!" But his shout, like the master's, was too late. Snapping lines, slippery with sleet, wrenched free from the hands that sought to grasp them. The thunder of freed sails heavy with ice drowned out even the roar of the sea. The deck tilted crazily landward.

Already, men were sliding down the sleet-slicked decks into the waters below. Passengers emerged screaming from the hatchways to be swept off their feet by the seas. Each new assault of the waves lashed the crippled ship into more frenzied motion, but none set her free of the bar.

The deck trembled with the onslaught of the seas and the cargoes cannonading against the hull. Eyes everywhere at once, Brandon sought to bring order to the deck's pandemonium. The master, too, was semaphoring wildly, directing such of the crew as had not been swept into the sea. His gestures were barely visible in the greying light of predawn.

Suddenly, Brandon remembered Melissa, perhaps trapped in some water-filled passage. He fought the urge to look for her. The *Endeavour* was his first responsibility. Yet in truth there was little he or the master could do to save the foundering ship.

The deck lurched and tilted more sharply. Loosened cargo smashed the rail. In the riggings above men lost their hold. Some fell screaming into the boiling surf, others crashed to their death on the deck.

Through the sleet that pockmarked the few smooth spaces on the sea, Brandon saw lights and dim figures scurrying on the shore. But the calls of rescuers and the cries of the drowning were alike snatched away by the wind.

A few hundred yards cut the *Endeavour* off from land with the finality of miles. To launch a boat meant death to the rescuers; to those still on board, swimming seemed as hopeless. Already, the spreading light of an angry red dawn showed broken figures washing up upon the shore.

Crawling along the sloping deck, in danger of sliding into the waves with each pitch and toss of the ship, Brandon fought his way from hand-hold to handhold toward the passenger hatchway. Planks and spars slithered past him, some finding their bruising mark.

In the luminescence cast by the angry waters Brandon saw a white, frightened face and small hands clinging to a rope dead ahead. "Hold on, Melissa! Hold on!" To reach and at least comfort Melissa he must struggle but a few feet more.

Then a massive wave convulsed the dying ship. His frozen fingers lost their grip. As he fought for a handhold her body swept past him, straight through a splintered gap in the railing where he had met her.

▪▪ ▪▪ ▪▪

HE PAUSED BUT AN INSTANT to get his bearings. Then he plunged in after her. The water's cold struck him like a blow. He gasped, choking on salt water as a wave slapped his face. How long could he survive the cold? How long could Melissa?

For a few panicked seconds the waves worked their will upon him, tossing him high, then sucking him under. He surfaced, fighting for air, shaking his head to clear the water from his eyes. At first he could see nothing but the waves, higher than his head, advancing upon him. Then a flash of white streaked past him. Melissa! He lunged for her. As another wave crashed upon them both he managed to grasp her skirts.

Down they went together, rolling over and over with the churning of the waters. Just as he knew he could hold his breath no longer the capricious ocean tossed them to its surface. He drew Melissa to him, tightening his hold. He got an instant's glimpse of the still pallor of her face. Is she already dead? No matter. I must get her to shore. How long could he withstand this frigid buffeting?

They were farther now from the sandbar and the ship. The waves contended less fiercely; they surged more consistently shoreward. Yet the *Endeavour's* sinking might yet pull them to the bottom of the sea. He trod water, gauging the rhythm of the rollers. If I can use their motion to my advantage, might there yet be a chance? How much time has elapsed? Hours, as it seems? Seconds, more likely. His heart was pounding heavily. His limbs were numbing fast, and he feared to lose his hold upon Melissa.

The waves seemed farther apart now. As each wave crested, he flung himself forward, hoping they moved in the direction of the shore. In the seconds between waves he swam as one possessed, towing Melissa behind him. Gasping and choking, panting with the effort, he contrived to surge forward as far as each wave would take him. They were moving shoreward steadily now, the pace of the great breakers slowing to their advantage.

He took a deep breath and tightened his grip on the child. He felt the slackness of her body, and his heart contracted with dread. But he tried to relax, to let the current work its will with him whenever it surged toward the shore. He must conserve what strength he had left. He felt deadly tired, his whole body numb, his thoughts no longer ordered but fragmented and vague. Melissa, looking at him with Serena's eyes . . . yes, those eyes . . . there was something about them, something important to know. The thought was swept away on the next wave.

A jolt shook his body. His feet, devoid now of all sensation, must have touched the bottom. A breaker smashed over his head, rolling and tumbling him and his burden. As it ebbed, he staggered to his feet, struggling to make his numb limbs obey him, fighting the fierce undertow by which the sea reclaimed its own.

Still clutching Melissa, he fell . . . rose . . . fell again. Now the water, between waves, was only waist high.

Instinctively seizing the right moment, he flung himself into a cresting breaker and let it carry them to shore.

Hands reached to help him as he staggered into the shallows. "Here!" he gasped. "Hurry!"

He thrust Melissa's limp body into someone's outstretched arms. Then his legs gave way beneath him, and he collapsed, face downward, sprawled full length and senseless upon the sands of the Barnegat shore.

CHAPTER ❧ 4 9

"MISSUS WAINWRIGHT! Missus Wainwright! Be ye in there?" the pounding at her door sent Serena bolt upright on the musty sacking of her bed. Her heart was thumping wildly. "Who is it?" Straightening the wrinkled garments in which she had lain down, expecting at any moment to hear that the *Endeavour* had come in with the dawn tide, she went to the door.

The gaffer who helped about the inn stood there, lantern in hand. "Missus Wainwright," he quavered, "be comin'—quick! The *Endeavour* be aground at Barnegat!"

Why was she not surprised? The old man peered at her, evidently expecting an outcry. But her face felt blank, her lips frozen. "I'm coming," she said tonelessly. She picked up her cloak and followed him out to her waiting wagon.

❧ ❧ ❧

SERENA AND HER GUIDE picked their way along the shore. The polished blue bowl of the sky, the sun-whitened froth upon the still-churning waves, were in brilliant, mocking contrast to the litter of the beach, bodies and cargo intermingled.

"So many," whispered Serena.

"And more's bein' washed up with each tide. The Shoals've got their own back this time." The man's voice held sorrow, but grim satisfaction, too.

Wreckers were moving among the corpses, brazenly wrenching crates and sea chests open, spilling their contents upon the sand to be picked over, then secreted in burlap sacks or kicked contemptuously aside. Women and children staggered under head-high loads of plunder, making for the shelter of the dunes where they might sort their booty in peace. Splintered planking and shreds of canvas washed up with every wave, tripping the scurrying figures. Men with makeshift litters threaded through the crowds to pick up the dead, indignantly scattering the ghouls whose hands darted over the corpses with the swiftness of crabs over carrion.

Serena saw a wrinkled crone squatting over a crumpled form clad in the shreds of a lace negligee. As the ghoul rolled the body over on its back, Serena gave a start of recognition. Madame Constanza. The singer who had flirted with Brandon. "No! Let her be!" The old woman paid her no mind but went about her business, tearing the jewels from the dead singer's ears.

Serena hesitated, but her companion tugged at her sleeve. Reluctantly, she passed by to continue her quest.

❧   ❧   ❧

THEY WERE NEARING the end of the beach now. A row of dunes halted their passage. Serena turned and looked back. The panorama stretched as far as she could see, a composite of greed and tragic devastation. But there was no sign of Melissa, no form small enough to be hers. Her companion had momentarily deserted her. Now he came back and tugged at her arm. "Missus, they say more of the dead be taken to the meeting house."

They were soon at the gates of the burying ground. Here the Quakers, by tradition, buried victims of shipwreck. Here the bodies were being assembled to be identified by their relatives or, that failing, to form yet one more of the rows of unmarked graves where unclaimed victims lay. At other times, the clapboard meeting house slept quietly within its low stone wall amidst its sheltering cedars. This is how I saw it long ago, from the crow's-nest of the *Audacious*. Was that a prophecy?

Today its peace was shattered. The low little porch was thronged with people tramping in and out; the wavery panes of the windows reflected a constant movement. The soughing of the cedar branches was drowned out by the wailing voices of women, the deep tones of men offering what comfort they could, the murmur and mutter of quest and questioning.

Serena and her guide picked their way along row upon row of sodden bodies. The faces of some had been covered; others stared sightlessly at the sky, the marks of their final struggle cancelled by the rictus of death.

Most were men, their sailors' garb in limp, clinging shreds, the calluses on their horny feet whitened by salt water.

"But why did the captain—?" Serena did not finish her question. Unknowingly, she clutched the withered hand of her companion. They had reached the end of the last row. Here, last year's scythed grass, bleached by winter, lay thickly upon the uneven ground that stretched to the forest's edge. In the brassy sunlight, black shadows of branches capered across the still forms of the dead.

The figure at the end had seemed familiar. Serena drew closer. She bent over the stout form in sober garments. The unacknowledged hope that Melissa had not been on the ship died as she recognized the face. It was one of Mistress Mansey's servants. "Oh, dear God!" she whispered. But where was Melissa? Floating in some cove? Wedged among rocks by waves reluctant to give up their victims? "Oh, dear God," she said again. "I can't bear this search much longer." Almost, it would be better to know Melissa dead than to be rent continually by hope's battle with despair.

She looked out upon the rows of silent corpses. "Why? Oh, why? Who was the captain? What fool ran the Shoals in the face of a spring tide and killed—killed all these people lying here?"

"The master, he be drowned, too. 'Twasn't his fault, Missus. It be none of his doin'. I heard tell it be the ship's owner. He be orderin' the master to beat the storm on threat of losin' his command."

"Who is the owner?" The words lay leaden on the air as Serena's numb lips moulded them. Why do I ask? I know the answer. Whose arrogance would demand its way the more insistently for being questioned?

"Cap'n Brandon it be. Cap'n Stuart Brandon."

"Of course." Serena's eyes begin to roll. The old man moved to catch her. "No. Leave me— Leave me, please." She slumped against a tree trunk, white-faced and trembling. "Oh, my God, Melissa—if your own father has killed you . . ." The old man shambled off to seek assistance.

&ε &ε &ε

"CHILD . . ." It seemed an endless time that she had stood here by the tree, too stunned to go on with her quest. The voice was Doctor Will's. Was this a phantom conjured by shock? She looked up. The tall, shabby figure before her was indeed the Black Doctor of the Pines. His kindly face was drawn with concern for her. But of course, she thought, as her mind began to function again. His goodness would bring him here to help, were he anywhere in the vicinity. Now I'm no longer alone. "Oh,

Doctor Will!" She threw herself into his arms, giving way to terrified weeping.

He held her firmly, stroking her hair, patting her, gentling her, speaking softly, over and over, that his words might penetrate her anguish. "No, child, no. Don't cry so. All is well, you see. She has been rescued. She is safe."

For some moments she seemed not to hear him. Then she drew back and looked up at him, eyes bright with hope in her tear-streaked face.

"Yes — she is safe in one of the cottages. A Captain Brandon swam to shore with her, they say." Serena gasped. "Come, child. Let us go to her." He put his arm round her shoulders to guide her stumbling steps as they left the burial ground behind them.

❧ ❧ ❧

MELISSA LAY ASLEEP. Her tangled curls, still damp, spilled across the pillow. Her face was grey and still. Deep shadows lay under her eyes, and only the slight motion of the counterpane revealed that she was breathing. Then she sighed deeply and shifted her position. A pale-pink froth bubbled from her mouth. Charity, keeping watch beside the bed, leaned forward and sponged it away.

"Oh, Doctor Will," cried Serena, "can she live?"

"Yes. There's danger of lung fever, and we must keep her warm. But she is young, and strong. With rest and care, she will recover." He placed a chair by the bed and guided Serena to it.

Serena took her child's hand in hers. How small it was, and pale, yet how much bigger than when last she had held it. The skin beneath the nails was tinged with blue. "'Lissa, it's Mama. Can you hear me?" The child's eyelids fluttered. The small fingers tightened on her own.

"Mama?"

"Yes — it's me, 'Lissa. Listen — you must sleep now, sleep and get well. Then I'll take you to a place called Weyford. We'll be together always."

For a time there was silence. Then Melissa murmured a word. At first Serena could not grasp what she was saying. Then she understood. *"Röslein."*

"All right, my darling. I'll sing. But rest now. You must rest." Serena drew a shaky breath. The first notes wavered perilously. Then her voice grew stronger, throbbing with relief and triumph. *"Röslein, Röslein, Röslein rot, Röslein auf der Heide . . ."*

Doctor Will turned away to hide his tears. He beckoned to Charity, and together they slipped from the room.

Chapter &. 5 0

TWO DAYS HAD PASSED. Stuart Brandon hitched Captain to a gatepost and entered the cottage where he knew Melissa lay. A tall, courtly black man by the hearth directed him to the small back bedroom. Beside a cot sat a woman. As he paused in the doorway she rose and came to meet him. It was Serena.

She gestured for silence and drew him into the main chamber. At her nod, the black man and a plump black woman went to keep watch in her stead. He caught just a glimpse of Melissa's small form before they drew the door shut behind them. The owner of the cottage was nowhere to be seen.

Serena glided across the room to stand by the front window. She turned to him then, her face held expressionless. Feeling a hesitancy unfamiliar to him, he came to her. In the harsh light of the sun-splashed morning he scutinized her face. It seemed to him he saw her intimately for the first time, as he had never quite seen her in the heat of their passionate engagements. The years had changed her but little: The erect carriage, the slender figure with its graceful curves, the unconsciously sinuous walk were still the same. Few men would fail to mark her passing.

But time had not left her unscarred. It had traced the finest of lines at the corners of her eyes. The radiant innocence was gone from her face. Her lips were set to the task of control. As she watched him approach, they tightened.

He was wearing old garments kept at his shipping docks: breeches, boots, and linen shirt, the attire he had worn on the night they first had met. She surveyed his tall figure and her lips twisted. Her expression told him the irony had not escaped her. Her gaze shifted from his face to the door of the room where Melissa was sleeping. She squared her shoulders and looked directly into his eyes.

He saw her eyes burning with scorn in the face he had sought so often to forget: those amber eyes—mirrors of every shade of her feeling, from the wildest of passion to the deepest despair. It was those eyes, in the face of a child, that had drawn him to Melissa. In that instant, before she spoke, he knew.

"Yes," she said, in answer to the question he had not needed to ask, "she is your daughter. And it is you who have near to killed her." Her proud posture faltered. She swayed slightly and clutched the window frame for support. But she fended off the hand he stretched out to steady her and straightened, rigid, to face him.

"So, Captain Brandon, we meet again." In her words he caught another echo of their past. "And we meet not at Weyford but at Barnegat. Your daughter lies near death beyond that door—and you the cause of it. *You!*" She all but choked, then stared at him, panting.

The silence grew between them, pulsing with words left unspoken through the years. The cottage stood remote from its fellows. No sound came to them from the village street, which dwindled to a sand trail a few paces beyond the dooryard. No sound came from the others in the house. They might have been alone as at their first encounter. He stared at her tear-streaked face and could think of no reply.

He saw that the lines of her face still curved upward, despite all the grief she had endured. He saw the shadows beneath her eyes, the pallor of her cheeks. And he saw the force of will that, but for that single out-burst, kept her lips firmly sealed. The face of Serena at eighteen, which had always, for him, overlaid and obscured her maturity, was stripped away. The girl was gone; a woman faced him, her face a mask enclosing her anguish, its angular planes bespeaking the effort by which she kept the mask in place.

And suddenly it seemed he knew all she had never told him: the strug-gles she had endured, her motive for an act that had seemed a betrayal—her liaison with Hiram Jonas—everything for which he had scourged her, over and over again. He acknowledged this, as he acknowledged the pride that had kept her silent. "Melissa, and the mother she was told had left her. How could I have failed to guess?"

She drew a breath as though to speak, then clamped her lips tightly, staring past him again to where Melisssa lay.

He touched her shoulder. "Serena, I know what you must feel now, but—"

She flung off his hand. "You, Stuart Brandon? *You* know what I feel?" The mask was gone, shattered by his touch, and her voice was harsh with pain. "When have you ever known how I felt, or cared, except as it served your desires?" Her voice rose. She gestured toward the closed door. "Your daughter lies in there, near to death, and it's your doing. She is youth, she is beauty, she is love—the only person who ever loved me for myself alone. She was all I had left of you. I wanted her to be everything that I could never be, all you and the world I live in denied me. And to give her that, I had to give her up, send her away, let her grow up thinking I had deserted her, hoping only that someday—"She covered her face with her hands. Then she dropped them and looked straight into his eyes again, scorning to hide her tears. "She is everything I worked for, gave up my good name for—and she nearly died because of you. She may die still." She looked wildly about her, then snatched up a cloak from the settle. "I must get out of here." Her voice was taut with loathing. Before he could stop her, she pushed blindly past him and ran out the door.

⁊ ⁊ ⁊

HE CAUGHT UP WITH HER by a wagon that was hitched to the low fence. Without looking at him, she climbed into the back and began jerkily shifting the contents.

"What are you doing?"

At first she did not answer. Then she said tonelessly, "I'm taking her home—home to Weyford. Will says she can be moved now."

"Let me help you."

She shook her head.

The door of the cottage opened. The plump black woman came out, carrying quilts and bedding. She glanced sharply at Stuart Brandon as she passed.

"Thank you, Charity. I'll soon be ready." Serena began spreading the quilts, arranging a makeshift bed. She looked up at him once, then away. She ignored the tears that streamed down her face and splashed onto the dusty wagon bed. In a voice held by effort to a tense monotone, she said, "It was you who gave the order to cross the Shoals, to race the storm. Wasn't it?"

Charity came out with another load of quilts. Barely noticing what he did, he took them from her and dumped them into the wagon. "Be 'bout twenty minutes," she said to Serena. "Will, he be gettin' her ready, and I think she'll eat some soup." Serena nodded but could not answer. "Have a care, Serena," said Charity, once more giving Brandon that measuring stare. Serena reached out and squeezed her friend's shoulder. A look full of meaning passed between the two women. Then Charity returned to the cottage, closing the door carefully behind her.

"Wasn't it?" asked Serena again, as though there had been no interruption.

He swallowed. The master had been at the helm, but in essence her accusation was true. "Yes. It was I who gave the order."

She had finished with the bedding now. She scrambled out of the wagon. "Of course," she ground out, not letting herself know how much she had wished the rumour false. "Of course it was you who gave the order. Why? Did the master oppose you? His death, too, must be laid to your account—and the deaths of all those people."

"That is true. And I must live with it all my life."

Now there were deep lines at the corners of her mouth; her eyes, tear-blurred and haunted, were sunk deep into their sockets. "I've seen you in that mood. I know what you are like. You see only your own wishes. You fear to be in error. Anyone who questions your slightest whim is your enemy. Reasons do not matter. Facts are meaningless. You weigh only the threat to your supremacy. Everything else—even people's lives— is so much flotsam blocking your course. How often has your fear of error servèd that other fear—your fear of what you felt for me?"

"Serena—"

"You're a coward, Stuart Brandon. Oh, spare me your tales of piracy. You're not a coward in battle—you're a coward of the heart. Spare me your tales of the women who have wronged you. I'm not one of them." An ironical smile briefly lightened her expression. " 'I'll not stake my life on the word of any woman.' You said that the night we first met. 'Those we love, we trust least of all.' You said that, too. Then if distrust be the measure, you loved me. What was it, that insistence of yours that I'm a trollop, but a weapon to fight off that love?" She laughed without mirth at the sight of his face. "I said you were a coward: What have you done but bolt every time you've come close to me? That night by the stream, when we rode back from Barnegat—" For a moment she was silent, swallowing convulsively. "And once I knew fully what you are—at Jonasville, when we met again—I knew I must protect Melissa from you, from even the knowledge of you, lest she be compelled like me to tell herself terrible lies."

"Serena, it was that night, when I saw you again, that I—"

"That you knew how much I meant to you? I can well believe it. I, too, that night—do you know how glad I was to see you? Now, I thought. Now we can all be together—" She looked toward the cottage door, fighting for control. It was still closed. "And how did you choose to acknowledge how you felt?" She flung back the strands of hair that had fallen about her face. "You taunted me about Hiram Jones. You called me a whore. Just what had you done to deserve my fidelity? And what would you have me do instead? Where was I to go, whom was I to turn to when you cast me out, when I lost my home and my inheritance because of one youthful act of folly—how was I, a woman, to support myself and my child? By marrying Caleb Sawyer, making both of us hostages to his madness? By becoming a barmaid, perhaps, or a whore who walked the streets while my child grew up in alleyways, a loveless bastard with no future?" Her voice rose on a tide of painful remembrance, then broke.

He said nothing.

"I tried," she said more quietly. "Dear God, how I tried. But when Caleb destroyed my work with Will—"

"When Hiram Jonas told me of that, I think I began to realize—"

"Realize what? That whoredom, sanctioned or unsanctioned, was the only choice left to me? Well, I chose the unsanctioned kind. It's easier to escape, for at least the law does not abet it. And as for the other kind— you've but to see what it's done to my sister. . . . It served you well, didn't it, to scorn me for what I'd no choice but to do, while you played upon my hopes and used my love for you to satisfy your lust. What a fool I was. Even back at Weyford, as late as that— Oh, what does it matter now?" Wearily, she climbed up to the wagon seat, shaking off his efforts to help her.

He came to stand beside her, looking up into her drained, white face. "Serena, I gave that order to sail, and others have paid far more dearly than I for my folly. But I saved Melissa's life at risk of mine. Does that count for nothing? Perhaps you're right in what you say—that opposition blinds me to reason. But there's this, too: I was so eager to see you that—"

"—that you brought along Madame Constanza to while away the hours you had to wait."

"I did not know she would be on the ship. I had not looked at the passenger list." And if I had—if I had seen the name Melissa Wainwright? Would the outcome have been any different? "She—Constanza—offered herself, but I could not go to her. I could think only of you. You were like no other woman I'd known before—"

She looked past him toward the cottage. The door stood open now, but no one was in sight. "Oh, what lonely nights I've spent praying to hear such words from you."

His heart leapt at the glow in her eyes, then subsided again. The light was not that of living fire but of embers—not the flame of yearning, but the faint glow of yearning recalled.

"Oh, yes," she said, "I hoped. All those years when I thought you were dead but felt you were alive, all these months since, when you have come to me and left again and come to me and left. Perhaps that's the fate of women—to wait and hope, wait and hope, for some man to make things right for them." She stopped. Her breath caught. "Of course," she said slowly, "that's what I did—I hoped for someone to save me: Papa . . . Doctor Will . . . Hiram . . . you. You above all. And I suppose in a way Hiram has. Now it's up to me to use his gift to assure I'll never need rescue again."

Brandon glanced over his shoulder. There was a bustle and stir by the doorway. Any moment his chance would be gone. "Serena—"

"You don't know yet why I had sent for you." Now those eyes burnt through him. "You've scorned Hiram Jonas. Yet Hiram has sent me enough money to buy your share in Weyford. He has freed me, for Melissa's sake, from the prison of my debt. Now there's only the prison of my love for you. And you've freed me from that yourself."

"And are you really free of it?" Something in her eyes, he was not sure what, told him there was hope, however she might deny it now. Or was it only his own hope reflected?

She made no answer. Again she looked toward the cottage. Doctor Will was coming down the path, carrying the sleeping Melissa.

Stuart Brandon stepped back as Serena climbed down from the wagon. Both watched as Melissa was settled in the wagon bed, the quilts tucked carefully round her. For a moment she opened her eyes.

"Mama—?"

"I'm here. Sleep, darling. When you wake up you'll be at Weyford."

"And you won't leave me?"

"Not ever."

Melissa snuggled into the quilts. She reached up to squeeze her mother's hand. Her eyelids drooped. She settled into deep, exhausted sleep.

Serena embraced the Black Doctor. "How can I thank you?" She turned to Charity, hugging her hard. "You'll be there soon?"

"Just as soon as I fetch 'Tate." Charity gave Stuart Brandon a quick, appraising glance. "Have a care, Serena. Safe journey."

Brother and sister went back to the cottage, turning once to wave. Serena climbed back onto the wagon seat. Silently, Brandon untied the reins and handed them to her. The horse stirred restlessly. She spoke to it once to reassure it but made no move to depart. He dared not speak.

"I loved you," she said. "I loved you for your boldness, for your courage. I loved you for what I thought you saw in me, even though you would never admit it. It was what no one else honoured, no one else saw— except Caleb, perhaps, in his twisted way. Not Father. Not Mother.

Only you." She sighed deeply. "I've cursed you, again and again, for telling
me terrible lies, making me hope, making me dream. But you never lied
to me. You are what you are; there's no subterfuge about it. It was I who
lied to myself. I was blind, like you, of my own will." She shook her head.
"No longer. I know what I've to do now. And I believe the day will come
when a man will love me for what I really am and, knowing that, will
trust my love for him."

"Serena, I do love you."

"It's too late." Now her voice was drained of all emotion. "I have the
ironworks, and I have Melissa. Do you think I would place her at the
mercy of your whims again?" She did not wait for an answer but tightened
her grip on the reins. "You'll see. Weyford will rise again. It will be what
it was in Father's day—and more." She turned, for a last time, to face
him. "There's no need for us to meet again. Lawyer Pettigru can bring
you the papers." She clucked to the horse. The wagon jolted forward.
"Farewell, Captain Brandon," she said.

He stood, finding no words to stop her, as the wagon gained speed
and rolled away. It moved faster and faster, the white dust rising behind
it, the dark shape of the Barrens ahead. Serena sat straight, her
shoulders tensely squared, as though waiting for merciful shadows to
grant privacy to her grief. As he watched, the Barrens reached out to en-
fold her.

He broke out of his trance then and took a step after the wagon. "Serena!
Serena! Wait!" There was no answer. He stood in the middle of the sand
trail, the dust of her passage swirling about his feet. "Serena! Serena—
please!" It was a word he had never thought to say to her.

The Barrens lay closed to him, dark and secretive.

"Please," he said again, but in a whisper. Gently the dust settled back
upon the roadstead, till no trace remained of her passage. It seemed he still
heard the rumbling of the wagon's wheels. Then the sound became one
with the roar of the distant surf, relentlessly pounding the Barnegat shore.

The Wainwright Chronicles

An Afterword

T HOSE FAMILIAR WITH Pine Barrens history will detect, in "Weyford," a likeness to Batsto, from which George Washington did indeed purchase firebacks—though not defective ones. It was Batsto, as well as the very real "nest of Rebel pirates" at Chestnut Neck, that the British sought to destroy in the battle of that name. But to the Richards family, who ruled Batsto so long and so illustriously, and to their descendants still active in Pennsylvania iron, the Wainwrights bear no intentional resemblance.

Other readers will see in "Doctor Will" more than a hint of James Still, the Black Doctor of the Pines who practiced a century later. They, like those who suspect that "Hiram Jonas" and his "Jonasville" were inspired by Hezekiah Smith and the lesser known of New Jersey's two Smithvilles, will not be wrong. But the personalities and personal lives of Hiram Jonas and Doctor Will as set forth in the Wainwright Chronicles are not intended to depict what is known of these two men.

Some minor characters are real enough: Tavernkeeper Nicholas Sooy, like Jesse Richards and others of that clan, is buried in Pleasant Mills churchyard. And, with the exception of Weyford, the ironmaking villages mentioned throughout really existed and a few, like Weymouth, can still be found on maps. Many details about them—such as the closing down of Atsion forge by its Quaker owner—are true to history or legend.

Joe Mulliner the Pine Robber really lived, and really crashed Barrens parties. But the tales about him so intertwine fact and legend that they can be disentangled no longer. Was he hanged at Burlington or, as one text has it, at Woodbury? "Woodlington" is both and neither. Was he really buried where his tombstone stood? No one knows.

While clearly inspired by such places and personalities, as some dialogue is inspired by "piney" talk, especially the use of "be" for "is" or "was," the scenes and events of the Wainwright Chronicles are intended to convey not a likeness but a feeling. None of the characters, with the foregoing exceptions, is modeled upon a real counterpart. Moreover, historical chronology and geographical exactness have sometimes been subordinated to the story's needs.

331

. Henry Charlton Beck's *Forgotten Towns of Southern New Jersey*, published the year I was born, sparked the interest that led, years later, to the idea of embodying the history and ecology of the Barrens in the Wainwright series. George Agnew Chamberlain's mystery *Midnight Boy* played its part. So did the historical works of John Cunningham and Arthur Pierce, as well as John McPhee's rendering of the Barrens of today. Those interested in learning more about the Barrens will find a wealth of material in these works.

Reverend Beck, though, was well aware that his Jersey journeys yielded more of folklore than of the kind of "fact" that satisfies formal historians. He knew, too, that many a minnow becomes a whale (or sometimes a shark) as its story is retold. He recorded the tales of Jersey nevertheless, and thereby preserved the essence of an era. It was Reverend Beck's books, not the tomes in historical libraries, that made the once-ignored Barrens come alive with "lanes and legends" crucial to the birth of a United States that now stretches from sea to sea.

I, too, suspect that "fiction" is sometimes truer than fact. Fact informs; fiction illuminates. The Wainwright Chronicles are written in that spirit.

Katherine & Clare

Some Phrases
and Expressions

ಶಿ

blast A furnace in operation is "in blast."

blowout, blowing out Taking the furnace out of operation, especially for the season.

clandestine retreat An unauthorized holiday; a drinking spree.

coaling The making of charcoal. Those who did so were known as colliers.

crane-berries Cranberries, so called because the crook of the stem resembles a crane's bill.

cripple A boggy area but with running water, or one where white cedars grow (see also *spong*).

draw the gate Release water into the channels to move the bellows.

flux The material that draws impurities from the ore, often limestone but, in Barrens furnaces, ground oystershell.

fingerboard A place where several roads come together (not the sign at such a place).

frolicking A celebration, often of a blowout.

jack, Jersey lightnin' Applejack.

make a muster Give birth to a child.

pigs, pig iron A term generally used in ironmaking for the bars formed from the molten iron when the furnace is tapped. In Weyford's day the molds were gutters in the sand.

spong A boggy area without running water, or where blueberries (whortleberries) grow. Pronounced "spung." (See also *cripple*).

stampers, stamping mill Machinery that crushes slag so that unsmelted ore can be used again.

whortleberries Huckleberries or blueberries.

woodjin A person steeped in woods lore; an expert hunter and tracker.

A Pine Barrens Book List

ॐ

A full bibliography for the Wainwright Chronicles is available for $5 postpaid from Wainwright Press, P.O. Box 288, Emmaus, PA 18049–0288. The books listed here are the most important, interesting, and comprehensive. All were in print when we went to press.

Boyd, Howard P. **A Field Guide to the Pine Barrens of New Jersey: Its Flora, Fauna, Ecology, and Historic Sites.** Medford, NJ: Plexus Publishing Company, 1991. A one-book reference library to take with you on explorations or to read before you go. Charming and accurate drawings by Mary Pat Finelli: trees, shrubs, grasses, flowers, bugs, birds. Invaluable.

Beck, Henry Charlton. **The Roads of Home: Lanes and Legends of New Jersey.** New Brunswick, NJ: Rutgers University Press, 1956. An update and expansion of the 1930s "forgotten towns" books. "The Man in the Iron Casket" and "The Black Doctor" may seem familiar.

Beck, Henry Charlton. **Forgotten Towns of Southern New Jersey.** New York: Dutton, 1936. Reissued 1961. New Brunswick, NJ: Rutgers University Press. The book that started it all: Ong's Hat, Sweetwater, Speedwell, Mount Misery, Batsto. Discursive and delightful, though much of what Beck writes about has vanished in the ensuing half-century.

McPhee, John. **The Pine Barrens.** New York: Farrar, Straus, & Giroux, 1968. A master writer explores the Barrens of the present day, from fire ecology to fox hunting.

Moonsammy, Rita; David Steven Cohen; and Lorraine E. Williams, Editors. **Pinelands Folklife.** New Brunswick, NJ: Rutgers University Press, 1987. The Barrens as experienced by the people who live there. The photographs are a treasure in themselves: cranberrying, basketweaving, glassblowing, musicmaking.

Book design by John Beck, The Bookmakers, Incorporated, Wilkes-Barre, Pennsylvania
Jacket design, map, and Wainwright Press logo by Elizabeth Dickson Graphics, Durham, Pennsylvania
Cover etching by Henrik Rådberg, 1895–1979
Photography by Richard M. Ross
Copy editors: Ruth M. Barker and Amy Kowalski
Set in Electra by The Bookmakers, Incorporated
Jacket printed by Zodiac Marketing Services, Wilkes-Barre, Pennsylvania
Printed and bound by Quinn-Woodbine, Incorporated, Woodbine, New Jersey

WAINWRIGHT PRESS, INC.

Lillian R. Rodberg, President and Publisher
Nancy E. Hopkins, Executive Director
Emmaus, PA 18049–0288

For each first-edition copy of *To Tell Me Terrible Lies* sold
Wainwright Press contributes one dollar to
Pinelands preservation.